House of Thorns

LEE MOUNTFORD

PROLOGUE

God, how long has it been?

Emily Harper gazed down the long gravel driveway towards the house ahead of her.

Erimus House.

She felt a swell of emotions as she trod over the loose stones, which crunched underfoot. It was dusk, with the sun hidden behind the large house, silhouetting the building against the dull sky.

Erimus House was three stories high and constructed primarily with large stone blocks, all cut square and butted neatly together. Much of the front elevation was covered in evergreen climbing plants that ran up the surface. Emily remembered them from when she was a child; she'd cut her hand quite badly on some of the thorns laced in amongst the greenery.

With the main door of the building facing towards her, Emily stared at the dominating front façade as she walked. No lights were on inside, which she found strange. *Wonder if I'm the first one here?*

Lengths of trimmed green lawn stretched off either side

of the drive, stretching to the tall boundary stone walls that ran around the perimeter of the property. The protective walls around the grounds were mostly covered with climbing plants as well, similar to the main house.

There were some hedges and planters in amongst the stretches of lawn, but Emily knew the *really* impressive garden was to the rear of the house—it was something Eleanore had worked hard on all those years ago.

Eleanore, Emily then thought. *She's probably dead now. She must have been, what, in her early fifties back then.* Emily tried to remember exactly how long it had been since she was last at the house—how long ago it had been since *that* night.

The night of the fire.

Thirty-plus years, easy, she thought to herself. *Which would put Eleanore in her eighties now. She could still be alive, I suppose. Wonder if she's still here?*

The house looked just like Emily remembered it. That meant the damage from the fire had obviously been repaired. She wondered briefly if Erimus House had ever opened its doors again after she and the others had been forced to leave.

Memories of her family—Ollie, Daniel, and Lucy—sprang up in her mind, bringing with them more surges of emotion. Emily stopped walking for a second and steadied herself as a tidal wave of melancholy enveloped her.

Those three weren't her family by blood, of course. Emily was an orphan. That's why she'd ended up at Erimus House in the first place, same as the others, but the bond she'd made with her surrogate siblings made them feel like brothers and a sister all the same. It had surprised her just how close she'd gotten with them, despite the relatively short amount of time she'd spent at the house.

They were *my family,* she told herself. *The only one I had.*

Before continuing on, Emily turned to look back at the large cast-iron gates behind her, which were set within the boundary wall. She glanced at the stone pillars on either side, each with a circle carved near the top, then looked through the gates to the outside of the property, wondering if she was crazy for coming back.

No, you're not crazy, you're fulfilling a promise, she told herself. *Plus, you'll finally get to see the others again.*

That thought filled her with both fear and excitement. It had been so long she didn't know how everyone would react to each other now. Would it be awkward? Would the love they'd shared all those years ago still be there?

Emily turned, pulled her coat tighter around herself, and ventured forward once more. She was exhausted—the long trek taking its toll on her. There was also a bite to the air, and she felt a scratching tickle in her throat that caused her to instinctively run her hand over her neck. *Hope I'm not catching a cold.*

The house grew larger and larger the closer Emily got. That mixture of happiness and sadness she'd felt when first seeing the house was still with her, but there was something else there as well, something that came close to overriding all the other feelings.

Worry.

Things had happened in the house back then. As a child, Emily just hadn't been able to explain them, but they had left her and her siblings terrified.

But you didn't see most of it, Emily reminded herself. Then, a correction: *No, at the end you did. But those things couldn't have been real,* she said to herself. *There's no way.*

Emily wondered how the others would feel about

everything. *If* they came, of course. *Hell, maybe I'll be the only one.*

It was a sobering thought. She *really* hoped the others would show, otherwise it would wind up being a completely wasted trip. A missed opportunity to catch up with people that, at one time, had meant the world to her.

Emily was about halfway down the drive, staring at the building, when she was reminded of the first time she'd approached the house. Déjà vu swept over her. She'd been apprehensive back then as well, worried that she wouldn't like her new home or the kids that lived there. Worried that her new guardian would be an awful person.

There had been some differences during that first walk, though. It was daytime back then, and she hadn't been walking alone.

Her thoughts went to the group of four people who'd been standing outside the main entrance of the house, all waiting to greet her.

Ground Floor

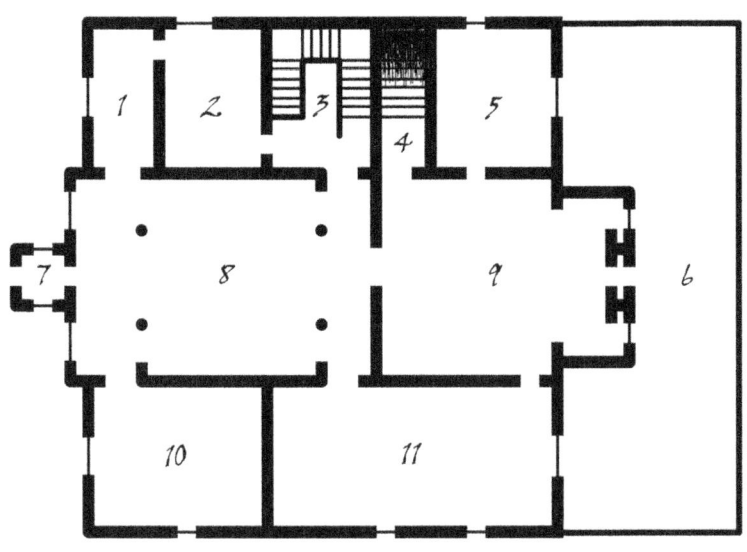

Ground Floor Rooms

1 - Den
2 - Study
3 - Stairs Up
4 - To Cellar
5 - Kitchen
6 - Patio
7 - Porch
8 - Entrance Hallway
9 - Dining Area
10 - Library
11 - Drawing Room

Middle Floor

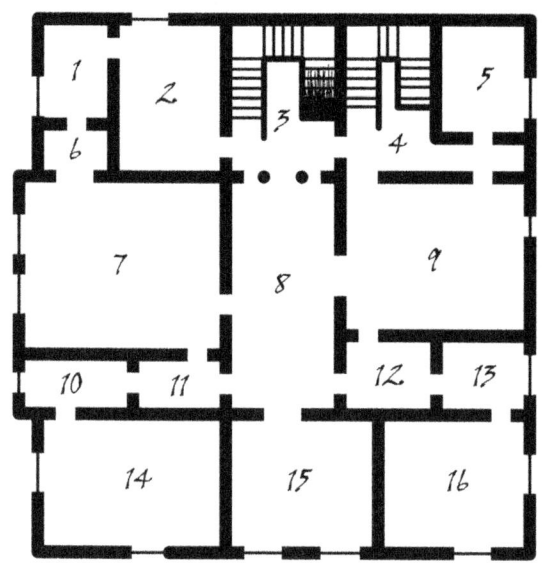

Middle Floor Rooms

1 - Changing Area
2 - Spare Room
3 - Stairs Down
4 - Stairs Up
5 - Store
6 - En-suite
7 - Dan's Room
8 - Hallway
9 - Ollie's Room
10 - En-suit
11 - Changing Area
12 - Changing Area
13 - En-suite
14 - Bathroom
15 - Snug
16 - Spare Room

Top Floor

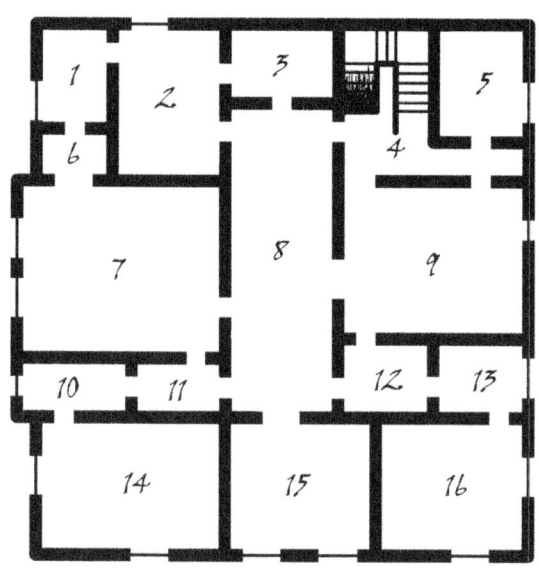

Top Floor Rooms

1 - Changing Area
2 - Eleanore's Room
3 - Spare Room
4 - Stairs Down
5 - Store
6 - En-suite
7 - Lucy's Room
8 - Hallway
9 - Emily's Room
10 - En-suite
11 - Changing Area
12 - Changing Area
13 - En-suite
14 - Bathroom
15 - Snug
16 - Spare Room

THEN...

CHAPTER
ONE

Emily stopped. Nerves gripped her—she just couldn't bring herself to move forward anymore.

What if they don't like me?

The hand that held hers gave a gentle, reassuring squeeze. 'It'll be okay,' the woman next to Emily said. 'This is a good place. I promise.'

Mrs. Clement was Emily's social worker. She was in her forties, with long brown hair pulled into a ponytail and thin framed glasses perched on her narrow nose. The social worker had spent a lot of time with the eleven-year-old since Emily's parents had died. That had only been five months ago, but it was something Emily still had to try hard not to think about. Whenever she did, it always made her heart hurt and she couldn't help but cry.

Only two weeks ago, Mrs. Clement had told Emily she'd found a place for the young girl. Somewhere for her to live and to now call home.

Erimus House.

The idea didn't sit well with Emily. She'd already had a home, and it had been snatched away along with Mum and

Dad. Plus, the new place's name alone sounded weird to her.

She stood halfway down the long driveway to Erimus House, the open gate behind her. The large building up ahead was *much* bigger than her old one.

Standing in front of the house, just outside its entrance, were four people: three children and an adult. The adult, a woman with grey hair cut into a bob, was smiling, while the children stared back at Emily with unreadable expressions.

'Come on,' Mrs. Clement said and started forward again, still holding Emily's hand and urging her onward as well.

The social worker was the closest thing Emily had left to a friend now, though she knew the older woman wasn't *really* her friend. Emily didn't doubt Mrs. Clement cared about her well-being, and the woman had always shown Emily a great deal of compassion and kindness, but Emily knew that, ultimately, Mrs. Clement was just doing her job. Now that Emily was being handed over, she likely wouldn't see Mrs. Clement again. Maybe once or twice for checkups, but that would be it.

Emily looked up to see Mrs. Clement focused on the way forward.

Someone else that will disappear from my life, Emily thought. She then gazed ahead again to the group waiting for her and found herself briefly wondering how long *they* would be in her life for.

Will I settle here? she thought. *Will the other kids welcome me? What if they don't like me?*

As they moved, Emily hooked the thumb of her right hand under the strap of her backpack, while her left hand remained holding on to Mrs. Clement. The social worker was also dragging a modest case along behind her, which bounced and juddered along the gravel. All of Emily's remaining possessions were in the case and the backpack. Her whole life... what was left of it.

As worried as Emily was, she still couldn't believe the size of the house she was going to be living in. It was three stories high with a pitched slate roof, multiple chimneys, and weathered stone walls that were a mix of sandstone and grey colours. There were also large swathes of green planters climbing up the walls.

The entrance door sat in a square porch that jutted out from the main building by a few feet, and there were two long windows on either side of the outcropping along the front elevation. The windows followed the same placements on the next floor up, though with an additional two in the centre replacing the porch, and those placements were repeated again on the top floor, but with shorter windows and higher sills.

At the very top of the elevation there was a single peak with an emblem in its centre. Emily narrowed her eyes to try and make out what the emblem was, soon realising it was just a simple circle etched into a rectangular section of stone.

'This place looks like a mansion,' Emily whispered to Mrs. Clement, who chuckled in response.

'Not quite, but it's big, isn't it? Plenty of space for you. You're going to love it here, Emily. Just give it time.'

Emily nodded... though she wasn't convinced.

She carried on the rest of the way in silence, keeping her eyes low but casting quick glances back up at those ahead.

The thought of Mrs. Clement leaving her behind made Emily's chest tighten. She'd noticed on the drive over how isolated the place was, seemingly in the middle of nowhere, with only fields around it. Those fields had been punctuated now and then by copses of trees, farms, and farmhouses. *Feels like I'm outside of civilisation.*

That thought made her sad, removed from the world, and it reminded her again that the only constant in her life in the last five months was going to soon leave her.

An urge to cry suddenly sprang up, growing stronger with every step, but Emily fought it with everything she had, pushing images of her parents out of her mind.

Don't let them see you cry, she told herself. *Show them you're strong.*

Back in school, Emily had seen how quickly other children could pick up on weakness, and how quickly that could be used against someone. If the kids in this house were mean, it would just give them ammunition straight out of the gate. She glanced briefly at the tallest child: a boy with shaggy blonde hair and light-blue eyes, wearing jeans and a red hooded top. He was taller than Emily, though looked to be a similar age, and wore a blank expression. If any of the kids were going to turn out to be bullies, Emily guessed it would be him.

The boy stood just to the right of the smiling woman, with the other two children on her left.

There was another boy in the group, this one quite a bit shorter than the first, and he had dark hair and brown eyes. He wore a light-orange polo shirt and pressed trousers. Emily struggled to place his age. And while he was shorter than the first boy, and also Emily, he wasn't the smallest among them.

That title fell to the last child, a girl with dark brown hair and eyes, just like the boy next to her. Her hair was long and flowing, kept away from her eyes by a pink hairband. Emily had no doubt the girl was the youngest of the group, and she wore a simple light-blue dress that stopped at her shins, as well as a silver locket around her neck. The small girl cast a kind smile over to Emily, and Emily instinctively smiled back, surprising herself. As worried as she was, that one gesture alone made her feel just a touch better.

She tried to figure out where she'd fit in with the group. If she had to guess, she figured herself to be the second oldest, behind the tallest boy. *Does that mean the youngest two will look up to me?* Emily could feel their eyes on her and guessed they were trying to appraise her as well. She also wondered what they made of her appearance. Emily was thin and above average height for a girl her age, with long chestnut hair, light-blue eyes, and a smattering of freckles across her nose and cheeks. She wasn't particularly outgoing, so she often tucked her head down so as to not draw attention to herself.

What do they think of my clothes? she went on to wonder. While the other children were hardly dressed fancily, their clothes were still clean and obviously ironed. Emily herself was dressed in light-blue jeans with frayed bottoms, trainers, and a brown-and-white-plaid flannel shirt with a vest beneath. Her hair was parted in the middle and left untied.

Emily stopped a few seconds later, now standing just a few feet away from the group, still clinging tightly to Mrs. Clement's hand.

The woman before her, still wearing a kind smile, crouched down. She was older than Emily's mother had been, though she didn't seem *old* old. Not like Emily's grandmother had been. She was thin, taller than Mrs. Clement, and wore a white jumper with brown linen trousers. Emily noticed a black rope cord from a necklace around her neck, though the bottom disappeared beneath her jumper.

The woman's grey eyes danced with intelligence, and when she peered at Emily, it felt like she was looking past the façade and directly into her soul. Emily had to fight the urge to step back behind her social worker to hide.

'And what is your name?' the lady asked.

Emily was aware the woman would have already known, but she answered anyway, trying to keep her voice steady and firm.

'I'm Emily,' she said. Then, after a moment, 'Emily Harper.' For some reason, Emily felt it important to give her last name, just in case anyone wanted to take *that* from her as well.

The woman held out a hand, though it took Emily a moment to realise she was supposed to shake, which she did. The lady's grip was gentle and soft, and it soon released.

'Pleased to meet you, Emily,' the woman said. 'My name is Eleanore Chambers. Thank you for coming to live with us. I really hope you find your new home here.'

Emily didn't say anything; she didn't know how to respond.

'I'm sure she will,' the social worker answered for her. Mrs. Clement then looked down at Emily. 'But I'll be back in a couple of weeks to make sure you've settled in.'

'Of course,' Eleanore said, glancing up at Mrs. Clement before then turning her eyes back to Emily. 'Let me introduce you to the other children.' She stood back up and gestured to her left to the big, blonde-haired boy. 'This is Oliver Thompson,' she said.

The boy glanced upwards to her, frowned, then looked back at Emily and rolled his eyes. 'It's *Ollie*,' he corrected.

To Emily's surprise, he then flashed a big smile and held out a hand. 'Pleased to meet you, Emily. Welcome to the house.'

He spoke with such confidence it threw Emily for a loop, and she just stared ahead at his hand for a moment. 'It's okay,' he went on. 'I know it's scary. But everyone here will be nice to you, I promise.' Emily fixed her gaze on him. The boy's expression was earnest, and he waited patiently. When Emily eventually shook his hand as well she expected his grip to be frighteningly tight, but it was just as gentle as Eleanore's had been.

'Pleased to meet you, Ollie,' she said.

His smile grew wider.

'This fine young man here,' Eleanore began, gesturing to the other boy, 'is Daniel Price.'

Daniel gave a polite, tight-lipped smile. He made as if to shake, then stopped, obviously unsure of himself. He looked just as nervous as Emily felt.

'Hi,' he said and gave an awkward wave.

'Hi,' Emily replied. 'Pleased to meet you.'

'You too,' Daniel said, but added nothing more.

'And lastly,' Eleanore continued, 'we have Lucy Clarke. Say hello, Lucy.'

'Hello,' Lucy quickly replied with a large smile, keeping her big, innocent eyes fixed firmly on Emily. She noticed dimples at the sides of the young girl's mouth and had no doubt Lucy would become quite beautiful as she got older.

'Hi, Lucy,' Emily said. 'Pleased to meet you as well.'

'You too,' Lucy replied, still smiling. She almost seemed excited. *Maybe she thinks she's getting a sister.* Emily had never had siblings, though she was surprised that the thought of it wasn't unpleasant.

But Emily quickly stopped herself. *This isn't my real family.*

Still, all the children appeared much more friendly than she'd initially feared. *Probably because we're all here for the same reason,* she told herself. Looking at each of them, she felt the realisation hit her hard: they had all lost their parents as well. These weren't just normal kids—they were going through the same thing she was.

That notion somehow helped.

'Now that the introductions are out of the way,' Eleanore went on, 'why don't we go inside? We'd all be happy to show you around the house, Emily, as well as the grounds.' She looked up to Mrs. Clement. 'Would you like to stay and join us?'

Emily looked up to the social worker to see the woman already gazing back down at her.

'Would you like me to stay?' she asked. 'I can if you want.'

Emily hesitated. She glanced away from Mrs. Clement and over to the children for a brief second, before looking back up. In truth, she dearly wanted Mrs. Clement to stay, to put off leaving... but something was stopping her from saying it. Emily realised she didn't want to appear weak and scared in front of the other children.

Eventually, her eyes settled on Ollie again, who was looking back with a sympathetic smile. He gave her a small nod. 'It's okay, you know,' he said. 'Do whatever you need to do. We all know it's scary.'

Is he reading my thoughts? she wondered. *No,* she realised. *He just knows what I'm going through.*

Emily hesitated a little while longer. She knew Mrs. Clement would have to leave soon regardless, so she figured why not just cut the cord now? *Show the others you can be strong.* And Ollie's kindness had boosted her confidence. While Emily didn't *want* Mrs. Clement to go at all, she couldn't stop it from happening. The social worker was responsible for a lot of children, and there were others that hadn't found their homes yet. Emily knew those kids needed Mrs. Clement more than she did now.

'I'll be fine,' Emily eventually said.

Mrs. Clement's eyes widened in surprise. 'Are... are you sure?'

Emily took a breath and smiled before nodding. 'Yes, I'm sure.'

The social worker knelt down. 'That's very brave of you, Emily,' she said, giving Emily a tight hug. 'And I'm so proud of you. But remember, I'll be back in a couple of weeks.' She then pulled away and added, 'If everything isn't okay, then we can try to find somewhere else.'

'Of course,' Eleanore interjected. 'You aren't going to be forced to stay here, Emily. Just see what you think and then make your decision.'

Emily looked from one adult to the other. She didn't realise she was allowed that much of a say in things. The way it had initially been put to her was that she either chose Erimus House or settled in for a *long* wait until somewhere else came up.

'Okay,' was all Emily said.

Mrs. Clement gave her a long, searching look. 'And you're sure you're fine with me leaving now?'

Emily smiled once more, hoping it looked confident, while she fought back the tears. 'I am,' she replied.

The social worker looked like she wanted to cry herself, and her expression was somewhere between sadness and pride. 'Then I'll leave you to get settled in.' She squeezed Emily's shoulder and stood up, turning her attention to Eleanore. 'I'll just bring the case inside,' she said.

'Nonsense,' Eleanore replied with a wave of her hand. She stepped forward and took the case from Mrs. Clement, easily lifting it up. 'Let me have that. We'll set it just inside for now until we show Emily around.'

'Thank you,' Mrs. Clement replied. She looked back at Emily yet again. 'Well, I guess this is goodbye for now, Emily,' she said sadly. 'I really think you'll settle in well here.' She then extended her arms. 'I don't think I'm supposed to be hugging you so much,' she joked, 'but I think I need it more than you.' Emily stepped forward and allowed herself to be swallowed up by another embrace.

Don't cry, don't cry, don't cry.

'I meant what I said,' Mrs. Clement whispered quietly. 'I'm so, so proud of you.'

Don't cry!

Emily felt her eyes fill with tears, so she buried her face into Mrs. Clement's shoulder, drying them on the fabric while gritting her teeth together in an effort to stop the flow. Mrs. Clement must have realised what was happening and allowed the hug to linger longer than it needed to until it was Emily that eventually broke away.

Finally, the social worker stood back up. 'I'll see you soon,' she said, then looked to the others and waved. 'Goodbye, everyone. Take good care of my girl here.'

'We will,' Ollie promised.

Then, after casting a final, lingering glance at Emily, the woman turned and started to walk back down the drive. Emily watched her go for a little while, immediately regretting her choice to be brave. Another hand soon found her shoulder. It was Eleanore.

'Come on,' the older woman said gently. 'Let's go look around. I'm sure you'll absolutely love this place.'

CHAPTER
TWO

Eleanore and the children moved aside, allowing Emily to step inside the single-storey porch. Emily looked down to see large, dark tiles beneath her feet. Each was square shaped and many had cracks in them. The small porch had tall, wooden-framed windows to the left and right walls, letting plenty of light inside.

While the outer door to the porch seemed surprisingly thin, the main door ahead—which hung open—was made from heavy stained wood and looked extremely solid.

Emily could see through into the space ahead, which looked to be a large entrance hall. Inside were more tiles, though these ones were lighter in colour and laid in diamond shapes, though none of these were cracked like the outside ones. In the centre of the area was a large, patterned rug—a mix of blues, burgundies, browns, and dull yellows, with a border around the edge as well as central motifs.

There were also thin, off-white columns in the hall: two set close to the entrance and another two farther towards the back, all running up and connecting to the ornate plastered ceiling. A chandelier hung down in the centre of the room. The light fitting had multiple arms that initially dropped down before swooping back up. The lightbulbs at the ends were all shaped like flames from candles.

'Step inside,' Eleanore said from behind. 'Take it all in.'

Emily did, keeping her thumbs tucked into the straps of her backpack. It was certainly a grand space, around eight feet wide by twenty feet long. While there were no stairs in the lobby, multiple solid-oak doors lined the walls, all stained a dark brown, with four panels set into each. The walls around them were a mix of two distinct plain wallpapers. An off-white paper ran up to about three feet in height, where it met a decorative dado rail. Above that, the wallpaper was coloured somewhere between a dull orange and a light brown, and that one continued up to the ornate cornices at the edges of the ceiling.

There were two windows behind Emily, one on either side of the entrance porch, allowing natural light into the space. However, given the room's length, the rear of the space still appeared rather gloomy.

Emily counted five internal doors around her, not including the main entrance. Two were close by, one on the left wall and one on the right, and another two were farther into the space towards the back, again to the left and right. The final door was straight ahead, beyond the columns, set into the rear wall of the room.

As Emily took a few more steps forward, the others filed into the room behind her. She heard Eleanore set down her case and close the main door, which squeaked as it moved and shut with an audible *click*.

She'd expected the others to move up beside her, but everyone gave her a respectful distance, which Emily appreciated. She took in more of the details, specifically the multiple, large pictures that dominated the walls, most of them showing painted landscapes. There was also a fireplace to the left midway along the wall with a white mantel surrounding it, which in turn had expensive-looking vases mounted on top. Emily also noticed a few cast-iron radiators dotted around the space, pressed into the walls between furniture that consisted of high-backed wooden benches with long cushions across the seats, low cabinets and bookshelves, and even an old chest, all the same dark oak as the internal doors, and all looking very expensive and old. There was a long-case clock, and Emily could hear the constant, gentle *tick, tick, tick* from it. The final thing she spotted was in the corner of the space up ahead, where a telephone sat on a small circular table. A black-and-gold receiver curved atop the black base that housed the rotary dial.

The whole space seemed extremely grand to Emily.

'You can choose where we go next, Emily,' Eleanore stated. 'I'll warn you, the layout can be a little confusing at first, but you'll soon get used to it. Now, to your right,' she went on, pointing to the door on the right closest to the main entrance, 'we have a library. It isn't a huge space compared to the rest of the house, but it's a nice area to relax in. If the book selection isn't to your liking, we can always get some more in.' She then pointed to the door on the opposite side of the library. 'There's a small den through there, and that gives access to a study.' Eleanore motioned to the right-hand wall again, this time to the door farther up. 'That is the drawing room. The children and I often play board games in there.' Next, she pointed to the door opposite that one. 'That is the stairwell, which will take you up to the floor above us. And finally,' she nodded to the single rear door, 'that is the dining room. The kitchen is just off that.'

'And so is the door to the cellar,' Ollie added while looking over at Eleanore. Emily couldn't be certain, but she thought she picked up on a hint of frustration in the boy's voice.

'Yes,' Eleanore replied with a frown aimed back at Ollie. 'But the cellar is out of bounds and always locked, as Ollie well knows.'

'Why?' asked Emily.

'The heating system is down there,' the older woman replied. 'The boiler, lots of old pipes and such. Not the safest place for children, so I keep it locked up.'

Ollie didn't say anything more. He simply looked back at Eleanore, his expression giving nothing away.

'So,' Eleanore continued, 'where would you like to go first, Emily?'

Emily looked around. 'Wherever you'd like,' she replied, unsure of where to pick.

'No problem, my dear,' Eleanore said. 'I can imagine this is all a lot for you to take in. Why don't we look at the library first, then we can work around to the dining room. From there we can also show you the rear garden.'

'That sounds good,' Emily replied.

'Perfect,' Eleanore stated. 'Why don't you set your backpack down with the case here? No need to carry it around the whole time. When we're done, I'll bring everything up to your room for you.'

Emily paused, hesitant about leaving her bag behind. It didn't contain a lot: a few more clothes and some of her favourite books. There was also a small picture book, filled with the only photos she had left of her family.

It'll be fine here, she quickly told herself. *No one will break in and take it.* She then forced herself to slip off the backpack, stride over to the case, and set the bag down next to it.

Emily was then led into the library, which was a corner room and approximately eight feet by eight feet. It had a thick green carpet on the floor, panelled walls, a window looking out of the front of the property, and another one looking out to the side.

She had expected the walls to be completely filled with bookshelves but found only four, though they were full height and all lined with old-looking fabric-lined books. Emily noticed there was yet another fireplace, and a portrait of a man sat just above it on the wall. She stared at the painting. If the man depicted there was famous, she certainly didn't recognise him. He looked to be a similar age to Eleanore, with brushed-back grey hair, a neat white beard and moustache, and he was clad in a smart suit. He stood in a regal pose, one hand on his hip and the other resting on a cane as he stared out with a blank expression and no hint of a smile.

A writing desk also caught Emily's eye, sitting just next to the front window. It was a walnut-oak design with two stacks of small drawers on the flat surface and many more drawers set into the main carcass. A single chair was positioned in front of the desk, tucked in neatly. There were also two sofas in the room, positioned in an L shape around a coffee table, each covered with ugly green cotton slipcovers. In addition, there was a single armchair, the fabric of it a darker green than the carpet. Emily spied another cast-iron radiator and noticed there was also another door inside the room, which she guessed led to the drawing room.

'This is a nice space to come when you want a little

alone time to read,' Eleanore said. 'Do you like to read, dear?'

Emily quickly nodded. 'I do,' she said. Losing herself in stories had become one of her key coping mechanisms, something to take herself away from the harsh reality of her new life.

'Fantastic,' Eleanore replied. 'Well, you can peruse the selection later on if you'd like. It's quite varied, though most of them are probably a little dry and boring for someone your age. That case over there,' she pointed to one of the bookshelves, 'is probably your best bet. Those books are more tailored to children and young adults. Now, if you'll follow me, we'll move on to the drawing room.'

'Do you use the fires much?' Emily asked before they started to move. She pointed over to the fireplace, which had a bed of coal within and an iron guard just in front of the opening.

'Sometimes,' Eleanore said. 'They used to be the only way to heat the house back when it was built, but that was a long time ago. A heating system was put in a while later, but that is getting on in age as well. The fires are nice on a winter's night when we can all curl up together. If you ever want one lit, please don't try it yourself. Just come and get me, okay?'

'Okay,' Emily replied with a compliant nod.

'Great,' Eleanore said. 'Now, if you'll follow me.'

The older woman led Emily and the others through the inner door of the library, where they exited into the drawing room as Emily had suspected. This was a longer space than the previous room, more than double the length, with three windows to the side wall and one to the rear that provided a view of the back garden. There was a fireplace again, this one without a portrait above it. The ceiling was mostly flat but with a decorative beading running across it, cutting the surface up into rectangles. The colour of the ceiling was a similar orange-brown mix from the walls in the entrance hall. A thick, berry-coloured carpet covered the floor, and there was more sofa seating and a small coffee table around the fireplace. Likely because of the size of the room, it contained more furniture than the library: another writing desk, half-height cabinets with stacks of board games on top, a circular table covered in cloth in one corner, and some small, beautiful dark-oak tables. While there was no portrait in the room, there *were* quite a lot of landscape paintings on the walls, and Emily gazed at each as she moved slowly forward, taking everything in before stopping eventually in the centre of the room.

As she did, she sensed a small figure move beside her. Emily turned and looked down to see Lucy, who was smiling back up at her. Emily returned the gesture, and for a moment, Emily had the feeling Lucy was going to reach out and take her hand, though she didn't.

'I like this room,' the young girl told Emily.

Emily didn't know how to reply. 'Really?' she eventually said.

Lucy nodded. 'We play games in here together all the time. It's always fun. Will you play with us sometime?'

Lucy's big brown eyes looked almost pleading in that moment, and Emily couldn't help but smile. 'Yeah, I'll play,' she replied.

'Will you be on my team for some of them?'

'Of course,' Emily said with a small laugh.

'Great!' Lucy said. She then looked over at the other two children. 'And we can beat the stinky boys.' She stuck her tongue out playfully at them. Emily saw Ollie laugh.

Daniel just smiled, his lips still pressed tightly together and hands behind his back.

'We spend quite a few evenings in here together,' Eleanore explained. 'Saturday nights especially.'

'Sounds nice,' Emily said.

Eleanore led them onward once again, and this time when they moved, Lucy stayed by Emily's side.

The older woman guided them out into the entrance hall and diagonally across it to the door on the opposite side near the front of the building. 'This is the den,' she said as they entered.

This space was darker than the others, with only a single window to the front. It was small, about half the length of the library, with more sofa seating across the back wall. Given the shallowness of the space, the natural light from the window easily reached the back wall, but the sides of the room remained quite gloomy. Like the rest of the house so far, the area smelled of old wood, and the air seemed heavy and musty.

Emily quickly noticed a door to her right, at the far side of the space. After letting her look around for a few moments, Eleanore took them through that door next.

'The study,' she stated upon entering. It was a touch larger than the den, but again only had a single window. The study, however, also had multiple light fittings overhead. There were four desks placed around the room, all facing a wall-mounted chalkboard on the back wall. 'We homeschool here,' Eleanore explained. 'The nearest school is quite a long trip away, I'm afraid, but I like to think I'm a pretty good teacher. Right, kids?' she asked the others.

Daniel gave a silent but firm nod, while Ollie's was a little more nonchalant.

'She is,' Lucy confirmed. 'We're learning about the Second World War at the moment.'

'Awful business,' Eleanore stated, 'but important to our history, so it's good to know about.'

The walls in the room were again panelled, this time white, and what floor was exposed was timber boarding, though most of it was covered in a large rug. There were two wardrobes in the room, positioned next to a fire-place. Emily also saw another portrait of the same man from before.

'Who is he?' Emily asked, pointing to the picture.

Eleanore approached and stood next to Emily as both stared at the portrait. 'That is Mr. Graves,' the woman said. 'Jasper Graves. He is the benefactor of this place. Shame he didn't get to see it up and running.'

Emily gazed up to her. 'He died?' she asked.

Eleanore gave a nod. 'He did, I'm afraid, before any of you arrived here. He was as keen to help children that needed it as I am. This was his home, actually, and it has been passed down through his family for many years. Initially, he only asked me to help, but when he found out he didn't have long left, he gifted the house to me and asked if I would run it as a children's home. He was a very kind man.'

Emily wondered if he had been Eleanore's husband, but given the different last names, she guessed not. *Maybe she changed it back after he died.* Regardless, Emily decided to ask anyway. 'Were you and him... you know... erm...'

Eleanore chuckled. 'Together?' She shook her head. 'No, it wasn't like that. But he was a good man, and it's because of him we have this place. Now,' the woman went on, 'let's keep going. Lots more to see.'

The group then took the door straight ahead and Emily

found herself in a stairwell. The stairs were to the left of the space and ran up to a half-landing, where they turned back on themselves and continued. There was a tall window on the half-landing that washed light down over them. The stairs themselves were timber with an extremely dark stain, almost black, and a patterned carpet runner up the centre. The balustrades were dark oak as well, though lighter than the treads, and the other side of the stairs were pressed tight against a side wall. All the walls were panelled, just like many of the other rooms, and were the same pale green as the drawing room.

Emily moved herself over to the stairs so she could look up. From her limited vantage point, it seemed to her like there was another wide hallway above them, and she saw two more columns close to the guardrail.

'We'll head up there shortly,' Eleanore said. 'But let's visit the dining room and garden first.'

After exiting out into the main hall once again, the group then walked through the single door in the far wall.

'You eat *here?*' she asked, gazing around.

'We do,' Eleanore replied. 'Every meal, all of us together.'

It was a far cry from what Emily was used to. Back home, she and her parents always wedged themselves into a square table in their kitchen, or used trays balanced on their laps while sitting and eating in the living room.

This, however, seemed so... formal.

That was mainly because of the large dining table central in the room. It was roughly rectangular, though the corners were rounded, and had two seats against each long side as well as ones at either end of the table. It was made of that familiar dark oak, which seemed to be a constant with the furniture. There were woven table mats in front of each seat, as well as a large circular one in the centre. Knives and forks were already set, along with glasses.

Just behind the table was a door with large glass panels set into it, giving access outside; there were also two full-height windows, one on either side of the door, allowing plenty of light into the space.

The floors were hardwood planks, the same dark stain as the stairs, and the walls were pale green, this time flat with wallpaper rather than the panels of some other rooms. Yet another fireplace was set into the right-hand wall, as well as two radiators.

Then there was the ceiling, which was the familiar brownish-orange coloured plaster, but in the centre was a huge circular moulding with a dull green border. A large, striking crystal chandelier hung down from the moulding, though it was currently switched off since the many wall-mounted lamps spaced around the room were on.

There were two other internal doors in addition to the one behind them, both on the left-hand side of the room. Emily was quick to notice a thick padlock on the one closest to them.

'What do you think so far?' Eleanore asked with obvious pride.

'The house is beautiful,' Emily replied. 'Different to what I'm used to, though.'

Eleanore chuckled. 'I can imagine. They don't make them like this anymore, which is both good and bad.'

Emily turned to her. 'What do you mean?'

'Well, as you said, the house is beautiful, and it's also full of character. But by golly it can get cold, even with the fires and radiators on. It's hard to keep warm here in the winter. We'll have to make sure to get you some more warm clothing—best to be prepared.' She then pointed to the internal door closest to the back wall. 'That's the kitchen,' she said. 'Come on, I'll show you.'

For some reason, Emily had expected the kitchen to be huge, picturing the kind of thing depicted on television shows set a long time ago, where servants in houses like this prepared food for the owners. And while the kitchen *was* big, it wasn't what she was envisioning, appearing much more... normal. Kitchen cupboards ran around the left-hand side of the room, pressed against the wall, and a window sat above the sink looking out over the garden. There was an island, and opposite that were two large cupboards and a refrigerator. Onions hung in sacks to her right, and there were a variety of plants in pots growing close to the window.

She also noticed a wall-mounted rack, which had sets of keys dangling from hooks on it. Emily assumed some were for the external doors and windows, but there were quite a few others dangling down as well, long, old-fashioned iron ones.

Unlike the musty smell of the other areas, Emily picked up the scent of herbs, onions, and fresh greens. 'I prepare the food,' Eleanore began, 'but I've also been teaching everyone how to cook as well. Do you have any experience in cooking?'

Emily shook her head. 'Not really.'

'Well, hopefully you'll enjoy it. Though we have a gas stove here,' Eleanore said, pointing to the large metallic cooker, 'so you have to be careful. We always ensure it's off when we're done. Right, kids? How often do we check?'

'Twice,' Lucy said. 'One time, and then again for a double-check.'

'Right you are,' Eleanore said. 'Because if the gas is left

on and it catches flame, well, the whole house could wind up ablaze in no time at all.'

'I'll remember that,' Emily said.

'Good. Not trying to frighten you, of course. Just safety first. But cooking can be very enjoyable. Lucy and Ollie certainly seem to like it.'

Emily looked to the other boy. 'What about you?'

He didn't say anything, so Eleanore spoke for him. 'He is picking it up well, but Daniel prefers getting his hands dirty in other ways.'

'I like fixing things,' Daniel replied in a soft voice. 'Putting things back together.'

'He's our little builder,' Eleanore said as she moved next to Daniel and put her arm around him to give him a squeeze. 'He even tried to help me with one of the radiators once. He was a huge help.'

Emily looked out of the window before her to the garden, which seemed to stretch on and on. When her parents were alive, they'd all lived together in a small terrace house; they'd had no garden at all, only a small backyard with hard concrete underfoot.

'Want to go see it?' Eleanore asked, nodding out through the window.

Emily nodded. 'Yes please.'

'Excellent,' the older woman replied. 'Follow me. I think you're going to love it.'

After a short trek back into the dining room, everyone filtered out through the rear door. Emily found herself atop a raised patio area looking down at the long garden, which must have continued on for a hundred feet before hitting a back wall lined with tall conifer trees. Over to the far right towards the back was a small football goal, a tennis net, a pole that held a ball on a rope, and even a climbing frame.

To the other side was a large shed, and closer to them were multiple planters, bushes, and flowerbeds.

'I expect you'll spend a lot of time out here,' Eleanore said. 'The children all love being outside, isn't that right?'

'We love it,' said Lucy, who was once again at Emily's side.

Emily turned to Eleanore. 'The garden is so neat. Do *you* cut the grass and water all the plants?'

'I do what I can,' Eleanore said, though she was shaking her head. 'But we also have a gardener that comes once every couple of weeks. Mr. Peterson. You'll meet him soon. He is a little gruff, likes to just get on with his work and not be bothered, but you'll get used to him. And he's very good at what he does. He's a bit of a handyman as well, so he helps out with the house, fixing things that are beyond Daniel and I.' She then turned and gestured to the garden furniture on the patio close to them, which consisted of a table and outdoor sofa under a covered gazebo. 'We sometimes have lunch out here if the weather is nice. And I'll often sit here and read while everyone is playing. If I'm not pottering around in the garden, that is. Actually, if you'd like, I can show you how to plant and tend to flowers. None of the others have really shown an interest in that kind of thing.'

Emily didn't know how to answer; she had no experience with gardening. 'I suppose I can try,' she eventually replied.

'That's the spirit!' Eleanore said. 'And if you don't like it, no harm done. Best to try new things—you never know, you might have green fingers.'

Emily looked down at her hands, frowned in confusion, then gazed over to Eleanore.

'You've never heard that expression before, dear?' she

asked. Emily shook her head. 'Ah, no matter. It's a term used for someone that likes gardening. That they have green fingers because they're always handling plants.'

'Oh,' Emily said, now understanding, though she still thought it was a silly expression.

'Do you like to play football?' Ollie asked her.

Emily nodded. 'I'm not great, but yes.'

'Awesome. We all have a kick about from time to time. I can help you get better. If I can teach Lucy to put the ball in the net from twenty yards out, I'm certain I can improve your game.'

Emily turned to Lucy with a smile. '*Twenty yards* out? Wow.'

'Yup,' Lucy replied with a beaming smile. 'Ollie said I'm better than Peeler.'

'Pelé,' Ollie corrected.

'Yeah, him,' the girl replied, shrugging. Ollie rolled his eyes with a grin.

Emily looked down to the garden again, from the short flight of steps that ran off from the patio, down to the lawn, and then off to the far wall, impressed at how much space was available and imagining all the things she could do in the garden.

'Want to have a look at the bedrooms?' Eleanore asked. 'You can finally see your own room as well.'

In truth, Emily just wanted to sit down for a while, but nodded anyway. 'Sure.'

'Then follow me,' the older woman said.

As Emily moved, she found herself next to Daniel, who quickly looked up in surprise. *He's definitely the nervous one of the group,* she thought to herself. All the kids had been so friendly already, so she didn't like the idea of any of them being nervous around her. Besides, she had enough nerves for everyone at the moment.

'Do you like living here?' she asked him quietly.

Daniel hesitated for a second. 'Mostly, yes,' he said with a nod.

'Mostly?' Emily asked.

'Well...' Daniel began, then paused for a moment. 'I miss how things used to be,' he eventually said.

'I get that,' Emily replied, feeling bad for him. She also found herself wondering about the circumstances that had drawn each of the children to the house.

'But, also, I don't like it here at night,' Daniel added as they stepped back into the dining room.

Emily turned her head to him with a frown. 'Why?'

He twisted his face and screwed his mouth up to one side, obviously debating whether to answer. 'It's just really... creepy,' he answered quietly, looking around at the walls carefully, as if he was scared they'd actually hear him.

Emily looked around as well. 'I can imagine,' she said, picturing how everything would look in the dead of night. The image brought with it a small shudder.

'And...' Daniel began, looking at her. *No,* she realised, *not at me. Past me.* She saw that he was gazing over to the door with the padlock.

'And what?' Emily prompted.

But Daniel just shook his head. 'Nothing,' he said in a tone that brought the conversation to a close, though Emily noticed he kept his eyes on the door until they left the room.

CHAPTER
THREE

The stairwell brought the group out directly into the wide hallway Emily had glanced at before, which was still narrower than the entrance hall on the lower floor and set perpendicular to it. The floor there was a lighter timber plank and covered by a long central carpet. The ceiling was flat with decorative coving to the perimeter, and the walls in the hallways were a mix of panelling and flat surfaces, all the familiar pale green from downstairs. There were also several side tables that stood against the walls. Seven doors lined the corridor, two close by on both the left and right just at the top of the stairs, another four farther down deep into the hallway. Finally, there was one straight ahead at the far end of the space.

The doorways looked much grander than the floor below, with mouldings to the jambs made to resemble columns, and ornate pediments at the heads. Emily noticed the ones to the two closest doors were curved, while the others were roughly triangular but with a deliberate break at the peaks.

'Why are they different?' Emily asked Eleanore, pointing to the door heads.

'Ah, good eye,' Eleanore began. 'It's from the days when servants used to tend to the house. You see, the curved heads that are unbroken showed the room inside belonged to an owner, so the servants weren't allowed to go in without knocking. However, when there is a broken triangular one, the servants could come and go freely.'

'That seems... mean to the servants,' Emily said.

Eleanore nodded. 'It does, doesn't it? It was a different time back then, of course, but even so, it doesn't sit right with me either. No need to worry now though, they're just interesting decorations, nothing more. They won't stop you from going anywhere. In fact, while you can access most rooms off this middle hallway, you can also make your way around pretty much the whole floor just by going room to room. They all have connecting doors for the most part.'

'Is my bedroom on this floor?' Emily asked.

This time, Eleanore shook her head. 'Ollie and Daniel are down here. Your bedroom is on the next floor up, with me and Lucy, if you're happy with that?'

'Sure,' Emily said.

'The floor layout on this storey and the one above is pretty much identical,' Eleanore explained. 'You'll soon get the hang of things. But through there'—she pointed to the left-hand-side door at the top of the stairs—'is another flight of stairs that takes you farther up. The next two doors in the middle of the corridor are for Ollie and Daniel's bedrooms, then the next two close by are the dressing rooms—'

'Dressing rooms?' Emily asked in surprise.

'Oh yes. You have to remember, the first families that lived here were all *very* wealthy.'

'But why can you get to the dressing rooms from the main hall?'

'Oh, there are doors in the bedrooms as well,' Eleanore said. 'Like I told you before, this place is confusing. Lots of rooms all interconnecting. For example, each bedroom also has an ensuite, which you get to through the dressing spaces.' The woman pointed to the door at the end of the hallway. 'That door takes you through into what used to be an antique room, but now we just use it as another game room, or a snug. There is a television in there, but we don't use it much. From there, you can get to a bathroom on one side and a reading room on the other. Also, I'll make you aware now that we don't lock doors here,' Eleanore said. 'But if it's a personal space, everyone always knocks before entering. That seems to suffice.'

'There is one door locked, though,' Ollie said. 'Remember?'

'How many times, Ollie? That is for your safety,' Eleanore said with a frown. She turned to Emily. 'But you have free rein everywhere else. Now, I won't show you Ollie and Daniel's rooms, since I'll leave that up to them, but I can show you the snug.'

Yet again, the group followed their guardian, footfalls reverberating and causing squeaks every other step. Once inside the snug, Emily was immediately greeted by a space that screamed relaxation. There were two low sofas, four bean bags strewn around, a couple of low bookshelves, and a fat-backed television in one corner, complete with an aerial sticking up from it and a sheen of dust over the screen. Two windows overlooked the side lawns, where Emily could just see the top of the boundary and the fields beyond.

'I don't like everyone spending too much time in here, if

possible,' Eleanore said. 'Better to keep one's mind active than just lounging about watching the television.'

Emily nodded, but still felt a little deflated. One of her favourite things to do had been snuggling next to her father to watch television with him after he'd gotten home from a long day at work. Most eleven-year-olds she knew wouldn't even hug their parents, let alone snuggle on a couch, but she'd loved it. Emily suddenly felt a pang of sadness and longing. Not noticing her change in mood, Eleanore led the way through to the reading room, which contained a tall bookshelf, another writing desk, and two more sofas.

'The bathroom is accessed from the snug,' Eleanore said. 'Both here and the story above. Well, it isn't really a snug above us, I use it for my yoga, but you need to come through the middle rooms on both floors regardless.'

'That's... strange,' Emily said.

Eleanore nodded. 'The house was designed before bathrooms were really a thing, so they were added later. Here, I'll show you.'

She moved to the side of the room and pushed the door open, showing a space that could have been big enough for a bedroom, but instead had tiled floor, tiled walls, a toilet, two sinks, a clawfoot bathtub, and large, partitioned shower.

'Just be sure to open a window if you use the shower,' Eleanore said. 'We don't have any extract installed, so the hot water can really fog up the room.'

'I will,' Emily said.

'Now,' Eleanore went on, 'how about we finally head upstairs and I can show you to your room? I'm sure you're eager to see it.'

'Yes please,' Emily replied, already confused by the

layout. In addition, exhaustion had started creeping over her. She hoped that after being shown to her room, she would be afforded a little time alone where she could gather her thoughts, and maybe even cry a little—she could feel the need building.

'The stairwell is through here,' Eleanore went on. Emily and the others followed back toward the stairs they'd just come up, but then the older woman took the door to their right, which brought them out into a smaller, much-less-grand staircase. The space was narrow, and the stairs carpeted in a simple grey, with white spindles and handrail. The stairs again ran up to a half-landing with a window, then continued back on themselves and up to the next storey. Straight ahead, however, was yet another door.

'What's through there?' Emily asked.

'Storage,' Eleanore replied. 'Feel free to take a peek inside, or I can show you another time. I keep sheets, bedding, toiletries... all manner of things, really.'

'I can look later,' Emily said, eager to keep going. The group took the stairs, and after reaching the top, Emily saw a door much like the one below that she guessed led to more storerooms. Everyone took a sharp right and came out into another hallway, this one a little longer than the one below, but with a noticeably lower ceiling. The arrangements of the doors replicated the middle floor, as did their decoration.

'So,' Eleanore began, 'Lucy's bedroom is in the middle on the right, and yours is that one on the left, just opposite Lucy's,' she said, pointing. 'Mine is tucked away in the corner.'

Emily gazed at the closed oak door—a thought struck her. 'Why don't you all sleep on the same floor?' she asked.

'Well, we could,' Eleanore began. 'There are certainly

enough rooms. But I wanted to make sure everyone's bedrooms were roughly the same size, to keep things fair. The four I've given you all are the biggest ones.'

'What about yours?' Emily asked.

'Not as big,' the woman replied. 'Plus, it's one of the coldest. Not right to give any of you a cold space. I think it was probably a guest or servant's room in the past.'

'But... do you not want one of the biggest ones?' Emily asked, confused. *Don't adults* always *get the biggest rooms?*

But Eleanore waved a dismissive hand. 'I don't need much space,' she said. 'Plus, I can handle the cold. The room is just fine for me.'

'And what about when other children come?' Emily continued. 'Won't they be left with smaller rooms?'

'Oh, there won't be any more children coming here,' Eleanore answered.

That took Emily by surprise. She'd just assumed, with the extra space, that people would keep coming until the house was full up.

'Really? You haven't mentioned that before,' Ollie said, clearly as confused as Emily.

'Really,' Eleanore confirmed.

'But why?' Ollie asked. 'There's more space.'

'Yes,' Eleanore replied, 'but unfortunately, there's still only one of me. Honestly, I'd love to have more children here, but I think I'll be stretched too thin if that happens. I want to make sure I give you all the care and time you deserve, and I think I can manage that with four of you. Any more and I'd just worry the attention I can give to each of you would be too diminished. You've all been through enough as it is. The last thing you need is the person looking after you being inattentive. Does that make sense?'

Emily watched Ollie take a moment, clearly thinking

about the woman's words. Eventually, he nodded. 'It does, yeah,' he said. 'Sorry, I just guessed—'

But Eleanore gave another dismissive wave. 'Don't apologise, it's quite alright,' she said. 'In truth, I probably should have discussed this with each of you before now, just so you knew what the plan was. But I think the five of us will make a good little bunch. Well, as long as Emily agrees to stay.' The woman glanced at Emily. 'But no pressure, my dear. Now... let's get you to your room.'

Eleanore approached the door first, and once beside it, she turned to face Emily with a smile. 'We can change the decoration if you want, to something that you like a little more. But for now, I hope it's to your liking.' She then nodded to the door. 'Go ahead,' she said in a gentle voice. 'Take a look.'

For the longest time, Emily didn't move; she just stared ahead at the door, rooted to the spot. For some reason, the idea of going inside made everything seem more real to her, more permanent—as if setting foot in the room would be fully accepting it as her own.

She looked at Eleanore.

'It's perfectly fine,' the guardian said. 'Take your time. I know this is a lot for you. We can always come back later, if you want?'

Emily stared back at the door, then shook her head. 'No, I'm fine,' she eventually said. 'I want to see it.'

Eleanore nodded and shuffled farther to the side. Emily took in a deep, steadying breath and stepped forward, grabbing the brass knob of the door handle, the metal cold beneath her fingertips. She twisted and pushed and the door drifted inwards with a slight squeak. Even from the hallway, Emily could see the room was *much* bigger than her old one. Finally, she stepped inside to take everything in.

In truth, it felt *too* big for her. Her old room was small, with a single bed pushed against one wall, but it was warm, cozy, and it was *hers.*

This new space, despite having plenty of furniture, still felt sparse, cold, and somewhat unwelcoming.

Don't cry, Emily told herself again.

The room had two windows that overlooked the side of the property, which let in plenty of light.

For some reason, Emily had expected to see a four-post bed with curtains around it. While there were no posts, the bed was still large, easily able to accommodate two adults. The duvet was white with a turquoise, flowery pattern—certainly not to Emily's tastes.

There was a hard-backed sofa just at the foot of the bed, facing away from it, with three leather cushions covering the seats. On the far wall opposite the sofa and bed was a fireplace and chimney breast, as per the lower floors, and the room had the pale green-panelled walls Emily had seen so much of already. The floor was the same dark wood as the stairs, which Emily didn't like either, and the hard surface only added to the cold feel of the room. Thankfully, most of the floor was covered with an enormous rug that even ran beneath the bed.

Two big double-door wardrobes provided plenty of storage, and there were two nightstands, a small circular table with a chair near one of the windows, some cabinets, and a long, low bookshelf. While there was ornate coving around the edges of the ceiling, the expanse of its surface was mostly flat, with only a modest ceiling rose holding a chandelier.

Even with all that, there was a lot of space between the bed and the fireplace. *Too* much space. In her head, bedrooms were supposed to be compact and welcoming, like stepping into a warm embrace, not an uncaring void.

You'll get used to it, she told herself, and quickly remembered how she'd often bemoaned the lack of space in her old room.

'Like it?' Eleanore asked, stepping into the room as well. When Emily turned, she noticed the other children waiting outside.

She met Eleanore's eyes and nodded. 'I do,' she said, not wanting to offend. 'Thank you.' However, it was all getting to be too much for her. Too much to take in. Too much change.

Eleanore bent down and placed a gentle hand on Emily's shoulder, studying her. 'Are you okay, dear?'

Emily gave a quick nod. Too quick. She was still fighting the urge to cry, and the question from Eleanore had only pushed her closer.

'Tell you what,' the adult continued. 'We'll leave you here for a little while to rest up. I'm sure this has all been a lot for you to take in. Just come down and see us when you're ready. Or wait until I call for dinner. It's entirely up to you. There's no rush. I'll bring up your things and leave them outside your room.'

Emily wanted to say thank you, but couldn't. She knew the effort of speaking would only make her tears spring free. So she nodded again, feeling her eyes grow wet.

Realising what was happening, Eleanore smiled, gave her shoulder a squeeze, and rose to leave. The woman then moved away, cast a final look back, and closed the door as she left. Emily heard everyone's footsteps walking away, leaving her alone.

I'm alone. Utterly alone.

She couldn't help but picture her mother and father again while she remembered the warmth of her family.

Don't cry, don't cry, don't cry.

But it was no use. Emily ran to the bed, jumped on it, buried her face into the pillow, and sobbed.

CHAPTER
FOUR

'Tell you what,' Eleanore began, talking to the other children as they reached the bottom of the stairs. 'Why don't you all go out to the garden to play for a little while? I'll take Emily's things up, then busy myself around the house. Wrap up just a touch before you go out, though,' she added, raising a finger. 'It's warm enough now, but it will get colder later in the day. Sound good?'

'Yes,' Ollie said, knowing she wanted to keep them all active and not thinking about Emily. 'Come on, gang,' he said to the others as he walked to the tall coat stand in the corner of the hallway. 'First one outside can decide what we play.'

He grabbed three jackets and started to move over to the dining room, but rather than following, Lucy approached Eleanore instead. Fidgeting with her hands, the young girl looked up to the older woman.

'Is... is Emily okay?' she asked. 'She looked sad.'

Eleanore bent down. 'Well, I think she is a little bit,' the woman said. 'She's been through a lot, like all of you, and it's just a lot to take in. So, it's important she has some time alone to process everything.'

'I don't want her to be sad,' Lucy said, looking down.

'That's sweet, honey,' Eleanore replied, gently placing a finger beneath Lucy's chin to tilt her head back up. 'But it's to be expected. Just give her time.'

Lucy nodded.

'Why don't you pick the game, Lucy?' Daniel suggested. Ollie looked to the other boy and smiled.

'You sure, Daniel?' Ollie asked. 'We were going to do first one out chooses. You've got a bit of a head start, you could get to the garden first.'

Daniel just shrugged. 'She'd still beat me,' he said. 'She's rapid.'

Ollie laughed. It was certainly true. 'You might beat *me,* though,' he said.

'Only because you always let us win,' Daniel replied.

'Not always,' Ollie countered, though that certainly wasn't true.

Eleanore stood back to her feet. 'Go on, all of you,' she said with a playful grin, 'before I decide to make you pull all the weeds from the garden for me.'

Lucy's eyes went wide as she laughed. The girl then turned and took off like a rocket, whizzing between Ollie and Daniel and out through the far door.

'Think we best catch her,' Ollie said to Daniel before the two boys jogged away as well.

'Be careful,' Eleanore called after them.

'We always are,' Ollie replied.

The pair soon found Lucy outside, making a beeline for the shed.

'I bet you she picks football again,' Daniel said, sounding a little disappointed.

'You don't like it very much, do you?' Ollie asked as the boys continued their jog.

'It's okay. I just prefer other things.'

Ollie knew the 'other things' he was referring to was playing with his Meccano sets, which were kind of like Legos for older kids, though Dan had also always been partial to hide and seek.

By the time Ollie and Daniel reached the shed, Lucy had already come back outside, football tucked under her arm. 'Will you go in goal, Ollie?' she asked.

'Sure,' Ollie replied. 'You two see how many you can get past me. But I warn you, I won't just let you score this time.'

Lucy scoffed playfully. 'You won't be able to stop me.' She dropped the ball down towards her foot and quickly kicked it back up into her hands to catch it. 'Is this called football or soccer?' she asked. 'I knew a boy back at school who always liked to call it soccer.'

'We call it football,' Ollie stated. 'It's soccer in America.'

'Why?' Lucy asked.

'They have their own version of football.'

'And it's different?' she asked.

'Very,' Ollie confirmed. 'It's more like rugby.'

'Then why don't they call it rugby?'

'Because it's... different.'

Lucy tilted her head and frowned. 'I'm confused.'

Ollie chuckled. 'Don't think about it too much.' He then looked over to Daniel, who was gazing back up at the house. 'What's up?'

'Nothing,' Daniel replied, still looking back. 'Just... what do you think of Emily?'

Ollie shrugged. 'She's nice,' he said. 'But Eleanore was right. She needs some time alone. Remember how you both felt when you first arrived? I think we were all the same. The first thing I wanted to do was cry. It took me a little while to come around.'

'Think she'll stay?' Daniel asked.

Ollie looked back to the house as well. 'I don't know. I hope so. She's like us, nowhere else to go. But we have to help her get used to everything. It's going to be hard for her for a while.'

'I know,' Daniel said. 'I feel bad for her.'

'Me too,' Lucy added.

'Well, we've all been through the same kind of thing,' Ollie continued. 'So, I think we'll be able to help. We understand her, because we know what it's like.'

'Losing our families?' Lucy asked, voice sad.

Ollie noticed she was rubbing a thumb over her locket, the football again tucked under one arm. He offered a sad smile. 'Right,' he said. 'We all helped each other, so we can do the same for her as well.'

Daniel gave Ollie a firm nod. 'We will,' he said with conviction. 'Then hopefully she'll stay.'

'She kind of has to,' Ollie added with a smirk. 'So Lucy isn't outnumbered by smelly boys anymore.'

'Smelly and *stupid* boys,' Lucy corrected, raising a finger and grinning.

The group then started their game, with Lucy and Daniel taking turns shooting at the goal while Ollie attempted to stop them. He saved some, let some pass him, and others he had no chance to save, regardless.

They continued playing for over an hour before things slowed and the trio sat down on the grass for a rest.

'Think we should play board games tonight?' Lucy asked. 'Emily might enjoy it.'

'We can ask her,' Ollie said. 'See how she's feeling and let her join if she's up for it.'

'I think she will be,' Lucy replied. She then stood up.

'Where are you going?' Daniel asked.

'Toilet,' she replied. 'I'll be right back. But I'm bored with football now. You can choose what we do next, Daniel.'

'Why don't *I* get to pick?' Ollie asked with mock offence.

'Because that's how it is,' Lucy shot back and stuck out her tongue, then skipped away towards the house.

Ollie just laughed and shook his head. He picked at the grass, resting one arm on his bent knee.

'Ollie,' Daniel began, 'can... can I tell you something?' He sounded hesitant.

'Of course you can,' Ollie replied. 'Anything. What's up?'

'I... didn't want to say anything in front of Lucy, but last night... I saw something.'

Ollie stopped picking at the grass, immediately interested. 'What?'

Daniel paused and drew in a breath. 'Well, I woke up in the night and couldn't get back to sleep. I was scared at first. I even... hid under my covers a little.' His face flushed.

'It's fine,' Ollie said. 'Don't worry. I know you don't like the house at night. It does feel a little creepy, honestly, but I keep telling you, we're perfectly safe.'

'I know,' Daniel said. 'But... I heard something.'

Ollie cocked his head to the side, intrigued. 'What did you hear?' he asked. 'The house is old and makes lots of strange noises.'

But Daniel shook his head. 'No,' he went on, 'it wasn't

that. I heard someone... walking outside our bedrooms in the hall.'

Ollie straightened up. 'Really?' he asked. 'Are you sure it wasn't a dream?'

Another shake of the head. 'No, it was... Eleanore,' he said.

'Oh,' Ollie replied. 'What was she doing?'

'Well, I heard her going down the stairs,' he said. 'I know it was that because of the creaking. I was... scared at first, before I realised it was her. Scared it was a... you know.'

'Ghosts aren't real, remember?' Ollie stated, repeating the mantra he'd told Daniel many times over the last few months.

'I finally realised who it was when I heard her cough. Because I was already scared, I kinda wanted to go see her.' The redness in his cheeks deepened further. The boy sighed. 'I wish I didn't get so scared.'

'It's fine,' Ollie stated, giving him a light, playful punch on the shoulder. 'Don't worry about it. We all get scared.'

Daniel flashed Ollie a thankful smile. 'Anyway, I managed to force myself to creep outside and walk to the stairs. I just managed to see her at the bottom. She was carrying a tray.'

'A tray?' Ollie asked with a raised eyebrow.

Daniel nodded. 'I couldn't see what was on it, exactly, because it was dark. But I think I saw some small bottles, maybe some water. And some...' he paused. 'I don't know if they were knives and forks or something. I couldn't see them, but I heard them clink. I wanted to shout to her to let her know I was there, but... I also wanted to see what she was doing. So I went downstairs as well, quietly. By the time I got to the bottom, I saw her go through to the dining room. I heard her put the tray down and... I'm sure she unlocked the padlock.'

'The lock to the cellar?' Ollie asked, now extremely interested. That door had always bugged him. Even if the cellar *did* house the boiler, he was confused as to why Eleanore had never shown any of them the space, even just to satisfy their curiosity. *I've certainly asked enough times,* Ollie thought.

It was made even stranger by the fact that they were given unrestricted access to the rest of the house. *Apart from the attic,* he remembered, but only because they needed a ladder to access it. And besides, Ollie had actually seen the attic once before.

The whole thing made Ollie even more certain Eleanore was hiding something down in the cellar. While he liked Eleanore and trusted her to look out for them, he still didn't like her concealing something from them.

Eleanore had always tried to allay his fears, of course, just telling him she didn't want them down there with the old equipment. He'd once asked why, if it wasn't safe, she was allowed to let children live in the house? She'd answered that the cellar had been inspected by someone prior to the house becoming a children's home and signed everything off, under the agreement children didn't play down there. He'd then been told to stop asking about it.

Regardless, Ollie knew any inspection would have been a long while ago, before he and the others had arrived—plenty of time for her to then get things down to the cellar if she wanted.

In truth, Ollie hated not fully trusting Eleanore, as she'd been so perfect in every other way.

'Did you go down to the cellar?' Ollie asked Daniel, prodding him to continue.

'I followed her, but she'd already closed the door behind her by the time I got there. The padlock wasn't there, but I'm pretty sure she used it on the inside after she went in, since I heard it being locked.'

'Strange,' Ollie said while in deep thought. 'I wonder what was on the tray, and why she was taking it down there.'

It wasn't really a lot to go on, and there could have been a rational explanation. Not really cause for alarm.

'That... isn't everything,' Daniel said. 'When I was standing outside the door, I'm certain I heard her say something.'

'Say something?' Daniel asked. 'What?'

'It was something like, 'Almost time, dear.' But I didn't hear any more.'

Ollie frowned in confusion. That *was* odd. 'Who was she talking to?'

Daniel shook his head. 'Not sure. The way she spoke, it was kind of like she was talking to herself, because I couldn't hear anyone reply.'

Ollie sat in silence for a few moments, turning everything over in his mind. After a while, Daniel spoke. 'Do you believe me?' the boy asked.

'Of course I do,' Ollie quickly replied with a nod. 'One hundred percent.'

Daniel looked relieved. 'Should we tell Lucy?'

Ollie considered this. 'Well, it's up to you. I won't stop you if you want to. But it might be best to hold off for now. Just in case she asks Eleanore about it.'

'Okay,' Daniel said. 'So... I take it you don't think we *should* ask Eleanore about it?'

After a moment, Ollie shook his head. 'No, not yet.

Probably best to keep it to ourselves until we can find out more. Do me a favour, though, will you?'

'What?'

'If you wake up and hear her again, come get me. Don't knock, just come straight into my room.'

'Okay,' Daniel replied. 'No problem.'

'Thanks, I appreciate that.'

Ollie had no idea what was going on down in that cellar, but he dearly wanted to find out.

CHAPTER
FIVE

Lucy finished up in her room and came out into the hallway. On her way back to the boys, she stopped and stared at the door to Emily's room. Lucy could have just used the main bathroom on the middle floor, but she had wanted to come up to the top just to see if Emily had finally re-emerged. The girl's door was still closed, and Lucy couldn't hear anything inside the room. Emily's case and backpack remained stacked just next to the door.

Lucy dearly wanted to check on their new arrival, and bit her lip as she stood motionless, tempted to just go over and knock. But she was mindful of what Eleanore and Ollie had said about Emily needing space.

Please stay with us, Lucy thought to herself. She'd never had any brothers or sisters while growing up, but now at the house, it felt like she had two protective brothers in Ollie and Daniel. They both looked out for her and made her feel safe. All that was missing was a sister.

She brought up a hand and gripped her heart-shaped locket, rubbing her thumb over the surface. Just as she started to turn away, the girl heard movement from inside the room and froze. She looked down at the handle as it turned and the door was pulled open. The other girl's head then peeked out—her eyes widened in surprise at seeing Lucy.

'Oh, it's you,' Emily said, 'I thought I heard someone moving about.'

'S-sorry,' Lucy stammered. 'I was just coming back from the bathroom.' She noticed Emily's eyes looked red.

'Okay,' Emily said, then paused for a moment. 'Why are you just standing there?'

Lucy bit her lip, unsure of what to say. *There's nothing wrong with the truth,* she then told herself. 'I... was thinking about coming to check on you,' she admitted. 'Everyone said you needed space, so I wasn't sure if I should do it or not, so I wound up standing here like an idiot. Sorry.'

Thankfully, after a moment, Emily smiled. 'It's okay,' she said. 'Thank you, Lucy. I appreciate that, but I'm fine.'

Lucy knew that wasn't completely true, as Emily had obviously been crying, but she didn't say anything. An awkward silence hung between the two.

'So,' Emily began, 'how long have you been here? At the house.'

'Six months,' Lucy said, then cocked her head to the side with a slight frown. 'Or maybe seven. I can't remember exactly. Something like that.'

'Were you the first one here?' Emily asked.

Lucy shook her head. 'Ollie was. Then me. Daniel came about two months after I got here. And... now we have you,' she added with a smile.

While Emily smiled in return, the expression didn't reach her eyes, and after a few seconds she glanced at the floor. Lucy quickly chastised herself. *Don't push so much!* 'If you like it here, that is,' she quickly added, but was unsure if that would make things worse. Lucy hesitated before finally adding. 'Do you want me to leave you alone for a little bit?'

After a moment, Emily shook her head. 'No, it's okay,' she said, opening her door a little wider. 'I think I'm ready to come out now, anyway. I don't want to just hide away in my room.'

Lucy let a big grin break out over her face. 'That's great!' she exclaimed. 'Though I'd totally get it if you did want to hide. I know Daniel liked to stay in his room a lot for his first couple of weeks. He's more... what's the word Eleanore used for him again? Erm... reserved. Is that right?'

Emily nodded. 'Yeah, that sounds right.'

'But Daniel is really nice, though. Very clever. He's just a little quiet.'

'I've noticed that,' Emily said. 'Nothing wrong with being quiet. I'm like that sometimes myself.'

'Oh, I'm not,' Lucy replied with a giggle. 'Ollie says I'm a chatterbox. He says I even keep talking in my sleep, just chattering on, but I don't believe him. I'm pretty sure he's just teasing me.'

The other girl laughed. 'Probably. Ollie seems to look out for everyone here, from what I've seen.'

'He does,' Lucy confirmed with a nod. 'He likes to make sure everyone is okay. I know he used to be an older brother before... you know. He had a little sister. Grace.' Lucy looked down. 'Not anymore though.'

'I see,' Emily said. 'That's sad. Do you know what happened?'

Lucy nodded. 'We've all shared what happened to us. But I think he should tell you about Grace. It's his story. We all have our stories. I don't mind telling you mine, if you want. You don't have to do the same. I know that would be hard.'

'Are... are you sure?' Emily asked with a surprised expression.

Lucy nodded. 'Of course.'

'And... and you won't mind if I don't want to talk about what happened?'

Lucy responded with a shake of her head. 'Nope. Not a bit.' She then took a small breath and rubbed her locket for a moment before beginning. 'I grew up on a farm. Dad worked a whole lot, most of the day and most of the night, and Mum kept the house all nice. I loved living there. As I got a little older, Mum started getting sick a lot, so she couldn't spend as much time looking after me.' She looked down as she recalled how things changed, her eyes fixed on her locket. 'Dad needed to keep working, as he said times were getting harder, so I was on my own a lot. I didn't have brothers or sisters or anything. Eventually, Mum got *really* ill, and... she died.'

'I'm so sorry,' Emily said earnestly.

Lucy smiled. 'Thank you. It was awful, and Dad really took it hard. He wasn't good at looking after children. I mean, he loved me a bunch, I know that, but he wasn't good at the normal stuff: brushing my hair, buying clothes, cooking, and 'keeping the house going,' as Mum had called it.'

'What happened to your dad?' Emily asked. 'Did... did you get taken away from him?'

'Oh no,' Lucy said. 'He tried for me, but he really missed Mum, and started to drink a lot. A lot of beer and whiskey. I kept trying to help him, but...' Lucy trailed off. She'd told the story a few times before, and while it was always hard, she knew she could get through it.

'It's okay,' Emily said. 'You don't have to—'

'No, it's fine,' Lucy insisted. 'Dad died a year and a half after Mum did. Heart attack, they said, but I think it was just a broken heart. And then...' She shrugged. 'I didn't have anyone. Not until I came here. Now, I have another family. I mean, I know it's not my *real* one, but sometimes it feels like it is.'

'I take it you like it here?' Emily asked.

'Yeah, I really do,' Lucy said. 'It's different from my old home, and it *does* get cold in the winter, like Eleanore said, but it's so big! Every day is like a little adventure. Ollie and Daniel are great, and Eleanore always makes sure we have everything we need. She just treats us as if we were her own kids. I mean, it's not the same as with Mum and Dad, but I know things could be a lot worse for me. I could have ended up anywhere. I've heard of places for kids like us that are just like big schools, everyone packed in. I definitely don't want to end up anywhere like *that*.'

'You mean an orphanage?' Emily asked.

'That's it!' Lucy replied. 'Yeah, an orphanage. They don't sound good.'

'No,' Emily said, 'they don't. Thank you for sharing what happened. That must have been tough.'

Lucy went to nod, then shrugged. 'It gets easier the more I talk about it. Suppose it helps being a chatterbox.' She then grinned, causing Emily to laugh.

'What's that?' Emily then asked, pointing to Lucy's locket.

Lucy looked down to it, still pinched between her thumb and forefinger. 'Oh, it's got a picture of Mum and Dad in it. Wanna see?' Without waiting for an answer, Lucy carefully unclipped the front, opened it, and stepped closer to Emily; she held it up, feeling the chain pull taut against the back of her neck. 'See?'

Emily leaned in and nodded, staring at one side, then the other. The left part had a photo of Lucy's mother, smiling and looking out, and on the right was her father, who wasn't smiling, but still looked happy.

'Wow,' Emily said. 'Your mother is beautiful.'

'She was,' Lucy said with a nod. 'Even at the end, when she was sick, she tried to make herself look nice. As much as she could.'

'And your dad looks big and strong,' Emily went on.

Lucy laughed. 'Oh yeah. When he picked me up, it was like I weighed nothing. He could keep me on his shoulders for *hours*, just walking around carrying me like I wasn't even there.' She giggled at the memory. *He couldn't do that after Mum died, though,* she told herself, then quickly exorcised the thought, concentrating on the good memories instead.

There was another brief silence between the two, then Lucy went on: 'You wanna come with me? We're all outside playing. You can join in. Beats being in that stuffy old room all day.'

'I suppose it does,' Emily said. 'Sure, I'll come.'

Lucy beamed another smile. 'Great! Make sure you grab a jacket,' she said, tugging at the one she was wearing. 'It's getting a little cold.'

Emily looked down at her case and bag. 'Gimme a sec,' she said, grabbing them both and moving them inside the room. Lucy watched through the open door as Emily rummaged through her backpack for a moment, then came back out while slipping on a thin fleeced jacket. She closed the door behind her. 'I'll unpack everything else later,' she said.

Unpack? Lucy thought. *Does that mean she's staying?* But she didn't ask—she didn't want to get ahead of herself.

After descending the stairs and moving out into the main hall, the girls ran into Eleanore, who was just stepping out of the library. She looked at Emily in surprise.

'Oh, you've decided to venture out? How wonderful.'

'Yeah,' Emily said. 'Lucy asked me to come outside and play. Said it would be better than sitting in my room alone all day. I think she's right.'

'Now, Lucy,' Eleanore began, with a gaze somewhere between being stern and amused, 'you weren't being too pushy, were you?'

'No!' Lucy quickly said.

'She wasn't,' Emily added straight after. 'Honestly, she wasn't pushy at all. I just... wanted to go outside.'

Eleanore smiled. 'Well, I'm happy to hear that, dear. The fresh air will do you good. Anyway, don't let me stop you, you two run along. Get to know each other and play. I'll call you in a couple of hours when dinner is ready.'

'Thanks Eleanore,' Lucy said. She then grabbed Emily's hand and pulled her away. Thankfully, she felt Emily allow herself to be led, rather than resisting.

'What games were you playing?' Emily asked.

'Football,' Lucy said. 'But I think we're all done with that for now. You can pick the next one. Or we can just sit and chat.' Then, as they broke through to the dining room, Lucy asked, 'How old are you? You're taller than me, so I guess you're older. You seem a little older.'

'I'm eleven,' Emily said.

'Cool! I'm nine,' Lucy replied. 'Daniel is eleven as well, but he's a little short for a boy, I think. Ollie is the oldest, he's twelve. So we're all pretty close together, I guess.'

'Yeah, I guess we are,' Emily agreed. 'Apart from Eleanore. Do you know how old she is?'

Lucy frowned as she thought. 'Fifty something, I think. I'm sure I heard her say that. But she's very fit for someone that old. She does loads of stretching all the time.'

'Yoga?'

Lucy nodded. 'Yeah, that's it. It must give her lots of energy, because she's always doing something.'

'Well, I suppose this is a big house for her to look after.'

'Sure is,' Lucy said. 'You know, I think it's good the rest of us are so close together. In age, I mean. We can all play and hang around and no one is too young or annoying.' Lucy then looked over to Emily and grinned. 'Unless you think *I'm* too young and annoying?'

Emily just smiled. 'No, Lucy, you seem lovely to me.'

'But a bit of a chatterbox, right?'

Emily, still smiling, held up her thumb and forefinger, with just a touch of space between. 'Maybe a teensy bit, but I like it.'

'Good,' Lucy replied. 'You can tell that to Ollie for me.' She pulled Emily on a little more forcefully. 'Come on, let's go before it's dinner time.'

'We have a few hours yet,' Emily said as they broke into a trot.

'Yeah, but that will *fly* past,' Lucy replied. 'So we gotta make the most of it.' Lucy then let go of Emily's hand and ran ahead. 'Keep up, slowcoach,' she called back with a giggle.

CHAPTER
SIX

Daniel and Ollie sat in relative silence for the rest of the time while they waited for Lucy to return. Daniel knew the older child was thinking about what he had just told him.

He wondered if he'd done the right thing. *It's probably nothing strange.* After all, Daniel hadn't been able to see what exactly had been on the tray, and Eleanore going down to the cellar wasn't hugely strange. *Maybe she was just checking on things.*

But then, that didn't explain *what* she'd said. 'Almost time, dear.'

Who is the 'dear'? he wondered. *Is there someone else here? And almost time for what?*

And why go down at that time, when she should have been asleep?

Daniel was tying together the stalks of two daisies he'd picked while he thought, his fingers working absentmindedly. When he looked up and back at the house, however, he raised his eyebrows in surprise.

'Emily's coming, too,' he said, feeling himself tense up.

Ollie looked up. 'Oh, cool,' the boy said. 'Brave of her to come out so soon.'

'Yeah,' Daniel agreed, remembering how long it had taken him to finally feel comfortable leaving his room.

I need to be braver, he told himself.

Ever since Daniel had first arrived, everyone at the house had been great with him.

Eleanore had looked after his every need, and cuddled him when he'd cried and gotten overwhelmed. Lucy had welcomed him with open arms, literally. She'd ran towards him as he'd first approached the house and hugged him tight, saying she was so happy someone else had come to live there. Daniel knew Eleanore had spoken to Lucy later about that, telling the young girl not to do it with new arrivals. Then there was Ollie, who had taken Daniel under his wing like an older brother.

Daniel was thankful for all of that, for their patience and protection... but he often felt like a burden. All he wanted was to look out for the others as much as they looked out for him.

But he knew that meant forcing himself to overcome his fear and fight his way out of his shell.

Both of the boys stood as the girls walked over.

'Look who wanted to come see us!' Lucy said with a big smile.

'Hi again,' Ollie said to Emily with a wave.

'Hi,' Daniel added as well, though he refrained from waving.

'How are you feeling?' Ollie asked.

Emily tilted her head from side to side, looking unsure. 'Okay, I guess,' she said. 'It's just all...' She trailed off, obviously searching for the words.

'A lot?' Ollie suggested.

Emily nodded. 'Yeah, a lot.'

'Don't worry,' he said. 'We all felt the same way when we first got here.'

'Lucy told me you were the first,' Emily stated.

'That's right,' Ollie replied. 'I got here maybe a year ago now. The place felt a lot bigger back then when it was just me and Eleanore.'

Emily turned to Daniel. 'And you got here a little after Lucy, right?' Daniel was tempted to just nod, but instead decided to push himself and speak. 'That's right,' he replied, copying Ollie. He tried to think of something else to say. 'I was scared at first,' he admitted. He then stopped himself. *Why did I tell her that?* Then he quickly added, 'But everyone helped me.'

'Even me?' Lucy asked, holding her grin.

'Even you, Luce,' Daniel replied.

'So what are we playing?' Emily asked. 'I hear you just got done with football.'

'Yeah, I'm bored of that now,' Lucy said as she stepped forward and performed a lazy cartwheel. 'Hide and seek?' she then suggested. 'Daniel likes that.'

'Only if we play it out here,' Daniel said. He *did* like that game, but not when they did it in the house. It was too big, and when you were hiding, it meant you could be a *long* way from anyone else.

'Wait!' Lucy suddenly said, dramatically slapping her own forehead. 'I said Emily could pick.'

Emily giggled and shook her head. 'It's fine,' she said. 'I'll go with the flow.'

Lucy frowned. 'Go with the flow?'

'Yeah, you know... go with what everyone else wants to do.'

However, Lucy's frown didn't fade. 'But why is there a flow?'

'Well,' Emily started, 'it's... erm.'

'If most people want to do the same thing,' Daniel began, 'then imagine them all flowing the same way. And if someone is going with the flow, they're following along with it, letting themselves be taken along. Like a stick in a stream or something.'

'Yes,' Emily added, 'that's it exactly. Thanks, Daniel.'

Daniel just nodded.

'I get it,' Lucy said, her confused frown finally disappearing. 'So... what does the 'flow' want to do? Hide and seek?'

When nobody made a suggestion, Lucy shrugged. 'Let's just go play on the climbing frame for a little bit,' she said. 'We can talk or something. Besides, I'm a little tired.'

'*You're* tired?' Ollie asked in feigned shock. 'I didn't know you *got* tired. You're a little bundle of energy.'

Lucy laughed. 'Maybe that's why I keep talking and can never sit still. Buuuut it has been a long day.'

She then looked to Emily for support. 'Climbing frame sounds good,' the new girl replied.

The group then walked over to the frame, which was made from thick wooden logs, all assembled in three distinct segments. There was an 'up-and-over' part with a net on each side, an enclosed space in the middle, and at the other end, a section with thinner interconnected logs in the shape of a dome. Lucy approached that segment, climbed to the middle, hooked her legs over one of the logs, and let herself dangle upside down, her long hair flowing freely towards the ground. Ollie then climbed up to the top, where he sat perched like a bird keeping watch over its nest.

Daniel gestured for Emily to go next. She smiled and started to climb, but it was clear she had no route in mind and didn't really know where she wanted to go. Eventually, she hauled herself up close to Lucy and pushed her bum through one of the gaps to sit while letting her legs dangle.

Daniel moved farther around the side to climb up, pushing himself closer to the top, where he settled. Eleanore had been right, it was getting a little colder now. It had been a nice day so far, but Daniel noticed the first signs of the skies starting to dull, which meant night was coming.

'Do you guys ever get out of the house?' Emily asked.

'We're outside now, silly,' Lucy replied.

'No, that's not what I mean. It's just... if you're home-schooled here, do you, like, just spend *all* your time at the house and in the garden? Don't you ever get to leave?'

'Oh, we do,' Ollie said. 'We often go into town with Eleanore. It's a bit of a drive, though.'

'How do you get there?' Emily said, turning to look up at him. 'I didn't see a car anywhere.'

'Oh, Eleanore doesn't drive,' Daniel explained. 'We get a taxi.'

'Ah,' Emily said.

'But we usually go about once a week, on a weekend normally,' Daniel went on. 'There's a big park there we enjoy playing in.'

'That's good,' Emily said.

'Did you think we were just prisoners trapped in here?' Ollie asked, grinning.

'Well, it *had* crossed my mind,' Emily replied with a laugh. 'But it's good to know you're not.'

'Honestly,' Ollie went on, 'it can feel a little... I don't know what the word is... like we're here a lot. It's nice spending time outside, and the house is huge, but for the most part we're always here. We do get to go out, sure, but it's different than before—for me, anyway. I had school, football lessons, and on weekends we'd go and see family. So, it takes a little getting used to.'

Emily gave an understanding nod. 'But you *did* get used to it?'

'Yeah,' Ollie said. 'And now I like it here. It definitely helped when Lucy and Daniel came.'

'Ollie said when I came I talked his ear off,' Lucy stated, still dangling.

'You did,' Ollie teased.

'Yup,' Lucy agreed. 'And you didn't stop me. Because you loooved it.'

'I'm just patient,' Ollie countered.

There was a brief pause before Lucy spoke up again. 'I... told Emily my story.'

'You *did?*' Daniel asked, looking over to the youngest of the group with raised eyebrows.

Lucy nodded, which looked odd since she was upside down. 'It just kinda... happened. Sorry.'

As far as Daniel understood it, they were supposed to all open up as a group, and only when the time was right. *Does that mean I have to tell my story now?* He didn't feel quite ready for that. It had been hard enough telling Ollie and Lucy the first time, and he barely knew Emily.

'Oh, don't worry,' Emily said. 'You guys don't need to tell me yours. I know it's personal.'

'Well,' Ollie began, 'since Luce couldn't wait, I don't mind going.'

But before he could continue, Lucy gripped onto the bars on either side of her and let her body roll down over itself as she supported her own weight. When her feet made contact with a log below, she adjusted herself into a sitting position. She then vigorously shook her head. 'I was getting dizzy,' she explained. The young girl then looked up. 'Go on, then, Ollie.'

Ollie chuckled. 'Yes, boss,' he said. After a brief pause, he started picking at the threads at the bottom of his jeans. 'Dad died first,' he said. 'He worked in a factory, and some idiot there got his sleeve caught in one of the big machines. Dad tried to help, but he was pulled in...' He trailed off for a moment. 'Anyway, it was hard after that. But me, my mum, and my sister Grace all carried on. I tried to make sure Grace was always okay, though I could tell she was struggling. One weekend when I was at football practice, Mum was on her way to pick me up, and Grace was in the car with her. They had an accident. They both died in the crash. The person that hit them had been drinking.' He shrugged. 'And that was that. I wasn't there for them.'

'I'm so sorry,' Emily said up to him. 'That's... awful.'

Ollie nodded. 'Yeah, but we've all had awful things happen. Lucy told you her story, Daniel has his, and you obviously have your own, so we've all been through it. Don't worry, though, you don't need to tell us yours now. Or at all, if you don't want to.'

'But... why do you all share them?' Emily asked.

Ollie shrugged. 'It was Luce that started it. She told me what happened to her. It made me realise I wasn't on my own, that someone else was feeling the same thing. So, I told her what happened to me. It kinda... helped.'

Daniel felt Emily's eyes fall on him and his body tightened again.

'Don't worry,' she quickly said. 'You don't have to say any—'

'No, it's okay,' Daniel interrupted. *Gotta be brave*. 'I... I don't mind.'

'Only if you're sure,' Emily added.

Daniel looked up to Ollie, who was gazing back down with an understanding smile. He gave Daniel a nod as if to say, *It'll be fine.*

'I was like Luce,' Daniel began. 'I lost my mam first.' He knew the others pronounced it *mum*, but in his family it had always been different. 'Cancer,' he said. 'Happened when I was eight.' Thinking of his mam, first when she was loving, fit and healthy, then when she was frail and weak, almost made him start crying on the spot. He fought on, however. 'Dad was a mechanic and ran his own business. During school holidays after Mam died, I spent a lot of time at work with him, watching him fix things. But when we were at home, he drank a lot, same as Luce's dad. Then one day when I got back from school, there were police and an ambulance at my house. They said he'd swallowed some pills. I wasn't allowed inside. In fact, I didn't ever get to go back inside my house. They asked me if I wanted to get my things, but I told the people looking after me what to grab. I just... didn't want to go back in.' He shook his head, feeling tears roll down his cheeks. 'I kept thinking I'd see him lying there on the floor, though I knew he wasn't really there anymore.'

Movement beside him caused Daniel to look up, and he saw Lucy climb closer. She placed an arm around his shoulder and gave him a squeeze.

He left me all alone, Daniel wanted to add. *He was supposed to be there for me but left me*. He didn't just want to say it, he wanted to scream it.

'Then not long after, I came here,' Daniel finished and

forced a smile. 'And Luce has been talking my ear off ever since.'

Lucy squeezed him tight once again. 'You're welcome,' she said.

There was a pause.

'You okay, Daniel?' Ollie called down.

'Yeah,' Daniel eventually said, wiping his eyes. 'You?'

'Yeah,' Ollie stated.

Daniel turned to Lucy. 'And you?'

Everyone always felt glum after sharing like that. He, Ollie, and Lucy had heard each other's stories before, of course, more than once, but each time the sessions were always accompanied by an odd feeling Daniel couldn't place, like it had brought everyone even closer together.

He hoped the moment had helped Emily in some way as well.

'I... I think I wanna go too,' Emily said, surprising him.

They all turned to look at her.

'Really?' Daniel asked.

'You sure?' Ollie added. 'There's no pressure. You don't have to—'

'No, I think... I think I want to,' Emily said. 'Well, if "want" is the right word.'

Daniel was impressed. 'Bit of advice,' he said. 'If you feel like you're struggling, just push through. It doesn't matter if you cry. I was a *mess* when I first told mine.'

'You weren't a mess,' Ollie said. 'We all cried. It's fine.'

'Well, there *was* a bit of snot,' Lucy jibed and Daniel couldn't help but laugh. Then, they fell silent and waited for Emily to begin.

'House fire,' she eventually stated, looking down at the ground. 'I wasn't there. I was staying at a friend's house.

Didn't have any brothers or sisters, it was just me, Mum, and Dad.' She took a breath. 'The fire actually started next door, but it spread to our house while everyone was asleep. There... there wasn't much left. One night my house was there, then it wasn't. One night my parents were there, then—'

Emily broke down crying.

In an instant, the others moved towards her. They helped Emily down to the ground and all three of them circled around and hugged her, embracing her from all sides. Daniel was in front and he felt one of Emily's arms wrap around his shoulders, her fingers gripping the back of his shirt tightly as her sobbing grew more intense.

There were no gentle utterances of 'Shhh' or 'it'll be alright,' because they all knew better. They just had to let her cry, let her get it out and feel what she was feeling.

Because it *wasn't* alright.

Daniel knew that. They all knew that.

It was awful and unfair and none of them deserved it. He started crying as well, and though he didn't sob and shake, tears still rolled down his cheeks freely. He heard Lucy sniff and realised she was doing the same.

The group just stood like that for a while—*for as long as it takes,* Daniel told himself—holding each other, letting Emily's pain flow out.

Her head dropped a little lower and Daniel felt it press into his upper chest, her hair tickling under his chin. It made him uncomfortable, simply because he wasn't used to hugging, not since his mother died. But he stayed put.

He didn't know how much time had passed, but eventually Emily lifted her head, her eyes red and puffy and wet.

'I'm... I'm okay,' she eventually said and lowered her arm from Daniel's shoulders. The group slowly untangled, with Lucy the last to let go.

Emily wiped her eyes with her sleeve, then took a breath and let out a long exhale. 'Woah,' she said. 'That was... something.'

'How do you feel?' Ollie asked.

Emily considered the question. 'Sad,' she eventually said. 'But... happy I shared, if that makes sense.'

'It does,' Daniel replied. 'For what it's worth, I'm sorry that happened to you.'

'Me too,' Lucy said.

Ollie put his hand on Emily's shoulder and squeezed.

'Well,' Emily started, 'I'm sorry for what all of you went through as well.'

'It's crappy, isn't it?' Lucy said, then covered her mouth. 'Is crappy okay to say?'

'You already said it,' Ollie replied. 'Twice. It isn't too bad, just don't let Eleanore hear you.'

Emily continued wiping her eyes. 'I must look a mess,' she said. 'Eleanore is going to know I've been crying.'

'Don't worry,' Ollie said. 'We have time before we go back in. Besides, Eleanore won't say anything. She knows sometimes we process stuff together. She doesn't press us unless we want to talk. She's actually really good like that.'

'Nice to know,' Emily said, sniffing. 'I could do with a tissue, though.'

'I'll go get you something,' Daniel said and turned towards the house.

'Oh no, you don't have to do that.'

'It's fine,' he said as he set off. 'Just wait here. I'll be right back.'

'Thank you, Daniel,' Emily called after him.

Daniel made his way to the kitchen, where he grabbed a couple of segments of paper towel from the roll. As he was leaving the kitchen, he saw Eleanore enter the dining room from the hallway. His eyes immediately flicked to the padlocked door before returning to her.

'Hi, Daniel,' she said happily. 'How are you all?'

'Good,' Daniel said. 'Emily is outside with us.'

'I know,' she replied. 'I saw her and Lucy heading out. How does she seem?'

'Okay,' Daniel said. He saw Eleanore glance down to the paper towels in his hand. 'For Emily,' he explained.

Eleanore just nodded. 'Say no more, and don't keep a lady waiting, Daniel. Tell everyone there's only a little while longer before dinner. I'll call you in soon.'

'I will,' Daniel said. He then headed back out, casting one last look at the locked door as he went.

CHAPTER
SEVEN

'How are you finding the food, Emily?' Eleanore asked from her position at the head of the table.

'Delicious,' Emily replied as she finished chewing her mouthful of chicken. The small amount of remaining meat was accompanied on the plate by a few leftover green beans. The plate had been stacked with mashed potatoes, gravy, and sliced carrots.

'Glad to hear it,' Eleanore said before she slipped her own fork into her mouth, grabbing two skewered carrot slices with her teeth.

There hadn't been much conversation as they'd eaten. Eleanore had initially asked everyone how the day had been, and they had all talked about what they'd been doing that afternoon—thankfully, from Emily's point of view, leaving out the stories the children had shared—but that had been it.

Now the only sounds were the clinking of cutlery on plates, or people's sips of water to wash down the food. Emily had been tempted to ask if there was anything tastier to drink, like orange squash or lemonade, but decided against it.

It was growing darker outside, so the lights were all on in the dining room. Though the chandelier was directly above the table, its light washed mostly to the side, keeping it from being too bright below.

'So,' Emily began again after setting her knife and fork down on her plate and crossing the two pieces of cutlery over each other to show she was finished. 'What are we doing this evening?'

'Board games!' Lucy stated, looking over to Emily. 'It'll be fun.'

Emily nodded. 'I'm okay with that.'

'Sounds like a good idea,' Eleanore said. 'Is everyone agreeable?' She looked to Ollie and Daniel, who both nodded. 'Excellent. Who gets to pick the game? I think Emily should do the honours, personally.'

'Oh, no,' Emily began. 'I don't want to—'

'Yes, Emily picks!' Lucy interjected. 'And the rest of us will just go with the flow.'

Emily heard Ollie snicker.

'Great,' Eleanore started. 'Well, when everyone is done, we'll get washed up and head over to the drawing room.'

'Can we light the fire?' Lucy asked. 'Make it all nice and cozy.'

'We'll see,' Eleanore replied.

'Please?' Lucy asked, making puppy-dog-eyes.

'As I said, we'll see,' Eleanore replied, though her tone made it obvious she'd give in.

Sure enough, not an hour later, everyone was seated around the coffee table in the drawing room while the fire crackled close by. Emily found the heat coming off it to be extremely soothing. However, it did nothing to stave off the feeling of tiredness that was ever increasing.

Emily had chosen Monopoly, simply because it was something she'd played before. Even though the game hadn't been going on long, Daniel had already taken a commanding lead, buying up properties strategically and watching the money roll in.

'Has everyone made you feel welcome on your first day, Emily?' Eleanore asked as Emily shook the dice and rolled.

'They have,' Emily replied as she moved her piece on the board. 'They *really* have. I was... really nervous coming in, but everyone has been so friendly, and that really helped.'

'They're good kids,' Eleanore said as she smiled at the others with pride. 'I can honestly say we've never had any trouble here, no fighting or arguments. Maybe the occasional squabble, but nothing important. Honestly, it amazes me just how well these three have gelled.'

'Emily will gel as well,' Lucy said. 'She's definitely one of us now.'

'Lucy,' Eleanore replied. 'What I have told you about being pushy?'

But Lucy shrugged. 'What? She is. I can already tell.'

Eleanore shook her head, but Emily just smiled. 'It's fine,' Emily said, then threw a wink at Lucy, who grinned in return. 'But like I said, everyone has made my first day much easier.'

'I'm so happy to hear that,' Eleanore stated as she rolled herself and moved her own piece across the board. She ended up on a space that Daniel owned—the boy had obviously been counting ahead, as he wore that familiar tight-lipped grin.

'Well, I guess Daniel is about to make even more money,' Eleanore said and handed over some notes.

'Thank you,' Daniel said as he happily took them, adding them to his piles of money that had been split by amounts, rising left to right from highest to lowest. Eleanore let out a sigh and wafted her hand in front of her face. 'Goodness, it's warm in here with that fire.' The older woman then slipped off her jumper, which showed the plain off-white t-shirt below. As she balled up her top and set it down beside herself, Emily noticed the rope necklace she was wearing—*maybe it's twine,* Emily considered—that held a ring at the bottom. Eleanore noticed Emily looking at it. She lifted her hand and rubbed the flat black ring with her thumb and forefinger. 'Looking at this?' she asked. 'I've had it a long time. Truth be told, I couldn't even tell you where I got it.'

'Does the circle mean something?' Emily asked.

'Not that I'm aware of,' Eleanore replied. 'Though in many cultures and beliefs, shapes are important. Circles, triangles, things like that. They all have certain connotations.'

'Mum wore a necklace,' Emily went on. 'A crucifix.'

'Was she religious?' Eleanore asked.

'Maybe a little,' Emily said with a shrug. 'But she didn't go to church or anything. Grandma was *very* religious, so maybe Mum just wore it to remind her of her own mother after Grandma died.' Emily gazed at the circle a little more. 'Are you religious?'

Eleanore hesitated. 'I'd say I'm more spiritual,' she said. 'I don't follow Christianity or anything like that, but... how do I put this... I do think there is more to life, or more to existence, than what we think we know.'

'So...' Emily began, 'you think there's more after we die?'

Eleanore gave a soft smile and nodded. 'I do, yes. I have no idea what that *is,* of course, but it's a personal belief.' She paused. 'Do you have any beliefs about what happens next?' The woman sounded hesitant, as if unsure whether or not she should bring up the subject.

Emily thought about the question. 'Not really,' she said. 'I just always assumed there was nothing. Dad believed that. But'—she shrugged—'who knows. I don't really like to think about it, to be honest.'

'That's understandable,' Eleanore said. 'It's not the most pleasant of topics. We don't have to talk about it.' No one raised any protest, so Eleanore changed the subject. 'How about tomorrow we head into town for a little bit? We can sort through your clothes before we go, Emily, and see if you have enough suitable for winter. If not, we'll get you some things.'

'Oh, I'm sure I'll be okay with what I have,' Emily said.

'It's perfectly fine,' Eleanore replied. 'And even if you decide against staying, you can take what we buy with you. There's a good bookshop as well. So we'll look through that.'

'Do we *all* get presents?' Lucy asked, hopefully.

'Tell you what,' Eleanore said. 'For being so welcoming to Emily, everyone gets something. But nothing that's going to break the bank.'

Lucy cheered and did a little fist pump.

The game continued for another hour or so until Daniel had eventually cleaned everyone out. Once it was done, Emily couldn't help but yawn. That, in turn, caused Eleanore to yawn as well.

'Dearie me,' the older woman said. 'It seems like it's

been a long day for us all. Is everyone tired?' There were nods around the room, and Eleanore checked her watch. 'It isn't very late, but an early night might be a good idea. How about we have a light supper and call it a day?' No one disagreed. 'That's settled, then. Emily, I know you haven't unpacked, but if you'd like, I can help you with that in the morning when we sort through your clothes. There is a toothbrush, toothpaste, shampoo, and soap already in your en-suite. Do you have clothes to sleep in?'

'Yes,' Emily replied. 'I kept them in my backpack.'

'Great. Well, let's get the game packed up, then grab some cereal. If anyone does want to stay up a little later, feel free, just don't be up *too* late.'

As it turned out, no one took Eleanore up on that offer, and after their supper, everyone said their goodnights—with Lucy giving Emily a tight hug—before retiring to their rooms.

Once inside, Emily retrieved her vest and pyjama bottoms, changed, then moved into the dressing area to find the en-suite.

As she entered the dressing room, she looked over to a door that gave access to one of the other rooms. She considered dragging a chair from the bedroom to push up against it and stop anyone from getting in.

Don't be paranoid, no one here will sneak in.

However, reality soon sunk in—as nice as everyone had been, Emily realised she hardly really knew them.

She decided against barricading the door, however, and examined the narrow space around her, which was lit by a single bulb with no lampshade. There was a long rail against one side of the room with scores of empty clothes hangers dangling from it. On the other side were two rows of stacked shelving, again empty. There was also a set of drawers and a taller storage unit with a cabinet door. The decoration was plain and white, though the white had started to yellow in places. At the end of the dressing room was another door that gave access to the en-suite. Emily stepped inside. The bathroom was small, with an enclosed shower, toilet, and single sink. A toothbrush and tube of toothpaste sat in a glass on the corner of the sink, with a bottle of handwash and facewash, both perched on the other corner. There was also a soap holder fixed to the wall close by, with what looked to be a fresh bar of green soap resting on it.

Emily quickly used the toilet, washed herself, cleaned her teeth, and then moved back into the bedroom. It was dark outside now, and quiet. It had been quiet when she'd been up in her room earlier, but that had been during the day, so while she'd been sad, Emily hadn't felt uneasy. Now, though, Daniel's words from earlier were replaying in her mind: *I don't like it here at night. It's just really... creepy.*

The chandelier was on, as well as the four wall-mounted lights and the lamp on her nightstand, yet the room was so big there were still pockets of gloom between the patches of light. Emily looked ahead to the window and could only see absolute blackness beyond it. She listened intently, hearing some quiet movement on the same floor as her—*probably Eleanore or Lucy getting ready for bed*—but other than that, nothing. The air felt heavy, somehow. She stepped forward, intending to look farther out of the window to find out what she could see, but stopped when she felt anxiety creep up from her gut. Instead, she grabbed a book from her backpack, switched off the main lights, and climbed under the covers, guided by her nightlight. The thick duvet was cool against her feet. She shuffled down, pushing her head back into the thick pillows, surprised at just how comfortable the bed was. It was so big she felt lost in it, especially when compared to her old one.

From there, Emily tried to read more of her story, but found herself just gazing at the pages for a while without really taking in the words, completely lost in thought.

The events of the day replayed over in her mind. She remembered the nerves she'd felt when first walking down the drive, and when first meeting the others—and then her surprise at just how nice they'd all turned out to be. She remembered the warmth and companionship she'd felt while playing the board game. She then thought about her big, cold room, and of the huge house that creaked and echoed, and the huge garden with more space than she'd ever need.

And on and on.

She also thought of Mum and Dad. Emily tried not to, but couldn't help it. She remembered how things used to be. They hadn't had a lot of money back then, but her childhood had been a happy one. Her mother, a nurse, was the most caring and compassionate woman Emily had ever known, and her father, who'd operated plant machinery on building sites, was also kind, patient, and very funny, never failing to make Emily laugh.

Things were always safe with them. Everything was... right. Until it wasn't.

Her parents had been gone for a little over five months now—not that long in reality, but even so, Emily often felt like they were still around, like this was all some kind of terrible dream. Sometimes she felt like she could somehow reach out *through* reality and grab them, pull them back, and correct the mistake.

Emily lowered the book and sniffed as she started to

cry again. In truth, she was surprised she had any tears left in her body, considering how much she had cried in recent months.

After a while, Emily thought about what she'd say when Mrs. Clement returned. The day had gone as well as it possibly could have, which pleased Emily. She knew that she was lucky—in relative terms—to have been chosen to live at Erimus House. Other kids in her position likely would have gone somewhere far worse.

But even so, it felt like if she agreed to stay, it would be somehow betraying Mum and Dad. It would make things permanent, as if that one choice was what would ensure her parents *stayed* dead. She knew it was stupid to think like that—it didn't make any sense—but the notion was there regardless.

Even so, deep down, Emily knew she was going to stay. Whatever internal hardships lay ahead for her, she believed Ollie, Daniel, and Lucy were the perfect people to face them with. They could help her. And she could help them, just like her mother had helped others.

Helping people is the right thing to do, her mother had said on more than one occasion. *If we don't have compassion, we don't have anything.*

That was true. Emily fully believed it. Her family hadn't had a lot, really—a small house, a small car, no fancy holidays abroad—but when it came to what mattered, they'd had *everything*.

Not anymore, though, Emily thought to herself as she rolled to her side, still sobbing. *No... not anymore.*

CHAPTER
EIGHT

Two weeks later...

In the two weeks that passed since Emily had arrived, she felt like she'd settled into a routine at the house. She liked that. People needed routines, even though they often thought they didn't.

On weekdays, they'd all gather in the study to be taught by Eleanore. To Emily's surprise, she found she liked this way of learning more than traditional school. Eleanore certainly seemed to be knowledgeable, and the topics were varied and interesting, going from the expected English, Maths, and Sciences, to things that were a little different, such as CPR—which Eleanore said stood for cardiopulmonary resuscitation—as well as lessons on the mythology of different cultures.

During the evenings, the children hung out and played together while Eleanore kept herself busy. Emily had visited the nearby town twice now and found it quaint and pleasant. There wasn't a mass of shops, as the town was very modestly sized—almost a village, really—but the bookshop there was a good one.

Other than going into town, the rest of the time on weekends was their own. Twice already, Emily had helped Eleanore in the garden, surprised to find she actually really enjoyed it; Eleanore had showed her how to trim and prune, explaining ways to care for the plants and encourage them to grow.

'To be a good gardener, you have to be a good nurturer,' she'd said. Emily liked that as well. She knew her mum would have been a good gardener if she'd tried her hand at it.

Eleanore had also given the children haircuts one Sunday afternoon, again surprising Emily at how adept the woman was. It seemed she was able to turn her hand to just about anything.

In addition to all that, Emily had met Mr. Peterson, the man who came to help with the garden. There wasn't much to the meeting, in truth, as Eleanore had simply introduced Emily, and he'd nodded in response. He'd then set about his work, which involved trimming all the lawns on a big, ride-on mower that he brought with him. He was a squat man with a big, bushy moustache and only a ring of hair around the sides and back of his head. He reminded Emily of a sea lion.

During the time since her arrival, Emily had expected constant questions about how she was settling in. Fortunately, everyone gave her the space she needed.

Apart from Lucy, of course, who would often ask if Emily had decided whether or not she was going to stay.

Emily always said she was, indicating she didn't really have a choice, despite what the adults had said to the contrary. That didn't seem to satisfy the younger girl, however, who obviously wanted Emily to *want* to stay.

It wasn't until the night before Mrs. Clement was due

to arrive again—while all the children were gathered in the snug—that Emily told the others where her heart was.

'Mrs. Clement will be here tomorrow,' she began. At the moment, both Daniel and her were reading on the sofa, Lucy was drawing on the floor, and Ollie just sat with his own thoughts.

'How are you feeling about that?' Ollie asked her.

'Fine,' she replied and cast a quick glance at Lucy. 'I'm going to tell her I want to stay here.'

'Really?' Daniel asked with a smile.

'Really?!' Lucy repeated with a bigger one.

Emily laughed. 'Yes, really.'

On the day of the social worker's arrival, the children were out in the garden when Eleanore called them back in. 'She's here!'

As they all made their way to the house, Emily found she was nervous, which was odd. She'd already made her decision, but the moment felt... significant to her.

Am I having second thoughts? she wondered. But as she considered it more, she knew that wasn't the case. Staying at Erimus House was the obvious choice.

The *only* choice.

When the children arrived into the main hall, Emily saw Mrs. Clement was already inside, talking to Eleanore. The woman looked over and locked eyes with Emily. She smiled warmly.

'Hello there, Emily,' Mrs. Clement said. 'How have you been?'

'Good,' Emily replied as she walked up to the woman.

'Feel like you're settling in?' Mrs. Clement asked, giving Emily a brief hug in greeting.

'I do,' Emily replied. She turned and gestured to the other children. 'Everyone has made me feel at home. And

Eleanore'—she nodded up to the other woman—'has been great.'

The social worker's smile widened. 'I knew you'd like it here,' she said. 'I'd heard great things about it from my colleagues. They were the ones who placed Ollie, Daniel, and Lucy, you know.'

Emily hadn't known that. In truth, she had no idea how the whole thing worked.

Mrs. Clement then looked back over to Eleanore. 'You sure you can't take more?' she asked. 'A lot of children need good homes like this.'

Glum expression on her face, Eleanore shook her head. 'Oh, I know,' she said. 'But I have my hands full with these four, I'm afraid.'

'I understand,' Mrs. Clement replied. 'Couldn't hurt to ask, though.'

Everyone soon settled in the drawing room, where Eleanore served Mrs. Clement tea and biscuits while the children each had a hot chocolate.

The conversation revolved around how the past couple of weeks had gone, and after around forty minutes, Eleanore lightly clapped her hands together. 'Okay, then,' she began. 'Ollie, Daniel, Lucy, you three come with me. Mrs. Clement and Emily need a little time alone, so let's give them that.'

The three children got up dutifully, and each cast Emily a glance and smile as they left the room with Eleanore. Emily felt her anxiety rise a little as Mrs. Clement remained seated. It was strange, since there was no reason to worry, but there was a knot in her gut regardless.

'It's great to hear you've taken to the place so well, Emily,' Mrs. Clement began. 'But now that we're alone, is there anything else you want to talk about?'

'Like what?' Emily asked.

'Any worries you have about living here? Concerns. Anything you didn't want to say in front of the others?'

Emily shook her head. 'No,' she said. However, Mrs. Clement held her gaze, as if to ask if she was sure. 'Honestly,' Emily went on, 'things are still hard for me. But... I do really like it here. And the other kids...' She then looked over to the door the trio had just left through. 'I dunno. It feels like they understand.'

'Well,' Mrs. Clement said. 'I suppose they do. You've all been through something most children will never have to deal with. If you've found companionship with the others, that's a good thing. A *really* good thing.'

Emily nodded, still looking at the door. 'Yeah,' she said. 'I know.'

'And you want to stay?'

Emily turned her attention back to the social worker and gave another nod. 'Yes, I do.'

A relieved smile washed over Mrs. Clement's face. 'I'm so happy to hear that.'

'I mean, I wouldn't have been able to leave anyway, right?' Emily asked. 'Not unless it was really bad here. I kind of guessed I couldn't really be too choosy.'

'I would have tried my best to get you somewhere else,' Mrs. Clement said. 'But I have to be honest, it does really help that you want to stay. Not that I had any doubts, of course.' The woman then looked down at her hands, which were fidgeting on her lap. 'Not everywhere is as good as this place, unfortunately.'

'Is... something wrong?' Emily asked, sensing there was more to it.

Mrs. Clement hesitated. 'Well, I'm not sure how much I should say. There is... another home that we send children to, a place we've used for a while. But this past week... well, let's just say something has happened and we've realised it isn't what we thought it was. Not at all. A lot of kids are going to need to be re-homed now.'

Emily's eyes widened. 'What happened there?'

But Mrs. Clement shook her head. 'Don't worry about it, that's for me and my colleagues to deal with. You just concentrate on enjoying your new home.'

My new home, Emily repeated in her head. Another pang of anxiety. She realised it was the finality of the situation that was causing her to worry. However, she knew that would have been the case no matter *where* she was. And by the sound of it, it could have been far worse for her.

There was a pause. 'Will... will you come back to check on me again?' Emily asked.

'I'll try,' Mrs. Clement said. 'It's just... this whole other situation is going to take some work to resolve, so it might be a little while before I'm back.'

Emily's heart suddenly ached for those children. *What did they go through?* 'It's okay,' Emily said. 'I'll be fine here. You don't need to worry about me. Just concentrate on the others.'

Mrs. Clement tilted her head to the side and gave a sad smile. 'You're such a good kid, Emily, you know that? So caring. Never lose that.'

Emily felt herself fill with pride. She'd heard similar compliments given to her mother, so to hear one directed at herself brought with it a feeling of warmth, like there was a connection there to the parent she'd lost.

Mrs. Clement stayed for another fifteen minutes or so chatting with them all, though mainly with Eleanore. They spoke about some final paperwork that Eleanore said she would complete and post back off, and then it came time to say goodbye.

'I'll try and get back soon,' Mrs. Clement said to Emily as they stood outside. 'I promise.' Yet the woman looked tired, and Emily knew deep down she probably wouldn't see Mrs. Clement again. But... that was okay.

After the social worker had left, Eleanore pulled Emily aside. 'I'm so happy you decided to stay,' she said. 'I know this place won't replace what you lost, but I hope it will come to feel like home to you. And if you ever need anything, just tell me. I'm always here for you. For all of you.'

'Thank you,' Emily said. She was feeling somewhere between happy and sad. Sad for what she'd lost, but happy for what she'd found. Eleanore stepped forward and hugged Emily. The child surprised herself at how hard she hugged the older woman back. 'Thank you for letting me come here,' Emily whispered.

'Oh, my dear,' she heard Eleanore say. 'It is my pleasure. But you never have to thank me for that.'

Emily then felt Eleanore kiss the top of her head. 'Now,' the woman said as she pulled away. 'You go hang out with the others. I'll fix us something special for dinner tonight to celebrate your decision to stay.'

'Sounds good!' Emily said.

After going outside, she saw the others down at the climbing frame. She paused on the patio and smiled, watching them for a moment. It didn't take long for Lucy to look over, and Emily saw her wave. She waved back and set off to them, finding herself eager to spend time with them once more.

CHAPTER NINE

Creak.

Daniel stared up into the darkness, his body tensing up. He'd woken from a troubling dream a little while ago, though he didn't know how long exactly.

The dream had involved his parents. They were shouting to him, but he was lost in complete blackness and couldn't figure out which way the calls were coming from. It had resulted in him stumbling about blindly, never able to find them.

Creak.

Someone was moving outside. Daniel gripped the duvet with tight fists, severely tempted to pull it over his head.

Probably just Eleanore, he told himself, wondering what time it was.

Then, outside, there was a gentle rattle of a tray. That confirmed it for him.

Should I go out and speak to her? Should I follow her again?

In truth, Daniel just wanted to stay under his covers.

But he remembered his conversation with Ollie a couple of weeks ago—the older boy had said to wake him up if Daniel ever saw Eleanore wandering around in the night again.

Daniel slowly sat up in bed and felt a slight chill on his exposed arms, since he'd worn only a white t-shirt and black jogging bottoms to bed. He considered what to do next, not really liking the idea of sneaking over to Ollie's room. It felt like a betrayal of Eleanore somehow. And besides, it had been such a good day, with Emily deciding to stay; he didn't want anything to ruin that. The meal they'd shared that evening was delicious, and dinnertime had been filled with more chatter than usual as everyone laughed and joked.

The day had felt special. Significant. As if everything was now complete.

So to ruin it all by spying on their carer, the woman who had provided all of that safety for them, felt... wrong.

At the same time, Daniel still did wonder what was going on down in the cellar. He'd thought about it often since seeing her the last time, sometimes convincing himself it was all nothing, other times leaning towards there being more to it.

Daniel then heard Eleanore descend the stairs. There was another rattle. A *clink*. Then... a sob.

Daniel frowned. *I must have heard wrong,* he told himself. *Why would Eleanore be crying?*

The sound had been quiet, but Daniel had been certain—it was enough to convince him to act.

Be brave.

He considered following Eleanore on his own, just to prove to himself he could be brave. But he'd made a promise to Ollie and decided to make good on that.

However, as Daniel swung his feet out of bed in the dark and found his slippers, he realised that by the time he fetched Ollie, Eleanore would likely already be down in the cellar. *And she'll* definitely *lock the door behind herself.*

It was then, as he stood up, Daniel changed his mind yet again, deciding to go it alone. *I can always come back for Ollie.*

He grabbed his dressing gown, slipped it on, and gently opened his door, pulling it slowly to avoid it creaking. He peered out into the dark as his chest tightened further.

The black was thick and uninviting, swallowing everything beyond a few feet outside of the room. As much as he wanted to, Daniel knew he couldn't switch on a light if he wanted to stay hidden.

Be brave!

He forced himself to step out into the hallway. As he did, he felt utterly exposed and vulnerable. Steeling his nerves, Daniel clenched his fists together and started to slowly creep towards the stairs.

I need to hurry.

But a thought struck Daniel the moment he placed his foot onto the first tread. *What am I going to do when I find her?*

He suddenly realised he hadn't thought that part through. He didn't want to confront Eleanore for fear of being told off, which left only following her, yet there was no way he could get through the cellar door without being seen.

And besides, Daniel really didn't want to go down there in the dark anyway.

He realised what he was doing was pointless. *Unless I can see what's on the tray*. At least finding that out would be something to share with Ollie. It could even help them figure out why Eleanore was sneaking around at night.

The plan satisfied him, so Daniel started moving down the stairs a little more quickly, keeping to the central carpet runner to help mask his steps.

Just as he was midway down the first flight, his foot met a tread—

Creeeak.

Daniel froze, unsure if Eleanore had heard. He waited, listening intently, expecting Eleanore to call out, or maybe even start walking back. He waited and waited before finally hearing a distant sound.

The padlock. No!

Daniel moved again, realising he was going to be too late. However, he still had to be careful not to make any more noise, and by the time he reached the main entrance hallway, he heard what sounded like the door to the cellar being closed. He tiptoed through the hall, listening to the *tick, tick, tick* of the long-case clock, and arrived to see the door to the cellar staircase was indeed closed. He let out a quiet sigh of disappointment and silently moved closer to the sturdy door, where he pressed his ear against the oak surface. He could hear movement, but it was getting farther away. And there was also... a small sob.

Why is she upset?

Daniel then tried to weigh up his choices. He could simply wait for Eleanore to return—maybe try to hide somewhere and watch her come out to see if there was anything interesting left on the tray. However, he had no idea how long she would be. *What if I'm sitting here all night?*

He didn't find the idea of waiting down in the dark particularly appealing.

Another option was just to go back to bed and forget the whole thing. That *certainly* had appeal. Ultimately, however, Daniel settled on going to Ollie's room and telling the older boy what he'd seen. That way, he'd be keeping his promise, and he also wouldn't have to wait all alone in the dark.

With the decision made, Daniel ventured back upstairs, still careful to be quiet, but now more confident he wouldn't be heard. He reached Ollie's door and stood outside for a moment, wondering if he should gently tap. Ollie had told him he didn't need to knock, but just waltzing into the room seemed... rude. It wasn't how they did things. Still, he didn't know how hard he would need to knock to wake the other boy. *What if the girls hear it?* Daniel didn't want to wake everyone else.

So, he took hold of the handle and gently turned it before pushing the door open. The layout of Ollie's room was the same as Daniel's, though it had been personalised with posters on the walls from the football magazines Ollie liked to collect.

Daniel stepped into the dark room and turned to his left, where the large bed was pressed against the same wall he was next to. The duvet was pulled up tight around Ollie's neck, who was facing away; Daniel was able to make out a lump of messy blonde hair on the pillow.

'Ollie,' he whispered. There was no response. He heard the other boy's slow, steady breathing continue. 'Ollie,' he said again, a little less hesitant.

Still nothing.

Daniel didn't want to call out any louder, so he moved inside the room and approached the bed, looking down at Ollie's form. Daniel reached out a hand and put it down where he assumed Ollie's shoulder was, then gently shook his friend.

'Ollie,' Daniel said again. However, it *still* didn't rouse the boy.

Daniel sighed. *He could sleep through an earthquake.*

With nothing else for it, Daniel shook Ollie again, this time much more vigorously. It *finally* worked and Ollie began to stir, his head lifting off the pillow.

'Huh?' the boy uttered groggily.

'Ollie,' Daniel whispered yet again.

Ollie's head turned a little, and Daniel could see his eyes were still half-closed. 'D—Daniel?' he asked, confused.

'Yeah,' Daniel replied. 'It's me.'

'What's going on?' Ollie asked, pushing himself up to a sitting position. 'What time is it?'

'I don't know,' Daniel said. 'I haven't checked. It's late, though. Really late.' He then considered what he'd said. 'Or it might be early, I suppose. Really early.'

Ollie scratched his head, eyes still half-closed. 'So what's wrong?' he asked. 'Why did you wake me?' A second later, his eyes shot open wider and he turned to fully face Daniel. 'Eleanore!' he quietly exclaimed.

Daniel nodded. 'I heard her again.'

Ollie then quickly threw his sheets back. 'Is she heading down?' he asked, quickly getting up. Daniel shook his head.

'She's already down in the cellar,' he said. 'By the time I got out of my room she was already going downstairs, and I thought I'd lose her if I came here for you first.'

'So... what happened?' Ollie asked, hugging himself to ward off the night's chill.

'I lost her anyway,' Daniel said with a shrug. 'She was too far ahead. And she locked the door behind her as well.'

Ollie retrieved his robe from the back of his door and wrapped it around himself.

'There's something else, though,' Daniel added.

'What?'

'I... I think she was crying?'

Ollie frowned and cocked his head to the side. 'Crying?' he repeated. 'Do you know why?'

'No idea,' Daniel answered. 'I mean, it wasn't full-on crying, but I heard her sniffling a few times.'

'Sniffling?'

Daniel nodded. 'Yeah, you know, like when you cry and sniffle to stop the'—he crinkled his nose—'snot and tears.'

'Ah,' Ollie replied. 'You sure?'

'Certain,' Daniel confirmed.

Ollie crossed his arms and looked down, clearly deep in thought. 'I *really* want to find out what's going on down there,' he said.

'Me too,' Daniel agreed. 'But... what do we do? We can't get in the cellar. Do we just... wait for Eleanore to come back and ask her what she was doing?'

Ollie shook his head. 'Doubt she'd tell us anything,' he said. 'And she'd probably scold us for sneaking around at night, even though she's doing the same thing.' Ollie thought some more. 'I say we go downstairs,' he eventually suggested. 'Maybe see what we can hear through the door.'

'What if she comes back?' Daniel asked.

'We hide,' Ollie replied with a shrug. 'We might even get a glance at the key she uses to lock up with. If we know what it looks like, it will make finding it later easier.'

'Y—you wanna go find the key?' Daniel asked. 'Like... steal it from her?'

'Well, more like borrow it,' Ollie clarified. 'And, yeah, maybe. I'm not sure yet.'

'You don't know where she keeps it.'

'No, no I don't, you're right,' Ollie said. 'It's certainly not on the rack in the kitchen with the others, you can tell just by looking that none would fit. But if I know what kind of key I'm searching for, that'd be a good start, right?'

'I guess,' Daniel said. He hadn't considered Ollie would want to just take the key. It made him feel uneasy knowing *he* could get into trouble for it as well, simply by association.

'Don't worry,' Ollie said. 'If I do try for it, I'd never let it come back on you. Besides, I don't even know *if* I'll do it. But I am going down there now—you coming?'

Daniel considered it, but already knew the answer. Despite worrying about getting caught, *he* was the one that had first noticed Eleanore, and *he* was the one that had alerted Ollie to the whole thing. It felt right that he went along to see it through. Plus, Daniel didn't want to succumb to fear yet again.

'Yeah,' Daniel said. 'I'm coming.'

'You sure?' Ollie asked. 'Don't feel like you have to. It's fine if you don't wanna—'

'No. I want to,' Daniel insisted.

Ollie smiled and patted him on the shoulder. 'Thanks,' he said, and then led Daniel out into the hallway. The pair made their way down the stairs and into the main hall on the ground floor. The ticking of the long-case clock was the only sound around them as the two boys crept silently onwards, making slow and steady progress, the darkness so thick they couldn't move quickly. It struck Daniel that on the two occasions he'd seen Eleanore out at night, she hadn't had a light with her, yet was fine moving through the shadows at a good pace.

Of course, she'd lived in the house much longer than

the rest of them, so the woman probably knew every step like the back of her hand.

As they walked past the clock, Daniel made a point to shuffle closer to it so he could make out the time: it was twenty past two in the morning.

'Wow,' Ollie whispered, pointing to the clock. 'Why is she up at this hour? It makes no sense.'

Eventually, the two boys reached the dining room and padded over to the locked door. The door was exactly like the others in the house, only this one had been fitted with a metal clasp that normally held the padlock. The lock wasn't there now, however, and the clasp hung open.

Ollie put his hand on the door handle and turned it. Daniel held his breath, hoping it wouldn't make any sound. The two boys eventually heard the latch of the door click open. Ollie then pushed, but something on the inside stopped the door from opening.

'I think she used the padlock inside again,' Ollie said before he gave the door another push just to be sure, and finally shook his head. 'It's no use.' He let go of the handle.

'Now what?' Daniel asked. 'Do we wait?'

Ollie nodded. 'Yeah, I think so.'

'But where?' Daniel went on. He turned to look around, but there weren't any obvious places to hide. Crawling under the dining room table was far too obvious and visible, despite the dark. Daniel also considered the kitchen. But once in that room, there wasn't anywhere else to go if someone came in.

As he continued to look, Daniel's eyes fell on the rear windows. He couldn't see the garden, or even the patio, just a sheen of black, as if someone had completely painted over the glass with dark paint. The boy then remembered his dream, where he'd been running through darkness just like that, desperately searching for his parents. As he stared, Daniel half expected to see something come swimming into view out of the darkness to press itself up against the glass. Maybe a ghost or a shambling zombie.

Neither of those things are real, he quickly told himself. Daniel fully believed that... in the cold light of day. But at night, when the shadows were at their deepest, something primal deep inside him took over, some instinct that taught humans to fear the dark.

Eventually, Daniel forced his eyes away and continued to think, but it was a struggle to come up with a solid plan. 'We could go in the library or drawing room,' he suggested. 'If we leave the door open a little, we can look out and maybe see her coming back out from the basement. We probably wouldn't see the key, but we might get a look at whatever she was carrying on the tray.'

Ollie considered it. 'We'd need to be careful she doesn't spot us,' he said as both of them looked back into the main hall. Then he turned to the kitchen. 'We could go in there.'

'I was thinking that,' Daniel said. 'But the door is so close to the cellar that if we're peeking out, Eleanore will see us.'

'Yeah... you're right,' Ollie said. 'I think the library or drawing room is the best we can do.'

The two boys made the quick trek over to the library. They pushed the door—which was already ajar—farther open and entered, careful to move the door back into almost the same position while still allowing them to see out.

After waiting for ten minutes, each trying to peek out at the same time, Daniel made a suggestion. 'Why don't we take turns standing watch? I can go first, then we can swap after a little while. That means one of us can sit down for a little bit.'

'You tired?' Ollie asked.

Daniel hesitated, but then nodded. 'A little, I guess,' he admitted.

'Not surprised,' the older boy went on. 'It's late. Or... early. Tell you what, I'll go first. You sit.'

'Are you sure?' Daniel asked.

'Of course. I'll let you know if I see her, or when I need to swap.'

Daniel was thankful and took a seat on one of the sofas.

When he'd woken up from his dream earlier, he'd been fully alert, his heart pounding. Then, after hearing Eleanor, his adrenaline had spiked again. Now, though, since some time had passed, tiredness was overtaking him again. He leaned his head back into the seat behind him and stared up at the ceiling. The window to the front wall still had its curtains open, but it let in only the smallest amount of moonlight from outside. Daniel felt that if he let his eyes close even a little bit, he'd simply slip off to sleep.

'It's good Emily has decided to stay,' he whispered over to Ollie, hoping some kind of conversation would keep him awake.

'Yeah,' Ollie whispered back. 'She seems like a good fit for us. I like her.'

'Me too,' Daniel replied, still looking up. Though he could see the ceiling, the darkness around him was thick; as his eyes started to glaze over, the shadows across the ceiling took on different shapes, sometimes even looking like faces. They weren't, of course, but it was interesting to observe.

For reasons he couldn't explain, his thoughts drifted back to a conversation between Emily and Eleanore a few weeks ago. It was something he had thought about often since.

'Ollie,' Daniel asked sleepily. 'What do you think happens after we die?'

In his periphery vision, he saw Ollie turn and look back at him. The older boy was silent for a long while. 'I don't know,' he eventually said.

'Do you ever think about it?'

Another pause. 'Yes,' Ollie eventually admitted.

'Me too,' Daniel said quietly. 'A lot. Especially since... well, you know.'

'Yeah,' Ollie replied. 'I know. What do *you* think happens?'

Daniel shrugged as he continued to stare. 'I don't know. I *hope* there's something else, but...' He trailed off. Eventually, he added, 'But you don't believe in ghosts, right?'

'Right,' Ollie confirmed.

'And you don't think this place is haunted.'

'It isn't,' Ollie stated. 'It *definitely* isn't. *You* don't really think it is, do you?'

'I... I guess not,' Daniel said. 'I mean, I haven't actually seen anything that would make me think it is. Just sometimes this place gets a little...'

'Creepy,' Ollie finished for him.

'Right,' Daniel said. He then let out a yawn he'd unsuccessfully been trying to hold in.

'That's just because it's an old house. It makes funny noises, it's cold, and it's dark. But there's no spirits or anything like that here with us.'

'I guess you're right,' Daniel said. 'I need to stop being so scared all the time.'

'Don't be too hard on yourself,' Ollie told him. 'You're really brave. Everyone gets scared, including me. But my mother always said it's how you act when you're scared that counts.'

Daniel let out a smile in the dark. 'Thanks,' he said.

The two boys grew silent, so Ollie turned to look out through the door again and Daniel continued to stare up at the ceiling. He just stared and stared, his eyes growing ever heavier with each passing—

Daniel felt himself jolted awake.

He quickly sat up straight, panic flooding through him.

I fell asleep!

With wide eyes, he looked up to see Ollie leaning over him, his arm outstretched and hand resting on Daniel's shoulder.

'I must have...' Daniel began. Then shook his head. 'Is she coming? Is Eleanore coming?' he asked in a louder voice than he'd intended.

But Ollie wore a relaxed smile.

'No,' he whispered back. 'It's been over an hour. I think she's going to be down there a while.' The boy yawned. 'And honestly, I can't keep my eyes open anymore.'

'I'll keep watch now,' Daniel said as he rubbed his eyes.

'No,' Ollie said. 'Come on, we'll just go to bed. If we both fall asleep down here, we might get caught. We can try again another night.'

'Are you sure?' Daniel asked, not against the thought of returning to his bed and still feeling exhausted.

'Yeah,' Ollie said. 'Come on, let's go.'

Once he helped Daniel up, both of them shuffled towards the door, where they peeked out again to make sure the coast was clear. They weren't able to see directly into the dining room from their position—it was far too dark—but they could listen, and the only sound was from the clock.

After that, Ollie led Daniel out into the hallways and they tiptoed across to the staircase, which they ascended, sticking again to the central carpeted area. Soon enough, they were back in the upper hallway, standing between both their rooms.

'Eventful night,' Daniel quipped.

Ollie laughed. 'Yeah, we're gonna pay for it tomorrow.' He covered his mouth and yawned. 'I'm gonna be tired all day.'

'Me too,' Daniel agreed. He turned toward his door. 'Well, sleep well,' he added. 'For the few hours of night we have left.'

The older boy nodded and turned away too. As both padded over to their rooms, a startling noise suddenly rattled through the house, rising up from below and shooting upwards, causing the very building to shake. The sound wasn't easily describable, sounding something between horrific wails and the roar of a jet engine. Not human, exactly, but... not far off.

Daniel tensed up and he instinctively spun to gaze wide-eyed at Ollie, who in turn was looking back with an expression of panic, something Daniel had never seen in the older boy before.

While the unnatural wailing soon died off, the house continued to rumble for a few moments after, with some of the pictures and wall hangings trembling on their hooks. Silence fell once more, though Daniel's ears were still ringing. He wanted to run over and hug Ollie for protection. However, he felt himself rooted to the spot in absolute fear.

'What—what the hell was *that?*' Ollie uttered as his head whipped around in the dark, looking left and right, eyes wide and frantic.

'I—I don't know,' Daniel stammered.

His body was still tight, braced for that awful sound to come back and the building to shake once more. Thoughts of sleep were now the furthest thing from his mind.

Both boys stood rooted for a while longer before Ollie eventually started to move, creeping back over to the staircase.

'What are you doing?' Daniel asked in horror. *Don't go back down there!*

'I need to look,' Ollie said.

'Stay up here, Ollie,' Daniel urged. He didn't want to go downstairs, and he dearly didn't want to be left alone, either. As Ollie continued to walk, Daniel had the idea to run upstairs to the girls if the older boy carried on, just so he wasn't on his own.

'I am,' Ollie said as he reached the railing and leaned over, looking down. 'I just want to see if I can spot anything.'

'You can't see the hall from here,' Daniel said.

'I know,' Ollie quickly replied. 'But there might be something...'

Daniel waited. 'Anything?' he eventually asked, but saw Ollie shake his head. 'What on earth could have made that noise?' Daniel went on, though he knew Ollie had about as much idea as he did. Ollie didn't answer and just continued staring down.

Another sound then startled Daniel, this one coming from upstairs. It took him a moment to realise it was from a door opening. Ollie had clearly heard it as well, as the other boy turned his head to his right, through to the staircase that led farther up.

Daniel finally found the strength to move and padded over to join Ollie; both stood staring through the open door to the rising staircase. They could just make out light footsteps at the top of the stairs.

'Lucy?' a whispered voice said. Daniel felt relief flood through him. It was Emily.

They then heard another door open, followed by hushed voices.

Daniel followed Ollie through to the bottom of the stairs. 'Emily,' Ollie called up, keeping his voice soft.

'Yeah,' Emily whispered down to them. 'Did you feel that?' she asked. She sounded worried.

'Yeah,' Ollie replied. He then looked to Daniel and flicked his head up the stairs in a *follow me* gesture. 'Wait there,' he called out.

Ollie and Daniel ascended the stairs, and as they turned on the half-landing, Daniel saw both Emily and Lucy at the top, both wrapped in their dressing gowns and staring down with worried expressions.

'What happened? What was that?' Lucy asked, pressing herself close to Emily, who had a protective arm around the younger girl.

'I don't know,' Ollie said as he and Daniel reached the top.

'The house was shaking,' Emily said, sounding utterly confused. 'It woke me up.'

'Me too,' Lucy said. 'Did it wake you two up as well?'

'Yeah,' Ollie replied immediately. 'I... felt the house shaking and came out to get Daniel.'

Daniel kept quiet, though he had to fight off a frown of confusion. *Why isn't he telling them everything?*

'Was it an earthquake?' Emily asked. 'I... I didn't think we got them in this country.'

'Could have been,' Ollie said. 'I don't know.'

Lucy then looked over to Eleanore's room. 'Do you think she heard it?'

Ollie and Daniel shared a look.

'Should we wake her?' Emily went on.

Ollie quickly shook his head. 'Best not, since she might still be sleeping,' he said. 'There isn't a lot she can do.'

'But... what do *we* do?' Emily asked.

At first, Ollie didn't have an answer. 'Honestly, maybe just try going back to bed,' he suggested.

'After *that?*' Emily asked in confusion.

'Did you hear a sound as well?' Daniel asked. 'Or was it just the shaking that woke you?'

Emily frowned and shook her head. 'Just the shaking,' she said. 'It seemed like it was stopping just as I opened my eyes. Did *you* hear something?'

Daniel hesitated. 'No, not really,' he said. 'Just... a rumble, I guess.' He didn't like lying, but felt compelled to follow Ollie's lead about keeping the full truth quiet—at least for now.

'Maybe it was a plane going over us,' Lucy offered.

'That could be it,' Ollie said. 'Good suggestion, Luce.'

She smiled and suddenly looked a little more relaxed.

'Do planes fly over here often?' Emily asked.

'No,' Ollie admitted. 'But it still might explain it.'

Emily seemed to be considering that. 'It would have had to be flying *really* low.'

'Look,' Ollie went on, 'let's just try to get more sleep. We can ask Eleanore about it in the morning. No sense waking her now. If we hear it again, then we can go get her. How does that sound? I know we've had a bit of a scare, but I'm sure it's all okay.'

The group all looked at one another and seemed to come to a silent agreement.

'Can... can I sleep with you?' Lucy asked Emily, looking up at the older girl with big, pleading eyes.

'Little freaked out, huh?' Emily asked. Lucy nodded. 'Sure you can,' Emily went on and gave Lucy a squeeze. She then turned back to the boys. 'I hope you two get back to sleep okay.'

'Us too,' Ollie added as he shared a look with Daniel. They waited for the girls to go into Emily's room, and after a moment, set off back down to the floor below. It was only when they were back out into the hallway that Daniel spoke up, still keeping his voice low.

'Why didn't you tell them?' he asked the older boy. 'About what we saw with Eleanore, and what we *heard?*'

'I was going to,' Ollie began. 'But... you know what Luce is like. She'd let it slip, or even ask Eleanore about it outright. If we're going to find out what's going on, then we don't want Eleanore to know we're on to her.'

'We could tell Emily, though,' Daniel suggested.

Ollie nodded. 'Maybe, yeah, but Luce was *right* there. Plus, Emily is new here. We don't want to worry her just yet. Though... yeah, I think we can probably trust her with it.'

There was a brief pause. 'Do you really think it could have been a plane?' Daniel asked.

Ollie looked hesitant. 'Maybe,' he said. But Daniel could tell the older boy wasn't convinced. Daniel wasn't either—he had been *sure* the sound had travelled upwards from below.

Another silence descended on them. Daniel knew he'd have to go back into his room now. Alone. He was tempted to ask Ollie if he could jump into his bed, but knew it would be weird, so he refrained.

'You okay?' Ollie asked him.

Daniel gave a firm nod. 'Yeah, just... a little freaked out,' he said. 'Like Luce.'

'I don't blame you,' Ollie said. 'I think we all are. Try to get some sleep. Hopefully we'll get the chance to chat about it all tomorrow. Sound good?'

Another nod. The boys said their goodnights and Daniel entered his dark room once more. He didn't bother to put the light on to guide the way and simply slipped from his dressing gown and dove into his bed, throwing his covers over himself.

He lay there unable to drop off for the longest time, his mind now in overdrive. He kept thinking about that awful noise, trying desperately to find a plausible explanation for it.

As he did, one thought kept coming back to him. *If the noise came from below, and Eleanore was down there... did she hear it? She* had *to.*

And then... another thought. *Did she cause it?*

It seemed impossible. How could Eleanore have made the building shake? There was no way the woman could have done that.

Even so, the notion stayed with Daniel until he eventually fell back into a deep sleep.

So deep, in fact, that he didn't hear the footsteps and light sobs go past his room twenty minutes later when Eleanore made her way back to bed.

CHAPTER
TEN

Perhaps not surprisingly, everyone seemed tired the next day. It had taken Emily a while to doze back off after returning to her room, and Lucy as well, though the younger girl had fallen asleep first.

However, the biggest surprise to Emily was that the most tired looking of them all appeared to be... Eleanore. Emily had assumed their guardian hadn't even felt the house shaking. Or... maybe she had, because she looked tired, with her normally sparkling and alert eyes now carrying bags beneath them.

Once down in the dining room, Lucy wasted no time in asking Eleanore about the previous night. 'Did you feel the house shaking?'

Eleanore just frowned. 'Shaking?' she asked in surprise. 'No, not at all. What do you mean? When did that happen?'

But there was something about the way she spoke that made Emily question if the woman was being truthful.

'Last night,' Lucy went on. 'We all got woken up because, well, like I said, everything *shook*. It was so weird. And scary!'

Eleanore cast everyone a glance, eyebrow raised. 'Did everyone feel it?' She was greeted with nods. Yet the woman just shrugged her shoulders. 'That's... strange,' she said. 'But no, I was sleeping. I didn't feel anything at all.' Her voice lacked her normal enthusiasm and energy.

'Do you have any idea what it might have been?' Emily pressed.

Eleanore was silent for a couple of seconds, obviously deep in thought. 'Maybe just a ground tremor or something.'

'Do you get them here often?' Emily asked.

Eleanore shook her head. 'Can't say we do. But I can't think of anything else that could have caused it.'

'A plane?' Lucy suggested.

'Perhaps,' Eleanore said. 'Are you all okay? It didn't scare you, did it?'

'Yes,' Lucy said. 'Well, it did at the time. I think I'm okay now.'

'Don't worry,' Eleanore went on. 'There's nothing to worry about. I'm sure it won't happen again. Now, I'm just going to fix everyone breakfast, so gather round the table in ten minutes.'

And that was that. Eleanore walked off; a few minutes later everyone ate their breakfast in an odd silence.

Emily wanted to ask more, and she could sense Lucy did as well, but no one said anything—Eleanore just stared down at her food as she ate. The whole atmosphere was off.

Given it was Saturday, the children went out into the garden together after they'd eaten, since they didn't have any school to do. Once out there, talk unsurprisingly returned to the previous night, with the group discussing possible explanations for why the house had shaken.

A low-flying plane, or possibly even a light earthquake, were still the only suggestions that made any sense to them. Soon after, though, Emily could sense Lucy was keen to move on from the topic, seeming like she'd grown bored.

'Come *on*,' she yowled. 'Let's have some fuuuun. It's dull just talking about that all the time.'

'Yeah, you're right,' Ollie said and glanced at Daniel. That was the second time Emily had noticed the two share a look that morning, and she felt sure something was going on there. She debated flat-out asking them about it right then, but decided to leave it. *Probably not my business, and I don't want to look too pushy.*

So, the children moved on to playing games. The sky was grey and Emily knew rain would come soon, so they made the most of the time they had by kicking the football around, though no one showed any particular enthusiasm. There was plenty of yawning from everyone. Eventually, they saw Eleanore approach.

'Emily,' she said as she reached them. 'Can I see you in the snug upstairs, please?'

Emily cocked an eyebrow. 'Erm, sure. Is... everything okay?'

'Oh yes,' Eleanore replied. 'Everything is fine. I just... well, I need to take a little sample of your blood.'

Emily's face fell.

'You... *what?*' she asked, shocked.

Eleanore held up her hands. 'It's perfectly fine, dear,' she said. 'I did it with the other children as well. Now that you're staying, I want to send a sample off to the local doctor here. I already have the paperwork completed to get you registered, but I have to also give them a blood sample.'

'But why?' Emily asked. She cast a glance at the others, yet found they didn't appear at all shocked.

'Well, firstly so they can check your blood type,' Eleanore explained. 'It's important to know. And they'll also run a few preliminary tests to make sure there are no illnesses or anything. Don't worry, there's nothing to worry about.'

'But... why don't we just get the doctor to come and do it?' Emily asked. 'Seems safer—'

'Oh, there's no need,' Eleanore said with a wave of her hand. 'I used to be a caregiver for my father when he was sick. I've taken plenty of blood samples and things like that. Much easier if I do it, rather than making them take a trip all the way out here.'

Emily looked at the others again with raised eyebrows and an expression that she hoped read, *Is she serious?*

'She's taken blood from all of us,' Daniel stated. 'It doesn't really hurt. Bit of a sting, then you're fine.'

'Just don't look,' Lucy said. 'You can *see* the blood coming out of the tube. It's... *blergh,*' she finished with a shiver.

Regardless, Emily was still hesitant. Having the woman take her blood just seemed so... odd.

'It'll be over before you know it,' Eleanore said, turning and beckoning Emily onward. However, Emily still looked at the others, unsure. 'Everything is clean and sterilised,' Eleanore went on.

'It'll be fine,' Lucy said. Emily turned her eyes to Ollie, who had said nothing throughout the exchange.

'And you all had it done?' she asked. The younger two nodded... and eventually Ollie did as well.

Emily stifled a sigh. She knew she could flat-out refuse, and she was tempted, but she thought that might cause a rift in the house. As the newest arrival, she didn't want to be the one to disrupt the harmony that seemed to exist there. Besides, if the others had gone through the same thing, and they were fine, what harm could it do? So, she moved away from the group and over to Eleanore, who smiled.

'Thank you, dear,' Eleanore said. 'I'll only keep you a minute.'

Emily followed the older woman up to the snug on the middle floor and, upon entering, she saw a high-backed seat with wooden armrests placed in the middle. Next to the seat was a plastic tray on a metallic stand. On top of the tray was a cannula in a clear plastic wrapper, some wipes, a roll of gauze, tape, a rolled-up belt, a box of rubber gloves, a small brown bottle filled with a liquid Emily couldn't identify, and *three* test tubes.

'How much blood do you need?' Emily asked, pointing to the test tubes.

'Oh, don't worry,' Eleanore said when she noticed what Emily was talking about. 'I won't be filling them all, just one—I always bring a couple more just in case.' She patted the chair. 'Please, sit down.'

Emily slowly made her way over to the chair. She gazed at the items a little longer before finally taking a seat. Butterflies fluttered in her belly.

'Place your arm on the armrest,' Eleanore instructed. Again, Emily complied. Eleanore then set about wrapping the belt around Emily's arm, just below her bicep.

'What's that for?' Emily asked.

'To reduce the blood flow at the bottom of your arm,' Eleanore replied. 'It'll plump up your veins for me.'

Emily repressed a shudder. 'Is that where you get the blood from? My arm?'

Eleanore nodded. 'Yes, below your wrist. You've never had blood taken before?'

Emily thought about it and eventually shrugged. 'Not that I can remember. I probably have at some point, I suppose.'

'It will be pretty much painless, I promise.'

' 'Pretty much'?' Emily asked.

Eleanore chuckled. 'Like Daniel said, just a little sting.' The older woman then put on a pair of the gloves and rolled Emily's arm over to reveal the more sensitive inner skin. The woman began to press on the flesh a few inches below Emily's inner elbow.

'What are you doing?'

'Looking for a suitable vein,' Eleanore said. 'Sometimes people have deep-set ones, which means it winds up being easier to get one on the back of the hand. But...' She then tapped the same spot three times. 'We have a good one here.'

'Great,' Emily stated flatly.

Eleanore then unscrewed the top of the small brown bottle and placed a length of cloth over the end before tipping it. She then righted the bottle and pulled the cloth away, revealing a wet patch on it. The room suddenly smelled like medicine and Emily couldn't help but wrinkle her nose at the sharp odour. 'Antiseptic,' Eleanore explained and wiped Emily's skin. Eleanore then retrieved the cannula and removed it from the packet. Emily felt her body grow tight as Eleanore pulled off the thin end cap that had been covering the needle. 'Just relax and be brave for me,' Eleanore said and moved the needle closer.

Emily's heart was hammering in her chest. *I don't like this.* She then remembered Lucy's words and diverted her gaze to the side of the room so she didn't see the blood being removed.

'There'll be a quick sting,' Eleanore said. 'One... two... three.'

Emily flinched as she felt the needle pierce and push through her skin. It did indeed sting, but the pain was fleeting. At least until Eleanore moved to grab a test tube, and Emily could feel the needle shift around under her flesh. It made her feel a little lightheaded and her stomach lurched.

'Nearly there,' Eleanore said in a soothing voice. Emily felt the needle move again as Eleanore screwed the end of the test tube onto the back of the cannula. The woman held everything firm for a few seconds. 'There we go,' she said, sounding pleased.

Emily couldn't help but open her eyes and glance down at her arm, where she immediately saw the clear tube filling with her crimson blood. It brought on another wave of light-headedness. 'Oh...' Emily uttered woozily.

'Just look away, dear,' Eleanore said. 'We're almost done.'

Emily did, closing her eyes and taking steady breaths. Eventually, she felt movement, so she opened one eye and saw that Eleanore had removed the test tube. Emily clamped her eyes shut again. She felt pressure on the point the needle met her skin, which brought with it another sting. Then she felt the needle finally pull free. More pressure, and when Emily finally opened her eyes, there was a folded piece of gauze taped to her arm, with just a tiny spot of blood showing through. 'All done,' Eleanore chirped. She then started to untie the belt from Emily's arm. 'I must say,' the older woman went on, 'you handled that very well.'

Emily looked down at the tray to see the vial of her blood lying on it, a stopper now on the end. Eleanore set the belt down at her feet.

'Is... is that it?' Emily asked.

Eleanore smiled. 'It is. You're all done and can go back down with the others now. *But,*' she said, raising a finger, 'I want you to make sure you drink plenty of water. Grab a glass as soon as you head down. Understand?'

'Yes,' Emily replied with a nod.

'Fantastic. I'll tidy up in here.' Eleanore helped Emily to her feet, and then held the young girl in place for a moment. 'Feel okay?' she asked. 'You aren't dizzy or anything, are you? Take your time.'

Emily stood where she was for a moment and looked to the floor, concentrating. She had felt a little dizzy earlier, but it had now passed. 'I'm okay,' she confirmed.

'Your legs aren't wobbly, are they?'

Emily shook her head. 'I'm good,' she reiterated.

'Super,' Eleanore said and let go of the girl. 'Remember, plenty of water.' Emily nodded again, then started to move away. When she was halfway from the room, she stopped and turned back. 'Something wrong, dear?' Eleanore asked, noticing her.

'Just... about last night,' Emily began. 'You *really* didn't feel anything?'

'Afraid not,' Eleanore said. 'Not a thing. I must have slept through it. Always been a deep sleeper. I wouldn't worry, though. This house has been standing a long time, a little tremor isn't going to hurt it.'

After a moment of consideration, Emily replied, 'Yeah, you're probably right.'

'Anything else, dear?' While Eleanore's voice was pleasant enough, Emily was still struck at just how *tired* the woman looked.

'No,' Emily said. 'Nothing else.'

'Great, then I'll call you all for dinner later. Go have fun.'

'Thanks,' Emily said and walked away, making her way down to the kitchen, where she poured herself a glass of water as instructed. She gulped down the first half, then stared out the rear window. In the distance, she could see Lucy almost at the top of the climbing frame, with Ollie and Daniel sitting on the grass close by. The two boys still looked deep in thought.

Yeah, something's definitely going on with those two, Emily told herself as she finished her water.

CHAPTER

ELEVEN

Lucy's eyes opened. She blinked repeatedly in the dark.

Why am I awake? she thought groggily. Then she noticed how cold it was and realised she couldn't feel the duvet on top of her. *Not again.* Lucy lifted her head and was just able to see the cover, which was bunched up at the bottom of the bed over her feet.

Must have kicked it down again in my sleep. It was something she did often. Lucy sat up and reached forward to grab the duvet—then noticed the door to her room was open.

Lucy's expression turned to a frown of confusion. The girl was certain she'd closed it before going to bed that night. *I always close it!*

The cold was biting, more so than the previous night, so she quickly pulled the sheet back up to her midsection; she was still sitting up, but at least now she had her legs protected. She leaned over and clicked on her nightlight, washing a portion of the room in a dull, yellowy glow.

She again looked over to the door and considered if it

had just drifted open somehow in the night. However, that had never happened before. Besides, it wasn't like there were any phantom drafts running through the house.

Maybe Eleanore checked in on me and accidentally left it open, she wondered. *Yeah, that might be it.*

However, it still left Lucy with a small decision to make. She could either lie back down and try to go to sleep, ignoring the door, or get out of bed to close it. That in itself shouldn't have been a foreboding task, but as the young girl peered out into the darkness of the hallway, anxiety rose in her gut.

I can't leave it open, she told herself, unable to stop from imagining someone outside looking back in as she slept. Lucy quickly screwed her eyes shut and shook her head, dislodging the unwelcome thought. Though she'd never vocalised it to the others, she found the house every bit as unsettling as Daniel did at night.

Still, that had never been enough to put Lucy off the house completely. Far from it, in fact. She *loved* it there. Just... sometimes at night, it could feel like there was something else out there in the shadows.

She quickly shook her head again. *Stop it! Stop scaring yourself,* she silently admonished. The girl then forced herself out of bed, knowing that ultimately, the door would need to be closed—she wouldn't be able to relax otherwise. Feeling slightly more protected by the light from her nightstand, she padded the short distance over to the door and took hold of the handle. However, as she glanced across the hall, she noticed that Emily's door stood open as well.

What the...?

She wondered if Eleanore had checked on each of them and had accidentally left both doors ajar. It seemed unlikely, though. Lucy peeked her head out into the hall and gazed over to Eleanore's room to find *her* door open as well.

In fact, so was every door she could see in the corridor.

A chill ran up her spine. Lucy knew there was no way Eleanore would have gone round and opened every single door individually before going to bed. No way at all.

As Lucy gazed around the hallway, her eyes settled on the doorway to the staircase. It was deep in the shadows, but she could just tell it was open.

And it looked like someone was standing in the dark, staring back.

Lucy's body tensed and she took half a step backwards, though she still gazed ahead, trying to make out if there really *was* someone or if it was just a trick of the brain. One moment she was certain, the next it seemed like it was just her tired eyes making familiar shapes out in the shadows—shapes that didn't actually exist.

She was tempted to call out, but refrained. Besides, she wasn't sure if she would actually be able to summon her voice to work with the tension gripping her. That feeling only intensified as the shadows seemed to move. When they did, Lucy was certain she saw a glint of light, as if someone's eye had caught a reflection of the light that trickled out from her bedroom. Again, it was hard to be certain, but Lucy felt like whoever was there—*if anyone is there*—had moved deeper into the staircase.

She listened intently, unable to move, rooted to the spot. A few seconds later, the girl heard a creak on the stairs. Then, after a few more moments, there was another, this time lower down.

'E—Emily?' Lucy uttered, though her voice was choked off by fear, barely even audible. 'E—Eleanore?' Slightly louder this time, but not by much. While Lucy still felt cold, she noticed it wasn't quite as severe as it had been when she'd first poked her head out of the room—which didn't make sense to her. Scenarios ran through her mind of who it might have been, realising it could have *only* been Emily or Eleanore. *But why would either be out of bed and walking around? And why open all the doors?*

She considered it *might* have been one of the boys, but that was more unlikely given their rooms were on the floor below. *Why wander all the way up here?*

All Lucy wanted to do was run back to bed and wrap herself up in the thick protective duvet. However, as appealing as that was, something else stirred in her when she gazed over to Emily's room. She realised she wanted to make sure the other girl was safe.

Not just her, but Eleanore as well.

However, that meant going farther out into the hall. Lucy bit her lip, terrified. Even so, the young girl forced her fear away and stepped out of her room—gripping her locket for comfort—because checking on Emily was more important than her own fear. She felt awfully exposed as she moved deeper into the corridor, step by step, hugging herself. She kept going anyway, letting her gaze remain on Emily's door mainly but every so often flicking a glance back towards the staircase. However, the farther away from her own light she got, the less she could make out.

Eventually, she reached the door to her friend's room and peeked inside. Again, the shadows were thick, but Lucy was just able to make out the form of the older girl tucked up under her covers, auburn hair strewn over the pillows.

Lucy could also make out the steady rise and fall of Emily's form breathing. While Lucy was tempted to go and wake Emily, just so she wasn't alone and scared, she held off. *Let her sleep.*

That means the person on the stairs was probably Eleanore, Lucy realised. Summoning even more bravery, she turned to move across to her guardian's room. Just as she started, a quiet sound gave her pause: the creaking of a door coming from the floor below.

Whoever it was, it became clear to Lucy they were opening things up on the level below now as well. And that became even more obvious when she soon heard another creak.

It has to be Eleanore, she told herself, though she couldn't figure out what the woman was doing.

Maybe someone is sleepwalking, Lucy then considered. She'd heard of people doing crazy things when sleep-walking.

Still, she felt like she *had* to be sure it was their guardian. Once she knew that, Lucy would be brave enough to go down and ask what was going on. With that in mind, the young girl moved steadily over to Eleanore's room. The meagre light coming out from her own room didn't stretch far enough to illuminate much.

Lucy looked inside but couldn't see beyond the dark, as the thick curtains over the windows were pulled shut. However, she *could* hear breathing. *If I get closer I might be able to tell.* The girl padded forward. She kept her steps as light as she could; the rug on the floor felt soft and tickly under her bare feet. She continued to the side of the bed, feeling her way forward with outstretched hands, eyes narrowed and focused, trying to pull in any slivers of light she could to make something out. Her midsection gently bumped against the side of the bed, so Lucy leaned forward. The breathing was closer now.

There was definitely a form under the sheets. Lucy stood motionless as she focused and her eyes started to adjust. Eventually, she was able to make out Eleanore's grey hair framing her sleeping face.

Confused, Lucy slowly turned around. *Then who was that?*

It took her a while to feel her way back out, but Lucy then left Eleanore's room and worked her way back over to her own bedroom, welcoming the light that spilled out. As she did, she tried to keep her emotions in check.

It has to be one of the boys. Maybe they're messing around? She didn't even want to consider the possibility it might not have been Ollie or Daniel. *Don't even think it.*

As she reached her room, Lucy glanced over at the staircase door. *Do I go down?*

The thought of doing that was even scarier than checking on Emily had been. However, the need to protect her brothers was just as strong as well.

Not brothers, she told herself. *Not really.*

Lucy then pondered on that thought. While she wasn't related to the others by blood, that didn't mean they weren't family. She glanced over at Emily's room. Lucy had only known the girl for a couple of weeks, yet she could already feel a strong bond there—and she couldn't imagine what the house would be like without the boys. Those two had always looked out for her and protected her, making Lucy feel safe.

They are *my brothers,* she told herself. *And Emily is my sister. We're a family.*

The thought filled her with warmth. It also gave her the strength to push on.

She considered first waking Emily, to tell the other girl what was happening and to also have someone there to accompany her down. But another part of Lucy also wanted to do this alone, to do it for the others. She walked forward to the staircase, still holding the locket, caressing it with her thumb.

That trinket was all she had of her mother and father. It was the most important object in the world to her now. In fact, the only nightmares Lucy really had were of losing it; each time, she would wake up sweating and quickly reach for it to make sure the locket was still around her neck. Wearing it made it feel like her parents were with her, and when she gently rubbed it, it was as if she was sending a hug to her parents in the afterlife.

As Lucy reached the stairwell, she realised she needed more light. *What if the light wakes the others?* she thought, looking back up the corridor. *If it does, then you can tell them what you were doing,* she then reasoned, as there was no shame in the truth. Besides, she was a good distance from either of their rooms, especially Eleanore's, so she doubted the light would reach them. With that, Lucy leaned inside and felt for the switch, before finally flicking it on.

She winced as a bloom of light assaulted her, a stark contrast to the heavy darkness it quickly replaced. After letting herself acclimatise, Lucy then slowly made her way down.

Once out into the hallway below, she found it a little easier to see, thanks to both the light from the staircase behind her and also the large window on the other stair's half landing. While it was still dark, it certainly wasn't as bad as the floor above.

As expected, Lucy found all the doors in the mid-storey hallway open.

After another deep breath to steel herself, the young girl quickly checked on the boys, Ollie first, then Daniel—both of them were sound asleep in their beds. Her body tensed up as she gazed up again.

Someone is in the house, she realised, given everyone was accounted for.

There was another creak of a door, this time from the ground floor.

Panic filled her. Though Lucy wanted to be brave for everyone, moving around on her own suddenly felt like a bad idea. As another door opened, however, she tiptoed over to the staircase railing just so she could look down, desperate to see who it was. While she wouldn't be able to see into the entrance hallway from her vantage point, she wanted to know if there was anyone at the bottom of the stairs. Once at the edge, Lucy braced herself and gazed over the railing, eyes narrowed again to try to penetrate the dark.

She stared and stared, down into the dark.

'Lucy?' a voice close by said, causing Lucy to jolt and let out a squeal. She whipped her head around in fright, heart pounding in her chest, terrified a stranger was close by.

To Lucy's eternal relief, she saw it was Eleanore, who stood in the doorway to the stairwell. The woman was wearing her plain white pyjamas and dressing gown, rubbing at her eyes with her brow furrowed in confusion.

'It's just me,' Eleanore said in a soothing tone. 'What are you doing up? Why are you down here?'

Lucy's heart beat rapidly in her chest and she couldn't help sucking in deep, steadying breaths. It took her a moment to answer. 'I... I heard something,' she eventually said.

'What did you hear?' Eleanore asked as she looked around. 'And why did you open all the doors?'

'I didn't!' Lucy quickly exclaimed. 'I heard them all opening. Someone is going around the house opening them all up. I *heard* them, Eleanore.'

The older woman frowned and tilted her head to the side. 'What do you mean?'

'Listen,' Lucy said and pointed over the guard rail. Eleanore moved closer and both peered down, waiting in silence, with Lucy praying that whoever was down there opened another door—just to prove her right.

Frustratingly, no sound came back up.

'I don't hear anything,' Eleanore said after waiting a little more.

'But I'm telling the truth,' the young girl insisted.

Eleanore stared at her, studying Lucy. 'Come on,' was all the woman said, expression unreadable. 'Let's get you back to bed. You need your sleep.'

'But someone is *down* there,' Lucy went on.

Eleanore just shook her head. 'No one is down there, Lucy,' she stated.

'There *is!*' Lucy snapped back, almost stamping her foot in annoyance. She caught herself, however, realising how forcefully she had spoken out—and in a tone she'd never used with the older woman before. Lucy lowered her head. 'Can... can we just go down and check?'

Eleanore sighed and placed a hand on Lucy's shoulder. 'There's no one down there, dear,' she said, voice gentle. 'Now come on, back to bed. It's too late to be wandering the house on your own. You could have tripped and fallen down the stairs.' Lucy felt Eleanore's hand on her shoulder as the woman started to pull Lucy away from the stairs.

'But—'

'But nothing, Lucy,' Eleanore stated. While she didn't raise her voice, this time there was an undeniable firmness to her words. 'Now let's go.'

She then ushered Lucy away from the guardrail. Lucy wanted to argue more, but held back, knowing it would do no good. Eleanore just wouldn't listen to her. *But why? Isn't she worried about what I heard?*

'Shouldn't we at least close Ollie and Daniel's doors?' Lucy asked.

'It's fine, they're still asleep,' Eleanore said. 'Now come on, back to bed. Don't make me tell you again.'

Lucy was marched upstairs. Once at the top of the stairs, Eleanore turned off the staircase light and then escorted Lucy over to her room, where she waited for the girl to get back into bed. Eleanore sat down on the mattress.

'Listen, Lucy,' she began. 'I just think you had a bad dream, that's all.'

'But then how come the doors are all open?' Lucy asked.

'Because *I* didn't do it.'

The look Eleanore gave in response made it clear she didn't believe what Lucy was saying. That stung. 'Be that as it may,' Eleanore began, 'I don't want you wandering around at night. It isn't safe. I can promise you, there's no one else in the house other than us. There's nothing here to worry about.' Eleanore then gently stroked Lucy's arm. 'Now, get some sleep.' She leaned forward and placed a light kiss on Lucy's forehead before flicking off the night light, standing, and starting to walk from the room.

'Wait,' Lucy called after her, causing Eleanore to turn.

'What is it?' the older woman asked, with more patience than Lucy had expected.

'Can... can you close the door behind you?'

Eleanore smiled and nodded. 'Sure,' she said. 'Now... go to sleep.'

The guardian pulled the door closed as she left, leaving Lucy alone in the darkness. The girl didn't feel sleepy in the slightest, especially since her mind kept replaying what had just happened. She just lay in bed and listened, trying to pick up any sounds of movement.

But nothing came.

The young girl considered if she'd made a mistake by not alerting one of the others. Maybe they could have helped and taken the lead—and then maybe they wouldn't have made as much noise and woken Eleanore. Or at least she would have had back-up when Eleanore did come down, someone to corroborate her story.

Lucy had no idea how long she lay in the dark, her mind going over things again and again. Eventually... she managed to fall asleep.

When she opened her eyes the next morning, light streamed in from between the heavy curtains. She felt exhausted and just wanted to roll over and sleep some more. There were no other sounds in the house, which meant everyone else was still asleep, so Lucy gazed over to the wall-mounted clock on the far wall. It was only five-fifty in the morning. She groaned and pulled the duvet farther up while rolling to her side, now facing her door. The girl's eyes widened.

The door was once again open.

CHAPTER
TWELVE

After breakfast that morning, the children expected to have lessons in the study, given it was a Monday, but Eleanore surprised them by saying they could have an extra day off. She said people seemed tired, so she felt they needed a longer break.

That was welcome news to everyone. However, there was one problem: the torrential rain outside.

All of the children had gathered on the mid-floor snug, each busying themselves. Ollie was seated on a sofa, knees up, with a sketch pad resting on his legs as he tried to replicate his favourite football team's crest. Emily and Daniel were on a different sofa, both reading, and Lucy was sitting close to the window, looking out over the grounds. Ollie wasn't sure how much she could see, given the amount of rain that cascaded down the glass.

He had already noticed the girl seemed out of sorts that day and looked tired. Ollie put his pad down and turned over towards her.

'Everything okay, Luce?' he asked her. Lucy blinked and

turned to him. Pensive, she chewed the side of her mouth. The other two glanced over to her as well.

'I'm... fine,' she said.

Ollie patted the seat next to him. 'Come on,' he said. 'Spill it. What's wrong?'

Lucy cast her gaze downward. 'If... if I tell you all something, will you believe me?'

'Of course,' Emily said.

'You don't even have to ask, Luce,' Daniel added. 'Of course we will.'

Ollie patted the seat again. 'Come on, don't sit over there on your own. Tell us. We can help.'

Lucy gave a thankful smile and moved over to him. In turn, Emily and Daniel came over as well, with Emily squashing on the other side of Lucy and Daniel perching on the arm just next to her. They all waited patiently for Lucy to begin.

'It happened last night,' the young girl started. 'I... I thought there was someone in the house with us.'

Everyone shared a concerned look with each other. 'In here?' Ollie asked, confused and concerned in equal measure. 'What do you mean?'

'Well,' she went on, 'I woke up in the night. I was cold because I'd kicked my cover off again. When I was fixing it, I noticed my door was open, and I'm sure I closed it before going to sleep. I know I did. When I looked out into the hallway, I could see Emily and Eleanore's doors were open as well.'

'Mine *was* open this morning,' Emily said. 'I just assumed Eleanore had just checked on me.'

'Same,' Daniel said.

'Yeah,' Ollie added with a nod. 'Mine too.' He remembered thinking it was odd when he saw it, but hadn't paid it much mind since then. He'd been the last one up, as usual, so coming out to see other doors open hadn't been out of the norm at all.

'See!' Lucy said. 'I didn't know what was going on. I thought it might have been Eleanore too, like you guys did. I, well...' She hesitated. 'I thought I saw someone in the stairwell, but it was too dark to know for sure.'

Eleanore, Ollie thought to himself with certainty. *Creeping around again. What was she up to last night?*

He tried to catch Daniel's eye, but the other boy remained focused on Lucy.

'I checked on Emily to make sure she was okay,' Lucy continued, flashing Emily a smile, 'And then went over to Eleanore's room.'

'That was really brave of you, Luce,' Emily said and gave Lucy a squeeze, causing the younger girl's smile to widen.

'Eleanore wasn't in bed, was she,' Ollie said confidently. Both Lucy and Emily looked up to him.

'She was,' Lucy said. 'Also sleeping. It wasn't her.'

'Huh?' Ollie replied, shocked.

Lucy nodded. 'Yeah. Sound asleep. At first, anyway. A few seconds later, I started hearing your guys' doors opening below me.' She pointed to Ollie and Daniel in turn. 'So... I went down and saw both of you were still in bed too.'

'Wow,' Daniel said. 'You're much braver than I am.'

Ollie couldn't help but notice how proud Lucy looked in that moment. He couldn't disagree with Daniel. The girl had certainly been brave, but he was confused. If the person sneaking around hadn't been Eleanore, then who the hell *was* it?

'You're certain you saw someone?' Ollie asked.

Lucy paused and tilted her head. 'No... not certain,' she admitted. 'But I heard them. I mean, I suppose the creak on the stairs could have been anything. But I heard the doors opening on the bottom floor too.'

'Did you go down there?' Daniel asked.

But Lucy shook her head. 'No, Eleanore woke up and came down before I could. After she scared me to death, she asked what I was doing.'

'What did you tell her?' Ollie asked.

'The truth,' Lucy replied. 'I told her what had happened, but I... I don't think she believed me. She wouldn't even check downstairs, just said there was nothing to worry about. Then she sent me back to bed.' Lucy let out a sigh, looking down at the floor a second time. 'Then this morning when I woke up... my door was open again.' Eventually, she raised her eyes and looked at the others somewhat hesitantly. 'You... you all believe me, right?'

Ollie was quick to nod, and he placed a hand on her shoulder. 'We do,' he said. 'Of course we do.'

'Yeah, we believe you, Luce,' Emily confirmed; Daniel nodded as well.

A relieved expression broke out over the young girl's face. 'So... who do you think it was?' she then asked.

Ollie thought on it but was confounded.

'Could someone have broken in?' Emily asked.

'The doors and windows are all locked at night,' Daniel replied. 'Well, the windows on the ground floor, anyway. So if someone *did* break in, they would have had to force their way inside. But I didn't see anything showing someone had.'

'Unless the doors *were* open,' Ollie suggested. 'Maybe Eleanore locked them after Lucy had gone to bed.'

'You mean... you think she let someone in on purpose?' Emily asked with a frown.

Ollie shrugged. 'Well, I'm not saying *that*, exactly. I'm just trying to think of an explanation. Maybe she forgot and locked up later, after seeing Luce. Could have given someone the chance to slip in and out.'

'Do you get strangers all the way out here?' Emily asked.

'No,' Ollie admitted with a shake of his head. He knew he was reaching.

'Besides,' Lucy began, 'I was awake for a little bit afterwards. I didn't hear the front door open. And I *would* have, because it clinks and rattles a lot.'

That was true enough, Ollie knew. 'Okay,' he said. 'I doubt anyone could have come in from outside, then. But if that's the case... it doesn't give us any answers.' He then saw Daniel looking back at him with raised eyebrows. The intent from the boy was clear. *Should we tell them?*

At first Ollie was hesitant—he didn't want anything getting back to Eleanore. Ultimately, however, Ollie knew the girls had every right to know what had been going on. In truth, he and Daniel shouldn't have kept it from them this long.

'There's... something else you should know,' Ollie began after giving Daniel a quick nod. 'Something Daniel and I have been trying to figure out.'

'What?' Emily asked—both her and Lucy's gazes fixed on him.

Ollie kept his focus on Daniel. 'You wanna tell it?' he asked. 'After all, you saw everything.'

All eyes turned to the other boy, who wilted under their stares. However, he nodded and took a small breath. 'Well,' he started, 'I've seen Eleanore walking around at night. Twice now. And both times she... went down to the cellar.'

Emily and Lucy shuffled around in their seats to fully face Daniel. 'Okay,' Emily began. 'Is that... well, is that so strange?' she asked.

'It was about two or three in the morning,' Daniel stated. 'And both times she was carrying a tray, though I couldn't make out what was on it.'

'How did you know she went to the cellar?' Lucy asked, eyes wide. 'Did you follow her?'

Daniel nodded. 'Yes, but I was too slow both times. I heard her opening the padlock, though. I told Ollie after the first time it happened, and the second time I woke him up so he could see, but Eleanore had already gone down and locked the door behind her that time too.'

'We waited for a little bit downstairs,' Ollie said, taking over. 'Hiding, to see if we could see anything, but it was taking too long and we were falling asleep, so we went back to bed.'

'How come you didn't tell us?' Lucy asked.

'We didn't want to worry you, Luce,' Ollie explained. 'Not until we knew what she was doing.'

'When did that happen?' Emily asked.

'The first time was the night before you arrived,' Daniel answered. 'The second time was recently, only two nights ago.'

Emily paused before asking. 'The same night the house shook?' Daniel nodded.

'You should have told me!' Lucy said and stood up. She looked annoyed. 'And Emily. We don't keep secrets.'

'You're right,' Ollie said, hands out. 'And I'm sorry.' He glanced at Emily. 'To both of you. Honestly, we didn't *want* to keep it a secret, but... well... like I said, we also didn't want to worry you both without reason. And most important, we didn't want Eleanore to find out we'd been watching her.'

'Why would Eleanore find out?' Lucy asked. After a beat, her eyes widened and she quickly folded her arms across her chest. 'You thought I'd tell, didn't you.'

Ollie shook his head. 'No, not on purpose,' he insisted. 'We were just worried it might accidentally... you know... slip out.'

Lucy just glared at him. 'I wouldn't have said anything, Ollie,' she stated. 'Not if you'd asked me not to.'

With a sigh, Ollie looked down, feeling terrible. 'I know, I'm sorry. I... thought I was doing the right thing at the time.' Eventually, his eyes met hers again. 'Sorry, Luce. We should have said something before now.'

'Yeah. Sorry, Lucy,' Daniel added.

The girl continued to stare at them, arms still folded, casting her glare from one to the other. Eventually, however, she relented. 'Don't keep secrets,' she said again. 'It's not nice.'

Ollie nodded. 'We won't. Not anymore, I promise.' He then caught Emily's eye as well. 'Sorry to you too, Emily,' he said.

The other girl smiled. 'It's fine,' she said. 'I get why you didn't tell me. I'm the new girl.'

But Ollie quickly shook his head. 'It isn't that,' he said. 'I mean, we didn't wanna say anything the first time because it was your first day. Then nothing happened again for a couple of weeks. After the other night, well...' He stopped, aware he couldn't say anything without upsetting Lucy.

'Because I was always in the way?' the young girl asked, as if reading his mind.

Busted.

'No,' Ollie lied, now feeling even worse. 'Look, I'm sorry,' he said again. 'I thought I was looking out for everyone, but clearly I didn't think it through. It won't happen again.' He gave Lucy his best puppy-dog eyes, mimicking how she did it, though he knew on him the expression would come off goofy. 'Please don't be mad at me.'

After a moment, Lucy rolled her own eyes. 'Fine,' she eventually said before flashing him a small smile. 'I forgive you.'

'Thank you,' Ollie replied.

Lucy turned to Daniel. 'You too, you dumb secret keeper.'

Daniel didn't say anything in response, just gave a tight-lipped smile and a nod of thanks.

'And Emily,' Ollie went on. 'You're *not* the new girl. You're one of us now. Don't feel like you aren't.'

'Okay,' Emily said. 'Thank you. But with all that out of the way, what do we think is going on? I mean, from what I can tell, Eleanore going down to the cellar late at night is a little odd, maybe, but it doesn't seem like anything to worry about. And it also doesn't seem connected to what Lucy heard last night. I mean, Eleanore was sound asleep for pretty much all of that.'

'There's a little more I need to share,' Daniel said. 'Though I agree, it doesn't sound like the two things are linked.'

'Go on,' Emily said to him.

'Well, the first night I followed her,' Daniel began. 'I heard her through the door to the cellar. She said something. It was kinda like she was talking to herself, only what she said was... weird.'

'What was it?' Lucy asked.

' 'Almost time, dear',' Daniel recited.

Ollie watched as the girls both frowned in confusion. 'And she wasn't talking to anyone?' Emily asked.

Daniel shrugged. 'I can't be sure, but I don't think so. And then, the night before last, when I heard her go past my room, I'm pretty sure she was crying?'

'Eleanore?' Emily repeated with a look of surprise.

Daniel nodded. 'Not loudly, but like... sobbing.'

'I wonder why she was upset?' Lucy then asked.

'Do you think...' Ollie began, but trailed off, unsure if he should voice the thought in his mind.

'Do we think what?' Emily asked.

Ollie didn't answer right away, still grappling with if he should pose the question. Eventually he decided to, just to see what the others thought of the notion. 'Well, do you think maybe Eleanore left the cellar door open last night, and the person that Lucy saw didn't actually come in from outside, but... *up* from down there?'

As he spoke the words, he realised just how much it sounded like a reach. While he had no idea what Eleanore *had* been doing, he seriously doubted the woman would just give a stranger free rein in the house. He immediately regretted asking.

The others were silent for a little while. Eventually, Emily was the first to reply. 'I mean, I don't know Eleanore as well as the rest of you, but so far she seems pretty responsible.' Then she frowned. 'Well, apart from taking my blood. I still think that was weird. She did it to you guys as well, right?'

'She did,' Ollie confirmed. 'A little while before you came to the house. She did us all together on the same day.'

'And she sent it all to the doctor?'

'I think so,' Ollie said.

Lucy shook her head, still seeming lost in her thoughts. 'Eleanore wouldn't let strangers into the house,' she said defiantly. 'No way. I don't know who I saw, but Eleanore *didn't* let them in.'

'Honestly,' Ollie began, 'I think you're probably right. I only said it because... well, because it popped into my head. Though at the same time, I don't understand why she wouldn't go down and check on what you heard, Luce. Isn't that a little strange? I mean, if one of my kids told me that, I'd want to check everything out just to be sure.'

Ollie immediately regretted his wording—they weren't Eleanore's kids. She was just their guardian. However, no one said anything about that.

'I suppose so,' Lucy admitted.

Everyone grew quiet. They had no answers.

'So... what do we do about it all?' Emily asked. 'Because I think we only have two options. Well, three really. One, we talk to Eleanore and confront her about what's been happening, see what she says. Two, we try and sneak down and watch her in the night and catch her in the act, like you guys tried to. Or three, we just... do nothing.'

'Do nothing?' Ollie asked.

Emily nodded. 'I'm not saying we *should* do nothing, but it's an option. We could just kind of ignore it all and carry on, just to keep the peace.'

Ollie scrunched up his face. 'Nope, don't like that,' he said, causing Emily to laugh.

'I didn't think you would,' she replied.

'If we speak to Eleanore,' Daniel began, 'we could get in trouble like Lucy did. It doesn't sound like she's open to talking about this.'

'Plus,' Ollie jumped in, 'if she *is* hiding something and

knows we're on to her, she'll start being a lot more careful, so it will be harder to find anything out if she denies it.'

'Then that pretty much just leaves spying on her,' Emily said. 'But it's going to be hard for four of us to keep hidden while we do it.'

'And we might need to do it all night, which means making sure we don't fall asleep,' Daniel said. 'That... won't be easy.'

'Actually,' Ollie began. 'There is a fourth option. If we're brave enough, that is.'

'Do go on,' Emily said. 'This sounds interesting.'

Ollie smiled. 'We get the key from her and sneak down to the basement ourselves.'

CHAPTER
THIRTEEN

The girls had appeared surprised at Ollie's idea. Daniel, though... not so much. Mainly because Ollie had already floated it to him before.

'I don't know,' Lucy said. 'Sneaking around at night is one thing. Stealing her key is...' She trailed off.

'I get it,' Ollie said. 'It's risky. But it might be the only way to really find out what she's doing, because she's not going to tell us. I'm sure of it.'

As Daniel watched Emily and Lucy, he could tell they were starting to be swayed. It seemed Ollie sensed it as well, so he continued to press. 'I'll do it myself,' he said. 'I don't expect anyone else to get in trouble for it. And if I *do* get down there, I'll tell you all what I find.'

After silent consideration, Emily shook her head. 'No,' she said.

Daniel saw Ollie's body sag in disappointment. 'Okay,' he said. 'It was just a thought.'

But Emily shook her head once more. 'Wait, that's not what I mean. You're *not* doing it on your own. It's not fair for you to take the blame for everything.'

'Really?' Ollie asked, now looking pleasantly surprised.

'Yeah, I'll help,' Emily said.

'We still need to watch Eleanore, though,' Daniel quickly interjected. The others turned to him.

'What do you mean?' Emily asked.

'We don't know what the key looks like. *Or* where she keeps it.'

'Right,' Ollie said. 'But we could try to snoop around her room when she's not there. The key is probably there somewhere.'

'But how do we know if we find the right one?' Daniel asked.

'Keep trying them all?' Lucy offered.

'It would take time,' Daniel said. 'And it's risky. If we take every key we find, there's a higher chance of Eleanore noticing something is missing. But if we only take one at a time, that would take a while and make this stretch out over days. Maybe weeks.'

'We could cause a distraction,' Ollie suggested. 'Then one of us could snoop. Though I agree, watching her one night to see the key itself would be a good start.' Daniel could feel Ollie's eyes on him, and a second later the older boy asked, 'Are you okay helping us as well? You don't have to. Don't feel pressured.'

'Of course,' Daniel quickly replied. He didn't *love* the idea, but he also wasn't going to shirk away while the others did everything.

'You sure?' Ollie went on. Daniel just gave a firm nod in response. Ollie then turned to the youngest of the group. 'Luce?' he asked.

However, the young girl was slow in replying. Daniel could see the obvious conflict on her face. 'I... don't know,' she said quietly.

'It's okay,' Ollie replied. 'Don't worry about it. We'll just try to keep you out of it so there's no chance you get pulled in and blamed if we're caught.'

'But... I don't want to be the only one left out.'

'We'll tell you everything,' Ollie said. 'You just won't need to help us search the room or spy or stay up late.'

Emily wrapped an arm around Lucy. 'Do what you think feels right,' the older girl said. 'No one here will judge you. We've all got each other's backs, right?'

Lucy nodded. 'Right.' She then took a breath. 'Okay, I'll help.'

'And you're certain?' Ollie asked.

'I am,' Lucy replied, sounding more confident now.

Emily squeezed her tight. 'Welcome to the spying club,' she joked. Lucy laughed, leaning into the older girl.

'Then we need a plan,' Daniel said. 'Are we staying up late tonight to see if we can see her again?'

More silent consideration. 'What time did you say she was sneaking around?' Emily said.

'Around two or three in the morning,' Daniel replied.

'Ouch,' Emily said. 'It's going to be tough to stay awake that long.'

'And harder to wake up at the right time,' Ollie added. 'It's not like we can set an alarm. Plus, I sleep like the dead.'

'Sleep like the dead?' Lucy asked as she cast a confused glance over at Ollie.

'Oh,' Ollie said. 'It just means I'm a really deep sleeper, so it takes a lot for me to wake up.'

'It's a shame it's raining so much today,' Emily went on. 'If the weather was nicer, I could have gone out in the garden with Eleanore and kept her busy while one of you searched the room.'

'That's... a really good idea, actually,' Daniel said. 'It's the one thing that keeps her out of the house for a few hours at a time.'

'Maybe next time we go to town, one of us can pretend to be ill,' Lucy suggested. 'That will give them a *lot* of time alone.'

Daniel nodded with surprise. 'That's... even better, Luce. Well done.'

'But,' Ollie began, 'that also means waiting.'

'Yeah, it does,' Daniel admitted. 'Though what's the rush? Might as well do it right if we're gonna do it.'

Emily nodded in agreement. 'Why don't we ask if we can head into town this coming weekend?' she said.

'But would she still go if one of us is feeling poorly?' Lucy asked. 'Or *pretending* to be. We've never left anyone behind before.'

Emily shrugged. 'We can try. If not, then we'll go with my plan of distracting her in the garden.'

Daniel looked around at everyone. 'Seems like a good idea,' he said. 'Does everyone agree?'

There were nods all around.

'I guess I can wait a little bit longer,' Ollie said with a shrug. After a moment, added, 'What about last night, though? With what Lucy heard. If someone is roaming the house...' He trailed off, letting his words hang over everyone.

Daniel thought it through for a second. 'Well, nothing happened to us while we were asleep,' he said. 'Doors were opened, but... that's it.' He turned to Lucy. 'Is there anything else you can think to tell us that might help?'

Lucy's eyes flicked to the side as she thought. 'I don't know,' she said. 'I don't think so. For a little bit, I did think it might have been a... you know... ghost or something.' She looked up to Ollie. 'But you don't believe in them, right?'

Ollie shook his head. 'Definitely not,' he said.

'But what if it *was*?' Lucy went on. 'We know that no one else came in. The doors and windows were all locked. It wasn't any of us, or Eleanore, so maybe…'

'Maybe the house is haunted?' Ollie asked. Daniel had expected some kind of scepticism or scorn in the older boy's voice, but was surprised to find there was none.

'Maybe,' Lucy stated.

Ollie shrugged. 'I can't tell you what to believe, but I *really* doubt it.'

'Regardless of what it was,' Emily interjected, 'we don't really have a choice other than to wait it out. If Eleanore didn't want to listen to you, Luce, then there's nothing else we can do about it right now. *But*… I think we make a pact. If one of us sees or experiences something odd, we tell the others straight away. Even if it's in the middle of the night.'

'I agree,' said Ollie. 'I'd sure want everyone here to come get me.'

'But it applies to you as well, Ollie,' Emily said. 'No trying to handle it all on your own just to protect us.'

'I… wouldn't do that,' Ollie said, fooling absolutely no one.

'You big liaaaar,' Lucy teased with a giggle.

'Okay, okay,' Ollie said. 'I promise I won't do anything on my own.'

'Good,' Emily replied.

'Who stays behind, then?' Daniel asked. 'On Saturday, I mean. Who pretends to be ill so they can search Eleanore's room?'

Ollie's hand went straight up. 'I'm happy to do it,' he said. Before anyone could argue, he went on: 'It's more likely she'd let me stay on my own, anyway. I'm the oldest and have been here the longest, so she'll be more open to it.' He looked at Emily. 'You've only been here a few weeks, so she won't let you stay on your own.' His eyes then found Daniel. 'She *might* let you,' he began, but Daniel held up his hand.

'She knows I get spooked by the house,' he said. 'So probably not.'

Ollie smiled. Daniel knew the boy had already been thinking the same thing but just didn't want to say it.

'And Luce,' Ollie said, 'I don't think she'd be happy with you staying, given you're the youngest.'

'No, I think you're right,' Lucy agreed. Then a cheeky smile formed over her lips. 'But won't you be scared here all on your own, with only the *ghosts* for company?' She held her arms up in the air, hands flopping up and down to mimic a ghost. 'Oooooooooo,' she said, copying the sound one might make.

Ollie just rolled his eyes. 'I think I'll be fine,' he said. 'Besides, if one shows up, I'll just ask *them* what's down in the cellar.'

'Be sure to ask them why they like opening all the doors as well,' Lucy quipped. Suddenly, her eyes went wide. 'Hey! Maybe we should do an Ouija board!'

'No,' Ollie said.

'We don't have one,' Daniel added.

Lucy tilted her head to the side. 'Couldn't we just make one on paper?' She nudged Ollie's drawing pad with her foot. 'Wouldn't that work?'

'Maybe not a good idea,' Emily said.

'You don't think they work?' Lucy asked her. 'I heard Mum and Dad talking about them once. Dad sure seemed to think it was real.'

Emily shrugged. 'I'm not sure,' she said. 'But why tempt fate, eh? I mean, we don't want to bring anything bad through, do we? It seems like we've already got enough to deal with.'

'Yeah... I guess you're right,' Lucy said. 'Who knows *who* we would end up speaking to.' She paused in thought. 'Though, if it did work, do you think we'd maybe get to speak to our...' She trailed off.

No one else said anything. Daniel turned his gaze down to the floor.

No, he told himself. *We can't speak to them. They're dead and gone.*

'Come on,' Ollie suddenly said with a clap of his hands. 'We have plenty of time to kill until the weekend. What should we do today?'

'Something fun,' Lucy suggested.

'Obviously,' Ollie replied. 'But *what?* Especially since we're stuck inside today.'

'Charades?' Daniel suggested. 'We haven't done that in a while.'

There were nods of approval. 'Charades it is,' Ollie said. 'I'll go first.' He stood up and walked out in front of everyone before turning around with his hands raised, palms held together, almost in prayer. Then, he opened his hands out flat.

'A book!' Lucy said eagerly.

Ollie nodded. This time, he held up four fingers.

'Four words,' Emily added.

Another nod.

Lucy giggled. 'No way you read a book with *four* whole words.'

Ollie frowned and his jaw fell open in mock offence. Everyone else burst out laughing. 'Wow. Thanks, Luce,' Ollie said, unable to stop from chuckling.

'Just messing,' Lucy said. 'I love ya, really.'

Ollie shook his head. 'Love you too, Luce.' He held his fingers up again. 'So yes, *four* whole words. Let's go.'

The group spent a full day playing and laughing together. Despite the nagging in the back of Daniel's mind, he enjoyed himself that day, feeling safe and secure in the company of the others.

CHAPTER
FOURTEEN

'Ollie!'

Ollie opened his eyes, feeling himself being shaken awake. It took all his effort to keep them open and stare straight up. His body *begged* him to go back to sleep.

Lucy was looking down at him, illuminated by his nightlight, which she must have switched on. As Ollie narrowed his eyes, he could see Emily standing just behind Lucy.

Something happened.

He pushed himself up to his elbow. 'What's wrong?' he asked, suddenly feeling tense. 'Are you okay?'

'Yeah,' Lucy whispered. 'But Eleanore went downstairs again.'

Ollie's eyes widened. 'Really?' He quickly pulled his covers back. 'What time is it?'

'Late,' Emily said. 'Around two. I woke up, thought I heard something in my room, but it was nothing. Couldn't get back to sleep, but then I heard Eleanore come out of her room a few minutes later.'

Ollie got up. 'Did you see her?'

Emily nodded. 'I opened my door a little to peek out after she went past.'

'Did she have a tray with her?'

Emily shook her head. 'Not this time. But... I'm pretty sure she was sobbing again.'

'Really?' Ollie asked, moving to grab his robe. The night air was colder than it should have been; the girls were wrapped up as well.

'Quite a lot, actually,' Emily went on. 'I mean, it was obvious she was trying to keep it under control from what I could hear—she kept sniffling and puffing out long breaths, but it wasn't doing much good. When she made it downstairs, I woke Lucy up and then came here,' Emily explained. 'We still need to wake Daniel.'

'Let's go get him,' Ollie said, flicking off his nightlight before moving out of the room, his mind trying to figure out what had their guardian in tears in the middle of the night.

'My door was already open again,' Emily whispered as they walked.

'Mine too,' Lucy added. 'And so was yours, Ollie.' Looking ahead, Ollie could see Daniel's door hung open as well, along with all others on that level. *What's going on?*

The group continued forward into Daniel's room and paused at his bed.

'Wakey wakey, sleepyhead,' Lucy said and gently shook the boy with one hand while flicking on his nightlight with the other. Ollie and Emily stood just behind her, looking down as Daniel slowly came to. The boy's eyes blinked open, then scrunched closed at the light that washed over him. He looked dazed and confused.

'Wh-what is it?' he eventually asked in a croaky voice.

'Eleanore is creeping around again,' Ollie told him. 'Emily saw her and rounded everyone up. You coming?'

Daniel slowly sat up and rolled his shoulders back before stretching out. He yawned, then nodded. 'Yeah,' he rasped, rubbing his face. 'Let's go.'

As Ollie had suspected, Eleanore was nowhere to be seen by the time the group made it to the ground floor. The padlock was gone again, likely on the inside once again. Ollie moved forward and gently tried the door just to be sure, but found it locked.

Ollie stepped back and turned to the others, who were all huddled together in the dark. A strange realisation crept over him—it felt somehow right that they were all together in this, all acting as one. He also realised just *why* he was so focused on getting to the bottom of it: because it was exciting. A break from the norm. A goal to work towards and a mystery to solve. As much as he loved and appreciated Erimus House, it occurred to Ollie in that moment that maybe he'd begun getting bored with the routine of the house.

'Should we find somewhere to wait?' Emily asked.

'Might as well,' Ollie said. 'Last time me and Daniel camped out in the—'

Lucy's sharp intake of breath cut him off. 'Look!' she said, her voice a loud, panicked whisper. She was pointing off to one of the rear windows. 'Did you see that?'

'See what?' Ollie asked as he gazed over. The long, thick curtains around the window were open. They were always open, acting more as decoration rather than having any practical use, and there was just enough moonlight outside to allow Ollie to see the edge of the patio. Even so, there was nothing out of the ordinary.

'Something moved,' Lucy said. 'I'm sure of it. When I

looked over, something... I dunno... kind of shifted to the side. Like someone was there watching, then stepped away.'

Ollie felt a creeping sensation work its way up his spine. Regardless, he forced himself forward to the window and pressed his nose to it, gazing left and right, trying to see if he could spot anything. He felt the others approach from behind.

'It went to the left,' Lucy explained, so Ollie focused on that direction.

'Anything?' Emily asked.

Ollie continued to look for a few seconds more. 'Not that I can see,' he said before turning to Lucy. 'Did you get a good look?' he asked. 'Was it a person?'

But Lucy shook her head. 'I'm not sure. I didn't see much, since it was so quick.'

'Could it have been an animal or something?' Daniel asked.

Lucy cocked her head to the side. 'Erm... I think it was taller, but... I guess I don't know.'

Ollie looked back outside again. This close, he was able to see past the patio area and deeper into the garden, though what was visible didn't stretch down to the far wall. He then pulled his head back and turned his attention to the rear doors, which were only locked with internal dead bolts.

'I'm going outside,' he announced to the others.

'No,' Daniel said. 'Stay here. What if Eleanore comes back up?'

'I won't go far,' Ollie said. 'I'll just step out so I can see farther down the back of the house. Just in case whatever Lucy saw is still there.'

He felt a hand slip into his, and when he looked down he saw Lucy standing next to him, smiling back up. 'I'm coming as well,' she said.

Ollie shook his head. 'Just stay—'

'*No,*' she interrupted firmly, giving his arm a defiant yank. 'No doing everything yourself, remember?'

'Yeah,' Emily added. 'You promised.' She looked to Daniel. 'We all go together, right?'

Though Daniel appeared hesitant, he still nodded. 'Yeah,' he said. 'We're a team.' He looked back to Ollie. 'We stick together.'

Ollie couldn't help but smile. 'Okay, team,' he said. 'Follow me. Stay close. It's gonna be cold out there, so brace yourselves.'

The oldest boy moved over to the door, everyone else staying huddled just behind him. Once there, he gazed out into the night again. After seeing nothing, he pulled back the bolt close to the handle, then opened up the ones at the top and bottom of the door. Finally, he pulled the door open while stepping back to let it swing inward.

While the air that rolled in to meet them did indeed carry a chill, it wasn't as cold as Ollie had expected.

Though it was reluctantly, he forced himself to step outside and out onto the cool paving of the patio.

Should have put my slippers on, he thought to himself as a chill ran up him, causing him to shudder. The surface was still damp from the rain earlier that day, but even so, he took another few steps forward. Lucy fell in beside him and took hold of his hand again as they moved down to the left-hand side of the yard, Emily and Daniel just behind.

While the corner of the house was visible, darkness swallowed up most of what was beyond that, so Ollie wasn't able to make out the boundary side walls. Yet as far as he could see, there was still nothing unusual.

'I'm going to check around the corner,' he said. 'Just to be sure. Feel free to stay he—'

'Let's go,' Lucy said with determination and took a step forward first, pulling Ollie with her. He had to move quickly to keep up and couldn't help but be impressed by her bravery. Neither of the other two lagged behind either, so the group soon reached the corner. It was a little darker there, given the shadows created between the boundary wall and the side of the house. However, now that he was so close, Ollie could fully see the far wall—the coast was clear.

'What about around the front?' Daniel suggested in a whisper. 'If someone was out here, they might have just moved down the side of the house.'

'Yeah,' Ollie said, 'let's check. Makes sense to do a full loop.' However, he also knew they'd left the rear door wide open. If someone continued all the way around, that would be an easy way inside for them.

'Let's close the back door first,' Ollie said. '*Then* we can check around the house. I don't like the idea of just leaving it open.'

Emily and Daniel led the way back, but as they walked, Emily caught her foot on a protruding edge of paving and fell to the side. No one had time to react other than Emily herself, who thrust out an arm towards the back wall to stop herself, which sent her hand deep into one of the climbing plants that ran up the building.

'Ahhh,' she cried out. Once she was steady, she quickly yanked her hand back, cradling it. Everyone hurried over to her.

'Are you okay?' Daniel asked.

Emily cast a scowl over to the wall climber. 'Bloody thorns,' she seethed through gritted teeth. Ollie noticed blood running down the side of the girl's hand.

'Erm... Emily,' he said and nodded down.

Emily looked down as well and laid her palm face up. There was a gash right in the centre, blood spilling from it. Lucy drew in a breath.

'That looks deep,' Daniel said with obvious concern. He lowered his head closer. 'Does it hurt?'

Emily was still wincing. 'Like a bitch,' she said through clenched teeth—Lucy's eyes widened.

The cut ran from just below the joint of her pointer finger and diagonally down to the heel of her palm. Though it wasn't gushing blood, she was still bleeding enough to concern Ollie.

'Careful,' Daniel said as more of it ran from the side of Emily's hand and dripped to the ground. He took gentle hold of Emily's wrist and extended her arm a little. 'You don't want to get any on your clothes,' he went on. 'Eleanore will spot it right away and ask what happened.'

'Good point,' Ollie said.

'She's going to ask anyway when she sees the cut,' Emily said.

'We need a towel or something,' Lucy added. 'So she can wrap her hand.'

'I'll go get one,' Daniel said. 'There are some in the kitchen drawers. I'll wet one and bring it back.'

'It's gonna get covered in blood,' Ollie warned. 'So we'll have to hide it after.'

'Yeah,' Daniel agreed. 'And sneakily wash it if we get the chance. Then put it back before Eleanore notices one is missing.'

'If we don't ruin it first,' Emily said. 'There's a *lot* of blood.'

Ollie flicked his eyes over to Daniel. 'You okay going alone?'

The younger boy nodded. 'Best only one of us goes. Emily might leave a blood trail across the floor.'

Yet as he looked closer, Ollie saw the reluctance on the boy's face. 'I'll come too,' Ollie said.

But Daniel shook his head. 'Stay with Emily and make sure she's okay,' he insisted. Ollie smiled, knowing the younger boy was pushing himself to be brave.

Daniel turned to leave, and as he did, Emily added, 'Thanks, Daniel.'

'No problem,' he said, setting off. Ollie watched him walk away, and though he wouldn't be going far, Ollie still didn't like the idea of them splitting up.

'It's falling on the patio,' Lucy interrupted, pointing down.

'Not much we can do about that,' Ollie said.

'We can stand on the grass,' Lucy suggested.

But Ollie shook his head. 'The paving is damp enough from the rain today. The grass will be *really* muddy, so we'd end up tracking mud back through the house.'

'I can't believe I was so clumsy,' Emily then said. She shot another glare at the wall climber. 'Why are there so many thorns in those things?'

'They're everywhere,' Ollie said. 'My first week here I was going to try to climb one of the boundary walls—not to escape or anything, just for fun—but there were loads of vines and thorns most of the way around.'

'They're probably there to stop people from climbing over,' Lucy suggested. 'And also to stop people from getting up to one of the bedroom windows.'

'Could be,' Emily said. 'Kind of like natural security, right?'

'Yeah,' Lucy replied. 'Or Eleanore doesn't know how to get rid of them.'

As they waited, all intermittently looking down at Emily's outstretched palm, Ollie happened to glance down towards the end of the garden, into the darkness that consumed everything. He narrowed his eyes.

Did something just move?

He kept on watching, almost certain he'd seen something shift in the shadows.

'What's up?' he heard Emily ask. As he turned back to her, he saw she was looking straight at him. Ollie peered back to the end of the garden again and continued to look for a moment, but eventually shook his head.

'Nothing,' he answered, then shuddered, suddenly feeling the cold again. 'How about we get back inside as soon as Daniel brings the towel?' he said. 'It's definitely getting colder.'

'What about checking the rest of the way around the house?' Lucy asked.

'Yeah,' Ollie replied. 'You're right. A quick loop and then back in. But I don't want to stay out too long, the temperature is really dropping.'

'Sounds like a good idea to me,' Lucy said.

Ollie let his eyes wander back down the garden again, unsure if what he'd seen had just been in his head or if there had been something down there.

'There he is,' Lucy said as she looked over to the kitchen window close by. Through the open blinds, Ollie spotted Daniel waving back at them.

∽

Daniel stood just before the kitchen sink, holding a grey hand towel under the running tap. His first instinct had been to put the tap on full blast, but he figured that would have made too much noise, since the kitchen was adjacent to the cellar stairs.

He had the towel fully stretched out and moved it around, letting the water coat the whole surface. Once done, he turned off the tap and bunched the towel up to wring out the excess water. After a few more shakes, he waved again to the others outside, pointed towards the rear door to indicate he was on his way, and began to walk out of the room.

En-route, he glanced at the rack that held the keys to the house. Eleanore was quite happy leaving the keys to the external doors and windows there in case anyone needed them, showing her trust in them all, but Ollie was right: it was clear none would fit the padlock to the cellar. *Obviously there isn't* that *much trust.*

There were other keys on the rack as well, which were for the many rooms to the house, though Daniel didn't know which went to which. For as long as he'd been here, those keys had never even been used.

Once he was back out into the dining room, Daniel noticed the temperature suddenly drop. His gaze shot over to the rear door, which he'd closed.

Suddenly he stopped short, his breath lodged in his throat as he glanced down into the entrance hallway.

There's... there's no way it's real, the boy said to himself as panic gripped him.

Yet the more he looked, the more he realised that his eyes *weren't* playing tricks on him.

There was a figure deeper in the space, standing close to the side wall that separated the hallway and the drawing room, just on the edge of a pocket of darkness. It was tall, *much* taller than Eleanore, and thin. The dark form wasn't exactly black, but something else, something Daniel couldn't quite comprehend. Its movements were quick and jerky, and its head twitched randomly, periodically flicking down to its shoulder.

Daniel noticed it had no clothes or hair, and it had its hands on the wall at the moment and seemed to be... stroking it, gliding its spindly fingers along the surface. The long fingers then moved over the frame of a picture close by, as if feeling their way around.

As much as Daniel wanted to look away, he couldn't, rooted to the spot and gazing forward. However, the boy did manage to summon enough strength to take small, careful steps backwards, not wanting to alert the thing—so far, it had remained oblivious to his presence.

Don't look, don't look, don't look.

His throat was dry and he could feel his heart thudding in his chest. A wave of pinpricks swept up Daniel's arms and back.

He continued to slowly retreat, step by step. He was thankful he couldn't see the face of the thing before him, since it stood in profile. The figure then made a noise that caused Daniel to jolt: the sound was quiet, somewhere between a *click* and a groan, and something Daniel had never heard before. If his friends asked him to recreate it later, he knew for certain he wouldn't be able to.

Eventually, Daniel made it to the door; the figure had become blurrier, claimed more by the darkness of the hall. When he reached out for the door, however, he bumped into it harder than he'd wanted, causing it to rattle in its frame.

The thing up ahead suddenly stopped, frozen motionless. It made the sound again. Then, slowly but surely, it started to turn its head towards Daniel.

Run! he told himself.

No longer worried about staying quiet, and desperate to get away, he spun, yanked the door open, and bolted outside, quickly ducking left and sprinting over to the others. Their heads all snapped over to him, all three of his friends wearing expressions of confusion and concern.

'What is it?' Ollie asked. 'Is Eleanore coming?'

Daniel reached them in a matter of moments, panting and shaking, standing close to Ollie while pressing himself into the older boy for protection. Daniel then pointed back towards the house, eyes wide. 'There's... There's...' It was hard to get any words out at all, and Daniel felt an overwhelming surge of terror so intense he almost started crying. 'There's something in there!' he eventually exclaimed.

'What do you mean?' Emily asked. Daniel felt Ollie drape a protective arm over his shoulder.

'What did you see?' Ollie asked quickly.

Daniel just shook his head. *How do I describe* that?

He looked down to see his hands trembling and realised he was still holding the damp towel. He quickly thrust it out to Emily, who took it, frowning in confusion.

'Come on, Daniel,' Ollie continued. 'What's in there?'

'I... I don't know,' Daniel uttered. 'I'm not sure *what* it is.' He was still panting, heart pounding; his wide eyes remained focused on the rear door to the house, where he half expected the thing inside to come lumbering out.

He felt Ollie's arm release and was shocked to see the boy start walking towards the door. Daniel shot out a hand and grabbed him. 'No!' he shouted. 'Don't!'

Ollie just placed a hand on his shoulder. 'We can't just stay out here all night,' he said. 'I'm gonna go look.'

'Don't!' Daniel repeated, terrified Ollie was about to walk into danger.

'What is it?' Lucy asked. 'Tell us.'

Daniel shook his head. 'I don't know,' he replied. 'I... I just don't know. But it *wasn't* a person.'

He saw the way Emily and Ollie looked at each other. *They don't believe me.*

'We'll all go,' Emily said. 'Stick together and just look inside by the door without actually going in.'

'We need to run away,' Daniel insisted as the urge to cry started to rise.

'There's nowhere we can run to,' Ollie explained. 'The front gate is locked, and we can't climb the walls.' The older boy then squeezed Daniel's shoulder. 'It's going to be fine, Daniel,' he said. 'I'll make sure of it. But I need to see who's in there.'

'*What's* in there!' Daniel corrected.

'Yeah,' Ollie said. 'I need to see *what's* in there. Just a quick look.'

Why doesn't he believe me? Why don't any of them believe me?

Even though he was terrified, Daniel gave a nod of confirmation, knowing Ollie would go anyway. Everyone huddled around the younger boy as they started to walk, Ollie in the lead and Emily and Lucy on either side of Daniel. He felt Lucy's small hand slip into his own. When he looked over to her, she gave him a warm smile. That gesture, plus having the others around him, bolstered him somewhat, filling him with a little more strength and bravery, as if he was siphoning it from the others.

Yet that didn't keep him from tensing up when they reached the open door. The group stopped, and they all gazed inside. From their vantage point, they were able to see into the entrance hallway, but not all the way to the far wall.

But the hall was empty.

'Where was it?' Ollie asked, his voice low.

Daniel pointed. 'There,' he said. 'It was standing in front of the wall to the drawing room, just... looking at it.'

'Looking at the wall?' Ollie asked.

Daniel nodded. 'Maybe it's gone farther inside,' he suggested.

'Why do you keep calling it... *it?*' Emily asked. 'Wasn't what you saw a *she* or a *he?*'

But Daniel shook his head. 'It—it wasn't either,' he said. 'I don't know how to describe it.'

They continued to stare. 'Do we go in?' Lucy asked, still holding Daniel's hand.

After a beat, Ollie nodded again. 'I think we have to,' he said. 'We can't stand out here all night.' Ollie then turned to glance back down the length of the rear garden. Daniel noticed there was something to the other boy's gaze as well —an ever-so-subtle hint of apprehension. Daniel also looked over to the garden, but saw only the darkness of the night. He gave a quick, questioning glance to Ollie, eyebrow raised, but the older boy just turned his head back to the house.

'Come on,' Ollie said. 'We'll go in.' He pointed down to Emily's now-wrapped hand. 'How is it?'

'It'll be fine,' she replied. 'The towel is doing the job, so I don't think I'm going to drip blood everywhere.'

Ollie nodded, then took a step inside. He kept moving forward and everyone filtered in behind, with Emily going next. Daniel let Lucy follow after that—not because he wanted to push her towards danger first, but because he wanted her in the middle of the pack, protected. He entered last, still keeping hold of her hand.

Once everyone was inside, they held their ground. 'Do we close the door?' Emily asked in a hushed whisper.

'What if we need to run?' Daniel quietly replied.

'Leave it for now,' Ollie said. He then started to creep forward. The others kept close, with Emily moving up next to Ollie and the four making a square formation as they entered the main hallway.

There was no strange figure anymore.

Daniel listened intently, trying to hear that strange sound it had made, but he could only hear the long-case clock and its relentless ticking.

'There's nothing here,' Ollie declared after they'd moved far enough to see the main door.

'But I *saw* something,' Daniel insisted.

'I believe you,' Ollie replied. 'But it isn't here now.'

Daniel looked around. All the doors in the space were open. 'Maybe it's in one of the rooms.'

'Then let's check,' Ollie said. The group then worked around the rooms sequentially, ducking their heads into each space, yet nothing was amiss.

'I... I don't understand,' Daniel said, mostly to himself, after they'd moved back into the centre of the main hall once more. 'I *saw* it. I really did.'

'Like Ollie said,' Emily replied, hooking an arm around his shoulder. 'We believe you.'

Daniel didn't think they were being completely truthful, but he appreciated it nonetheless. 'Then... where did it go?'

No one had an answer. Daniel wondered if they should check the upper floors next, but had a feeling they would just find the same thing. Somehow, he just knew it was gone. At least for now.

'Wait here,' Ollie said.

'Where are you—' Lucy began, but Ollie pointed to the still-open rear door.

'Can't leave that open all night,' the older boy said and paced quickly to the rear of the house. Daniel didn't want him to go alone, even if it was only a short distance, and watched the older boy intently. He noticed Ollie pause at the rear door before closing it, again peering out into the back garden.

When Ollie returned, Daniel asked, 'Is there something out there?'

Ollie shook his head. 'No. Thought I saw something before, but it was nothing.'

'You sure?' Daniel asked. *Maybe it was the same thing I saw. Or another just like it.*

'I'm sure,' Ollie confirmed.

'So... what now?' Lucy asked. 'Do we go looking upstairs? Or do we go back to hiding and see if we can spot Eleanore come back up? That was the plan in the first place, right?'

'Yeah,' Ollie said. 'That was the plan. What does everyone think we should—'

His words cut off and his eyes became unfocused. Ollie blinked a few times in confusion.

At the exact same time, Daniel felt his whole world shift, like a pulse rose up and overcame him, drowning his vision in white that rose upwards. He felt unsteady on his feet, head swimming while he struggled to keep his balance.

'What... What's going on?' he slurred, shaking his head. He tried to see the others, but white had overtaken everything. Even when he closed his eyes, it was all Daniel could see.

'H—help,' he heard Lucy say, voice weak.

I need to sit down, Daniel quickly told himself as he felt the strength from his legs suddenly disappear.

Yet he didn't get the chance to sit. Daniel simply fell, losing consciousness before he even hit the floor.

CHAPTER
FIFTEEN

Eleanore's eyes drifted open. The all-encompassing whiteness had vanished. She could see again.

The woman was in the belly of the house, down in its depths, lying on the floor. She looked up at the gurney next to her and felt her heart break.

It's done. No going back now.

The woman sobbed. That had been the hardest thing she'd ever done. Not the hardest event she'd *experienced*, but it wasn't far behind.

The second step had been completed. One final part, once she was ready. If she was *ever* ready.

I need to. I can't stop now.

Eleanore knew she couldn't do it straight away, though. She wasn't strong enough. She needed time. Things would be finalised with the last step. Everything would be permanent then.

Even so, she could still do something to speed everything up after that. Again... if she was strong enough. It had been promised, and what was planned.

But the woman would need to build herself up to that.
Covering her face, Eleanore continued to cry.
It will be worth it, she told herself. *It will all be worth it.*

CHAPTER
SIXTEEN

'Wake up.'

Emily felt something push against her shoulder. Her eyes blinked. Once her vision focused, adjusting to the light that came in through the front windows, she saw Eleanore standing above her, nudging Emily with the toe of her slippered foot.

'What are you all *doing* down here?' the older woman asked in obvious confusion. She was wrapped in her dressing gown, like she had been the previous night.

Emily quickly sat up and saw Ollie, Daniel, and Lucy around her, all stirring as well. She realised she was in the main hallway downstairs. It took Emily a moment for her memory to come back, but she soon remembered going downstairs with the others in the dead of night, cutting her hand, feeling faint, and then...

Did we all black out? Emily asked herself in confusion.

'What... what happened?' Daniel mumbled as he looked around.

'That's what I'd like to know,' Eleanore said from

above, arms folded across her chest. 'Why were you all sleeping down here on the floor? And Emily, what happened to your *hand?*'

Emily instinctively twitched her hand in response and felt it throb. The towel had come loose in the night and lay on the floor, soaked red. Crusty, dried blood also coated Emily's palm around the angry cut. She had no idea what to say, so she immediately looked to the others for help.

'We couldn't sleep,' Ollie quickly said. 'So... we decided to come down together. Maybe get a hot chocolate or something.'

Eleanore raised a questioning eyebrow. 'You *all* couldn't sleep?' There was no small amount of scepticism in her voice.

'Yes,' Ollie said as he slowly got to his feet.

'And then, what?' Eleanore continued. 'You just decided to curl up and sleep here on the floor?' The woman shook her head in annoyance. 'Emily, tell me what happened to your hand.'

'I... cut it,' was all Emily said.

'I can see that,' Eleanore replied. 'But *how?*' The woman briefly paused. 'Did you drop a glass or something?' She squatted down and gently took hold of Emily's wrist. 'Is there still glass in there?'

'I...' Emily began, yet had no idea how to continue.

Eleanore narrowed her eyes. 'What in the world?' she uttered. 'There's a...' The older woman trailed off, then moved her other hand closer to Emily's palm. Emily tensed as Eleanore delicately pinched something between her fingernails—causing Emily to jolt in pain—and pulled whatever it was free. Emily looked to what Eleanore had retrieved.

'It's a thorn,' the older woman exclaimed. She then cast Emily a frown. 'You all were outside, weren't you?'

Emily looked down.

'Yes,' came Ollie's voice. 'We were.'

'Why?' Eleanore demanded. 'You should be asleep at night, not playing outside. You'll catch a death of cold. What were you thinking?' She looked down at the others, who had remained sitting on the floor. 'And you *still* haven't told me why you were all just sleeping here.'

The children all cast each other confused glances, clearly all thinking the same thing. *Do we tell her the truth?*

'Well, come on,' Eleanore went on. 'Out with it. What have you all been up to?'

Ollie started to help everyone up to their feet.

'Answer me,' the older woman demanded.

'First,' Ollie replied, 'you tell us what *you've* been up to.'

Eleanore frowned. 'What do you mean?'

Ollie glanced at the others, obviously seeking their approval to continue. Emily gave him a nod.

'You've been sneaking around at night,' Ollie continued, his tone steady. 'We've seen you. Going down to the cellar. Why?'

Emily noticed the older woman's face fall—but only for a moment before she quickly caught herself. 'Don't try to change the topic,' she said. 'I asked you a question.'

'And we asked *you* one,' Ollie shot back. 'What have you been up to?'

'I don't have to answer to you,' Eleanore replied with a hint of anger. 'It's none of your concern.'

'It is when we wake up to find every door in the house open,' Ollie said. 'Well... all apart from one. And it is our concern when Lucy sees something in the night that scares her.'

Eleanore turned her gaze to Lucy, and the younger girl shrank back. 'What is he talking about?'

'You know what I'm talking about,' Ollie answered instead of the younger girl. 'A few nights ago, something woke her up and scared her. You woke up as well, but refused to go check on what Lucy was talking about.'

Realisation washed over Eleanore's face. She waved a hand. 'That was nothing,' she said. 'Lucy just had a bad dream and scared herself. Nothing more.'

'But you didn't even *check*,' Ollie went on.

'Because it was *nothing*,' Eleanore repeated.

'Well, Daniel saw something last night as well,' Ollie said. 'Right here in the hall.'

But Eleanore just shook her head. 'Nonsense. You're all just spooking yourselves. Now tell me, why were you outside?'

'We saw something,' Lucy said. 'Or at least I did. So we went out to look.'

Eleanore pointed at Emily's hand. 'And tried to scale the walls by the looks of it.'

Emily shook her head. 'No, I just tripped and fell, then put my hand out to stop myself and cut it on the wall plants. Honest.'

Eleanore let out a long sigh. 'See what happens when you mess around in the middle of the night? You all should have been asleep in bed, not sneaking around in the dark.'

'We just want to know what's going on,' Ollie said. 'That's all.'

'*Nothing* is going on,' Eleanore stated, sounding so earnest Emily could almost believe it. 'And how long have you all been spying on me like that?'

'Long enough,' was all Ollie said.

Emily watched as Eleanore drew in a deep breath, held

it, then closed her eyes as she pinched the bridge of her nose. Everyone waited until she finally opened her eyes again and exhaled. 'And the reason for sleeping here on the floor?'

There was no response. *How on earth do we explain that?* Emily thought. *We don't even know what happened ourselves.*

She remembered feeling dizzy, the room spinning, the sheer *whiteness* of everything, then falling. Thankfully, they had all been on the large central rug, rather than hardwood floors.

But why did we all faint at exactly the same time?

'Answer me,' Eleanore pressed. 'When I came u—down here, you were all lying here.'

'We just... fainted,' Ollie finally admitted. 'We don't know how or why, but we just did.'

'Fainted...' Eleanore began, but trailed off as she studied Ollie with an intense stare.

'Yes,' Ollie confirmed. 'I just remember feeling dizzy, then... nothing until you woke us up.'

Eleanore's gaze moved around to each child before finally falling back on Ollie. 'You're telling me the truth?' she asked.

Ollie nodded. 'Yes.'

'He's not lying,' Lucy said. 'That's what happened. I felt the same way.'

Emily had expected the older woman to accuse them all of lying once again, as the story certainly seemed outlandish, but Eleanore just stood and stared, obviously in thought.

She believes us, Emily realised. That was something. Had she been in Eleanore's shoes, Emily doubted she would have believed it. How do four people just pass out at the exact same time?

Not unless there was something going on to cause it, Emily realised.

'Do any of you still feel dizzy now?' Eleanore asked.

Emily glanced at the others. She felt fine, really, except for being really tired. Exhausted, even. It was as if she hadn't actually slept at all.

'I'm okay now,' Emily eventually replied.

'Me too,' echoed Lucy.

Then it was Daniel's turn. 'Yeah, me as well.'

Ollie didn't say anything. Eleanore looked over to him. 'Well?'

'I'm fine,' he eventually said.

There was another sigh from the older woman. She folded her arms across her front once again, though this time lower, just in front of her belly, giving off an aura much less stern than before.

'Okay,' Eleanore eventually said. 'I want you all to go to your rooms. No teaching today. I'm guessing everyone is tired?' The group slowly nodded. 'Then go get some sleep. You can rest until lunchtime. But tomorrow it's back to learning as normal.' Her voice then dropped. 'And there will be no more sneaking around at night. Is that clear?' The group again shared glances with each other, unsure how to answer. 'Is that *clear?*' Eleanore repeated, this time much more forcefully.

'Yes,' Lucy eventually replied with a nod.

'Promise me,' Eleanore went on.

'I promise,' Lucy said.

Eleanore turned her eyes to Daniel, who looked down. 'Promise,' she said.

'I promise,' Daniel replied.

Emily felt the woman's gaze descend on her next, and Eleanore waited expectantly with a raised eyebrow. 'Well?'

'I promise,' Emily eventually said.

Finally, it was Ollie's turn, but he was standing with his arms folded as well. 'Promise me, Ollie.' He said nothing. 'If not,' Eleanore continued, 'then you will *all* be punished and grounded. No games or playing for a week.' Still nothing. 'On top of that, I'll start locking your doors at night to keep you inside. Now, I'd really rather not do that, but look what happens when you sneak around on your own.' She pointed to Emily's hand again, but still kept her strong eye contact with the boy. 'So... what will it be?'

Ollie hesitated, but Emily saw the tension in his arms dissipate. His head sagged. 'I promise,' he finally said.

'Good,' Eleanore replied. 'Now, I'll say this and I want you to listen: you are all *safe* here. There is no one else in the house. Whatever you think you've seen, it's your imagination, or something else perfectly explainable.'

'Will you at least tell us why you keep going down to the cellar at night?' Ollie prodded.

Eleanore clenched her jaw... then slowly relaxed it. 'I check up on the equipment down there from time to time,' she said. 'I like to do it when you're all asleep, so no one feels the urge to follow me down. Now, that's the end of it,' she concluded with finality. 'Off to bed, all of you. Think about how you've behaved and hopefully we can all move past this.'

Emily started to reach down for the towel. 'Actually, wait,' Eleanore said, and bent down to retrieve it instead. 'The rest of you go up. Emily, come with me. I want to check over that cut and put some dressing on it.'

'Okay,' Emily replied. She watched the others trudge by, each giving her a glance on their way past. Finally, they'd all disappeared through the doors to the stairs. Once there, she heard them start to ascend.

Eleanore then took hold of Emily's hand once more and looked it over. 'It'll need a good clean,' she said. 'I'll warn you, it might sting a bit, but we don't want an infection spreading.'

'I understand,' Emily said.

'Good. Now, go take a seat at the dining room table and wait for me. I'll go get the things I need.'

'Where from?' Emily asked.

'My room,' Eleanore replied. 'Stop asking questions.'

A few minutes later, Emily was sitting at the table as instructed, facing Eleanore, who was just beside her on a seat of her own.

Eleanore had set out her supplies on the table, which included a bottle of antiseptic, some medical wipes, some rubber gloves, a roll of medical tape, some small lengths of white cloth, and a clear plastic bag of cotton wool.

'Now,' Eleanore began, 'we'll be done in just a jiffy, but you'll need to be brave. This is likely to hurt more than the needle. But as I said before, we need to make sure an infection doesn't take hold.'

'Doesn't it need a doctor?' Emily asked.

'Goodness no,' Eleanore replied with a chuckle. 'Nothing we can't handle here. Now hold out your hand, palm up.'

Emily did, watching nervously as Eleanore retrieved one of the wipes. 'First, I'll use this sterile wipe,' the woman explained. 'Just to clean it all out. Then I'll clear around the wound with antiseptic. After that, it'll just need a dressing and then you're free to go. Sound okay?'

Though Emily nodded, she wasn't certain. *How* much *is it going to hurt?* she wondered, but didn't ask. *Just grit your teeth and bear it,* Emily told herself, repeating something her mother had often said to her. *You're strong.*

However, the stinging from the sterilising wipe was enough to make her jump. Emily instinctively tried to snatch her hand away, but Eleanore held it firm, as if expecting her reaction.

'I know,' Eleanore said in a soothing tone. 'It'll be over soon. Just be brave a little longer.'

The stinging made it feel like Emily had grabbed a fistful of nettles. Her palm throbbed in pain. Regardless, she held firm, and managed not to flinch any more as Eleanore continued to work.

'Very good,' the woman finally said as she set the wipe down on the table. She then lowered her head to Emily's palm to look closer. 'Yes,' she said, 'I think that will do it. Now, I'm just going to clean around the cut. This shouldn't hurt as long as we don't get the antiseptic in the wound, so hold completely still, understand?'

'Yes,' Emily said and clenched her teeth together, forcing her arm and hand to remain as still as a statue, despite how much she wanted to pull her arm back to safety. Eleanore got to work again, and with every stroke, Emily expected a fresh surge of pain. Thankfully, the older woman proved to be a steady hand, and before she knew it, Emily's wound was cleaned and fully dressed. Clumps of cotton wool were covered with a white length of material, and it was all held in place with the medical tape.

'All finished,' Eleanore stated. 'How does the dressing feel?'

In truth, it felt cumbersome, and Emily wasn't able to make a fist. Still, at least the cut was protected.

'It's fine,' Emily replied. 'How long will I need to wear it for?'

'I'll check it again tonight before bed,' Eleanore said.

'See how it's healing. We may need to replace the dressing again, but it's not a big job. Hopefully you won't need to wear it longer than a day or two.'

Emily gave an appreciative nod as Eleanore released her hand. The young girl didn't know what to say next, especially when Eleanore continued to hold eye contact.

'You all had a busy night,' the older woman eventually began.

'I guess so,' was all Emily could think to say in reply.

'Why did you go along with it, dear?' Eleanore then asked. Her tone wasn't confrontational or accusatory, simply curious. 'Coming down with everyone last night?'

'Because,' Emily began after a beat. 'We all wanted to know if there was something going on. I guess we thought it was weird seeing you up so late at night.'

'You *all* thought that?' Eleanore asked. 'Or just *some* of you? Were you pressed into helping?'

'We all thought it,' Emily quickly confirmed.

'I see,' Eleanore said. 'Well, like I said before, there isn't anything strange about it. I don't always sleep well, so sometimes I get things done at night. That's it. That's all. Nothing sinister.'

'Okay,' Emily replied, then followed up with, 'why don't you sleep well?'

'Oh... well, I'm not quite sure,' Eleanore said. 'I've always been that way, I guess.'

Though Emily couldn't be certain, she felt Eleanore was lying. Or at the very least holding something back. Emily remembered how Eleanore had been sobbing when walking around the previous night.

Is she ill? the girl wondered. *Did she find out that something's wrong with her?*

Is it something to do with one of us?

Emily refrained from asking, fearing Eleanore wouldn't take kindly to the question.

Then another thought struck her.

'Can I ask you something?' she began.

'Of course,' Eleanore replied. 'What is it?'

'Did...' Emily paused. 'Did you ever have kids of your own?'

Eleanore took a second before replying, 'Why do you ask that, dear?'

'Just curious,' Emily replied with a shrug. It was something she had wondered about before. Eleanore had never mentioned kids, and with the woman being in her fifties, it meant any children would likely be in their twenties or thirties now.

'No, I never did,' Eleanore replied.

'Oh,' Emily said. 'Can... Can I ask why?'

'You can,' Eleanore said with a patient smile. 'At first, it was because I never met the right man. But later in life I found out that even if I *had* met someone, it just wasn't going to be possible for me.'

'Not possible?'

Eleanore nodded. 'Sometimes, ladies can't bear children. I always wanted them, but grew to accept the way things were.'

Emily had no idea how to respond, suddenly feeling awful for bringing it up. 'Sorry for asking,' she said and felt her cheeks flush.

But Eleanore gave a kind laugh. 'It's perfectly alright, Emily. Please don't be sorry. It's a natural question to have.'

'So is that why you wanted to help other kids?' Emily asked.

Still smiling, Eleanore nodded. 'That's right. I'll be

honest, at first I looked at it as getting what I wanted, in a roundabout kind of way. Kids of my own. But... I soon changed my thinking when I realised just how desperate some kids were. I knew it wasn't about me and what I wanted. It was what the children needed. That was around the same time I met Jasper, who thought the same way I did.'

'Jasper?' Emily asked, then it clicked. 'Oh, Mr. Graves. The benefactor.'

'That's right,' Eleanore said.

'He didn't have children either?' Emily asked.

'No,' Eleanore said. 'But he wanted to help, just like I did. He was quite wealthy, but *very* generous, always looking out for other people.'

'And why didn't he have kids?'

'Because sometimes men have issues getting women pregnant as well,' she replied. 'I suppose the two of us had something in common in that regard, both unable to have children of our own.'

'And so you set this place up?'

'Yes,' Eleanore said. 'But poor Jasper didn't get to see it through. However, he left behind everything I needed to make sure his dream was fulfilled.'

'Wasn't he married?' Emily asked. 'No wife for him to give everything to instead?'

'No,' Eleanore confirmed. 'Another thing we had in common, I guess—no luck in relationships.'

Not knowing how else to respond, Emily just nodded. 'That's sad,' she eventually said. 'What did he do? You know, for work?'

'He worked in languages,' Eleanore said.

'So he was smart?'

'Very,' Eleanore replied. 'He actually specialised in old

languages that aren't really spoken today. He was something of an expert in his field, as I understand it.'

For a second time, Emily couldn't think of what else to say. So, the two sat in silence for a little while before Eleanore eventually laid a hand on Emily's shoulder. 'Look,' the woman began, 'I am aware things might feel a little odd now after what just happened, but I need to make sure things get back to normal. I'm responsible for the safety of all of you, and I can't have you wandering around at night. Not least of all because growing children need their sleep. I think this is the first time I've ever had a cross word to say to any of you, so I'm aware how lucky I am to have four kids like you under my care. And it's *because* I understand that, and because I take it seriously, that I'm going to do the right thing by you all. That means giving you a loving environment, but that also means stamping out unacceptable behaviour as I need to. You've all lost so much and I refuse to fail you. So please, put a little trust in me, Emily; I swear you'll be completely safe and happy living here. Does that sound fair?'

Emily took a moment as she gazed into Eleanore's earnest gaze. 'It does,' the girl eventually said with a nod. 'I'm sorry,' she then added.

What Eleanore said made sense to Emily, but the girl was aware the woman was still holding something back.

'Thank you,' Eleanore said. 'Now, go get a little more sleep. I'll call you all for lunch if you don't wake up before then.'

After retreating to her room, Emily tucked herself tightly under her covers. There, she couldn't help but think about what Daniel had said he'd seen the previous night. It seemed an outlandish claim, and the obvious explanation was that he had been mistaken—an overactive imagination seeing shapes in the shadows that weren't really there.

But then, Lucy had claimed to see something as well.

The more she thought about it, the more Emily's eyes grew heavy, and it didn't take long for sleep to claim her once again.

CHAPTER
SEVENTEEN

'We can't just ignore what happened,' Ollie said.

Everyone was gathered at the end of the back garden, standing close to the rear wall in order to keep out of earshot of Eleanore. She was much farther up, working on some flowerbeds. The children had kept their distance from her for most of the day after lunch and had now pulled even farther away to discuss recent events. It was late afternoon, so the sun had just started its descent.

'I know,' Lucy replied to the older boy. 'But things feel weird. I just want them to go back to normal.'

Ollie's head dropped. 'We need to stick to the plan,' he said. 'She's hiding something. I say we be really good all week and push to go to town this weekend, like we agreed, and then I'll pretend to be sick. There's no reason anything should change from what we decided to do.'

Daniel watched on without saying much, unsure how he felt about the whole thing.

'But we *promised* her we'd be good,' Lucy shot back.

'What do you two think?' Ollie asked, looking to the others.

Daniel stayed quiet, allowing Emily to go first.

'Honestly,' Emily began, 'I... just don't know. I understand what you're saying, Ollie, but if we keep pushing we'll just end up locked in our rooms at night.'

But Ollie shook his head. 'She wouldn't do that to us,' he said. 'It's just a threat.'

'I don't know,' Lucy chipped in. 'She sounded serious to me. I think she would.'

'All the rooms are connected,' Ollie went on. 'That means she'd have to lock up *every* room on the top two floors to stop us from getting out into the hall.'

'I still think she might do it,' Lucy said with a shrug.

Ollie finally turned to Daniel. 'What about you?' the boy asked. 'I mean, you're the one that saw something. Do you just want to ignore it and pretend things are back to normal?'

Daniel considered the question. He slowly shook his head. 'No,' he replied. 'Not really. But I do think we need to stop for a little while.'

'Why?' Ollie asked.

'To let things calm down, like Lucy said,' Daniel went on. 'Eleanore knows what we're up to now. She's going to be very careful, watching us all the time. If we wait a while—'

'How long?' Ollie interrupted.

'I don't know,' Daniel answered. 'Long enough that she trusts us again.'

Ollie threw his hands up in the air. 'But that could take weeks. Or months, even.'

'I know,' Daniel conceded.

'We can't wait that long.'

'But why not?' Lucy interjected. 'Nothing's going to happen to us.'

'But you saw something as well,' Ollie stated. 'How can you say that?'

'I *think* I did,' Lucy went on. 'But I don't know *what* I saw, really.'

Daniel watched as Ollie folded his arms across his chest and looked down, jaw tense. The older boy had always been so patient with everyone, but that patience now seemed to be wearing thin. 'All the doors were open,' Ollie said. 'You heard them being opened that night. We've all seen it now as well. Surely *that's* something to be worried about.'

'Ollie,' Lucy said, 'do you really think Eleanore would put us in danger?'

'What?' A pause. 'That's beside the po—'

'*Do* you?' Lucy pushed. 'Despite whatever she's doing in the cellar, do you really think she'd let anything bad happen to us?'

Daniel could see the conflict on Ollie's face. 'No,' the older boy eventually conceded.

'Me either,' said Lucy. 'Look,' she went on as her eyes gazed down at her feet. 'After what happened with my parents, I honestly thought I'd be on my own forever. Lost and scared and just... alone.' She looked up again and Daniel saw her eyes were glistening. 'But since I came here, I'm happy again. I don't want to...' She paused. 'I don't want things to change, Ollie. And if we push things too far, I'm worried Eleanore will... will...'

'Will what?' Emily asked, putting a hand on Lucy's shoulder.

'Send us back or something,' Lucy blurted out quickly. 'And we'll be split up and I'll have no family again.' While

Lucy didn't sob, a tear started rolling down her left cheek.

Emily's hand moved over to the younger girl's far shoulder and hugged Lucy into her.

Daniel then turned his eyes to Ollie. The older boy no longer looked annoyed, just sad. For the longest time, nobody said anything.

'Okay, Luce,' Ollie eventually said. 'Okay. I won't ruin anything. I'll wait, as long as you all think we should.'

Lucy smiled and stepped forward from Emily, wrapping her arms around Ollie's waist and burying her head into his chest. 'Thank you,' she said.

'It's okay,' he whispered. 'But if anything else happens, then we need to act. Is that fair?'

Lucy didn't verbalise a reply, but Daniel saw her nod, her face still pressed into Ollie. The older boy looked over to Daniel again.

'You sure you're happy with that too?' he asked. 'After what you saw, can you just go back to normal?'

That was something Daniel had been struggling with all day. In truth, he didn't know the answer yet. One thing he *did* know, however, was that he didn't like being on his own at any point now. Just going back to his room earlier that day had been difficult, and that was when the sun was shining.

What will it be like at night?

Daniel had already struggled with the house when it was dark. Now things would be ten times worse. However, even taking all that into account, what else could they do? His point about Eleanore keeping a more watchful eye on them still stood.

'I... think that's all we can do,' Daniel eventually said, still torn. 'For now.'

Ollie nodded. 'Then we'll hold off,' he said. 'But if any of you get scared or see anything weird, you come get me. Agreed?'

'Agreed,' Daniel said, and Emily quickly echoed it.

'Yeah,' Lucy added, voice muffled by Ollie's blue hoodie.

Silence washed over them again, and eventually Lucy pulled away. Her eyes were red, but the tears had stopped.

'What about us passing out last night?' Emily went on to ask. 'Because that was really weird.'

'Yeah,' Daniel said. 'And Eleanore kinda brushed that off as well.'

'*Kinda* brushed it off?' Ollie said. 'There's no 'kinda' about it. She wasn't bothered at all.'

'Do we need to see a doctor?' Emily asked.

'I don't think so,' Daniel said, earning a questioning glance from Emily. 'Think about it,' Daniel went on, 'it can't have been because we're sick or anything. That couldn't have caused us to all faint at the same time. No way.'

'Maybe there's something wrong with the house,' Ollie offered. 'Like, I don't know, a gas leak.'

'I've been thinking that as well,' Emily said. 'Do we speak to Eleanore and ask her to get it checked out? When we told her what had happened, I got the feeling she believed us, which surprised me. Maybe she'll listen about getting someone in. Even if just Mr. Peterson has a look.'

'Maybe she did something down in the cellar,' Daniel went on to say, verbalising the thought just as it struck him. 'When she was messing around with the equipment.'

'Wouldn't she have passed out as well?' Ollie asked.

'Maybe she did,' Daniel replied. 'We didn't see her till

the next morning. Could be that she fixed whatever she did wrong and just isn't telling us about it.'

'That's just a guess,' Lucy said. 'You don't know that. We don't know anything.'

'True,' Daniel admitted. 'But if we don't speak to Eleanore about it, what else can we do? I mean, I don't know who we should be calling. Do any of you?'

The others shook their heads.

'So do we wait and see if it happens again?' Emily asked.

'Yes,' Lucy quickly added. 'And if it does, then we'll do something about it. It could have just been a one off.'

'But a one off *what?*' Ollie asked.

'I... don't know,' Lucy said. 'But we're all fine now. Let's just wait, like we agreed. Okay?'

Ollie looked down and nodded. 'Fine, I guess,' he said. 'Everyone agree?'

Daniel and Emily nodded. He understood Ollie's frustration, but in the end, what could they really do? They were just kids. If Eleanore didn't listen to them, they were stuck.

'How's your palm, Emily?' Lucy then asked.

They all looked down at Emily's hand, still wrapped in dressing. 'It's okay,' she said. 'Stings if I move it too much.' She turned to look at the wall right next to them, much of it covered with the same climbing plants she'd hurt herself on. 'Stupid thorns,' she said. Lucy giggled. 'I wonder if we can talk to Eleanore about getting them taken out,' Emily mused. 'Maybe that's something that Mr. Peterson can help with.' She took half a step closer to the wall and lifted up her good hand, brushing some of the leaves away and revealing some ropey vines all lined with spindly thorns.

'Doubt it,' Daniel said. 'It would be a huge job and would take forever.'

'I suppose,' Emily agreed. She then narrowed her eyes. 'Huh.'

'What is it?' Daniel asked as he saw Emily lean closer.

'Careful,' Lucy warned the older girl. 'We don't want you hurting your other hand.'

'What's that?' Emily asked, pointing.

The others moved around her to see—Daniel noticed straight away what Emily was looking at: a perfect circle carved into the stone.

'Oh those,' he said with a nod. 'Yeah, they're all over. Haven't you spotted them before?'

Emily cocked her head to the side, clearly thinking. 'There's some on the entrance pillars near the main gate, right?'

'Right,' Daniel said. 'They're at regular intervals along the boundary wall as well. I've seen quite a lot of them. They're also on the main house, dotted around.'

'But what *are* they?' Emily asked.

Daniel shrugged. 'Just a kind of decoration, I think.'

'Why a circle?'

'I don't know,' Daniel replied. 'They've been here as long as we have, I think. Though...' He pointed to the circle. 'They don't look as old or worn as the actual stone. So they were probably carved in more recently.'

'Strange,' Emily said as she gazed at the shape. She then released the planting to let it fall back into place.

Daniel didn't think it strange at all, in truth. Sometimes old buildings had things carved into them. It was what it was.

'Doesn't Eleanore wear a necklace with a circle on it?' Emily asked.

'Oh yeah,' Daniel said in realisation. 'You're right.'

'Think it's all connected in some way?' Ollie asked.

However, Daniel shook his head. 'I mean, those carvings might have been there before Eleanore even came to the house. And... well, they're just circles. It's a pretty common shape.'

'I suppose,' Ollie said.

'Maybe Eleanore got the necklace to remind her of the house,' Lucy suggested. 'Maybe she likes the circles.'

'Makes sense,' Emily stated.

'Kids!' came Eleanore's voice from the distance. The older woman was on her feet now, all her gardening things packed up in a fabric bag that dangled from her hand. 'I'm going to fix dinner,' she went on. 'You have twenty minutes, then I want you to come in and get cleaned up.'

'Yes, Eleanore,' Lucy shouted back.

Nodding, the woman turned and walked back to the house.

'Think things will still be awkward at dinner?' Emily asked.

'Probably,' Ollie replied. 'But I'm sure it will pass.'

Daniel stared up at the building as Eleanore disappeared inside. He was still conflicted about holding off investigating, despite having told Lucy they would.

Are we doing the right thing?

He thought again about the thing he'd seen the previous night. *Can we really ignore something like that?*

However, in the cold light of day, a natural doubt crept into his mind. It had been so fantastical and bizarre at the time.

Did... Did I really see anything at all?

CHAPTER
EIGHTEEN

Three months later...

Lucy held her breath and listened to the creaking of the floorboards draw ever closer.

Creak. Creak. Creeeak.

They were just outside now, outside the wardrobe she was hiding in. Her back was pressed tightly against the closet's rear as she sat on its floor, clothing hanging down around her. She held her breath.

No, don't open the door. Go away. Go away.

The person outside took hold of the handle.

'I know you're in there,' a voice said from the other side. 'And I'm gonna find yooouuuu.'

No! No, no, no. Not yet. Go away. Pleeease. Not yet!

The wardrobe door was flung open, causing Lucy to squeal and giggle.

Daniel stood outside, a big smile on his face. 'Found you!' he declared. 'And you're the first, so you're *it* next time.'

'No fair!' Lucy replied with fake annoyance. However,

the act was foiled by the way she couldn't keep the grin off her face.

'Why isn't it fair?' Daniel asked, helping her out of her wardrobe.

'Because I didn't *want* to be found first,' she said with a laugh. Daniel chuckled as well.

'Sorry,' he said, not sounding it at all. 'You must have moved and bumped something. I heard you when I was walking past your room. Plus, you left your door open.'

Lucy thought about that and almost slapped herself. She *had*. She'd been in such a rush to hide that she hadn't remembered to close it behind her.

'Well, guess I'll help you find the others now,' she said. 'Any ideas where to start?'

Daniel shrugged. 'We can try their rooms, I guess, but I think that's too obvious.' He grinned. 'What sort of idiot would hide in their *own* room?'

Lucy playfully punched his arm. The pair then continued to seek for the others, wandering the house.

Lucy's heart felt full.

It was Sunday, the last day of the weekend, and the children had nothing else to do but play together and laugh. The house was colder now, with the autumn months having set in, so everyone was wearing extra layers. All the radiators were on, of course, but the house was simply too big for them to completely warm it up.

Eleanore had been down in the library, reading, and sipping an herbal tea the last time Lucy had seen her.

It felt like things were back to normal now. Eleanore had stopped sneaking around in the night as far as they could tell, and even Daniel had started to relax in the house again.

There had been one incident since, but only Lucy knew

about it. Two months ago, she'd awoken in the night, having kicked off her covers again, and she'd heard something moving outside her room in the corridor. That was also accompanied by some weird sounds—like moaning, interspersed with an odd clicking. But by the time the girl had summoned the bravery to look out, the coast was clear. Afterward, Lucy had looked out of her window, and just on the periphery of what she could see, she'd been certain there had been things moving around outside. Four, maybe five figures, mostly swallowed by the night.

But strangely, the girl hadn't been scared watching them disappear into the darkness.

Lucy had an idea of what was going on. At least, she thought she did. Even if Ollie didn't believe in such things, Lucy understood there was no other explanation. Those things *were* ghosts. More importantly, those ghosts were not a threat.

They were just... there.

With a house as old as the one they lived in, it wasn't really a surprise to Lucy. And so, after that night, she had stopped being scared by the whole thing. So what if they shared the house with a few extra people? Those people had obviously been there longer than the kids had, and they even kept to themselves for the most part.

What was more, it actually brought Lucy a kind of comfort. If there *were* ghosts in the house, that meant death wasn't final. And *that* meant her parents still existed out there, somewhere.

And someday, I'll get to see them again.

So Lucy embraced that knowledge. Even if the others didn't believe in it, that wouldn't change her mind. All that mattered was they were all together, the house was safe, and there was no longer any distance or awkwardness between the children and Eleanore.

Things were as they should be.

Everyone had all spent the previous day in town, where Eleanore had bought them all hot chocolate, and then talk had turned to Christmas and what kind of presents everyone wanted. Lucy knew that, realistically, it was *far* too early to be getting excited for Christmas, yet she couldn't help it. In her mind, autumn was the start of the build-up, and nothing could convince her otherwise.

Lucy and Daniel continued their searching for several minutes and eventually found Ollie on the top storey in a spare bedroom, where he was hiding under the bed. Emily, however, had proved to be a more elusive quarry.

With Ollie now on the hunt with them, the trio searched the house from top to bottom but came up empty-handed. Eventually, they ended up back on the ground floor and wandered into the room Eleanore was occupying—she was still reading, seated on the sofa with the fire on. The blazing heat from it felt good.

'Have you seen Emily?' Lucy asked her.

'*Luce,*' Daniel interjected, 'We can't get help, remember?'

Eleanore chuckled. 'Don't worry, I won't say.'

Before anyone could say anything else, the group heard the back door open. The trio walked out to the main hall and saw Emily standing in the dining room, wrapped up in a coat, scarf, and wool hat. Her cheeks were bright red.

'You guys are rubbish at searching,' she said, rubbing her gloved hands together.

'You were *outside?*' Lucy asked. 'But why? It's so cold!'

'I didn't think you'd look out there. And I was right.'

'So why come in?' Ollie asked.

'Because it's so cold,' Emily said, parroting Lucy. 'I couldn't stay out anymore. But since the rest of you already got caught, I guess I win.'

The girl made her way towards them, taking off her hat, coat, gloves, and scarf as she approached. She hung them all up on the coat stand, though still had on her thick cotton jumper.

'I have to search now,' Lucy said with a sigh. 'I was caught first.'

Emily nodded as she rubbed her hands together yet again. 'Fine, but can we wait a little bit so I can warm up first?'

'Yeah,' Lucy said. She pointed to the library. 'The fire is going. That will help.'

'Ohhh, good idea,' the older girl said. All four of them then filed back into the library, where Eleanore looked up from her book again with a smile.

'Having fun?' she asked.

'Yeah,' Emily replied as she approached the crackling fire and held her hands out before it. When she did, Lucy noticed the faint white line on her palm. The scar there was the only remnant of the cut Emily had gotten a while ago. 'I just need to warm up a little,' Emily continued.

Eleanore laughed again. 'Maybe don't hide outside anymore today,' she suggested. 'You'll end up catching a cold.'

'Don't worry,' Emily replied, shivering. 'I wasn't planning on it.'

Lucy took a seat while she was waiting, and Daniel did the same, though Ollie stayed standing.

'Whatcha reading?' Lucy asked Eleanore as she gazed down at the fabric-lined book in the older woman's hands. She then read the black title across the spine. '*Bleak House?*'

the girl read aloud with a crinkled nose. 'That sounds... dull.'

Eleanore chuckled. 'Yes, I suppose it does. It's Charles Dickens.'

'Is it good so far?'

Eleanore nodded. 'Yes. But I've read it before, many times.'

'So why read it again?' Lucy asked. 'I mean, if you know what's going to happen, what's the point?'

'Oh, well,' Eleanore began, 'I guess it's like wearing a pair of old, comfy slippers. You know what you're getting, and there's something nice about that. Plus, there's always a chance you'll notice something you didn't pick up on before.'

'I guess that makes sense...' Lucy said. 'Do you think I'd like that book?'

Eleanore shrugged. 'Feel free to give it a try. The language might be difficult for you to follow, but I think you're bright enough to figure it out if you work at it.'

'What's it about?'

'Well, there's a lot to it, but basically the story is about a family who are hoping for an inheritance and the wait they go through for the fortune.'

Lucy frowned and stared at the book. She then shook her head. 'That's okay,' she said. 'I don't think I'd like it.'

'Like I said,' Eleanore went on, laughing again, 'there's more to it.'

'I believe you,' Lucy replied. 'But... no, not for me.'

'Fair enough,' Eleanore answered. 'It is a bit dry, I'll give you that.' She looked around at the bookshelves. 'Tell you what, why don't we all go into town again next weekend and load up on some new books?'

'Sounds great!' Lucy exclaimed.

'Yeah, that would be fantastic,' Emily added. 'Something new would be perfect.'

'Excellent,' Eleanore said. 'Then it's set.'

Eventually, Emily moved away from the fire, sufficiently thawed out. 'I haven't seen Mr. Peterson in a while,' she commented.

'Oh, he'll be back,' Eleanore stated. 'But in the autumn and winter months, there isn't as much to do in the garden. Nothing I can't handle. I think he's due next month to give the lawns their final cut until next year.'

'He's always so grumpy,' Lucy, said giggling. 'Isn't he married or anything?'

'He is,' Eleanore said. 'Do you think that getting married should stop someone from being grumpy?'

'Well... yeah,' Lucy replied. 'If he's married, he should be happy, right?'

Eleanore tussled Lucy's hair. 'Actually, yes,' she said. 'I guess that is how it's supposed to be. But I think Mr. Peterson is just grumpy by nature. It's how he's wired.'

'And his wife is okay with that?' Lucy asked.

Eleanore shrugged. 'She must be.'

The youngest girl then shook her head. 'When I get married, my husband won't be grumpy. No way. We'll both be happy.'

She saw Eleanore cock her head to the side. 'Is that something you want?' she asked. 'To get married?'

'Of course!' Lucy replied, as if it was obvious. 'And to have children as well.'

For some reason, Eleanore's expression remained stoic for a few seconds before a smile finally washed over her lips. 'Well, that's a nice dream. I hope it comes true for you.'

'Why wouldn't it?' Lucy asked.

Eleanore shrugged. 'Sometimes it just doesn't.'

It suddenly dawned on Lucy, and she had to refrain from wincing. She felt Emily's eyes on her. *It didn't work out for Eleanore, did it?*

Lucy quickly wanted to apologise, but didn't know where to begin, so she stayed quiet while thinking how best to broach it. Eleanore went back to her book, and more time passed with Lucy sitting, saying nothing. Then, it was simply too late.

'Go along,' Eleanore then said to them. 'Keep playing and enjoying yourself.'

Lucy kept to the back of the line as everyone moved out of the room. She was worried she'd upset Eleanore, and dearly hoped she hadn't. *What can I do to put it right?*

Then it came to her.

She paused at the door, turned, and walked back, quickly pacing over to Eleanore. The woman looked up with a raised eyebrow. Lucy bent down and hugged her tightly.

'Goodness,' Eleanore said. 'What's this for?'

'Because I wanted to,' Lucy simply said. After a moment, she felt Eleanore's body relax, and an arm fell on Lucy's back to return the embrace. Lucy gave it a moment before pulling away.

'Go on and play with the others,' Eleanore said again and tussled the girl's hair once more.

Lucy nodded and rejoined her friends out in the hall, feeling better about herself.

'Are you all ready to go hide?' Lucy asked. There were nods of approval, yet Lucy could sense reluctance, even from Daniel, who loved the game the most. 'Is everyone bored of hide and seek now?' she asked them.

She noticed Ollie and Emily both look over to Daniel,

waiting to see his response. The younger boy nodded. 'Yeah, a little,' he said. 'Should we do something else?'

'Sure,' Lucy replied. 'What?'

She then noticed Ollie's gaze had drifted back down towards the dining room. She knew what he was thinking about: the door to the cellar, which was locked up tight as always. The girl then managed to catch his eye and frowned, as if to say, *stop thinking about it.*

Ollie rolled his eyes and nodded.

While they had promised to hold off investigating for a while, Lucy *really* hoped the boy would let it go permanently. Things were good again. Perfect. No need to snoop.

The group finally settled on board games, which they played for a few hours before having dinner with Eleanore. After that, they all spent time back in the library, each of them reading by the blazing hot fire, creating an atmosphere so relaxing and comfortable it didn't take Lucy long to start falling asleep right there on the sofa.

Eventually, all the children retired to bed for the night. As Lucy lay wrapped up in her warm duvet, she smiled to herself, utterly content and happy.

Everything's alright again, she told herself. *And nothing is going to ruin it now.*

CHAPTER
NINETEEN

Eleanore pressed her palm against Ollie's forehead as the boy lay in his bed, looking glum.

'There's no temperature,' the woman said.

Emily, Daniel, and Lucy were gathered in Ollie's room alongside the woman. After gathering downstairs that morning, they'd soon noticed Ollie had been slow to appear. Emily knew that was normal, as he usually slept in longer than the others, but when she'd gone up to check, he'd complained about feeling ill.

'I don't feel hot,' Ollie replied. 'Just sick. Like I'm going to throw up. Dizzy too. And tired. *Really* tired.'

'Why don't you come down for breakfast?' Eleanore suggested. 'See if you can eat something. It might just be hunger. I'll make you some plain toast to see if you can stomach that, okay?'

But Ollie shook his head and curled his lip. 'No thank you, I think that would just make me vomit.' He then gagged a little, as if the simple thought of toast was pushing him over the edge.

'You just want to stay in bed?' Eleanore asked as she

moved her hand away and rested it atop Ollie's, which was lying by his side.

Ollie nodded. 'Yeah. I'll be fine. I just want to sleep.'

'Okay,' Eleanore said. 'You're obviously coming down with something. I wonder if it's a virus.' She looked to the others. 'Give Ollie some space today, kids, alright? Just in case. We don't want it spreading.' Everyone else nodded. 'And no trip to town today,' Eleanore added with a sad smile. 'We can't leave Ollie here alone.'

'But that's not *fair*,' Lucy began, sounding hurt. 'We were gonna get new books and...' She caught sight of Ollie and trailed off. She then gazed down. 'Yeah, of course. Sorry, Ollie,' she added.

The boy forced a smile. 'It's okay, Luce.' He then turned his eyes towards Eleanore. 'Please,' he went on. 'Don't ruin anyone's day because of me. You all go into town and have fun. I'll just stay here in bed.'

'Oh no,' Eleanore said. 'I won't be leaving you here on your own. What if something happened while we're gone?'

'What could happen?' Ollie asked. 'I'm just gonna be lying in bed, probably sleeping. Please,' he said. 'Everyone has been looking forward to it all week.'

'Well,' Eleanore said. 'What if you're sick while you're asleep and choke?'

'But that could happen anyway,' Ollie replied. 'You'd all be downstairs and wouldn't know. Come on, Eleanore, I'm twelve, I'm not a kid anymore.'

Eleanore just laughed. 'You *absolutely* are, Ollie,' she said. 'But you... are getting older, true, and you've been quite responsible.'

'It's okay, Ollie,' Lucy said. 'I don't want you to be left here on your own. That isn't fair.'

'No, what isn't fair is me ruining everyone's plans just

cause I'm sick right now. Just go have fun. I'll be here when you get back.'

Emily watched as Eleanore studied the boy. 'Are you absolutely sure?' the woman asked.

Ollie nodded. 'Yeah. Certain.'

Eleanore squeezed his hand. 'Are there any books you want me to pick up for you?'

'Maybe some football magazines?'

Eleanore nodded. 'Of course. Now, I'll go get you a glass of water and a bucket in case, well, you know.'

'Yeah...' Ollie said. 'In case I throw my guts up.'

Eleanore crinkled her nose. 'Yes... very well put,' she replied dryly. 'The rest of us still need to have breakfast, so I won't be booking a taxi for an hour or so yet. But I'll check on you again before we head off.'

'No problem,' Ollie replied and shuffled himself farther down into his bed. 'I'm just going to sleep.'

'Of course, dear,' Eleanore said. She gave his hand another squeeze and stood up, before sweeping her hands at the others to usher them out. 'Let's leave Ollie in peace, everyone.'

'Bye, Ollie,' Lucy said with a wave. 'And thank you.'

Ollie smiled. Daniel and Emily said their goodbyes as well and filed out of the room, with Emily at the rear. She cast a quick glance back to Ollie before she left. As she did, one thing became absolutely certain to her.

He's faking it.

CHAPTER
TWENTY

After he heard the wheels of the taxi head off down the driveway, Ollie bolted up to the top floor to look out over the front of the property. From his position, he watched the car eventually make its way through the open gates at the front, where it turned out onto the country road. He then waited a few more minutes until the vehicle was completely out of sight, just to make sure they didn't suddenly head back for some reason.

Perfect, he said to himself. While Ollie guessed he had a full three hours alone in the house at the very least, he still wanted to work quickly, so he ran over to Eleanore's bedroom.

Ollie had been inside her room before, but only when Eleanore had been present. Now, he had free rein.

Over the past three months, Ollie had struggled to keep his promise to Lucy—he *really* wanted to get into the cellar. Recently, his curiosity had won out. Not least because a few nights ago, when he'd woken in the night with an awful need to pee, he'd looked over to the open door to his dressing space and had been certain something had been looking back at him.

However, no sooner had Ollie clicked on his nightlight than it had vanished. He'd forced himself to look into the dressing room and en-suite as well, but still hadn't found anything.

Ollie didn't have the same beliefs as Lucy about the supernatural, so he had to wonder if it was just his imagination. Even so, the incident had ignited Ollie's desire to know more, so he'd decided to put the plan into action. Alone this time. He had no idea if the others believed he was really ill—he thought Emily had looked a little sceptical—but as long as they didn't rat him out, it didn't really matter.

He did feel bad about not having run it past the rest of them, but then, if he was only looking around a little, what harm could it do?

Eleanore's room was much like the ones the children had, only a little smaller. It contained the same style double bed, two large wardrobes, and dressing cabinets and drawers; the floor was timber planks with a large rug in the centre, which covered most of the area. The bed was neatly made and there wasn't a thing out of place.

Ollie started searching. The first wardrobe he looked in contained Eleanore's modest selection of clothes and little else. Next, Ollie moved over to the other wardrobe... but found that one locked.

Strange. What happened to her rule of not locking doors?

Ollie wasn't exactly surprised—though he knew he had to get inside. *Where would she keep the key?* He then had a horrible thought. *What if she keeps it with her and took it into town?* He then wondered if she would have the key to the cellar on her person as well. If so, his whole plan would turn out to be for nothing.

Hoping against it, the boy got back to searching. He checked the obvious places first: the drawers and cabinets, the nightstand, the dressing area, yet turned up nothing. Undeterred, Ollie continued, hoping to find some secret compartment or something in the open wardrobe, though he knew he was growing desperate. Ollie even forced both tall wardrobes away from the walls a little, which took a lot of effort, just to see if either had something taped to the backs. He was left disappointed and had to reposition the heavy pieces of furniture before continuing. Ollie even resorted to looking under the mattress on the bed.

There has to be something.

He stared around the space, eyes carefully scanning every facet of the room. Eventually, he felt his gaze fall on the rug. *I wonder,* he thought to himself.

While some of the rug was pinned down by the bed, well over half protruded from under it and ran farther into the room. Ollie lifted the loose end and rolled the rug back towards the bed, coughing at the dust he kicked up. Once it was rolled right back completely, he stood up, keeping his foot on the roll to ensure it didn't unfurl. He gazed at the floorboards.

Then... he felt a smile creep over his face. *Bingo!*

One of the floorboards had previously been lifted, with a larger gap around it than the others and no screws in the corners. It was close to the bed, and even if the rug hadn't been there, Ollie didn't think he'd have noticed if he hadn't specifically been looking.

After squatting down, he was able to slip his fingers down the sides of the loose plank and lift it up, then set it aside. In the revealed space, he saw the deep floor joists running from one side of the room to the other, and the inner surface of the ceiling board below that.

Resting just on top of the board was a wooden box.

It had a walnut finish and black metal hinges. Ollie reached inside and retrieved it. The lightweight box was only around six inches by three inches, and thankfully didn't appear to be locked. The boy let the rug roll back out and took a seat on the bed before setting the box on his lap. He couldn't help but notice a sense of trepidation run through him. Regardless, Ollie undid the clasps and opened it up.

Two keys sat inside, resting on a burgundy lining. Both were small. One was iron, and its dark colour matched the handles and hinges on the locked wardrobe. The other key was small and plain silver. *That looks like a key to a padlock.*

Ollie's eyes lit up with excitement and the boy snatched up both keys. As he did, he glanced again at the burgundy lining of the box, noting a few small, dry stains, all little more than droplets where the colour had darkened. At first he wondered if they were blood, but quickly dismissed the thought, realising it could be anything.

Ollie gazed down at both keys as they sat in his palm, his smile widening. *Which to use first?*

The cellar had been his main goal, of course, but the locked wardrobe was a new consideration to him. Plus... it was right there. That alone made his decision a quick one. He had plenty of time and could rush down to the cellar afterwards.

Can't have been much more than 20 minutes so far.

The boy stood, pocketed the silver key, and paced over to the wardrobe, where he used the key in the lock. It fit perfectly. Ollie turned it and heard a satisfying *click*, then pulled both doors open.

Upon seeing what lay inside, he had no idea where to start and simply took in everything he could. The first thing he noticed was that the interior of the wardrobe wasn't like the rest of the ones in the house. It was instead fitted with rows and rows of shelving, from top to bottom; in addition, some small compartments with droppable doors had been constructed.

The shelves at his eye level contained various bits of medical equipment. He saw needles, syringes, even scalpels, all neatly stored in metal cups or plastic containers. There were the bottles of antiseptic, as well as other liquids he didn't recognise. Just bottles upon bottles—he assumed they were medicine, yet none were labelled. There were also packets of unmarked tablets, some thermometers, cannulas, gloves, tape, pieces of cloth, even a stethoscope. While Ollie knew Eleanore kept first-aid equipment in the house, he didn't realise the woman's collection of medical supplies was so... vast.

While impressive, it wasn't really the kind of thing he was looking for.

Ollie then started rummaging through more of the compartments. Some were empty, but many were not. He found a manila folder in a particularly wide compartment, and after quickly flicking through, saw some legal documentation concerning him and the other three children becoming the legal responsibility of Eleanore. He knew reading through everything would be a time-consuming task, so he decided to put everything back.

There's got to be more, Ollie told himself, but couldn't find much that really piqued his interest. He was about to quit and lock the wardrobe up when he glanced down at the bottom of the cupboard. After narrowing his eyes, he then stepped back and realised there was a section of space unaccounted for beneath the closet's floor. It could be that it was just dead space, but wanting to be sure, Ollie knelt down and started to press on the wood. When he pushed on the far left-hand side, the right end popped up, making it obvious the sheet of timber was not screwed down. He was then able to easily slide the floor out and set it down.

As he'd thought, there was a large pocket of space inside. And in it sat another manila folder, and on top of that a single envelope. Though the envelope had probably once been white, it had yellowed over time, the surface was wrinkled, and the edges were curled. It wasn't sealed, and when Ollie pulled it out and opened it up, he saw a clutch of Polaroids inside, all held together by an elastic band.

The boy quickly took off the band and studied the first photo. The image had clearly aged—the whites were *too* white, bleaching out much of the detail. Even so, Ollie could see the smiling face of a younger Eleanore as she ducked down, arms out wide and encircling four children of varying ages.

The kids were arranged oldest to youngest from right to left, and Ollie guessed the boy on the right was probably around his own age. Next was a boy and a girl, who looked to be similar ages and could even have been twins. Lastly was the youngest child, a girl, who Ollie guessed might have been seven or so. They all shared enough facial similarities that Ollie figured they were siblings. All had brown hair and most were smiling, though the youngest just looked grumpy, like she didn't want to be in the shot at all.

Eleanore looked to be in her late twenties or early thirties in the photo, her hair longer and mostly brown.

Ollie kept flicking his eyes to the children, then to

Eleanore, then back again, trying to see if there was any similarity between them. He thought there was, and he saw it most in the eldest girl.

Her children! he realised. *It has to be.*

He continued to stare, trying to determine if he was jumping the gun. It was *possible* they were related, he knew, entirely possible. But if not, who were they to her? Clearly important enough to keep pictures of.

And where were they now?

He flicked to the next picture. It showed two of the four children sitting on the floor, each with wide, silly grins that showed their teeth, chocolate surrounding their mouths. A small plate sat between them, remnants of a cake on it.

The third one had three of the children together. The one after had all four together again. The one that followed showed the oldest and the youngest standing side by side. Ollie continued to flick through. Some photos showed Eleanore in them as well. Some had younger versions of the children.

While he couldn't be certain, it looked to Ollie like the photos were all taken in the same house. However, it *certainly* wasn't Erimus House, even if it did have a similar feel. As the boy continued to flick through the fat wad of photos, something struck him.

Who's taking these?

While Eleanore could have taken the ones she wasn't in, there were many pictures showing her and all four children together. That meant there had to be a sixth person with the camera.

It wasn't until he got close to the back of the stack that another person was shown. It was a man. He was sitting in a chair, with the youngest child on his knee and the others flanking him on either side.

Ollie frowned. The man, who had neatly cut brown hair and a trimmed beard, looked familiar to him, though it took Ollie a few moments to place it.

The benefactor! he realised.

Jasper Graves looked younger in the images than in his portraits, but it was definitely him.

She had a family? Ollie wondered. *Has Eleanore been lying to us all this time?*

He then considered if maybe they were other orphans. Maybe he and the others weren't the first. Even so, that still meant Eleanore had been lying about the past. And where was the house in the pictures? None of it made sense. Surely a children's home prior to Erimus House would have been mentioned.

Keep moving, Ollie told himself. *You're running out of time.* Plus, the cellar was what he *really* wanted to see.

He bound up the photos again and slipped them back in the envelope, then set the envelope on the floor next to him. Next, he retrieved the folder and opened it up. As he did, a single sheet of loose paper slipped out and fluttered to the floor. When Ollie gathered it up, he saw it was a handwritten note. He knew what Eleanore's handwriting looked like, with her elegant loops and leaning letters that artfully dipped and rose. This wasn't hers. While certainly legible, it was far more messily scrawled.

Even though Ollie was itching to get to the cellar, he read through the short note.

T̲ʜᴏʀɴs ᴏғ Eʀṣᴇᴛᴜ.

The Ouroboros have already been set. Everything is marked. The three stages can be executed.

1. The black.

Call them. Refer to the texts and the rite. They will observe and form the circle. Form the night.

2. The white.

The offering in thorns. Be strong.

3. The red.

The binding.

Then... it is time. And remember... be wary of the white flame.

OLLIE FROWNED and reread the page again, completely lost. An offering? A binding? The white flame?

What on earth?

It sounded like the ravings of a lunatic. While clearly not written by Eleanore, Ollie wondered if they were the scribblings of Jasper Graves. If so, it shed a whole new light on what Ollie knew about him.

He sounds crazy.

Ollie was half tempted to take the page and hide it somewhere, maybe under his mattress, so he could show the others later, but he knew if Eleanore found it was missing he would be the only suspect.

So, he put the note back in the folder, placed it and the envelope into the wardrobe once more, reset the base, and finally locked everything up. After that, Ollie went about putting the cupboard key back in its box, which he placed between the joists before replacing the floorboard and rolling out the carpet once more so everything was back to normal. He knew he'd have to get back into the box when he was done with the cellar key, but at least this way if Eleanore and the others came back early, nothing would look amiss and he could just hold on to the key.

If he wasn't caught red-handed in the cellar, of course.

Satisfied that everything in the room looked right, Ollie made his way downstairs, the words from the note still circling in his mind.

'Call them... They will observe.'

Who are 'they'?

Eventually, he found himself back in the dining room, staring at the cellar door. While looking, he allowed his eyes to flick to the closest window to him, which opened out onto the rear garden. He remembered back to the night where Daniel had claimed to see something.

You saw something too, Ollie thought. *No,* he then argued against himself. *You just* thought *you did.*

Even so, he couldn't help but remember the jittery, jerky movements of the figures he'd *thought* he'd seen.

Time to get on with it, Ollie then told himself as he pulled out the key. The boy took a breath and inserted the key easily into the lock, which popped open after a single turn.

I'm in! He felt another tingle of excitement.

Yet he just stood still for a moment, staring down at the padlock that hung from the latch, dangling open. *I'm... in,* he told himself again, but it wasn't with excitement this time, it was more... disbelief. He'd been wanting to get inside for months now. And now he'd finally done it.

It felt like a big deal.

After shaking his head, Ollie removed the padlock, wondering what to do with it, given it was far too bulky to fit in a pocket. *If I just leave it lying on the floor, someone will see it as soon as they walk in.*

He considered hanging it from the inside, like Eleanore did, only not locking it. *That'll be good enough.*

Padlock in hand, Ollie finally pulled the door towards him, hinges creaking. Inside, the boy saw a flight of stone steps run down into sheer darkness, which was about as welcoming as strolling into the mouth of a shark.

Thankfully, there was a grey light switch housed on a square metal box just to his left inside the room, so Ollie flipped it.

Flickering lights came to life farther down in the space, blinking and strobing before finally settling into a constant stream, coming from a single yellow bulb about halfway down the steps. At the bottom, Ollie saw a concrete floor level out and run off before soon meeting a rusty metal door, though the boy could only see the bottom of it thanks to the sloping bulkhead over the steps.

Another door, he said to himself, hoping this one wasn't locked.

Ollie steeled himself and set off, taking the steps slowly and steadily. His ears were on constant alert for the sound of an approaching car or the front door opening. And also, just in case he heard something coming from ahead.

When the boy finally reached the bottom, he saw that there was no handle on the new door, and certainly no lock. There was only a push plate, which he pressed his hand against.

It took more strength than he'd expected to force the door open, and he actually struggled to hold it ajar while he felt along the wall just inside the room for a switch.

Soon enough, however, he found one, and light poured out of the ceiling, coming from yellow strip lighting. Ollie stepped fully inside and took everything in: large pieces of ground-mounted machinery, wall-mounted control boxes, thick steel pipes fixed to the wall. Ollie realised instantly that Eleanore had indeed been telling the truth about the cellar, at least to some degree—it certainly didn't look safe for children.

The space ahead was deep, and walkways were situated between the rows of machinery. Ollie let the door close behind him and moved onward. The air felt heavier, which shouldn't have been a surprise given there were no windows for ventilation. The walls were solid, exposed block, the ceiling concrete, and the floor square stone slabs.

Eventually, Ollie reached the far wall and frowned in confusion.

There was nothing unusual that he could see, just more machinery, some empty buckets and a mop, more control boxes, and... nothing beyond that.

There has *to be more,* Ollie told himself. He then walked back up to the door, using a different aisle this time, but it was just more of the same.

This can't be right.

While the large room was dim, with pockets of shadows between some of the bulky equipment, there really wasn't any place Ollie could see that could be hiding something. He did three full loops around the rectangular cellar, but each time got the same result.

He was about to give up when he finally caught a glimpse of something in one of the corners on the far side of the room. There was a piece of machinery standing alone that Ollie realised wasn't actually connected to anything. Its wires and cords were all wrapped up neatly and tied around it. What was more, the piece of equipment—and Ollie had no idea what it was—sat on wheels, with plenty of space to the right for it to be moved away.

I wonder.

Ollie took hold of the machine and heaved it sideways as much as he could. It took considerable effort, but it eventually glided away from the wall. He kept it moving, only stopping when what was beneath was fully exposed.

There was a hatch in the cellar floor.

The door of the hatch was metal—once silver, but a lot of the surface was now coated in rust. There was a single ring pull-handle in the door that sat in a depression.

While Ollie now had another way forward, he felt a wave of trepidation wash over him—he didn't want to go even *lower*. Suddenly, the safety of the main house above seemed a long way away.

Even so, Ollie forced the worry from his mind and reached down for the handle before lifting the hatch with a strain. As the door swung up higher, the light from the cellar streamed down into the dark void—

Illuminating a face that looked back up at him.

Ollie let out a shriek and let the hatch drop closed with an almighty *clang*. He scuttled backwards in shock, tripping on his own feet and landing on his rear.

That wasn't human! he realised in panic.

Ollie kicked his legs out as he desperately scrambled backwards, eyes wide and fixed firmly on the closed trapdoor. He fully expected the door to raise back up and for that... *thing*... to peek over the lip and stare at him with its many eyes.

Its scores of eyes had seemed to shift around its face, with tiny pupils like pinpricks that slid over the milky surface of the eyeballs. The image of the thing was seared into Ollie's mind, including the darkness that had appeared to bleed into the thing, making the edges of its form hard to make out. Even so, he could still tell it had the form of a person, with no other features to its face besides the mass of roving eyes, some set deep into the dark form, others protruding outward, and all looking off in different directions.

What was more, the thing had just been standing there,

at the bottom of a run of ladders, unmoving in the darkness and looking up. Like it had been waiting.

It can't have been real, it can't have been real, Ollie told himself over and over again, though he didn't really believe that. The boy was able to push himself back to his feet, where he ran unsteadily over to the door. There, he fumbled with the pull handle and eventually heaved it open. Ollie slapped the inside light off and bolted out to the steps, letting the heavy door close behind him. He then sprinted up the steps, higher and higher, but the toe of his left foot clipped one of the steps, sending him sprawling upwards to smash his elbow against the concrete. Ollie quickly looked back to stare down at the door, terrified any minute it would start opening. Thankfully, it remained closed.

Ollie pushed himself back up and got to the top of the steps in double quick time, where he switched the light off and bolted out into the dining room, forcing the door closed behind him and pressing his back against it. Ollie was panting, drawing in quick, shallow breaths, unable to calm himself down.

Lock the door, he told himself—he froze, realising the padlock was still inside the door. That meant he'd have to open it back up and face the darkness once more.

He closed his eyes and clenched his teeth together. All he had to do was open the door enough to reach his hand in and snatch back the padlock, yet he couldn't bring himself to do it. It just seemed like a monumental task. *What if that thing followed me out? What if it grabs my arm?*

Still panting and close to hyperventilating, Ollie knew he had to do something. He couldn't just stand against the door, hoping to keep it held shut. He could either get the door locked, or run.

He took a deep breath. Then another, exhaling quickly, building himself up—if the door was locked from the outside, he'd feel at least a little safer in the house.

Do it!

Ollie spun, yanked the door open, and reached his hand inside to grab the lock; however, it didn't come away from the latch as easily as he'd hoped. Instead, it snagged, making him fight and fumble with it.

Come on!

Eventually, Ollie pulled it free, and slammed the door shut before resetting the lock once again. He took a small step away from the door, trying to make sense of what he'd seen.

It clearly hadn't been human, but... what?

Likely the same thing Daniel had seen, he realised, now feeling guilty for not believing the other boy. And maybe the same thing he'd seen at the bottom of the garden as well. Then he wondered if there was more than one of those things lurking about the house. The thought of it made his skin crawl.

Cellar finally locked, Ollie bolted, sprinting back through the main hallway and over to the stairs, which he bounded up before sprinting to his room and slamming the door shut behind him. Once inside, he just stared at his own door, terrified something would open it. Part of him wanted to climb under the covers and hide until the others returned, but he didn't want to block his view and not be able to see what might be coming.

Over the next few minutes as he stood watching the door in anticipation, Ollie was finally able to stop his body from trembling. Then, after almost half an hour with no sign of anything, he slowly moved to the bed and sat down, keeping his eyes on the door and listening intently.

It was only then that he remembered he still had the padlock key nestled in his pocket. While he knew he probably still had time to get it back upstairs, he couldn't bring himself to leave his room. Instead, he just waited where he was, sitting on his bed and staring at the door for another hour and a half until Eleanore and the others returned.

CHAPTER
TWENTY-ONE

Something happened, Emily said to herself as she entered the kitchen. Ollie was ahead of her, standing at the sink and pouring himself a glass of water. Emily didn't want anything from the kitchen herself. She'd just followed Ollie in to catch him alone.

'Come on,' she said to him. 'Spill it.'

He turned to face her. 'Spill what?'

'Whatever you found while you were here alone,' Emily went on, keeping her voice low enough that no one outside the room would hear.

'I don't follow,' he said. There was a look of confusion on his face, but it was forced.

Emily rolled her eyes. 'Well, you're clearly not ill. You came down from your room as soon as we all got back, and you haven't been back to bed since.'

'Like I said to Eleanore, I'm feeling a little better.'

'Mmm-hmm,' Emily replied with a slow nod. 'And you've been really quiet since.'

'Well, I'm not *completely* better, but I just don't want to sit in my room all day.'

But Emily shook her head. 'You're such a fibber,' she teased. 'You stayed home so you could look around and snoop, like we planned to do before. I'm not an *idiot*, Ollie, so come on... spill it. What did you find?'

He turned his back on her and took a sip of his water. Then, it was his turn to shake his head. 'I didn't snoop,' he said. 'And I didn't find anything.'

After staring at him for a second, Emily folded her arms over her chest.

'That's not what we agreed on, Ollie,' she stated.

He looked back. This time his frown of confusion was genuine. 'What do you mean?'

'Before,' Emily began, 'when we agreed to look in the cellar, we promised to share whatever we found. Just because you went ahead without us knowing doesn't mean you get to keep everything to yourself.' The boy continued to stare at her. It wasn't an angry glare, more a searching one, like he was weighing something up. 'Come on, Ollie,' Emily continued with a sisterly tone, 'you can tell me anything.'

He sighed and his body sagged. 'It's... hard to explain,' he eventually said.

Emily walked closer to him. 'That's okay,' she said. 'Just try, I'll listen. Is it... is it bad?'

His hesitation told her everything. 'Well, there's more than just *one* thing, I guess. But the main—' Yet before he could continue, the door to the kitchen was flung open and Lucy bounded in.

'Hiya,' she said in a sing-song voice. 'How ya' feeling, Ollie?'

The older boy turned away from them and looked back down at the drink in his hand. 'Fine,' he said to Lucy with his back to her, not letting her see his dour expression.

'All better?' she asked and came close to the pair.

'Getting there,' he replied before finally looking at her and giving a forced smile.

The younger girl moved over to him and hugged him around the waist, trapping Ollie's dangling arm against his side. 'You know,' she said, 'sleep is the best thing if you're sick. Even if you're getting better, it'll help. Mum always told me that.'

'Thanks but... I'll be okay. I just don't wanna go back to bed yet. I slept plenty when everyone was in town.'

'You haven't read your football magazines we got you yet!' Lucy went on as she eventually released Ollie.

'I will soon,' Ollie said. 'Probably tomorrow.'

With Lucy present, Emily knew there was no way Ollie was going to share what he'd uncovered. In Emily's head, Lucy deserved to know just as much as the rest of them, but she didn't want to put Ollie on the spot, given how reluctant he'd initially been. *I need to get him alone again.*

It suddenly struck her that, as big as the house was, it was actually difficult for any of the children to get alone time with each other, other than when they went to bed. The four seemed to spend all their time together in a big group. In truth, it had never felt odd or smothering to Emily, and though she'd only been in the house for a quarter of a year, she felt like she'd known the other three for decades. There was a bond there she hadn't felt before with others. Even her friends back at school—some of which she *had* known for years—hadn't been as close to her as Ollie, Daniel, and Lucy were now.

As Emily tried to figure out how she could pull Ollie away from Lucy, Daniel wandered in, and she knew it just wasn't going to happen. *Not yet, anyway.* In that instant, she decided to wait until they were all in bed, then she could just sneak down to his room and knock. It was the only time she knew for certain she could get him alone.

So, Emily waited, biding her time. Eleanore asked Ollie a few times during the course of the day if he was fine, and each time Ollie just answered with a simple, 'Yeah.'

Eventually, when it was time to turn in for the night, Emily watched Ollie, noting he seemed somewhat... apprehensive, even saying he wasn't tired and would keep playing games if any of the others wanted to stay up with him. However, everyone else was exhausted after a full day, so he begrudgingly went up to his room at the same time they went to theirs. Emily gave it a little over an hour, and once the house was completely silent, she snuck from her own room and crept down to Ollie's. There, she knocked and waited.

'Who is it?' she heard Ollie say.

'Emily,' she replied. 'Can I come in?'

After a couple of seconds, she heard him approach the door and it opened. 'What's wrong?' he asked, looking serious.

'Nothing,' she said. 'Just wanted to talk.' She then nodded deeper in the room and repeated her earlier question: 'Can I come in?'

After a beat, he stepped aside. 'Sure.'

Emily entered the room, which was lit by his single bedside lamp, and Ollie closed the door behind her—but not before peeking briefly out into the hallway.

He then came closer to Emily, yet said nothing.

'You were going to tell me something earlier today,' Emily began.

'Was I?' he asked.

Emily sighed. 'Stop avoiding it, Ollie,' she said. 'Just tell me.'

Ollie took a breath. 'Fine,' he said. Then, Emily listened.

She listened as Ollie told her about what he'd found in Eleanore's room and listened when he said he still had the key to the cellar and needed to get it back to its hiding spot. She then listened to how he'd finally made his way down into the cellar as well, and how he'd found a trapdoor.

She also listened to what he said had been waiting under that trapdoor: the multi-eyed horror that had been staring back up at him.

He asked her if she believed him. At first, she didn't know how to respond, but after seeing how scared the normally brave boy was, she just nodded.

'I do,' she told him. Then she asked the obvious question. 'But... what do we do about it?'

Ollie had no answer, and neither did she.

CHAPTER
TWENTY-TWO

Eleanore sat at the dining room table in the dark. It took everything she had not to cry, knowing if even a single tear rolled free, the wellspring that followed would be uncontrollable. She knew she couldn't act just yet. It was too early, and some of the children might still be awake.

But tonight was the night—if she was strong enough.

She'd been having this internal battle for months now. Everything had been ready for a while. It just needed the last push. The final step of the three.

Three was an important number in so many ways, though most of which were unknown to normal people.

Eleanore wasn't the only one that was enlightened, of course. The Children of the New Sun knew. They'd taught her. It was *their* knowledge she was using.

No, not theirs. They stole it.

Just like she'd stolen it from them.

Eleanore blinked hard as she remembered the Children, the people she knew there, and what they had taken from her.

Don't. Push it out of your mind, she told herself, feeling sadness and anger build in equal measure. Thinking about it would only lead to her sobbing. If that happened, the children might hear. Better they remain asleep.

Because not only was she going to take the final step, but she was going to go beyond what was needed. It would be better that way, and while harder now, it would make things easier later.

After all, Eleanore knew she couldn't go on like this anymore, and she needed to hurry everything up. She'd put on a brave face for long enough.

She considered retrieving the note from the wardrobe and reading it over again. In truth, that single page was little more than a cheat-sheet. The full transcripts were 'down there,' but Eleanore knew everything she needed. The brief note was just something she read over every now and again to try and keep focused.

No, she told herself, *no need for the note tonight. Just action.*

After taking a sip from her tea, which had been forgotten about and was now stone cold, she gazed out of the rear window.

Her breath immediately caught in her throat.

A watcher stood outside, staring back in at her. Its face was a mass of eyes, all of which were fixed on her; its ethereal form faded in and out of the dark.

Be calm, she told herself. She knew it wouldn't hurt her. Eleanore had caught glimpses of them before. Every time the sight had sent a chill up her spine.

They had been in the house for a while now, of course, ever since she'd released them. They'd been studying the property, everything within the markings. From the boundary walls, to the very books on the bookshelves, and even the words on the pages.

Everything.

They observed, experienced, and... remembered. Always in the dark. Their job was finished now, so they just remained, keeping to the shadows from where they'd been pulled.

Yanked from one eternal dark into a new one.

From black, to white, to red.

Now it was time for the red. It had been time for a while.

Come on, Eleanore, you need to be strong.
For them.

CHAPTER
TWENTY-THREE

'I think we should tell the others,' Emily eventually said to Ollie. 'It's only right.' She couldn't deny that what Ollie had told her had really freaked her out.

'But what if we scare them?' Ollie said. 'Because it sure scared me.'

'I know,' Emily replied. 'I understand that, and it probably will, but I still think they should know. They deserve to.'

'Do you think it's the same thing Daniel saw?'

'I...' Emily hesitated. 'I mean... probably. I don't know.'

'I think that's where they've been coming from,' Ollie went on. 'Under the house. That's why Eleanore keeps the cellar locked up. She knows about them, I just *know* it. I think it's why she keeps going down there.'

'Well, we need to speak to her too,' Emily said. 'After we've told the others.'

'But she'll lie, just like she did the other times,' Ollie replied. 'She could have told us all this before now, but she didn't. She told Lucy nothing was out there, even though there was!'

'Maybe she really doesn't know about those things?' Emily suggested. She was still struggling with Ollie's story herself—not that she thought he was lying, but it was just... a lot. If Daniel hadn't had a similar experience a few months ago, she would have thought Ollie had just been mistaken.

Lucy saw it too.

'I thought about that,' Ollie said. 'But why else lock the cellar up?'

Emily shrugged. 'Because it isn't safe for us, maybe?' Ollie frowned. 'I'm not saying it's definitely the case,' Emily was quick to point out. 'Just that it, you know, *might* be. I mean, we just don't know yet. That's why we should confront her. What else can we do besides that?'

Ollie hesitated. Eventually, he nodded. 'You're right.'

'We talk to Eleanore after we tell the others, see what she has to say. Give her the opportunity. Because despite all this, she's been good to us, right?'

'Yeah... she has,' the boy conceded. 'But if she knows about those things, that's big, Emily. It means we can't trust her, and that we need to get out of here. I mean, we probably already need to do that.' Another pause. 'Do we wake the others and tell them now?'

'I have no idea,' Emily said. 'Maybe wait until the morning?'

'Why? With those things—'

'Those things haven't done anything to us so far, and it's been months,' Emily pointed out. 'Just... if we go up and wake Lucy, we might wake Eleanore as well. Are we really ready to face her about it right now? I'd rather we all do it together, with everyone on the same page.'

Ollie held her gaze. His frantic expression softened. 'I understand that,' he said.

'Do you think we should try to get the key back before we confront her?' Emily asked.

'I don't think we'll get the chance,' he replied.

'We could wait a few days before talking to her, give us an opportunity to—'

'No,' Ollie said. 'I think we tell Daniel and Lucy tomorrow, then speak to Eleanore straight after. We need to get it over with.'

Emily suddenly held up a finger. 'Shhhh,' she whispered and cocked her head, listening.

Someone was coming upstairs.

CHAPTER
TWENTY-FOUR

Even as she climbed the stairs, Eleanore was struggling with doubt and apprehension. *Maybe not tonight. Maybe tomorrow.*

She'd been saying the same thing for a long time now. The more she put it off, the easier it was to just keep kicking it down the road.

And the harder it was to act.

That day had been a good one. In fact, things had been good in the house ever since the children had come close to realising something was up a few months back. *I should have acted then, as soon as the second step was complete.*

Though in truth, she knew that would have been too much for her. That step had taken almost everything she had in her, and she had to mourn behind a façade of normality. It had almost broken her.

As the woman reached the mid floor, she glanced down the hallway towards Ollie and Daniel's rooms. Both doors were closed and the lights were off. She then continued farther up to the top story, seeing the same for Emily and

Lucy's rooms. Finally, she entered her own bedroom and sat down on the bed.

It was getting harder to act like things were normal in front of the children. There had been a few times she had come close to just breaking down. She knew she couldn't put it off any longer—if she did, Eleanore knew she just wouldn't act at all. Then everything would be for nothing.

And what would become of *him?*

No, she needed to make it happen. And tonight was the night.

She looked down at the rug beneath her slippered feet. After taking a breath, she got up once more, then rolled the rug back. She didn't remove the floorboard straight away, instead just stared down, trying to build herself up. All she needed was the key. Everything else was down there.

Eventually, Eleanore pulled up the floorboard and retrieved the box from between the joists.

Open it. Just do one step at a time. She then forced herself to open the box and peer inside. Her eyes went wide.

There was only one key.

CHAPTER
TWENTY-FIVE

After hearing Eleanore go up to the floor above, Ollie had flicked his nightlight back on, though both he and Emily stayed silent for a while.

'I didn't even realise she was still awake,' Emily eventually whispered.

'Me either,' Ollie replied. 'Give it a minute before you go back to bed, though, otherwise she'll catch you.'

'And you'll be okay sleeping on your own?' Emily asked him, knowing if *she'd* seen what he had, there was no way she'd be okay sleeping alone. 'I mean, you could knock on Daniel's room and sleep with him for the night. He wouldn't mind.'

'Seriously, I'm fine,' Ollie said. 'Thank you for looking out for me, but I'm okay.'

Rapid footsteps suddenly thundered back downstairs, causing both of them to pause. The heavy steps moved over to Ollie's door.

'Ollie!' the voice of Eleanore snapped as she knocked harshly. 'Ollie, open up this instant!' More knocking.

Emily and Ollie just stared at each other in shock. Yet

before they could say anything more, the handle turned and the door swung inwards. Eleanore stood in the opening, still dressed in her clothing from that day; her eyes quickly settled on Emily with a confused frown.

'What are *you* doing here?' she asked, though it was close to sounding like a demand.

'Erm...' Emily's brain couldn't summon a response quick enough.

'She just wanted to make sure I was alright,' Ollie said. 'And that I wasn't still sick.'

Eleanore quickly entered the room and closed the door behind her. 'Is that right?' she asked as she moved over and stood before them, arms folded. She looked furious, though her gaze remained fixed on Emily.

'That's right,' Emily eventually said. Eleanore said nothing. She just glared.

'It's true,' Ollie insisted.

Eleanore's gaze then settled on the boy. 'You weren't *sick* today,' she said, her voice curt. 'You've been snooping around, haven't you?'

The comment confirmed Emily's fears—Eleanore obviously knew the key was missing.

'No,' Ollie shot back. 'I've been in bed pretty much all—'

'Don't lie to me!' Eleanore didn't quite yell, but she came as close as Emily had ever seen her.

'I'm not lying,' Ollie replied. It was unconvincing, even to Emily.

Eleanore simply held out her hand. 'The key.' This time, the demand was absolute.

Ollie maintained eye contact with her. However, he didn't move. 'Do you know what's down in the cellar?' he asked.

Emily watched Eleanore's face carefully. While the older woman tried to keep a steady expression, Emily saw it in her eyes: *She knows. Or at least, she knows something.*

'I don't know what you mean,' Eleanore eventually replied. Emily had to give it to her, the woman sounded more convincing than Ollie had. 'There's nothing down in the cellar.'

Ollie just scoffed and shook his head. 'And the stuff in your wardrobe?'

'You *have* been snooping.'

'Because you wouldn't tell us the truth!' Ollie shot back. 'You've been keeping things from us. Who are the four kids? And why are they in photos with you and Mr. Graves? Did you have kids with him? You told us you never did, and yet—'

'Enough!' Eleanore shouted as she raised her palm. Emily felt her eyes widen.

'And that weird note,' Ollie continued, ignoring her. 'Something about thorns and watchers?'

Eleanore looked down and drew in a deep breath, obviously fighting to hold back her anger. 'And you know about all this, Emily?' she asked.

Ollie interjected. 'She doesn't—'

'I do,' Emily stated. She gave Ollie a quick nod, trying to convey it was okay.

'So you're both in it together?'

'No,' Ollie was quick to say. 'The others didn't know what I was planning. I stayed home and did it myself. I only *just* told Emily what—'

But Eleanore turned and moved towards the door, stepped out into the hall, and shouted, 'Daniel, Lucy, come here now!'

'They don't know anything,' Emily insisted. Eleanore didn't acknowledge her, just shouted for the others again.

And again.

Eventually, Daniel's door opened and the boy emerged, hair messy and rubbing his eyes.

'What happened?' he asked.

Eleanore beckoned him over to her. 'Come here and stand with me,' she stated. 'Quickly.' Daniel complied, and his brow furrowed in confusion as he noticed Emily and Ollie. 'Lucy!' Eleanore shouted, moving to the bottom of the stairs.

She called twice more, before Emily eventually heard a small voice reply, 'Coming!'

There came the sound of Lucy's footsteps, and then she appeared in her night robe. Eleanore ushered both her and Daniel over into Ollie's room. 'What's going on?' Lucy asked.

'Everyone turn and face me,' Eleanore insisted once everyone was inside. She raised a finger. 'And keep your focus on me. *Only* me. Understand? No looking at each other.'

'I'm... confused,' Daniel said and turned to look at Emily and Ollie.

'*Here!*' Eleanore snapped and Daniel quickly looked back to her. 'Now, do you two'—she pointed to Daniel, then to Lucy—'know what happened today?'

Both children cast each other a look, which caused Eleanore to click her fingers, like she was drawing the attention of two dogs. 'Eyes on me,' she said. 'Now, I'll repeat again, do you know what happened today?'

'We... went into town,' Lucy said with some hesitation. 'Is that what you mean? Did something happen in town?'

Eleanore studied the younger girl, then turned to the boy. 'Daniel, any idea?'

'I don't know what you mean,' Daniel stated, shaking his head. Emily felt bad for them both, as they were obviously confused as to what was happening.

'I told you,' Ollie began. 'No one else knew.'

'Knew what?' Lucy asked.

'I found the key to the cellar today,' Ollie told her.

'Ollie!' Eleanore snapped. 'Not one more word—'

'She kept it under the floorboards in her room,' the boy went on defiantly.

'You... found the key?' Lucy asked. 'But we said we weren't gonna...'

She trailed off as Eleanore's head snapped over to her. 'Gonna *what?*' she asked sternly. Lucy's eyes flicked over to Ollie, but Eleanore repeated herself. 'Gonna *what,* Lucy? Finish that sentence.'

Lucy looked down guiltily. 'We weren't going to look for the key.'

Eleanore gave a sigh. 'So you were all plotting?'

But Lucy shook her head. 'No! We talked about it a while back, but then said we wouldn't.' Her scowling eyes fell on Ollie again. 'We all *agreed* we wouldn't.'

'What did you find?' Daniel then asked.

'That isn't the point, Daniel,' Eleanore snapped. 'I told you it isn't safe for children down there.'

'There was a floor hatch,' Ollie interrupted, keeping his eyes on Daniel. 'And when I looked in—'

'Enough!' Eleanore said again.

'I saw something,' Ollie carried on, ignoring the woman entirely. 'I think it was the same thing you saw before. It was just there, looking up.' When Daniel didn't say anything, Ollie continued, 'So I ran. Slammed the hatch and went to my room.'

'Ridiculous,' Eleanore said, shaking her head.

'It's true!'

Eleanore held up a hand. 'No it isn't, Ollie. It's an obvious lie.' However, Emily cocked her head to the side. *Am I imagining it, or does she sound a little relieved?* Like she had been expecting something else.

'Why don't you believe us about this?' Ollie demanded. 'We're telling the truth! Lucy was telling you the truth a while back, but you wouldn't believe her either.' He took a breath but continued before Eleanore could respond. 'Actually, I think you *do* believe us. I think you know there are things in this house and you're just trying to convince us we're wrong.'

'There's nothing in the house bedsides us, Ollie,' Eleanore said.

The boy just shook his head, exasperated. 'Lies! And why don't you tell us about the weird note in your wardrobe, the one that talks about watchers and the reddening and white flame and stuff?' Eleanore shook her head in annoyance, but Ollie continued, 'Or the photos in your wardrobe that you kept hidden? The ones of the other kids and Mr. Graves.'

'What other kids?' Lucy asked.

'She has photos,' Ollie went on. 'From when she was younger. There are four kids in them. Mr. Graves is in some of the pictures as well.'

Lucy turned her eyes to Eleanore. 'You had kids?' she asked. 'You *told* us you never had kids.'

'And you said you weren't married to Mr. Graves,' Daniel added.

Eleanore clenched her teeth. 'You're getting it all wrong.'

'Then tell us,' Ollie said. 'Because the way it looks to me... there were four of them and four of us. Are we just... what... the replacement or something?'

Eleanore screwed her eyes shut. Emily saw the woman's jaw flex as it tensed. 'They're just children I used to know,' she said. 'Children both me and Mr. Graves knew. They were important to us.'

'*Your* children?' Ollie asked.

'No, not mine,' she said. 'And not Mr. Graves', either.'

'Then whose?' Emily questioned.

'It doesn't *matter,*' the older woman shot back, opening her eyes again. 'They aren't in my life anymore.'

'Are they... dead?' she asked.

'No,' Eleanore replied, quickly shaking her head. 'Heavens no. They just grew up and have lives of their own now. That's it. That's all there is to it. I keep those photos because it was an important time in my life. That's it.' She looked over at Ollie. 'You're getting the wrong idea about all of this.'

'Then why didn't you show us them before?' Ollie asked.

'Do I ask to see all the photos you kept?' she replied. Eleanore then pointed to Lucy, specifically to the locket she wore. 'Do I insist on seeing the photos in your locket, Lucy?'

Lucy reflexively gripped the locket, looked down at it, then shook her head. 'No,' she replied.

'Exactly,' she replied. 'Because I know some things are private.'

Emily had no idea whether or not the older woman was telling the truth. She'd always thought she was good at reading people, despite her age, but at the moment she was at a loss. None of the other children said anything.

Eleanore continued: 'I thought after the silliness a few months ago, things had finally gone back to normal, but obviously not.' She flicked her eyes to Emily. 'I asked you back then to trust me, yet it seems you aren't able to do that.' She looked up to the others as well. 'None of you were. So, until I can trust *you*, your bedroom doors will be locked at night. No more wandering around.'

'You can't do that!' Ollie argued.

'I can and I will,' Eleanore stated calmly.

Ollie shook his head. 'No, what if one of those things—'

'There are no things!' Eleanore yelled. Her hands clenched into balled fists by her side. 'Now enough!'

Emily then heard sobbing. She looked to her side and saw tears rolling down Lucy's cheeks. 'Please stop fighting,' the girl whimpered. 'Please.'

'It's okay, Luce,' Emily said, moving over to the younger girl. She put her arm around her, and Lucy suddenly flung herself into Emily and buried her head into Emily's chest. The young girl's sobs grew more intense. 'Shhh,' Emily went on. 'It's all alright.'

'It isn't,' Lucy replied, her voice muffled. Then the young girl moved her head back and she glared at Ollie with a look of rage Emily had never seen before. 'You *promised!*' she yelled, surprising everyone. 'You promised! Things were good and you ruined them! You ruined everything! Why?'

'I...' Ollie started, but trailed off for a moment. 'Lucy... I...' he eventually went on. 'I just needed to know.'

'But *why?*' Lucy asked, pulling herself away from Emily. She then marched up to Ollie. Emily noticed Eleanore was just watching things develop, looking equally as surprised as Ollie did. Lucy then poked the boy in the chest, teeth clenched. 'You said you wouldn't, and you did it anyway,' she snarled.

'I said I'd hold off for *a while,*' Ollie argued back. 'Three months was long enough.'

'But you still didn't check with us!' Lucy went on. She shuffled forward even more, now coming chest to chest with Ollie, eyes blazing with fury. 'But you thought you knew best, didn't you? Well... you don't!'

'Luce,' Ollie began, voice soft. 'Aren't you listening? Didn't you hear what I *saw* under the cellar?'

But Lucy threw her arms up in the air. 'So *what?*' she replied. 'They won't hurt us. They're just... there.'

Emily frowned, now even more confused. 'Luce... what do you mean?'

Lucy turned to her. 'Those things,' she said. 'They don't *do* anything. They aren't mean. They're just... here with us. Like ghosts.' She looked back at Ollie. 'I know you think you know everything, but you don't! I mean, the thing you saw... did it even try to get you?'

Ollie hesitated. 'No, but—'

'*Exactly,*' Lucy stated. 'I bet it was just standing around minding its business until you bothered it.'

'How do you know so much about them, Lucy?' Emily asked.

Lucy shrugged. 'I saw them a little while ago. Nothing happened. They don't want to hurt anyone, so there's nothing to be scared about. In a way, it's kind of... nice.'

'Nice?' Ollie asked in disbelief.

'Yes!' she snapped. 'Because they're ghosts. Whether you want to believe it or not, they are. And that means, after what happened to our parents...'

'Go on,' Emily prodded after the girl trailed off.

'That there's *more*,' Lucy said, straightening up, as if challenging anyone to argue with her. 'More after we... you know. And that's a good thing. So we should just leave them alone—or, even better, be nice. I know they look funny, but so what?'

Emily was still aware Eleanore was just watching on, staying silent.

'Do you know anything about this?' Emily asked the older woman.

The hesitation told Emily everything, but a moment later, Eleanore slowly shook her head. 'I'm afraid I don't,' she eventually said. Lucy made as if to speak, but Eleanore held up her hand to quiet her. 'But I'm not saying you're wrong, Lucy. Just that... I don't know. What I *do* know, however, is that you are all safe here. I keep telling you that, and I mean it.'

Lucy jabbed at Ollie again. 'And now Eleanore is probably going to send us back and split us up, all because of you!'

'What do you mean, Lucy?' Eleanore asked with a frown.

Lucy drew in a breath and took hold of her locket. Her worried eyes met Eleanore's. 'That you'll get sick of us always being naughty and say you don't want us anymore. Then you'll send us back and we'll all get split up.'

Eleanore's eyes widened. 'Oh, my dear, no,' she said and held her arms out. Lucy ran to her and was embraced in a hug. 'No, honey,' Eleanore continued. 'I would never do that.' She then squatted down and took hold of Lucy's hands. 'Now listen, dear,' she went on in a comforting tone. 'I won't be 'getting sick of you' or 'sending you back,' understand? And I'd *never* split you all up. Ever. I'm a little mad, sure, but I'd never *ever* consider doing that.'

Lucy sniffed and nodded. 'Well... you seemed more than a *little* mad,' she said quietly.

Eleanore chuckled. 'Maybe a little. But don't ever worry about me not wanting you all here, okay?'

Lucy gave another nod. Eleanore then slowly got back to her feet. 'It's late,' she announced. 'We'll discuss this tomorrow. I want everyone to go to bed now and get some sleep. I *will* be locking the doors, but we can talk tomorrow about how long that lasts for. Is that clear to everyone?'

After a moment, there were nods all round, even from Ollie, who remained staring down at the floor. Emily knew the telling off from Lucy had hurt him.

'Good,' Eleanore went on. 'Now, everyone back to your rooms. I'm going to go down to the kitchen to get the keys.'

More nods. Emily knew they would still be able to get around, given the rooms were interconnected, and found herself wondering if Eleanore had forgotten that. Then again, they wouldn't be able to get out into the hallways to move between floors, so maybe that was all the woman cared about.

Around ten minutes later, when Emily was tucked up in bed, her door opened and Eleanore poked her head inside, her face illumined by the night light. 'All settled in?' she asked.

'Yes,' Emily replied.

'Good,' Eleanore said. 'Now, straight to sleep, okay?'

After Emily nodded, Eleanore reached in and flicked off the light. As she pulled away, Emily spoke. 'Eleanore,' she began.

'Yes, dear?'

'I'm... really sorry about before,' she said. 'We didn't mean to upset you. I'm sorry we snooped. It wasn't right of us.'

Even through the dark, she could see Eleanore smile. The woman's eyes also glinted, as if wet. 'Thank you, Emily,' she said. 'That's nice of you to say. Just get some sleep and tomorrow we can put all this behind us.'

'Okay,' Emily said. 'I will.'

Eleanore finally closed the door, so Emily rolled to her side and stared out into the dark, thinking about what Ollie had found, what Eleanore had said, and also about Lucy's tirade. Everything felt weird again, and Emily had to admit that despite Eleanore's subterfuge, Lucy *had* a point: things had been good in the house.

In fact, they had been good ever since Emily had first moved in. Coming from such heartbreak, being placed in Erimus House had been a Godsend.

She just hoped they hadn't ruined it. She also thought about what Ollie had accused Eleanore of: the four of them were replacements for the children in the photo, whoever they were. Emily considered that. Even if he was right, was it really such a bad thing? They were all replacements to each other in some way. Eleanore a replacement parent to them all. Emily, Daniel, and Lucy replacement siblings for Ollie. The kids a replacement for their new guardian.

A family of replacements.

Yet despite that, Emily had found people she could love. Replacement didn't have to mean *bad*. It just meant... different.

And she knew for certain that she didn't want to have to find replacements in her life again, especially not so soon. She wanted this to stick. For all of them to be together.

Though it took a long while, sleep eventually claimed Emily. She dreamt of her parents again.

CHAPTER
TWENTY-SIX

After waiting for a few hours, Eleanore silently crept through the house and checked on each child, carefully unlocking each door as quietly as she could before peeking inside. They had all been asleep.

That was good. But it also meant she needed to use this moment to push through right to the end.

No turning back, no more putting it off. Tonight is the night.

She was sitting on her bed, her face a mess of tears as she cried in silence.

First, she had to go back down beneath the cellar. There, she could take the final step—rubedo, the reddening. After that... well... then she intended to speed things up.

However, even the thought of it made her sick and forced even more tears from her. Her body shook. She couldn't help but think about Lucy standing up to Ollie, how much passion she'd shown. And of Emily's heartfelt apology exactly when Eleanore had needed to hear it. That girl certainly had great empathy. She also thought of Ollie

—for all he went against Eleanore, he was just standing up for those he loved, something she couldn't help but admire. He was their protector. Selfless—even if he didn't always think things through. And poor Daniel, shy and reserved, and as quiet and deep as an undisturbed well.

All such beautiful souls. Could she really do it?

It's for them, she told herself. *You have to see it through.*

Though... Eleanore knew that wasn't the whole story. It was very much for *her* as well.

She continued to cry in silence.

CHAPTER
TWENTY-SEVEN

'**O**llie!'
 The boy was violently shaken. Another panicked cry came. 'Ollie!'

Not only was Ollie being shaken, but he was also forcefully dragged up into a sitting position. 'Wake up!'

It was Daniel.

Ollie was completely disoriented. However, he managed to squint over at the other boy. Daniel stood next to Ollie's bed, a look of sheer terror etched on his face, which was illuminated by the dull glow of Ollie's nightlight.

A sinking feeling grew in Ollie's gut.

'What's wrong?' he asked, still dazed, but forcing his legs out of bed. He noticed an odd smell in the room.

'I think there's a fire!'

Ollie froze. 'A... *what?*'

Daniel yanked at the boy and pulled him up from the bed. 'A fire!' Daniel repeated and pointed over to the door. That's when Ollie saw it: flickering light around the edges of his door, accompanied by smoke slowly drifting in through the gaps. *That's what the smell is.* There was also a distant crackling sound.

Oh no!

'We have to get to the others!' Ollie stated, his mind springing into action. He ran over to the door and yanked it.

'They're locked,' Daniel said. '*All* the ones to the corridor are, remember? I had to run through them all just to get in here. We're stuck!'

'Do you know what happened?' Ollie asked. 'How it started or... *anything?*'

Daniel shook his head. 'No. I had a nightmare and woke up. Then... I smelled something funny. That's when I realised what it was.'

Ollie shook the door again in desperation. Eventually, he let go of the handle and stepped back. 'Okay,' he said, taking a breath that was thick with the smell of smoke. 'We need a plan. Eleanore has the keys. So, we have to wake her and get her to let us out.' He then looked up to the ceiling, took in a deeper breath, and bellowed: 'Eleanore! Eleanore, wake up! Eleanoooore!'

Daniel joined in as well, with both boys continuously screaming up at the ceiling. At first, there was no response. Then, a muffled voice called back down from directly above. It was Emily.

'What's happening?' came her faint voice.

'Fire!' Ollie cried out.

There was a moment of silence. 'Fire?' the confused voice yelled back.

'Yes!' Ollie screamed. 'Wake Eleanore up! She has to let us out!'

After a few more moments, he heard Emily start to yell for Eleanore, accompanied by banging on the walls.

While the girl above continued to try to alert the older woman, Ollie looked around, not content to just rely on that one course of action. His eyes settled on the window. *If I can climb down, maybe I can break a window and get back inside.* From there, he knew he could head up to Eleanore's room and wake the woman himself. Or, if something had happened, get the keys to let the others out.

'I'm going to climb down,' Ollie said to Daniel.

'You're... *what?*' Daniel replied in shock. 'But the wall is covered in thorns. And if you fall, you could... you could die.'

Ollie considered this, but shook his head. 'We're only one floor up. If I fall, it would hurt, but I don't think I'd die —I'd just land on the porch roof. Besides, we can't just wait around. I'm gonna get back inside and come let everyone out.'

He walked quickly to the window. Even before he got there, he could see an orange glow wash up from outside. When close to the glass, he gazed down and saw the flickering light was spilling out from the windows beneath, illuminating the immediate area outside the house.

Ollie tried to slide the window up. It came a little way, but was stopped by the restrictor fitted to it, leaving only a few inches of space. He realised he should have expected that—the restrictors had been in place as long as Ollie had been there. A safety measure, according to Eleanore, to stop anyone from opening the windows too far and falling out.

There has to be a way to disable it.

The boy ran his hand across the window frame and found a long metal latch set into the sash casing. He fumbled with it, tilting his head to look down, but couldn't figure it out.

'Let me try,' Daniel said. Ollie stepped aside and let the

younger boy work. Daniel didn't look at what he was doing, simply cocked his head and gazed to the side as he let his fingers feel their way across the latch. Then...

Click.

Daniel smiled and pulled the window all the way up, which made the crackling grow louder.

'Good work,' Ollie said with a wave of relief, immensely grateful Daniel's mind worked the way it did. *Because God knows how long it would have taken* me *to figure it out.*

'There was a small release button a little farther up,' Daniel explained.

Both boys then peered outside. The night air that rolled back in was refreshing, which only made Ollie realise just how polluted with smoke the bedroom was. Both he and Daniel then pushed their heads out a little farther.

It's a long way down, Ollie realised. *Even to the porch roof.* His stomach tied itself into a knot. The amount of orange light that spilled out from the porch windows indicated the fire had spread inside the small space as well.

What happens if I fall through into the fire?

Ollie gritted his teeth together. Dangerous or not, he knew he had to go, just to make sure the others were safe. He could still hear Emily shouting from above, and a second later realised Lucy had joined in as well.

'I'm going to climb down with you,' Daniel stated with grim determination.

Ollie turned to him. 'You don't have to,' he said. 'Just wait here and I'll let you out. I promise. I won't run away and leave you all behind or anything.'

'I know,' Daniel said. 'You'd never do that. But if there are two of us climbing down, that way... if one of us falls and hurts ourself, the other can still get the girls and Eleanore free.'

Ollie smiled and patted Daniel on the shoulder. 'See,' he said. 'I always knew you were brave. I'll go first, though, okay?'

'Okay,' Daniel agreed.

Ollie then took a breath and turned to gaze back down below once more. Smoke billowed past him to the outside air. *That's probably a good thing,* Ollie told himself. *Help stop the house from getting clogged up.*

He then thought about the smoke rising farther up to the girls. With that in mind, he stepped back and yelled up to them. 'Emily! Lucy! Open your windows!' He took a deeper breath. 'Open your windows!' he screamed again. 'It'll help with the smoke!'

'Okay!' he eventually heard Emily shout back down. *She must be so scared,* he thought to himself, remembering how her parents had died.

The thought gave Ollie renewed determination; he ran over to his wardrobe and pulled out some trainers, quickly laced them to his feet, and threw on some jeans as well as a coat over the t-shirt he was wearing. It was less about warding off the cold and more about not getting cut up by thorns on his way down.

'Put something on yourself,' Ollie said, throwing some clothes over to Daniel. 'Saves running around to your room again.'

'Will they fit?' Daniel asked.

'Well enough for what we need,' Ollie told him.

When Daniel was ready, both boys approached the window again. Ollie turned side-on and sat on the windowsill, pushing his hip outwards, ready to swing his legs over the lip.

'Be careful,' Daniel said. 'Here, let me help lower you down.'

'Thanks,' Ollie said. He took hold of Daniel's outstretched hand, then twisted his body to allow his legs to move out into the open air. Once in position, he gripped the windowsill with his free hand and lowered himself a little as he tried to blindly find purchase with his feet.

After a couple of moments with no luck, he looked down, doing his best to ignore the drop and instead try to spot a suitable foothold. He couldn't really see anything he could use.

Eventually, Ollie tried pushing one of his feet in through the wall planting—thorns scraped at his calf. There, his toe found a tiny ledge, the top of a protruding brick edge, and pressed down. It wasn't much, but it was something. However, climbing down seemed like an impossible task, since there was simply nothing else to grab onto.

He considered using just the planters themselves to hold on to, thinking he could wrap his hands in the sleeve of his jacket for protection and climb down that way, ignoring the pain and scratches.

The orange light that spilled from the porch windows was incredibly strong, and the cracking—now rumbling— of the fire was terrifying.

Sounds like it's an inferno.

The boy lowered himself down a little more, and he had to stop his body from shaking.

'Ollie,' Daniel suddenly warily from above.

Ollie gazed up, immediately noticing the constant stream of smoke that billowed out from around the boy. Daniel was wide-eyed, pointing down and just ahead, deeper into the front garden. Ollie followed his hand and his breath caught in his throat.

There were more of those things.

A cluster of six of them stood just at the edge of the light, merely... watching—watching Ollie, watching the house, watching everything. He could even make out the mass of glinting eyes on each of their faces.

Ollie's body locked in shock at seeing them—his foot slipped and he felt his body drop. He gripped Daniel's hand tightly and his fingers dug into the windowsill as he let out a yelp of shock.

In an instant, he felt Daniel's other hand grab the collar of Ollie's coat. 'Hold on!' the boy shouted.

Ollie's legs kicked and dangled helplessly.

I'm gonna fall, he thought to himself in panic. He couldn't help but glance down again in horror.

Then, a thought struck him: *Maybe I should let go. It's one way down. The quickest.* He reasoned that the fall probably wouldn't kill him, and he just needed to make sure he didn't wind up so hurt he couldn't keep going. Ollie knew it was a stupid idea, but climbing down would take a *long* time, and it was clear from the loud roaring of the fire that time was something they just did not have.

'Let go of me, Daniel,' Ollie said, still looking down, trying to ignore the things that still stared at him.

'What?' Daniel shouted in shock. 'You'll fall!'

'I need to get down faster,' Ollie replied. 'I'll be fine.' He looked up and forced a smile. 'Don't worry, I bounce well enough, so it won't hurt. Nothing to worry about.' He gave a laugh that he tried to make sound genuine, but it came out nervous. Daniel just shook his head.

'That's *stupid*,' he said and gripped Ollie's hand ever tighter. 'I'm not letting go.' The boy tried pulling Ollie back up, straining with his teeth clenched, but simply didn't have the strength.

'Daniel, it isn't that far to the porch roof,' Ollie argued.

'What if you go *through* the roof?' Daniel shouted back.

Ollie looked down again. He had no idea how strong the roof was, so it was certainly possible. Then, he heard glass shatter. Flames erupted from both the left and right of the porch. He imagined crashing through the roof and falling right into the flames. In panic, Ollie suddenly swivelled his head back up. 'You're right!' he shouted back. *What was I thinking?* 'It's a stupid idea. Pull me back up!'

Ollie began to kick frantically, trying to find his footing again. He felt one trainer come loose and fall free, followed by stinging scratches across the top of that foot.

'Ollie, you're—you're slipping!' Daniel said, panicked.

'I... I know,' Ollie replied. His body inched lower as Daniel's grip started to falter.

In that moment, Ollie knew with certainty he was going to fall. And it was all his own doing for being so bull-headed again. He just prayed the flat roof of the porch was strong enough to hold his weight.

Given he could see the surface of the roof bubble and blister, Ollie didn't hold out much hope.

He slipped farther down, hearing some kind of commotion above. Ollie took a breath, waiting for the inevitable.

Yet just as his body started to drop, another pair of hands grabbed him. Stronger this time, and they arrested his fall in an instant.

Ollie's head snapped back up, where he saw Eleanore leaning out of the window beside Daniel, arms outstretched, holding on to Ollie's jacket at the neck and shoulder.

The woman gave a roar of exertion and Ollie felt himself heaved upwards. It was enough that he was able to take hold of the windowsill himself with both hands. The older woman kept pulling until Ollie finally rolled back inside, where he dropped to the floor, filled with a wave of relief.

He coughed, the thick smoke inside the room in stark contrast to the night air outside. Eleanore squatted down next to Ollie, placing her hands on his shoulder again.

'Ollie, are you okay?' she asked, sounding frantic.

Ollie nodded and noticed Emily and Lucy were standing close by as well, both huddled together in their nightgowns.

Both looked terrified.

Lucy had her locket gripped tightly in one hand, the thin chain necklace pulled taut.

'What... What happened?' Ollie asked her. 'Why is there a fire?'

'I don't know!' Eleanore replied as she pulled Ollie to his feet. 'Lucy and Emily woke me. I'm... I'm so sorry I locked you all in. I shouldn't have done that.' She looked at each of them, eyes wet. 'I'm so sorry.'

'We need to get outside,' Ollie said. He truly believed she *was* sorry—he could hear the genuine, terrified regret in her voice—but now wasn't the time for apologies. It was time to escape. 'Is everyone alright?' he asked the girls. They looked scared and confused, which was no surprise at all.

'I think so?' Emily said.

'How do we get out?' Lucy asked. She cast a worried look back at the now-open door. 'The fire downstairs sounds... sounds...' She trailed off.

'I know,' Eleanore said. She turned everyone to face each other in a tight huddle and held her arms around them, encircling them all. 'Now listen, all of you. I don't know what happened or how it started, but I'm going to get you free. I need you all to be brave, stay close together, and just follow me. Understand?'

'We're going downstairs, aren't we?' Emily asked with hesitation.

Eleanore gave a slow nod.

'No!' Lucy exclaimed. 'We can't. The *fire* is down there! There has to be another way!'

'I don't think there is, sweetie,' Eleanore said. 'But don't worry. Like I said, stay together and we'll be out before you know it. I promise.'

'We'll need the key,' Daniel said. Eleanore turned to him with a raised eyebrow. 'For the front door. It's an old-style lock, so we'll need to get the key from the kitchen.'

'The back door doesn't need a key,' Emily replied. 'It's just a few bolts, so we can get out that way.'

'I have all the keys on me,' Eleanore then said. She shook the side of her dressing gown and Ollie heard the clinking of metal come from within one of the pockets. 'I grabbed everything earlier when I got the keys to the other rooms. I just wanted to keep them all on me.'

'But we can't get through a fire!' Lucy exclaimed.

Eleanore bent her head lower and laid a hand on the young girl's shoulder. 'Keep holding your locket tight, dear,' she said. 'I promise you, we'll all be fine. It will be hot and loud down there, but we'll be safe outside before you know it.'

'But... what will happen to the *house?*' Lucy asked, eyes sad.

The house is gone, Ollie knew, though he didn't say it.

'Someone will notice the fire,' Emily gently told the younger girl. 'It'll be really bright in the night, so someone will phone the fire brigade, I'm sure. Hopefully they'll get here and put it out before it spreads too far.'

Ollie knew the older girl was just placating Lucy, but he was glad of it. Anything to get them moving. Besides, the point about someone seeing the fire and alerting the authorities was probably true. Ollie just wasn't sure there'd be much left to salvage by the time they got there.

Lucy's eyes held Emily's gaze. The younger girl was obviously sceptical, but she nodded regardless.

'Okay,' Eleanore went on. 'Is everyone ready? Because we really need to move.'

The kids gave each other quick, worried glances.

'We're ready,' Ollie finally said. 'I'll stay at the back. Everyone follow Eleanore, understand?' His eyes settled on the youngest girl again. 'I'll make sure you're all alright.'

Lucy gave him a grateful, tight-lipped smile.

'Come on, then,' Eleanore said as she moved forward, looking back to make sure everyone followed. Emily and Lucy stayed close to the guardian, with Daniel just behind them and Ollie taking up his position at the rear. They were packed closely together, except for Ollie, with the oldest boy deliberately leaving a couple of feet between them so he could see what was coming ahead.

The group progressed as one, with Eleanore leading them swiftly out into the mid-floor corridor, which was flooded with smoke. Ollie felt it tickle his throat and chest with every breath.

The doorway to the stairs was open, allowing orange light to stream through and illuminate most of the corridor; thick plumes of dark smoke floated out and rose up to the ceiling. The sound of the fire below was a roar.

'It's so loud,' Lucy exclaimed.

'I know,' Eleanore said, 'but try to ignore it.'

The group paced quickly over to the stairs. En-route, it occurred to Ollie that the stairwell might well be an impassable inferno, and if it was... then what? There wasn't any other way out. *Not without dropping out of a window.*

As they entered the stairwell, however, he could see the way down was relatively safe, though thick smoke still drifted upwards, obscuring some of their view.

'Let's go,' Eleanore said, sounding uncertain. Even so, she set off quickly down the stairs. Everyone followed, keeping pace and packing themselves close together. As they hit the half landing, Ollie could see the conflagration through the open door at the bottom—the leaping flames looked taller than the children.

Ollie's chest tightened.

'I can't go down there!' Lucy suddenly shouted. She dropped to her rear on one of the steps and hugged herself, wide eyes looking down at the flames. Eleanore quickly crouched down and took hold of the girl's shoulders.

'Yes you can, Lucy,' she said. 'You're stronger than you think.'

'But I don't *want* to!' Lucy shouted back. 'I... I don't want this place to burn down. I want it to be okay.' The girl started to sob. 'I don't want to leave.'

'I know, sweetie,' Eleanore said. 'But we can't stay here. It isn't safe. You know that. We just have to get outside, then we can get help. Everything else will just... work itself out.'

'But I don't *want* it to,' Lucy went on, her head dropping as her voice cracked on the last word. The small girl's body shook amidst her sobs. Though there wasn't much room on the stairs, the other three children moved closer to Lucy and they all enveloped her in a hug.

'It's okay, Luce,' Emily said. 'Everything will be fine. I promise.'

'You don't *know* that,' Lucy replied. 'We might all get split up when we get out.'

'Don't think like that,' Daniel said. 'We'll all still be together.'

But Lucy shook her head. 'We won't. I know we won't.' Ollie noticed the girl was gripping her locket so hard her knuckles were going white—it was also getting harder and harder to breathe on the stairs.

We can't stay here.

He leaned forward and gently placed his forehead against the back of Lucy's head. 'I need to get you out of here, Sis,' he said. It was the first time he'd used that word, yet it didn't feel weird. 'When we're out,' he went on, 'we can figure everything else out together. But I won't let anyone split us up.' He then wrapped his arms around Lucy from behind and hugged her tight. 'But we can't do any of that if we stay here and suffocate. So please, come on. Let's get out of here. All of us. Together.'

Lucy eventually lifted her head. Her eyes and cheeks were wet, but she was smiling. 'You called me—'

'I know,' Ollie said, grinning as he gave her a squeeze. 'It felt right. So... what do you say? Should we get moving?'

Lucy nodded, still smiling, and everyone helped her back up to her feet. There was a smattering of coughing from the group as they descended closer to the ground floor. When they reached the doorway, Ollie was struck by the wave of heat that enveloped him.

Eleanore held up an arm in front of her face as if to ward off the heat and moved through, beckoning everyone else to follow once she was out into the entrance hallway.

Just as the children moved through the open doorway, Lucy suddenly stopped mid-step with a jolt—the right-hand-side of her gown had gotten caught on the strike plate in the door frame.

She quickly yanked at the gown and Ollie thought he heard it rip. She yanked again in panic, but couldn't get the gown free. Emily then reached a hand out and quickly unsnagged the girl before offering a quick smile.

'Come on!' Eleanore urged them from the hallway. The children quickly moved out towards her, forcing their way through the wall of heat.

Daniel gave a gasp of horror when they emerged; all the children had to shield their eyes, wincing as they observed the fiery chaos around them.

The flames were everywhere.

The blaze was more intense to the back of the hallway, and the dining room looked to be completely engulfed from what Ollie could see. But there was still plenty of danger out in the entrance hallway. In fact, as Ollie turned his head, he realised they had been lucky to emerge through the stairwell door when they had—the fire was creeping along the walls ever closer to it, now almost on top of it. Any longer and their escape route would have been blocked.

'Come on,' Eleanore shouted again over the crackling and roaring. 'Stick close together.'

The children all instinctively squeezed themselves nearer to each other, tightening up their huddle. The moment was so intense, Ollie felt like breaking down and crying as his heart hammered in his chest.

It's so hot!

It was insanely bright as well. The long rug in the centre of the hallway had caught fire, kicking up smoke in the blaze. When Ollie looked up, he saw the flames were even spreading across the ceiling. Thankfully, there was space around the perimeter rug between it and the walls, so the group could pass in relative safety without being consumed by the fire.

Unless the ceiling caves in, Ollie thought ominously.

But despite there being an unobstructed route to it, the main entrance itself was surrounded by flames. In fact, it looked horribly warped, with large gaps around its edges. The fire had obviously gotten through those gaps—even at that distance, Ollie could see flames inside the porch. He cast a look back to the dining room once more, briefly considering that the rear door might be the safer route. But things were even more intense through there. It actually looked as if the fire had started in that direction somewhere.

'We can't get through!' Lucy shouted, pointing ahead to the porch. Her other hand still gripped her locket, shaking terribly. Ollie noticed the chain was pulled so tight it was digging into Lucy's skin on the back of her neck.

'Wait here!' Eleanore called. 'I'm going to unlock it and make sure we can get through.'

Ollie put his arm around the younger girl as Eleanore ran off to the door while fishing around in her gown pocket. Ollie glanced around the room again. Some of the windows were ruined, with the glass shattered in many places and wooden frames fully ablaze. If the door was a no-go, the windows *might* be an option, though it was far from ideal.

Lucy began to cry again. Her face screwed up into anger.

'It'll be okay, Luce,' Ollie said, resting a hand on her shoulder. The hand holding her locket was still shaking, more and more, until finally...

Snap.

The chain broke, pinging free just behind Lucy's neck. The girl looked down at the locket in her hand in shock. 'No!' she cried, staring at the chain that dangled from either side of her fist. 'No! I can't have broken it, I *can't* have!'

'Don't worry,' Emily said to her, lowering her head to match Lucy's eye level. 'We can fix the chain. Just keep the locket safe.'

Lucy continued to gaze down at the locket, tears flowing down her cheeks.

Suddenly, a screeching sound caused everyone to look back up. Ollie saw Eleanore wrestling with the warped door, trying to force it open while dancing flames licked at her arms and face. Even from that distance he saw the key in the lock, but it turned out unlocking the door had only been half the battle.

'Wait here!' he ordered the others and ran towards Eleanore to help. As he approached, he saw she already had the key to the outer door ready, gripped between two fingers.

'Stay back,' Eleanore warned as Ollie arrived. He noticed she had one of her hands tucked into her sleeve as it gripped the edge of the door with it, pulling at the door. The exposed hand that held the key also yanked at the door, and the area of skin that pressed against the wood was red.

The flames from inside the porch jumped out, the heat now almost unbearable.

Ollie tucked his own hands into his sleeves and took hold of the door as well, feeling the heat seep through the material. He heaved along with the older woman, but it was difficult to force the buckled door open any more than the half a foot it had already come. The warped outer edge of the bottom of the door was wedged against the floor. Ollie yanked and yanked, feeling the heat around him grow. The flames from inside the porch snaked out farther, coming close to his face, but Ollie didn't relent.

'Ollie, go back with the others!' Eleanore shouted at him.

'You can't do it on your own!' he yelled back and kept going, eyes closed, grunting with exertion. He yanked and heaved and struggled, giving everything he had to force the door open. Through it all, the boy kept images of Lucy, Emily, and Daniel at the forefront of his mind.

He also thought of his sister, Grace. He'd failed her, but he wouldn't fail the others.

The images gave him even more drive, and he and Eleanore began to heave the door repeatedly, yank after yank, now both in step with each other. The door shunted and moved. Then again. And again.

Finally, to Ollie's eternal relief, the door was open wide enough to fit through. Of course, the external door to the enclosed outer porch still remained. If that one had gotten stuck as well, things would be more difficult given the leaping flames that clung to the porch walls.

'Get the others,' Eleanore shouted as she dashed through and got to work on the next lock. Ollie saw some of the flames take hold of the woman's gown at the hem.

'Eleanore!' he called. She didn't listen and continued with the lock. Ollie soon heard a *click* a moment before Eleanore swung the door open with little effort, allowing a blast of night air to wash in. The flames jumped in response, coming closer to Eleanore, almost washing over her face, but the woman managed to duck out of the way just in time.

She turned to him. 'Get the others!'

Ollie nodded but pointed to the bottom of her gown, where the fire had begun spreading upwards. Eleanore's eyes widened. She quickly slipped from the garment and threw it aside. Ollie didn't wait any longer and ran back to the other three.

'It's open!' he shouted and beckoned them to move. He quickly shepherded them over to Eleanore, who was now standing back inside the main hall, waiting for them.

'We're going to sprint through,' she declared in a loud voice. 'Don't think about anything. Just run. Okay?' After a second, she stepped aside. 'Go! Now!'

She then patted both Emily and Lucy on the backs.

'I don't want—' Lucy began.

'Just follow me, Lucy,' Emily told her, holding out her hand. 'I've got you.' She tugged at the girl. Lucy hesitated, turning her pleading eyes to Emily. Emily just smiled in response. 'I'll keep you safe, Luce, always,' she said.

Lucy gave a shaky nod and turned her eyes forward. A look of determination washed over her. 'Okay,' she said. The girl then dropped her locket into her right-hand gown pocket and took hold of Emily's hand.

'Show me how fast you are, Sis,' Emily said. 'See if you can beat me out there!'

A smile crossed Lucy's lips. 'Just try to keep up,' she said.

Both girls then ran.

Lucy moved ahead, pulling Emily with her, and the two weaved past the first door and out into the porch. While the fire was stronger there, neither girl broke their stride, and within moments they were out into the night.

Thank God, Ollie thought with relief.

'Now you two,' Eleanore said to Ollie and Daniel. 'Be quick.'

Ollie cast a look at Daniel. The poor boy looked terrified. Before he could encourage the younger boy though, Ollie heard an ominous creak come from the roof of the porch.

'Now!' Eleanore shouted.

Ollie was about to grab Daniel to force him onward, to not give the boy a chance to hesitate, but was shocked when Daniel actually grabbed and pulled *him* instead.

Both boys sprinted. The roof of the porch groaned again. They didn't stop.

Ollie felt a blast of heat as they ducked past the inner door. Flames jumped up at his face, but he remained focused on the way forward. There was yet another creak from above. Ollie tensed.

Both boys then leapt through the outer door, not stopping until they crashed into the waiting Lucy and Emily. Everyone spilled to the ground in a tangle of bodies, faces stained with soot and sweat.

Ollie quickly turned his head back to see Eleanore making her way through as well. His eyes turned upwards —the roof of the porch was fully ablaze. It creaked again. He held his breath.

Don't cave in.

Just when he thought the whole thing was about to come down on her, Eleanore made it outside. The porch held.

The woman then swooped over to the children and embraced them all, sobbing and panting.

'We need to get away from the house,' Ollie said, urging everyone back up. 'Just to be safe.' When others nodded agreement, he ushered the group deeper down the drive.

They trotted as one along the gravel and eventually

came to a stop, utterly exhausted, gulping in huge breaths, bent double with hands on knees.

'Sit,' Eleanore told them, pointing at the grass off to the side. She guided them over and everyone dropped down close to each other. Eleanore knelt down behind them all, arms around Ollie and Emily, with Daniel and Lucy wedged in the centre. Lucy was sobbing.

Ollie felt Eleanore squeeze them all tighter.

He looked back up to Erimus House, which continued to burn.

CHAPTER
TWENTY-EIGHT

Emily didn't know what to say. It seemed none of them did.

They all squished themselves close together to help ward off the cold night. The heat from the blazing house helped a little, but they weren't close enough to get much of it.

Lucy continued to sob. Emily kept her arm around the younger girl, rubbing her back. After hearing a small sniffle from behind, Emily glanced back and saw Eleanore was in floods of tears as well, though she was crying mostly silently.

Emily felt for the older woman. The home she had cultivated for all of them was now being destroyed, scorched to ashes right in front of their very eyes.

'What will happen to us now?' Lucy asked. Her small, sad voice broke Emily's heart.

'I... don't,' Eleanore began, then tried to clear her throat. 'I don't know, sweetheart.'

'We're going to be taken away, aren't we.' It wasn't a question.

A slow nod. 'I think so,' Eleanore admitted.

'Will we all be able to stay together?'

'I hope so,' Eleanore replied. 'I really do.'

'Can the house be fixed?' Daniel asked. 'You know, rebuilt? If they stop the fire in time, so the structure isn't too badly damaged, then maybe—'

'I honestly don't know, Daniel,' Eleanore said. 'I wish I did.'

Lucy's sobbing increased, so Emily hugged her again.

As Emily looked back up to the house, she saw the fire was spreading upstairs, with its light flickering out through the windows. And there, in Ollie's bedroom, Emily spotted the silhouette of a figure looking back out.

It's one of those things, she realised, feeling her eyes widen. She raised her hand.

'I see it,' Ollie said.

Lucy lifted her head, paused, then lowered it again. 'They wouldn't have hurt us, you know,' she said.

'Do you see it too?' Ollie asked Eleanore.

There was a long, *long* pause. 'I do,' she finally said.

'What will happen to the ghosts?' Lucy asked.

'I don't know, Lucy,' Eleanore replied. 'I don't even know that they *are* ghosts. I don't know what they are.'

Despite the strange sight in the house, there didn't seem to be any fear among the group, as far as Emily could tell. She wasn't really scared either. There was only a tired, resigned feeling about the future.

As everyone stared at the house, Emily was certain she heard sirens in the distance. For the longest time, no one said anything.

'If we can put the house back together,' Eleanore finally began. 'Like Daniel said, then... would you all come back?'

'Yes!' Lucy quickly replied. 'Of course. We all would, right?'

The other three nodded as well. Emily herself didn't hesitate, despite what was currently on the middle floor watching them. She realised it was because she felt Lucy was right about those things. After all, nothing had actually happened to any of the children, despite the presence of the entities. *They won't hurt us,* she told herself, as if the thought had just dawned.

'And what if you were all a little older?' Eleanore went on. 'If I called you, would you still come back to see me? Come see each other?'

'Of course,' Daniel said.

'Promise me, then,' Eleanore continued, her voice almost dreamlike.

'We promise,' Emily replied. She realised she was a little light-headed, which wasn't surprising given the amount of smoke she'd inhaled.

Their guardian gave a sad smile and hugged them all tighter as she cried.

Emily felt Ollie, Daniel, and Lucy press into her, Eleanore squeezing them all. The girl closed her eyes, enjoying the feeling of the others being so close to her. Being right... there.

NOW...

CHAPTER
TWENTY-NINE

Emily stood before the main door of the house, butterflies in her stomach, hands with a slight tremble. It was an excited nervousness mixed with apprehension.

The house seemed empty, with no lights on as far as she could tell, and no sounds coming from within.

She raised her hand and knocked on the enclosed porch door. Then she waited. After a second, Emily cast her eyes around the front of the house. The windows were just like she remembered, and she wondered if they had been repaired after the fire or if they'd been replaced outright. The climbing wall-plants were present, thicker than before, and she wondered if they were still laced with thorns.

The now-barely-perceptible scar on her palm tingled as if responding to her thoughts.

Taking in a breath, Emily knocked again. She cast her eyes up to the darkening sky. It would be night soon. If no answer came, did that mean she'd need to leave? She was exhausted, and the thought of the long trip back home was *not* appealing.

She rubbed her eyes. They felt dry, like her eyeballs were lined with sand. She ran her hand down to the front of her neck, which was tingling again, and she rubbed it, trying to extinguish the dry tickle.

She knocked a third time.

Eventually, realisation sunk in, creating a lead ball in her stomach that flattened the butterflies.

No one is here.

A wasted trip. But more than that... she wouldn't get to see them again. To Emily's surprise, the thought almost made her tear up.

She sighed, then looked down at the door handle and cocked her head. *I wonder.*

Emily reached out a hand, feeling the cool brass of the handle on her palm. She paused, turned, then pushed.

The door opened.

She watched it drift farther into the entrance vestibule, a confused frown on her face. *Why would it be open too?*

The heavier inner door opposite her still stood closed. *Surely that's not unlocked as well?*

But after stepping inside, she found that door also swung inwards with a long *creak*. The space before her was dark, but the dim light from outside pushed the shadows back around the entrance. The sight of the entrance hall from decades ago, again just as she remembered, caused her to pause.

'Hello?' Emily eventually called out. Her voice echoed down the entrance hall. No response, but as she gazed into the darkness, memories of first seeing that hallway flooded back. She remembered walking through it along with the others, at the time flooded with a sense of awe. It had been so different, so much more grand than what she had been used to.

Emily was taller now, of course, making the space seem less imposing but no less impressive.

'Hello?' she said again and stepped fully inside. A strong breeze rolled in behind her, sending a shudder through her. She closed the door, the resulting *thud* echoing down the wide hall.

Once the sound faded, she was left with a heavy silence. Something felt wrong. Off. Like it was *too* quiet. Then she remembered that the space had always been filled with the ticking from the long-case clock. While the clock was still standing at the side of the space, it made no sound. *Must be broken,* she thought, though was still amazed it had survived the fire.

'Hello!'

She called out louder this time, hoping someone was there. *Surely there* has *to be if everything is unlocked.*

But no one showed themselves. No one called down from upstairs.

What's going on?

It occurred to Emily that perhaps she was just the first to arrive. *But no, that wouldn't make sense,* she realised. Even if she was the first of the four to arrive, there still should have been someone waiting to let them all in, someone to greet them: Eleanore, if she was still alive, or someone else.

The one who had called them back in the first place.

Called me *back,* Emily then told herself. *You don't know that the others got the same message.*

She wondered if she should search the house, just to be sure she was alone, then idly strolled through towards the dining space, stopping just outside of it to look in. More memories flooded back. She stared at the furniture.

They've restored everything, she realised.

Her eyes then drifted over to the door to the cellar, where a padlock was in place again.

Her brow furrowed in confusion. *The cellar is still blocked off?*

She remembered what Ollie had told her all those years ago, about finding a hatch down there to an even lower level, and what he said was looking back up at him.

She'd seen one herself on the night of the fire, while they all huddled on the grass outside.

She glanced around the room.

Are they still here in the building now? she wondered.

A creeping sensation rose in her gut. As did the temptation to leave.

Instead, Emily wandered back to the main hall, and then—almost on autopilot—headed over to the staircase. She looked up the flight of stairs, suddenly longing to see her own room.

She crept up the steps and came out onto the mid-floor hallway. Once there, she immediately noticed all the doors were closed. She cast glances over to Ollie and Daniel's rooms. There was a temptation to see what the bedrooms looked like now, but she resisted, feeling like it was wrong looking in their rooms without them there. She smiled as she remembered the rule about knocking before entering from decades ago.

Continuing her exploration, Emily ventured to the top floor and moved to stand between her own and Lucy's room. Just like below, all the doors on that level were closed, including the one to Eleanore's room.

But Emily focused on the door to her old room. Apprehension filled her as she reached for the handle. *I wonder if the rooms have changed much?*

Though she remembered she hadn't actually changed

too much herself back in the day, leaving it pretty much as it had been when she'd moved in.

Emily held her breath and opened the door. A flood of nostalgia and melancholy hit her as she entered and took in the details.

No way!

She started to tremble, sinking under the wave of memories. She gazed at her bed, ran a hand over the duvet. She even sat down on it to feel it sink under her. It felt familiar. *So* familiar.

Like home.

Emily lay down on her side, head sinking into the pillow, tears running from her eyes.

It felt like she was finally back where she belonged. Strange, considering she'd only lived there for less than a year as a child. But Erimus House had been important to her. The people who *lived* there had been important.

They had been family.

The exhaustion she felt was building, mixing in with the emotion that surged through her. She closed her eyes as she remembered the past, remembered her happy life there.

It didn't take Emily long to drop into a deep sleep.

CHAPTER
THIRTY

When Emily opened her eyes again, it was completely dark, to the point she struggled to see the hand she brought before her face. She reached over towards the nightstand and fumbled for the switch, which she eventually found. Red light bloomed from the space just beside her. After blinking a few times in confusion, she realised the lampshade—which looked as she remembered—must have some kind of red filter on it now, which was more than a little odd.

She sat up in bed and looked over at the window. It was completely dark outside, so she could see nothing but black beyond the glass.

How long did I sleep?!

She quickly stood and walked up to the window, peering out, yet there was no light at all—not even moonlight.

Emily heard a door open and froze.

The sound was distant, down on the middle floor at her best guess. She quickly walked to her door, opened it, and peered out, seeing the corridor was utterly dark as well.

Though she found a light switch, she frowned—the light that flooded the hallway was red again.

Why would they use red lampshades everywhere?

'Hello?' she called out as she walked over to the stairs. 'Is anyone there?'

She paused when she heard someone running on the floor below.

Whoever it was sounded small; the quick footfalls ran down the next flight of stairs to the ground floor.

What the...

After forcing herself to move, Emily descended to the next floor down, emerging onto the mid-floor again. She saw that the light was on—red again—and the doors to both Ollie and Daniel's rooms were open.

Someone was standing in the doorway to Daniel's room, looking back out at her, bathed in red hallway light.

'Oh,' Emily said, drawing to a stop, body tensing. She suddenly wondered if this man—who seemed just as surprised to see her as she was to see him—had been there the whole time, or if he'd entered while she was napping. She guessed it was the latter.

Unless he was sleeping as well.

The stranger was a similar height to Emily and had a kind face, brown eyes with thick crow's feet at the sides, a trimmed beard, and hair in a loose side parting. While most of his hair and beard were brown, there were swathes of grey, and Emily guessed the man was likely somewhere in his forties.

'How... how long have you been here?' she asked, wary.

'Erm... not long, I don't think,' the man replied. He gave a nervous, tight-lipped smile. Emily felt her eyes widen.

'D—Daniel?'

The other man's face dropped. He cocked his head to

the side. She saw realisation sweep over him. 'Wait, *Emily?*' he asked in shock.

She couldn't believe it. After all this time, she was face to face with one of them again. A swell of emotion rose up inside and she had an overwhelming desire to just lunge forward and hug him.

'I... I don't believe it!' he said, and his smile widened, reaching his eyes. 'I just don't believe it!' he then repeated and laughed. He held his arms out awkwardly. 'Do we... you know?'

Emily swept forward and embraced him, hugging Daniel tightly. 'Oh I can't believe it's you!' she said, fighting an urge to cry. 'I wasn't sure if anyone else would turn up!'

'Me either,' he replied as the tight embrace lingered. 'The house was empty when I got here a few hours ago. I shouted but... no one answered.'

Emily finally pulled away. 'Really?' she asked with a cocked eyebrow. 'I did the same. It was still light when I arrived, but the house seemed empty.'

Daniel's eyes knitted in confusion. 'Huh,' he said. 'It was still light when I got here too. Odd that we missed each other. I just... had an urge to see my room again, then lay down and... I must have passed out.'

'That's exactly what happened to me,' Emily said. 'Weird, no?'

'*Very* weird,' Daniel agreed.

Emily couldn't help but stare at her old friend. She laid a hand on his shoulder. 'Look at you,' she said. 'Shy little Daniel is all grown up.'

He laughed and nodded. 'Yeah, I guess I am,' he said. 'But it's Dan now. Daniel always seemed too... formal.' He then stepped back and gestured to Emily. 'And look at *you*. You're beautiful, Emily.'

She blushed. 'Aw, you're too kind,' Emily replied with a dismissive wave of her hand. She then moved a stray length of auburn hair that had fallen over her face.

'Shame everything looks eerie all in red,' he added, pointing up to the ceiling lights.

'Yeah,' she said. 'I really don't know what's up with that.'

'Me neither,' Dan replied. 'Not a great design choice.'

Emily glanced around the hallway. It looked eerie in the red light, but other than the hue, it was exactly as she had remembered it. Her gaze settled on Ollie's open door. She narrowed her eyes, pointing to it. 'You don't think...'

'That Ollie is here as well?' Dan asked. 'Maybe. I heard someone run downstairs. Perhaps that was him? And if so, maybe Luce is here too.'

'Yeah, I heard someone running a couple minutes ago,' Emily confirmed. 'Should... should we go see?'

Dan nodded. 'I think so.' He glanced up at the ceiling. 'Was there anyone else upstairs with you?'

'Not that I saw,' Emily replied. 'The door to Lucy's room was closed, but I didn't look in.'

'And... Eleanore's?'

'It was closed as well,' Emily confirmed. 'Though... do you think she's still alive? It's been a long time.'

'I have no idea,' Dan answered. 'But *someone* invited us back here, so... maybe. I wasn't sure if it would be just us four, or if there would be others?'

'Others?' Emily asked.

'Yeah,' Dan went on. 'I have a feeling the place might have been repaired after the fire and carried on as a children's home. I wondered if other people that spent time here would have come along as well.'

'Ah,' Emily said. 'Yeah, I'd considered the same thing, actually.'

Dan stepped farther away from his door and closed it behind him. 'I still can't believe we both passed out in our rooms,' he said as they walked over towards the stairs.

'Strange,' Emily said. 'Though... I *was* exhausted. It's been a long day. I wonder what time it is?' She checked her watch as they walked. 'Woah, ten past three in the morning,' she confirmed.

'Really?' Dan asked. 'Wow.' He then glanced at his own watch. 'Yeah, ten past three exactly.'

The pair reached the ground floor and moved out to the entrance hallway, with Emily flicking on every light she passed, each red. 'They have the whole *house* set up like that?' she asked in disbelief.

As she gazed down the length of the hallway, Emily noticed movement through the door to the dining room—a figure ducked out of view. She didn't see much, but enough to know that it was a young boy with blonde hair.

'Did you see that?' she asked Dan, quickly pointing.

'I did,' he confirmed. Dan then called out: 'Hey, are you okay?'

'Who was that?' Emily asked. Yet the boy didn't show himself, remaining hidden.

'No idea,' Dan replied. 'I mean, I'm pretty sure no kids are still living here, so I'm guessing he came along with someone.'

Emily paused. 'Ollie!' she said.

Dan turned to her and frowned. 'Ollie would be our age now, Emily.'

She rolled her eyes and shook her head. 'No, Danie— Dan. I mean, maybe the boy came along *with* Ollie. It might be his son. The blonde hair is kind of a giveaway.'

'Ah,' Dan replied, then nodded. 'That... actually makes sense. But what is he doing up and wandering around at this hour?'

'No idea,' Emily said. 'But Eleanore would have thrown a fit about that back in the day.'

Dan laughed. 'Yeah. She *really* didn't like our late-night snooping.'

Emily turned back towards the stairs. 'I wonder if that means Ollie is still up in his room? Maybe he's asleep.'

'Maybe,' Dan replied. 'But honestly... this whole thing is odd.'

'I know it is, you're right. But... I'm so glad you came.' She turned to face her old friend again. 'Seeing you after so much time, well, it's amazing.'

Dan smiled. Then the front door suddenly opened. Both Emily and Dan spun to see a woman enter.

Initially, Emily had hoped it was Lucy, but the lady that stepped through and looked up to them with surprised eyes was much older, easily in her seventies. She had grey hair that still held a few streaks of brown, her hair was parted in the middle and hung down to her shoulders, and her face was heavily lined with age, jowls on either side of her chin. Despite the woman's obvious age, her brown eyes looked alert and full of life.

'Oh,' the woman said, startled. 'Hello.' She then shivered and closed the door behind her. 'Glad to see some other people made it.'

'Erm... yeah,' Emily said as she regarded the woman, who was around half a foot shorter than Emily. 'You arrived late, huh?'

'Late?' the lady asked. 'What do you mean?'

'It's three in the morning,' Dan explained.

'Really?' The woman's eyes widened. 'I... I had no idea. So... what are you both still doing up?'

Emily and Dan shared a look. 'Long story,' Emily said. She then smiled and extended her hand. 'My name is Emily.'

'And I'm Dan,' her friend added.

The other woman's face fell in shock. Her mouth hung open. She just stared at the pair, wide-eyed, bringing a hand up to her chest.

'Emily and... Dan?' she asked. 'Dan as in... *Daniel?*'

'That's right,' Dan replied with a nod. 'And... who are you, if you don't mind me asking?'

Emily's hand was still extended before her, waiting to be shook, yet the woman just continued gazing at Emily. It felt like she was peering into her soul.

'It can't be,' the woman said, and her aged voice cracked.

'Why not?' Emily asked. 'Do you... know us?'

Tears started to spill down the old woman's face. She gave a slow nod, fighting to stop from breaking down completely.

'It's me,' she said as her bottom lip trembled. 'Lucy.'

CHAPTER
THIRTY-ONE

Dan paused, repeating the name again and again in his mind, certain he'd misheard. He *had* to have misheard.

'L—Lucy?' Emily asked, clearly just as confused as he was. 'As in, little Lucy, who lived here with us?'

The old woman nodded, eyes still wet.

'That... that isn't possible,' Dan eventually said. 'The Lucy we knew was younger than us, and you're...' He hesitated. 'I don't want to be rude, but you're obviously older. Did... did you live here with an Emily and Daniel as well? What year was that?'

Given her age, Dan assumed the woman might have lived in the house before him and the others, but that didn't make sense when he remembered that they were the first batch of children there. There *were* no others before the four of them.

'I know this doesn't make sense,' the woman said. 'I... I can't explain it. You've both grown, but I can *tell* who you are. Don't... don't you see it with me?'

Dan stared at her, remembering the little girl from his youth, then trying to imagine if that person could actually be the old woman before him. The more he looked at her, the more he realised there was a similarity.

His body grew cold.

'It can't be,' he said, shaking his head. 'There has to be some other—'

'Do you still have the scar on your hand, Emily?' the woman asked. 'From where you cut yourself on the thorns outside?'

Dan's mouth fell open. Emily slowly raised her hand to reveal a faint line across her palm.

'No...' he uttered. 'It... it can't be.' *This doesn't make sense.*

The woman gave a sad smile. 'You both still look so young,' she said. Tears continued to run down her cheeks and she hugged herself, obviously just as confused as the two of them were. In that moment, she seemed so small and scared.

It is her, he realised with uneasy acceptance.

Not giving himself a chance to think about it, he stepped forward and wrapped his arms around her, pulling Lucy in for a hug, unable to stop himself. 'Luce,' he said, his voice unbelieving. 'It... it's really you!'

'This can't be real,' came Emily's voice from beside them. 'It's a dream or something. It has to be.'

Lucy held out an arm, inviting Emily into the embrace. 'Maybe,' the older woman said. 'But *God,* I've waited so long to see you all again.'

Emily hesitated, then finally stepped forward and joined in. She began to sob. Dan felt a wash of emotion as he hugged the two women tighter.

He echoed Emily's words in his mind: *this can't be real.*

It was impossible. He knew it was. And even before seeing Lucy, too much about the whole situation was flat-out weird, from both him and Emily falling asleep in their rooms at the same time, to the red lights from every fitting in the house.

Maybe Emily was right, he considered. Maybe it *was* all a dream. His mind swam with confusion and fear, yet also with joy at seeing the girls again after so long.

A thought then struck him, and his body locked up. He suddenly remembered the blonde-haired boy he'd seen running earlier.

Dan raised his head and looked over to the dining room door; a face was peeking out from the side, the same blonde-haired boy.

And though the distance between them was too great for Dan to make him out clearly, he found himself wondering if the little boy could actually be...

'Ollie?' he called out, causing the embrace to break. The boy ducked away.

Both Emily and Lucy followed his gaze. 'Wait, Ollie?' Emily asked. 'Did you spot him? Is he here?'

'The little blonde boy we saw earlier,' Dan explained. He glanced at Lucy, then back to Emily. 'Do you think maybe...'

Emily just looked at him, clearly not understanding. Then her eyes widened, his words dawning on her. 'It can't be,' she said. 'That was just a little boy...' But then she glanced at Lucy as well.

'Ollie, is that you?' Dan called once more as he stepped forward.

The boy didn't show himself, instead remaining hidden. *It can't be him,* Dan told himself as he continued walking. Emily and Lucy fell in behind him.

'Ollie, if that is you, buddy, there's nothing to be scared of,' Dan began. 'It's us. Dan, Emily, and Lucy.'

'You're lying,' a young voice immediately called back. Upon hearing it, a flood of memories washed over Dan: thoughts of the protective older boy that had always looked out for him.

The voice was Ollie's, no question about it. It made Dan pause.

It can't *be! This is fucking insane!*

'I... I know this doesn't make a lot of sense,' he said in a gentle voice, 'but it is us. You can come out. There's nothing to be scared of.'

But Dan knew there was *lots* to be scared of. The situation was madness, and the worry that sat in his gut had started to turn to panic as his mind searched for a rational explanation.

'Who are you all? Why are you here?' the boy called out.

Dan hesitated before answering. 'I came back because of a promise to Eleanore,' he explained, continuing to take steady footsteps forward. 'And you?'

'I... don't know,' the boy replied. 'The same, I think, but... I don't know.'

'Can we see you?' Dan asked.

'You aren't who you say you are,' the boy stated firmly. 'Why are you lying? Who *are* you people? What are you really doing here?'

Though Ollie's voice was mostly steady, there was a hint of panic there.

'Ollie,' Dan said. 'It *is* us. I can't explain it, but it is. Please, just let us see you.'

Emily took a gentle hold of Dan's arm, forcing him to stop. She gave him a small smile, then looked over to the door. 'Ollie,' she began. 'I know this is scary, but we can't figure out what's going on if we can't talk to you. Please, just come out. Don't hide.'

Silence. The trio waited, all eyes fixed on the open doorway. Eventually, the boy stepped into view. Dan's breath caught in his throat.

CHAPTER
THIRTY-TWO

Lucy's hand found her mouth as she gazed in disbelief at the boy. She felt lightheaded, her legs weak, and struggled to hold herself upright.

It wasn't right.

Ollie had always been bigger than her, older, and always their protector. *Lucy* was the baby of the group, yet now she was older than all of them. On top of that, Ollie looked like he hadn't aged a day since that night.

The boy stood motionless, regarding them with wary eyes. It was obvious he was scared, but he still wasn't shirking away.

'Oh... Ollie,' Emily said, her words breathless. 'It's... it's really you.'

'You *can't* be the others,' he said firmly. 'You're too old.'

'I... I know,' Emily said. 'It doesn't make sense to us either. How... how long have you been here?'

Ollie cocked his head. 'What do you mean?'

'I mean... in the house,' Emily said. 'How long have you been here?'

The boy paused, obviously thinking. 'I don't know. I

just remember waking up in my bed, then coming out of my room when I heard someone.' He looked at Emily. 'I didn't recognise the voice, so I ran down here. I didn't know what was happening.'

'Are you okay?' Lucy asked him.

Ollie hesitated, then nodded. 'I suppose so. But I want to know who you really are, and why you're here. Where are my friends??'

Lucy gave him a sad smile. 'We *are* your friends, Ollie.'

He shook his head and folded his arms over his chest. 'No, you can't be. Stop lying.'

'I'm not,' Lucy insisted and walked out in front of the others. The boy didn't give an inch and stood defiantly even as Lucy came close. She then lowered herself down to his level, her knees aching and popping. They were still a few feet apart, but Lucy held her smile while maintaining eye contact. 'It really is me,' she said. 'It's Lucy.' She then grasped her locket between her fingers and held it up. 'Remember this?'

Ollie's body tensed and his eyes widened. 'Where did you get that?' he whispered.

'I've always had it,' she replied. 'It helped me after my parents died. But not as much as you three did.' She turned back to Emily and Daniel, then gazed at Ollie once more. 'Remember that time when you pretended to be sick, so you could stay behind at the house and try to get into the cellar? I was so *mad* at you.' She laughed as she spoke. 'God, that seems such a long time ago now.'

She saw Ollie's eyes well up. 'But... but it *wasn't* that long ago,' he said, his voice cracking.

Lucy nodded, not knowing what else to do. She held out her arms wide. 'It's okay,' she said to him. 'I know this is confusing. We're confused too.'

The boy paused; his bottom lip wobbled. 'Luce,' he eventually said in a quiet voice. 'Is it really you?'

Lucy nodded. 'It is, Ollie. The same annoying chatterbox from before.'

Ollie suddenly ran forward and flung himself into Lucy's embrace, nearly knocking the woman down to the ground in the process. She held on tightly to him, feeling him tremble as she hugged him.

'W-what's happening?' Ollie asked in a terrified voice. In an instant, the other two swooped over and crouched down close to the pair, putting their arms around Lucy and Ollie.

The group stayed like that for several minutes as the boy started to cry.

CHAPTER
THIRTY-THREE

Ollie didn't want to let go.

He couldn't understand what was going on, but he felt if he broke the embrace, then he would be forced to face their current situation, and he didn't want to do that. He didn't want to try to make sense of it.

Because he had no clue where to begin.

They all looked so different to him. Lucy especially, but even Dan and Emily both looked to be in their forties, though Emily certainly still bore a strong resemblance to when she was a child: the same light blue eyes, auburn hair that was a touch lighter now, and a similar facial structure.

Eventually, he felt Daniel pull away. 'We need to figure out what's happening here,' the man said.

Thinking of Daniel as a man was messing with Ollie's head. *He has a beard and everything. While I'm still a... boy.*

Ollie looked up to see Daniel gazing around the hallway, eyes searching. Emily got to her feet alongside Daniel. Lucy, however, remained crouched, arm still around Ollie.

She looks so old, Ollie thought to himself. *Little Luce, now an old woman.*

'Hello!' Daniel suddenly called out. 'Hello? Is there anyone else here? Someone answer me!'

'What are you doing?' Emily asked in shock.

'There has to be someone here that knows what's going on,' he replied. Then he bellowed again: 'Eleanore, are you here?'

His voice reverberated around the hallway, then faded to silence a few seconds later. There was no response. Daniel started to pace in agitation. 'This is insane,' he said.

'I know,' Emily told him, 'but we need to keep calm.'

'Maybe it *is* all a dream,' Lucy suggested. 'I don't know how else to explain it.'

'A dream?' Ollie asked as he looked up to her. 'You think we're all sharing a dream?'

'I have no idea, Ollie,' she replied with a kind smile. 'I'm just trying to make sense of it.'

'But *whose* dream would it be?' Ollie asked, even as he knew it would be his. If that was the case, the others would just be a figment of his imagination.

Maybe I'll wake up soon in my bed, and the others will still be young and in their bedrooms where they're supposed to be.

And all the lights won't be so red *anymore.*

'Wait,' Emily said, her face a frown of confusion. She seemed to consider her next words before speaking. 'Does anyone know *why* we're actually back here?'

'What do you mean?' Dan asked.

'Exactly what I said,' Emily replied. 'Do we know the reason we all came back?'

'Well, because we were called,' Dan said. 'We're keeping the promise we made to Eleanore, right?'

Emily nodded. 'Yes,' she said. 'But *really* think about it.

What specifically brought you back here now, Dan? Was it a letter, a phone call? I mean, why have we all chosen this specific moment to come back? Because I'll be honest, I... can't even remember.'

'I...' Daniel began confidently, but quickly trailed off. 'I don't know,' he finally admitted, looking down. 'Jesus Christ, why don't I know?'

'I'm the same,' Emily said. 'I just remember getting here, filled with the notion that I was *supposed* to be here, that I was called back. It's only now, when I try to think about it, that I realise I can't remember what actually brought me back. I mean...' She hesitated. 'I can't even remember *how* I got here. It's all a blank. I just remember being at the gate.'

Ollie felt Lucy's body tense beside him.

'You're... you're right,' Daniel said. 'I can't remember either. Only being at the gate, like you.'

'I'm the same,' Lucy added. 'I just remember it being dark out and trying to find my way to the front door. Then I saw you two inside. But...' She fell silent for a brief moment. 'I don't remember actually taking a trip here.'

'But how can we forget why we came?' Daniel asked. 'Or how we got here?'

Emily shook her head and hugged herself. 'I don't know,' she said. 'Before I really thought about it, it just kind of made sense. I didn't even think to question it initially. But now...'

Ollie felt Lucy take a deep breath. 'I'm scared to ask this,' the older woman began. 'But... what's the last thing any of you actually remember? Before being at the gate, I mean.'

All eyes fell on her. There was silence for the longest time.

'I can't remember... anything,' Dan eventually said. His head snapped up. 'Jesus Christ, I can't remember anything. Nothing! Nothing about my whole bloody life!'

Emily brought both hands to her face. 'Me neither,' she said. 'What the hell is going on? Why can't I remember?'

Ollie realised he couldn't recall much either. He started to shake, utterly confused and terrified.

Wait... I do remember something.

'The night of the fire,' he said to the others as he pushed himself to his feet. 'I remember that part clearly, sitting out on the grass with Eleanore.'

After a brief pause, Emily spoke. 'Yeah, I remember that too. And the time in the house before it. Even back before I came here. I remember losing my parents.'

'I do as well,' Lucy added. 'But I can't remember anything after the fire. I couldn't even tell you what happened the minute after we were all gathered on the grass.'

'We... we saw something in the window,' Daniel said. 'Remember that? One of those... things. It was in one of the upstairs rooms, looking back out at us.'

'That's right,' Emily stated. 'The same things that you all saw in the house. The... what were they again?'

'Ghosts,' Lucy said. 'I always thought they were ghosts. Still do.'

'Were they even real?' Dan asked. 'I remember them, but just assumed it was our imagination as kids.'

'They were definitely real,' Ollie said, helping Lucy as the old woman struggled to get back on her feet. She gave him a nod of thanks. Ollie continued, 'I saw one under the trapdoor in the cellar, remember?'

'Even Eleanore didn't deny they were real on that last night,' Lucy said. 'She saw it in the window as well.'

'But... no one remembers anything *after* that night?' Emily asked.

Silence. Daniel sighed heavily.

'It's like the memories are right there, beyond a wall of fog. Just... *there*... waiting to be grabbed, but I can't reach them.' He started to pace again, then eventually his eyes settled on the front door. 'I'm going outside,' he stated.

'Why?' Emily asked.

'Because I need to see what's out there.' He started to walk towards the door. 'Maybe there's a clue on how we got here.'

'Daniel,' Lucy said loudly, causing him to stop in his tracks. He turned to her. 'We'll all go together, okay?' Lucy said. 'No running off on your own.'

After a moment, Daniel nodded. 'Okay. Also, it's... just Dan now, Luce,' he said.

'Oh,' Lucy replied. 'Any reason for that?'

'I... I don't know,' Dan said with a shrug. 'I... can't really remember, to be honest. But I know I go by Dan.'

'Well, that's fine,' Lucy told him. 'Dan it is. Just don't run off ahead. We'll figure this out together.'

All Ollie could do was watch on. There was a new dynamic in the group that unsettled him. Well, *everything* about the situation was unsettling, but he'd always seen himself as the leader, the protector—yet now he was a child surrounded by adults. They'd grown up, while he was just stuck as a boy. He felt Lucy's arm over his shoulder, and she squeezed him protectively.

He stepped away.

'Are you okay?' the old woman asked him, glancing down with a look of concern. Ollie could still see the young girl in her facial features, though it was now trapped beneath a mask of old age.

'I'm fine,' he said, offering nothing else. Yet all he wanted to do was shout, *This is wrong. I'm the oldest. I'm the one that looks after all of you!*

He stayed silent.

Lucy looked as if she wanted to say more as well, though instead just nodded while giving a tight-lipped smile, reminding Ollie of Daniel as a kid.

He's Dan now, Ollie told himself. *Not Daniel.* The name felt strange, further emphasising how different things were now.

Everyone made their way over to the main door. En-route, Ollie became aware of the adults circling around him protectively. He knew they probably didn't even realise they were doing it, but it made him want to bolt free and run to the head of the pack, retaking his normal role.

Once at the inner door, Dan opened it to reveal the entrance porch beyond. There was only thick blackness past the windows there, showing the starless night that engulfed everything. Dan then walked forward and opened the outer door as well.

'It's so quiet out there,' Emily eventually said. 'I can't even hear any cars in the distance.'

'Well, it's three in the morning,' Dan said. 'Probably not many cars out on the road at this time. But I take your point. There aren't any insects, or even the sounds of a breeze. Just... nothing.' Dan then checked his watch and frowned. 'Strange,' he said.

'What?' Emily asked.

'My watch is still showing ten past three AM. To the minute.'

'Maybe your battery died,' Emily said as she raised her hand and checked her own. But she frowned as well. 'Huh, maybe mine has as well? It's showing the same time.'

Ollie wasn't wearing a watch, and neither was Lucy, so he turned and leaned his head back into the main hallway so he could look over at the long-case clock. It showed ten past three as well, but the hand that ticked the seconds away wasn't moving. Moreover, he realised the old *tick, tick, tick* that had always filled the entrance hallway was now gone.

It made the knot in his stomach tie itself even tighter. *What is going on?*

'Come on,' Dan said as he slowly stepped outside. 'Let's see what we can find.'

Ollie expected to feel the temperature drop in the night air, yet he found it wasn't cold, actually no different from inside.

There was no moon or stars overhead, so Ollie could only guess they were obscured by clouds. Not that he could make out the shapes of any clouds either; it was like a black sheet of glass overhead.

'Something isn't right out here,' Dan stated as he looked around. The only light was the red hue washing out from inside the house, just enough to illuminate the immediate area out front. When Ollie looked back at the building, he saw the walls were completely covered with the wall planters, making him unable to see the blocks beneath. He *could* make out thick, thorny vines that snaked between the greenery, however.

Dan started walking again, with purpose this time, crunching over the gravel driveway. The others jogged to keep up.

'Slow down,' Emily said.

'Sorry,' Dan said, yet he maintained his pace. 'But I really need to see what's going on.'

As they moved away from the house, the already

meagre light levels dropped further, and seeing anything at all became challenging. However, for reasons Ollie couldn't explain, he could still make out his immediate surroundings and could even see where the grass met the edge of the drive. *Something* was letting them see a few feet around themselves, though he had no idea what.

Eventually, the group stopped just before the main entrance gates. Once there, Ollie felt his stomach drop.

He couldn't actually see the gate itself.

Instead, there was just a mass of wall climbers, vines, and thorns. They also coated the walls on either side of the gates, looking thick and black in the night.

'No,' Dan said and took a step forward. 'No, this can't be.'

'We're trapped,' Emily stated. 'What the hell is going on?!'

'We're not trapped,' Dan replied, though he sounded far from confident. He moved closer to the wall. 'I'm going to climb it.'

'Dan, wait!' Emily said.

'Yeah,' Lucy added. 'You're going to get hurt. Remember what the vines did to Emily's hand.'

'I'll be fine,' Dan stated. But just as he reached forward, he halted—Lucy gasped and drew in a breath.

The vines on the wall and gate were *moving*.

'What the hell!' Dan quickly stepped back.

Ollie watched in horror as the vines pulsed and slithered, the long thorns coating their lengths extending out like the thistles on the back of a porcupine.

A sound then drew their attention, coming from their right. The group turned as one to stare into the darkness.

It was a giggle.

No, Ollie thought. *Not quite*. It was like something was

trying to giggle: a non-human mouth attempting to imitate something it had heard. It was the creepiest sound Ollie had ever heard in his life. It came again a few seconds later, with others then joining in, until Ollie was certain he could make out four separate voices.

'What *is* that?' Lucy asked.

The strange giggling grew closer, followed by dull shuffling, like feet sliding over grass. Ollie felt his chest grow tight. He pushed himself closer into Lucy, whose protective arm again found its way around his shoulders. Ollie made no attempt to step away this time.

'Hello?' Dan called out.

More giggles. More shuffling. Closer and closer.

'I—I think we need to go back inside the house,' Emily said.

Dan continued to stare into the dark, but nodded. 'Yeah, I think you're right.'

The group started to slowly back away.

Just as they were about to turn and jog, he heard Emily draw in a sharp breath. 'Look!' she exclaimed.

Ollie froze as four shuffling beings came into view. They broke through from the dark, pushing into the edge of his vision: four faceless, humanoid things. They were about his size, and their bodies were smooth and featureless beyond the misshapen forms of their twisted limbs. Their arms and legs were different lengths, causing their gait to be unsteady and movements erratic.

Their smooth skin appeared to be a dark grey, though it was hard to be certain. The giggles continued, but given the things had no mouths, Ollie wasn't sure how they were making the sounds.

'Run!' he shouted to the others. Not waiting around, he quickly took hold of Lucy's hand and set off, pulling the older woman along with him but careful not to yank her over.

Dan and Emily ran as well, taking up a position just behind Ollie and Lucy. The four of them kicked up gravel during their run back down the driveway. Panic gripped Ollie and he cast a look back as he ran, gazing past Dan and Emily, yet the darkness was too thick to see the strange giggling things anymore. He could still hear them; their sounds carried over towards the group, though getting fainter by the second.

'What the hell were those things?' Emily shouted.

'This can't be real,' Dan said. 'It... it *can't* be.'

Ten seconds later, the group stormed through the front door again, slamming it closed behind them, before doing the same with the inner door. Lucy bent over, breathing deeply, her hand on her chest; the others panted as well, all bathed in an eerie red light.

Ollie put a hand on Lucy's back and rubbed it. 'Are you okay, Luce?' he asked, feeling a strange, sharp pain in his own head, but ignoring it to focus on the older woman.

'I'm... okay,' Lucy said, drawing deep breaths. 'My chest is a... a little tight.' She winced in pain and Ollie worried the woman was having a heart attack. Eventually, her expression eased and she straightened up. 'Thank you, Ollie,' she said. 'I'm okay. Just out of breath.'

Emily and Dan had gathered around, both breathing heavily, with Dan holding his side. 'Are you two okay?' Ollie asked him.

'Stitch,' Dan explained, then looked back at the front door. 'This is a dream,' he said. 'It has to be. No way any of this is real.'

'Are those things still coming?' Emily asked.

Dan slowly approached one of the front windows and

peered out. 'It's too dark to see much,' he said. 'But I can't spot anything.' He turned his head so that his ear was closer to the window. 'Can't hear anything, either.'

'What *were* they?' Lucy asked, having finally slowed her breathing.

'Were they the same things we used to see here?' Ollie asked. 'Like the one I saw in the cellar?'

'I'm not sure,' Lucy said. 'They seemed... different. These made noise, whereas the others didn't.'

'They did, though,' Ollie replied. 'Wasn't it a kind of clicking sound?'

Lucy paused, then nodded. 'You're right,' she said. 'But they certainly didn't giggle.'

'That's true,' Ollie said.

Lucy went on. 'And they looked different as well. Those things outside just looked... wrong.'

Ollie was about to say the watchers looked *wrong*, especially considering the cluster of eyes on their faces, but refrained.

A silence then fell over the group, each member struggling to make sense of the madness they found themselves in.

'We need a plan to get out of here,' Dan finally said. 'And after that, a way to get home.'

Emily hugged herself. 'But Dan,' she began, voice quiet. 'None of us know where 'home' is.'

Ollie saw Dan's body sag. 'I know,' the man eventually replied. 'But... we can't just stay here and—'

A loud, monstrous roar silenced Dan. Ollie jumped in shock as the furious sound reverberated around them. After a few more moments, everything faded to silence.

'What the hell was that?' Emily asked. All eyes faced the door to the dining room.

'It sounded like it came from the cellar,' Ollie said, his body locked in fright. A moment later, the four of them moved closer to each other, huddling together as they continued to stare.

'Listen!' Lucy said, voice an urgent whisper. Ollie heard it.

Thud.

It was a distant, dull sound, muffled by the door to the cellar, but Ollie could tell what it was.

Thud.

Heavy footsteps. Impossibly heavy. Something huge was making its way up the cellar stairs.

Thud.

The roar came again. Angry. Desperate. Horrifying.

'What do we do?' Lucy asked in a fear-filled voice.

'Upstairs!' Emily stated. 'Quick!'

They moved as one, but Lucy stumbled right as they set off and fell to her knees. Ollie immediately started to pull her back up, and Dan and Emily quickly moved closer to help as well.

'Are you okay?' Ollie asked Lucy, glancing back towards the dining room in panic.

'Fine,' she said, heaving herself back up.

Thud.

Thud.

Thud.

Ollie was certain he could feel vibrations through the floor underfoot.

'Is the door to the cellar locked?' Lucy asked.

'I think so,' Dan said as they started to move again. 'I saw the padlock when I first got here.'

Thud. Thud. Thud.

'I'm not sure a padlock can hold whatever that is,' Emily added—and Ollie found himself agreeing.

Thud.

'It's got to be at the top of the steps now,' Lucy exclaimed. The group stopped to look back.

There was an almighty *crash* and a sound of splintering wood. Ollie saw the remnants of the cellar door slide across the floor past the open dining room doorway.

Thud. Thud.

Whatever it was, it was out now. Ollie held his breath, staring forward, unable to get himself to move.

Thud.

'Jesus Christ...' Dan uttered.

A towering thing came into view through the doorway, turned to them, and bellowed out another horrifying roar.

CHAPTER
THIRTY-FOUR

Everyone instinctively pressed themselves into one another, huddling as close as possible as they stared ahead at this new horror, all of them rooted to the spot. Emily's mind struggled to accept what she was seeing. The monstrosity slowly ducked through the doorway, large hands holding the jambs firmly.

It was a man, or at least had the appearance of one, but was over eight feet tall, broad-chested, and completely naked. The thing's thick arms were lined with dark hair, matching the matted hair on the protruding chest, all covered in pale skin. In addition, the entire body of the thing was wrapped with what Emily initially took to be barbed wire, but what she soon realised were vines lined with long thorns.

Those vines were *moving*, snaking around the huge body as if they were alive, their spiky protrusions cutting into the skin. The tendrils ran down the man's thick arms, extending past his hands and clinging to the door frame he held on to, only coming free of it as he took another footstep, farther into the entrance hall.

While its body was terrifying enough, to Emily it was the thing's head that was most disturbing. The skin from the broad shoulders extended upwards like a hood, wrapping over the head, hiding most of it. There was also a vertical tear in the front of the cowl of skin, so the face was visible. It glared at them with a snarl on its face and a wild look in its glinting eyes. The skin of the face was red and leaking pus, like the top layers had been burned away, leaving some tendons visible in the cheeks.

Ollie's screams continued. No one seemed able to move. Finally, after what was likely far too long, Emily was able to act. She grabbed Ollie's arm and shouted, 'Move!'

The hulking thing took another step forward, the vines around its legs and feet scraping across the floor.

The group reacted to Emily's order, and they quickly ran over to the door to the staircase. Another roar from behind caused Emily to jolt. Lucy cried out in horror, but everyone kept going, dashing through to the stairs and thundering up them.

'Jesus Christ, Jesus Christ, Jesus Christ,' Dan repeated over and over from his position at the rear of the group. Everyone ran through into the mid-floor hallway, where they paused.

'What now?' Lucy asked, panicked.

'Do we hide?' Ollie added.

Emily didn't know what to say. She knew they couldn't run forever, but hiding meant they might get trapped.

'It's coming up!' Dan exclaimed.

The thudding footsteps were heavier on the stairs, and they'd begun moving quicker. There was another booming yell, again filled with rage and desperation.

Please wake up, Emily told herself, now certain this had to be a nightmare.

Though... she knew there was another explanation. The notion had popped into the back of her mind a while ago, but Emily had quickly pushed it away, unwilling to entertain it.

'Do we go up to the next floor?' Lucy asked as she looked around the space with wide eyes, desperately searching.

'It's coming!' Ollie shouted. 'We need to hurry!'

'Upstairs,' Dan finally decided. 'Quick. Run!'

The group set off again, shooting over to the next stairwell and dashing as fast as they could up to the top floor. Emily kept a close eye on Lucy, who was ahead of her and next to Ollie. That amount of running couldn't be good for someone in their seventies.

'Keep quiet,' Dan whispered as they moved farther into the top-storey hallway, which was still washed in red light. 'We've been making too much noise.'

'But where do we go now?' Emily asked in a hushed whisper. She could still hear the entity moving below; it sounded like it had come out into the mid-floor hallway.

Her mind raced to try to find an idea. All she could think was to take refuge in one of the bedrooms. *But then what?* There were only so many places they could hide.

Her breath caught in her throat as she heard the huge thing downstairs approach the staircase. It then began to ascend, heavy footsteps slamming on the stairs.

'Damnit,' Emily seethed through clenched teeth. Now they *had* to hide—they couldn't just stand out in the hallway to be found. She glanced around again. The door to her room was open, whereas Lucy's and Eleanore's were both closed. Then there were the doors to Eleanore's yoga room and spare room, which were closed as well.

One good thing about the layout was the interlinking

rooms, so if their pursuer entered the room they were in, the group could still run and work their way around the house.

But she knew they couldn't run forever, especially with the vines outside blocking their escape.

Emily then focused again on her own room, not able to think of anything else. 'This way!' she said in a hushed whisper.

She led the others into her bedroom, all of them being as quiet as possible while still moving quickly.

Thud, thud, thud.

With the sound of every footstep, Emily's chest felt tighter. Her body trembled and she couldn't get it under control. All she wanted to do was drop down, curl up into a ball, and sob.

'Close the door,' Dan whispered as everyone hid in the room. Emily did, acting as quickly and quietly as she could.

Thud, thud, thud.

She could tell the man was upstairs now, in the hallway close by. His almighty shriek of anger caused the group to push themselves closer together yet again.

She caught the attention of the others and brought a finger up to her lips. *Shhhh.* They were all wide-eyed but nodded their understanding.

Thud.

The man outside began his advance down the hallway, drawing closer. Emily listened to every heavy, terrible step. *He's going to find us.*

They waited, everyone holding their breath. Then, just as the footsteps reached the outside of the door... silence.

'We need to run,' Dan whispered to them.

Boom.

A thunderous blow struck the door and it splintered,

nearly shattering. Everyone screamed. There was another blow against the door and it flew inwards off its hinges, revealing the towering man standing outside. He grabbed the jambs of the doorway and yanked, pulling away entire sections of the wall, causing rubble to fall to the floor. Emily shrieked in horror.

Thorn-covered vines continued to slither around the man's body like they were alive, and at that close of a distance, Emily could see they actually ran *into* his body, penetrating the flesh at some points and exiting at others.

'Go!' Dan shouted. 'Run!'

Jarred from her staring, Emily bolted, pushing Lucy and Ollie ahead, and Dan pressed into her from behind. Emily glanced back mid-stride, seeing the huge man step away from the door. She heard his movement outside, realising the thing was quickly making its way down the hallway and keeping parallel to them.

'Keep going!' Dan yelled as Lucy and Ollie squeezed into the dark dressing room. Yet before they could make it through to the other side, a huge arm burst through the side wall close to them.

Emily instinctively ducked down, but then saw the meaty hand grab Lucy around the throat, the man's fingers actually meeting on the other side of her neck. Lucy's eyes widened and she let out a strained gasp. The old woman looked back at Emily in horror... and was then quickly yanked out into the hallway, her body breaking through the wall and sending a shower of rubble down to the floor.

'Lucy!' Ollie screamed, holding out a hand impotently but keeping back as the plaster and broken block work continued to fall, piling on the ground. Through the hole, Emily could see that the man still had hold of Lucy; she kicked her legs as she dangled in his grasp, mouth open and struggling for air. The elderly woman's eyes bulged and her face reddened.

Emily knew she had to help Lucy, yet she couldn't force herself to move and just stared, aghast.

She felt Dan move past her, which finally was enough to spur her to action. Emily followed him quickly out through the hole, coughing on the cloud of dust, and into the hallway. Both then stopped just before the huge entity.

'Let her go!' Dan screamed. He shot forward and grabbed Lucy by the waist, trying to wrestle her free. In response, their attacker simply raised a foot and kicked out, hitting Dan in the chest and sending him flying backwards like a ragdoll. Dan cried out in pain as he hit the wall behind him and dropped to the floor, where he lay wheezing.

Ollie then burst free from the hole as well. 'Stay back!' Emily ordered him, running towards Lucy instead. Before she could do anything useful, the nightmarish man swung his arm, smacking Emily across the face with tremendous force, the thorns cutting into her flesh as the blow sent her sprawling backwards.

From her place on the floor where she lay in pain, she was able to see Ollie charge forward next, emitting a high-pitched cry as he ran. Emily wanted to shout out to him again, to tell the boy to stop, but her head swam and it was difficult for her to focus. The boy was swatted away just like she had been, and his small body sent bouncing across the floor farther down the hallway. He slowly rolled to his back, sobbing in obvious pain.

With all of them down, it left no one to help Lucy, who continued to flail in the grip of the attacker.

'Lucy!' Emily managed to croak out. She turned to her side to push herself up, but the pain in her head stopped her cold, every movement causing a fresh bloom of agony. She felt blood trickle down her face, which stung from the lacerations.

The man raised Lucy higher up. Lengths of vine snaked from the end of his arm and started to slither over Lucy's panicked face. Her kicking became more frantic.

Then... the vines began to burrow into her flesh.

'No!' Emily finally managed to shout. She forced herself forward, but the world around her shifted again and she fell, unable to keep her equilibrium.

Dan was starting to move as well, but slowly, *very* slowly; Ollie remained on his back, sobbing. Emily could only watch as the huge man raised his other vine-wrapped arm and swung it back across Lucy's face.

A shower of blood rained down as chunks of flesh were torn from the side of Lucy's head.

'Noooo!' Emily screamed.

The man struck again, tearing free more skin. The vines from the arm that held Lucy wormed deeper into her head, pulling at the skin. The old woman's eyes looked like they were going to pop out of her sockets.

Emily was finally able to crawl forward, ignoring the pain and nausea that swam through her. The attacker continued to strike poor Lucy, alternating his focus between her head and dangling body. Torrents of blood rained down to the rug below. Her fighting and kicking grew weaker and weaker with every savage blow.

'Lucy,' Emily sobbed, holding out an arm towards her friend. *No, not just my friend,* she told herself, *my sister.* The young girl that had welcomed Emily with open arms and shown Emily nothing but love and warmth.

Eventually, Lucy stopped twitching and her body hung limp, blood cascading down, and her face a mess of exposed red flesh. Seeming satisfied, the huge man simply released her, letting Lucy's body crumple to the floor with a wet *squelch*.

The man then turned. Emily held her breath as he briefly faced her, yet kept turning, eventually coming square on to the door to the staircase. He started to walk forward, each footstep slow and heavy as before.

Emily was sobbing. She kept casting glances over to Lucy's unmoving form, before looking back at the assailant, who now seemed happy to leave, his work done.

The hulking man had clearly targeted Lucy specifically, but Emily couldn't work out why.

She continued to crawl towards the others as she sobbed. The pain was finally starting to slowly recede. She was eventually able to get herself up to her hands and knees, drawing closer to Lucy's body. She noticed Dan start to crawl nearer as well, blood trailing from his mouth. Eventually, Emily reached the old woman and drew in a gasp.

Lucy's face was a chewed-up mess of flesh, with one eye gone and the other staring up at the ceiling. There was blood everywhere, coating Lucy's torn clothes and the rug beneath her, so thick it wasn't able to soak into the fabric and just pooled atop it.

'This—this can't be happening,' Dan uttered as he shuffled next to Emily, looking down at their dead friend. 'Lucy... no.'

'Is... she okay?' Ollie called, his voice slurred. Emily turned to see the boy was dragging himself along the floor as well, a gash across the side of his face. 'No, Ollie,' Emily told him. 'Don't look.'

'Is she okay?' he demanded in reply.

Just as she was going to order the boy to stay back, Dan shouted, 'Look!'

Emily initially turned her gaze back to Lucy, hoping Dan had spotted signs of life, but he was instead pointing over to the side wall where the giant had pulled Lucy through.

One of the watchers stood there now, focused on the hole with its many eyes. Emily's body tensed up. *What next?*

The being's dull skin was bathed in red light, and it jerked and flinched as it simply gazed ahead, slowly rubbing its hands up and down the jagged sides of the opening. It *chirped* and *clicked*, making inhuman sounds.

What's it doing?

Emily watched in amazement as the wall started to... reform. The rubble on the ground slowly faded away and the opening became whole again, with the wallpaper-covered wall phasing back into being.

The whole thing took close to a minute to finish, but once the process was done, it was impossible to tell there'd ever been a hole there to begin with. Not even dust remained on the floor.

The watcher then slowly turned to them, revealing more of its form. This was as close as Emily had ever been to one before, and its visage caused revulsion to lurch up in her gut. It was thin, with long arms and featureless flesh, reminding her somewhat of the giggling things outside. The limbs of the watcher, however, were all in proportion to each other, despite being elongated.

But it was the creature's face that caused her to recoil most: a mass of bulbous eyes bunched centrally, pushing out from each other like frogspawn, with tiny black pupils drifting across the surface of each. The strange entity didn't move; it just continued to look at them, standing perfectly still. Emily was reminded of Lucy's theory on them being ghosts that had lived in the house far longer than the children had.

Though Emily didn't want to see the awful sight again, she couldn't help but turn back to Lucy's body. Blood still oozed out of the openings in the old woman's flesh and the air was thick with the smell of copper.

Emily paused.

Lucy's remaining eye... moved, rolling in what was left of the socket, settling directly on Emily. Emily tensed up and leaned forward, taking Lucy's bloody hand in her own.

'Lucy?' she whispered, astonished that the woman was still alive. She couldn't imagine how much pain Lucy was in, and couldn't help but think the woman would have been better off dead, given what was left of her. Though Emily knew that was probably just a matter of time now, as much as it crushed her to think it. There was simply no coming back from the injuries.

The sound of a door opening caused Emily to look up. She braced herself, expecting some other horror to come at the group. However, as she gazed over to Eleanore's room, she saw her former guardian standing in the now-open doorway, grey hair still in a bob and looking exactly as Emily had always remembered her.

It was like she hadn't aged a day since the night of the fire. Just like Ollie.

Eleanore's face was contorted in anguish as she gazed down at Lucy, tears forming in her eyes. 'Quickly,' she eventually said to them, motioning to her room. 'Bring Lucy inside.'

CHAPTER

THIRTY-FIVE

Dan looked down at his blood-soaked hands. He and Emily had just set Lucy down on Eleanore's bed, and though Ollie had wanted to help, Dan had refused, trying to keep the boy at a distance.

No way a child should see this.

Blood pooled on the surface of the duvet below Lucy, who lay motionless, save for the slight rise and fall of her chest.

Ollie tried to come closer again, but Dan intercepted him at the foot of the bed. '*Don't*, Ollie,' he said as he shook his head. 'You don't want to see.'

'She's my friend too,' Ollie said, defiance in his tear-filled eyes. 'My *sister* too.'

'I know,' Dan said. 'But... trust me.'

It felt odd talking to Ollie in such a way, the dynamic that of an adult and a child, but Dan couldn't help it. It was instinctual. Ollie *was* still a kid, as unbelievable as that was.

Dan glanced at the now-closed door to the room, straining his ears to make sure nothing was approaching. His eyes settled on Emily, and he saw that she had nasty-looking cuts across the side of her face. He was tempted to ask her if she was okay, yet she didn't seem to be bothered by it, despite the wounds running with blood. She was just focused on Lucy, staring down at the older woman with concern.

Dan then turned his attention to Eleanore, who was looking at Lucy as well, hand over her mouth and face locked in confusion. Dan noticed her glance over to Ollie.

'Eleanore?' Dan eventually said, drawing the woman's attention. 'What's going on here? Do you know what's happening?'

She gazed at him. A sad smile broke out over her lips. 'Look how much you've grown, Daniel,' she said, clearly holding back tears. Her eyes flicked over to Emily. 'You too, Emily,' she said. The woman briefly focused on Ollie again, and after a second she quickly looked away.

'Do you know what's happening?' Dan repeated, yet Eleanore stayed quiet, seemingly in shock. *Maybe she's just as confused as the rest of us.*

'How long have you been here?' Emily asked her.

Eleanore shrugged. 'I... don't know.'

'Do you remember arriving?' Emily went on. 'Or have you been here the whole time?'

'I... don't really remember *anything*,' Eleanore said. 'Not since the fire, to be honest. Other than walking down the driveway back to the house, that is. I felt the need to come to my room and once there I just... fell asleep.'

'Same as the rest of us,' Dan said, though it suddenly hit him that they hadn't gotten Ollie's story about that yet.

'And you don't know anything about what's going on?' Emily pushed. 'About the things we've seen here, why we can't remember anything, or the reason our ages are all different, or what that thing was that did this to Lucy?'

Eleanore slowly shook her head. She glanced at Ollie once again, action seeming reflexive, like she couldn't help it.

Dan sighed. 'Eleanore, I need you to be honest with me,' he said, sensing she was holding back.

'I—I don't know anything,' she replied in a trembling voice. 'No more than any of you.'

Emily stepped closer to the woman. 'Eleanore,' she said in a kind, patient voice, 'I can't tell you how good it is to see you again. Part of me just wants to wrap my arms around you and give you a hug, but the situation here is pretty desperate.' She pointed at Lucy. 'She isn't going to make it,' Emily went on, keeping her voice quiet, trying to hide the words from Lucy. 'And I'm worried that monster will come back for us. So if you know *anything*...'

In response, Eleanore just knelt down and took hold of Lucy's hand. Dan noticed the dying woman's fingers twitch and tighten in response. Though he didn't want to, he couldn't help but let his eyes drift up to Lucy's ruined face again.

Wait!

'Oh, my poor Lucy,' Eleanore said. 'My poor, sweet little girl.'

Dan caught Emily's eye and motioned to Lucy's face. A look of amazement washed over Emily.

While Lucy was still a mess, her face had... changed. The wounds and gashes looked less severe, like they had begun to close.

That isn't possible.

Though in truth, much of what Dan had already witnessed since waking in that damn house again shouldn't have been possible.

A nagging thought he'd been having reared its ugly

head again, fighting for attention Dan didn't want to give it.

It can't be that. He pushed it away.

Eleanore brushed a strand of bloody, gore-soaked hair back from Lucy's face. Dan watched in amazement, witnessing some of the wounds close up before his very eyes.

'She's... getting better,' Ollie stated as he stepped closer.

'How?' Emily asked as she moved to stand opposite Eleanore on the other side of the bed.

Lucy's breathing started to grow deeper, more regular, and another ragged cut slowly closed back up. The torn flesh around her jaw was healing before Dan's eyes as well, and when he looked farther up her face, Dan noticed *both* of Lucy's eyes were looking at him.

He had no idea how, but the other had reformed.

Everyone simply stared at the sight before them in amazement, standing silently until not a single wound remained on Lucy, though she was still covered in blood. On top of that, the woman now looked... *younger.*

Eleanore glanced over to Emily. 'Would you bring me a towel?' she asked.

Emily, still staring in shock, simply nodded, then quickly strode off to the en-suite.

Suddenly, Lucy started to sob. Dan and Ollie instinctively inched closer to her.

'Luce?' Ollie asked, voice full of concern as Eleanore started to stroke the crying woman's forehead.

Emily soon returned with a wet towel and she handed it to Eleanore. The older woman began to delicately dab Lucy's face, slowly cleaning away the blood.

How has she gotten younger?! Lucy now looked to be in her early forties, similar to Dan.

He then glanced at Emily. The wound across the side of her face was now gone as well, healed up completely.

'What... happened?' Lucy asked, voice weak and frightened, no longer sounding aged.

'Shhhhh,' Eleanore gently replied. 'It's all okay.'

'It isn't okay!' Dan snapped. '*None* of this is okay. This is a... a... a nightmare!'

Eleanore didn't look at him, just squeezed Lucy's hand as the woman started crying—not just crying, howling. Emily quickly leaned over Lucy and hugged her. Dan moved close to Lucy's legs and put a gentle hand on her waist; Ollie made his way next to Emily and hugged Lucy as well.

They all stayed that way for a while as Lucy continued to sob. Though Dan didn't understand how she had healed and de-aged, the relief was overwhelming.

'Eleanore,' Emily eventually said, looking gravely up at their former guardian. 'You know something about what's happening here, don't you?' Eleanore didn't answer, just continued cleaning Lucy's face. 'Don't you,' Emily persisted. Still no answer.

Emily took a breath. 'Eleanore, be honest with me. I need to know. Are we...' She hesitated as her voice cracked. After taking another deep breath, she pushed on. 'Are we dead?'

Dan froze. He had been thinking the same thing, but he'd been too terrified to face it. Tears spilled from Eleanore's eyes. She cast a look at Ollie, who was still only a boy, then her eyes finally met Emily's. Eventually, the woman gave a slow nod.

Dan's heart froze.

'I'm so sorry,' Eleanore said.

CHAPTER
THIRTY-SIX

Emily couldn't believe what she'd just heard, even if the notion had been nagging at her for a while.

'No,' Dan said, shaking his head vehemently. 'No, we can't be. We *can't* be dead. That makes no sense.'

Eleanore looked at him with sad eyes. 'It's... it's true, Daniel,' she said as tears continued to flow.

'It can't be!' Dan snapped. 'We're conscious! We clearly *exist!* If we were dead, it would just be nothing!'

Eleanore shook her head. Lucy's sobbing started to increase at hearing what was being said, her eyes firmly fixed on Eleanore.

'If we're dead, then where are we now?' Emily asked. 'Where is *this?* Why are we back in the old house?'

'It's... a lot to explain,' Eleanore replied.

'Try *really* fucking hard,' Dan stated, glaring at her.

'Did we die the night of the fire?' Emily asked. 'Because that's the last thing I remember. The last thing *any* of us seem to remember.'

Eleanore shook her head again. 'No,' she said. 'At least, I don't think so.' She gave another glance at Ollie, who was wide-eyed with shock. 'I think we continued to live our lives after sitting and watching the house burn that night. Then, when we did finally die, we...' She trailed off.

'We what?' Dan demanded.

'We came back home,' she said.

Emily felt her strength leave her. She almost flopped forward onto Lucy, only managing to catch herself at the last moment. Her head swam, the world around her twisting and spinning. It was all too much to take in. Her throat burned again, the tickling feeling growing stronger than it had before.

Dead? Can we really be dead?

Emily wasn't sure if she believed it, still clinging to the hope this was all some kind of awful dream, or that Eleanore was just plain wrong.

Wake up! Please wake up! she begged herself.

'How come we all look different ages?' Dan asked.

Eleanore continued to look at Lucy. 'We come back as we died,' she said quietly.

Emily felt a twist of pain in her gut. Her eyes fell on Ollie. Tears welled up.

No! The poor boy!

Ollie started to tremble, eyes growing wet. Emily quickly ran to him, wrapping him in a big hug just as the boy broke down crying.

'It isn't true,' Dan stated. 'It just *isn't!*'

Eleanore did not reply.

Emily held on to the sobbing boy, squeezing him tight. He lifted his head and looked up to her with eyes so big and so wet and so scared that Emily couldn't associate them with the strong older brother she once knew.

'Emily, are we really dead?' he asked. Emily's heart broke for him again; she fought against her own tears.

'I... I don't know,' she said.

Eventually, Lucy pushed herself up to a sitting position, drawing everyone's attention. Dan sat closer to her and rested a hand on her shoulder. 'Luce,' he said. 'Are... are you okay?'

She sniffed. 'It hurt so much,' she said in a weak voice. Seeming to be in a daze, Lucy stroked her own arms, looking down with a far-off stare.

'We tried to help,' Dan said. Emily picked up shame in his voice.

Lucy quickly looked at him. 'I know you did,' she said, and put a hand on his shoulder. 'Oh Dan, I know you did.' She then hugged him, moving much more easily than she had before the attack.

When they finally released each other, Dan said, 'Lucy... do you know you look... *different?*'

She frowned. 'Different?'

Dan nodded. 'Everything has healed up. Your face, your arms, your skin, it's all okay again. But... you look... younger. *Much* younger.'

'Wait, what are you talking about?' Lucy asked in confusion. Dan looked around, then saw a hand mirror on Eleanore's dresser, so he quickly retrieved it and handed it to Lucy.

After looking at her own reflection, Lucy's face fell. 'What in the world?' Her eyes quickly fixed on Eleanore. 'How?' she asked.

'I don't know,' Eleanore replied, for what had to have been the tenth time that night. However, Emily picked up the hesitation in her voice.

'You need to start being honest with us,' Emily said to her, from her position on the floor where she continued to hold Ollie. 'You obviously know far more than we do, so start explaining everything. If we're dead, then what is this place? Because it sure as shit isn't Heaven!'

'Is it Hell?' Lucy asked in panic.

'No,' Eleanore quickly said. 'It isn't either of those things. This is... something different.'

'Define 'different,'' Dan ordered.

'It's... hard to explain,' Eleanore said, all eyes on her. 'Just... think of it as a kind of... purgatory, I guess. A place separated from Heaven or Hell. Our own afterlife.'

Emily frowned. She felt anger roil in her gut. 'What does that even *mean*, Eleanore?' she asked, teeth clenched. 'Our own afterlife? It makes no sense. And what the hell was that monster that attacked Lucy?'

'Or the four things we saw outside?' Lucy added.

'And the watchers that lived here? What about them?' Dan threw in. 'You knew about them even back then, didn't you.' His voice was loud, rage bubbling just beneath the surface.

The barrage of questions caused Eleanore to shrink away. 'Please,' she said, 'don't get angry or shout at me. I'm going through the same thing you all are.'

'But *you* seem to know why!' Dan seethed.

Emily took a breath. 'Eleanore,' she said. 'Just start at the beginning. Tell us *everything* you know. And I mean everything.'

Eleanore paused. 'I... don't think it would make you feel any better, Emily. I really don't.'

Emily had no clue what to make of that statement.

'Try us,' Dan said. 'Because we need to know what you do, so we can try to figure something out.'

'There's nothing to 'figure out,' Daniel,' Eleanore said. 'This just... *is*.'

'Just 'is'?' Dan asked. 'Are you saying this is how things

are going to be forever? Trapped in this bloody house, and constantly attacked and hunted?!'

Eleanore stood to her feet and moved back, looking down, the bloody towel still in her hands. 'S-stop getting angry with me,' she sobbed.

Emily moved next to Dan and placed a hand on his shoulder, hoping to calm him. She knew if they wanted answers, they needed Eleanore talking, not scared or upset. 'Eleanore,' she said again, as calmly as she could. 'You owe us an explanation here. Just tell us what you know. We won't get angry or raise our voice. Promise.' She looked at Dan, who eventually nodded. 'So just tell us. Please. We deserve to know.'

The older woman fidgeted with the towel, smearing more blood over her fingers. She took a slow breath. 'Like I said before, after we died, we came here. We came home.' Emily bristled. This place didn't feel like 'home' to her, not anymore. Apparently not noticing her reaction, Eleanore continued, 'The things in the house with us now, they aren't evil. We don't have to be scared of them.'

'Not scared?!' Dan snapped—Emily didn't blame him. 'Look what happened to Lucy!'

'I know,' Eleanore quickly said, taking half a step back. 'I know. I... I didn't think it would be like this.'

'You did this to us, didn't you?' Ollie said, speaking for the first time in several minutes.

Emily looked down to the boy, who had stopped sobbing and was staring at the older woman, gaze furious. His hands were balled into fists.

'*You* brought us here,' he went on.

'It... it wasn't supposed to be this way,' Eleanore repeated. 'I... I didn't know it would be like this.' She started shaking her head, looking like she was on the verge of a breakdown. She shrunk down, reminding Emily in that moment of a cornered fox. 'I can't do this,' Eleanore said as she started to cry again. 'I'm sorry.'

Then... she ran, bolting past Emily with surprising speed. Before anyone could even reach for her, she'd darted out the door and slammed it closed behind her.

'Wait!' Dan shouted, jumping to his feet, but Lucy grabbed his arm.

'No, don't!' she yelled. 'Don't leave me.'

It was enough to make Dan pause.

'We won't leave you, Luce,' Emily promised.

'But we need to know what's going on,' Dan added.

'But what if... what if that thing is still out there?' Lucy asked, her voice filled with fear. Dan looked back to the door, yet Lucy kept a tight grip on his sleeve, trying to pull him back. 'Please, Dan, just stay here.'

Emily heard Eleanore's running footsteps fade away. *If that thing* is *still out there, will it attack Eleanore too?*

Dan allowed himself to be pulled down to the bed, where he sat next to Lucy. Everyone remained silent, trying to take everything in.

When she started to process things, Emily felt herself reeling, her mind struggling to make sense of it all. She felt sick. 'Do... you think it's really true? What Eleanore said?' she eventually asked the others.

They were slow in responding. 'No,' Dan said. 'No, I don't. It can't be.'

'But... what other explanation is there?' Emily asked. 'I mean, we can keep saying this is all a dream as much as we want, but the dream isn't ending.' She then raised her arm and pinched the skin on the back of her hand, hard enough to hurt. 'I felt that,' she said, looking at the red mark left behind. 'But if it was a dream, I shouldn't have been able to feel that, right? Isn't that what they always say?'

Dan just shrugged. 'No idea,' he said, gaze falling down to the floor.

More silence.

Emily couldn't help but stare at Ollie. If what Eleanore said *was* true, the boy would have died shortly after the fire, given how young he looked. It was hard enough for Emily to accept her *own* death, but it was somehow worse trying to come to terms with Ollie dying so early in life. *I can't imagine what he's going through at the moment.*

'What do we do?' Lucy asked, still hugging herself on the bed.

The group just cast lost glances at each other.

'Eleanore knows more. I'm sure she does,' Dan said. 'We have to find her and get her to tell us everything.'

'That means going back out th-there,' Lucy said as she pointed to the bedroom door. 'What if *it* is still there?'

'But we can't just stay in here, Luce,' Dan said.

'Easy for you to say, Dan,' Lucy replied. 'That thing didn't come for you. It didn't rip you up. It came for *me*.'

Dan looked down again, seeming ashamed.

Emily knew there was no good response. Lucy was right.

'What do you think, Emily?' Dan asked her.

Emily paused. 'I... I don't know,' she eventually said. 'I don't really want to go out there, but... we *need* answers. There *has* to be something we can do here.' She didn't know if that was true, but the alternative was too awful to process: *do we just stay in this purgatory forever, stalked constantly by that monster?*

'I'll go,' Ollie suddenly said. Emily stared down at him

in shock. 'You can all stay here,' he went on. 'I'll find Eleanore and talk to her.'

Emily shook her head. 'No, absolutely not.'

'I'll be fine,' Ollie said, putting on a brave face that Emily saw through immediately. *He still wants to be our protector*.

'Ollie, no,' Dan said. 'If anyone is going out there alone, it will be me.'

'Why?' Ollie challenged.

'Because,' Dan continued. 'I'm... you know...'

'A grown up?' Ollie asked, folding his arms over his chest. 'Is that it?'

'Well... yeah.'

Ollie took in a deep breath. 'Well, to me, we were all just children only yesterday. At least that's what it feels like. And yesterday, I was the oldest and I looked out for you guys.'

Dan's expression softened. 'You *did* look out for us, Ollie,' he said. 'All the time. We loved you for it. We *still* love you for it. You were our big brother.'

'And I still am, Dan,' Ollie said. 'So let me do this.'

Dan hesitated, clearly struggling with his response. Emily bent down and took Ollie's hands in her own. 'Ollie,' she said. 'I can't imagine how you are feeling at the moment, and none of us understand what's going on. But... things are different now. I don't know why, but the rest of us are older. I know that must be hard, but we can't let you run around on your own out there.'

Ollie held her gaze. 'But if we're dead, what difference does it make if someone is an adult or child? What does it matter?'

Emily opened her mouth to respond, yet nothing came out. She had no answer. Regardless, she knew she couldn't let Ollie go out on his own, no matter what justification he tried to give.

'We go together,' Lucy eventually said. Everyone looked over at her and watched as she carefully swung her legs out of bed and placed her feet on the floor.

'But... I thought you didn't want to?' Dan said.

Lucy glared at the door. 'I don't. I *really* don't,' she said. 'But I don't want anyone going alone. And... you're right. We need more answers.' She looked down again, staring at her feet, as if hesitant to stand. Finally, she pushed herself up.

'Can you stand okay?' Dan asked, taking hold of her arm to help.

Lucy nodded. 'I actually feel... fine,' she replied. 'Better than when I first got here.'

Dan let go, so Lucy took a careful step. Then another. Then she walked normally around the bed. Emily was still shocked at how much younger her friend now looked. Despite the areas of dried blood that still clung to Lucy's face, Emily couldn't help but notice how beautiful Lucy had grown up to be.

'So, where do we think Eleanore has run off to?' Dan asked.

'She can't be far,' Emily said. 'It's a big house, but not *that* big.'

'Why don't we go down into the cellar first?' Ollie then suggested.

Emily turned to him. 'Why?'

'To see what's down there. And not just in the cellar, but *under* the cellar. Eleanore was obviously hiding something down there. Maybe we'll find something that will help make sense of things.'

It was an interesting idea. Then another thought

sprang up in her mind. 'Wait,' she said and walked over to the far side of the room. 'I wonder.' She squatted down, taking hold of the end of the rug. 'Everyone move away,' she said.

Ollie smiled, clearly knowing what she was thinking. Everyone stepped off the rug, which Emily rolled back to reveal the floorboards beneath.

'That one,' Ollie said, pointing to the floorboard with the largest gaps around it. Emily dug her fingers into the space and was able to lift the plank. In the space underneath, bathed in the red hue from the light above, was a box.

'It's still here,' Emily said as she retrieved it. Everyone gathered around, and once she opened it up, she saw the two keys inside.

'Nice idea, Emily,' Ollie said to her. Emily smiled. For a moment, she was eleven again, appreciating a compliment from the older boy.

Emily grabbed both keys. 'Might as well take them with us,' she said.

Lucy nodded to the wardrobe. 'Do we look in there too?' she asked. 'So we can search through the things Ollie saw back then?'

'Like the photos?' Emily asked.

'And the note,' Ollie added. 'That thing was *weird*.'

Emily looked to Ollie, then to Dan, and finally to Lucy. 'What do you all think?'

'I think we should find Eleanore first,' Dan suggested. 'I mean, if we can just get her to tell us what she knows, it'll be a whole lot quicker. Though I know that means leaving the room. But honestly, if that thing comes back, are we really any safer in here?'

'No,' Lucy admitted. 'But, if we have the photos and the

note, we can confront Eleanore with them, make her tell us the truth about them—about *everything*.'

Emily could sense how hesitant Lucy was to go back out, and she couldn't blame the woman. She couldn't imagine how painful the brutal attack had been. Maybe staying in the room a little longer to give Lucy a reprieve would be a good thing.

'Let's just take a quick look,' Emily said.

'Yeah,' Lucy agreed.

Emily looked to Dan. 'Just to see?'

After a moment, Dan nodded. 'Sure,' he said. 'I kind of get the feeling we have plenty of time here, anyway.'

Everyone gathered around the wardrobe as Emily opened it up. 'There's a compartment at the bottom,' Ollie said. He bent down and pressed on the floor of the unit; the other end of the floor popped up, and he was able to remove that section of wood.

Inside the gap was a thin folder with an envelope sitting on top. 'The photos are in the envelope,' Ollie said.

Emily picked it up and pulled out the photographs. She started to go through them, handing each one off to Dan when finished. Dan then passed them to Lucy, and she in turn to Ollie.

'Any ideas about who the kids are?' Emily asked.

'I always thought they were brothers and sisters,' Ollie said. 'They kind of have a similar look to each other.'

Emily nodded.

'You might be right,' Dan said as he took the first photo and studied it. 'But how do they know Eleanore?'

'And Jasper Graves,' Ollie added. 'He's in some of the later photos.'

'Do you think it's possible Eleanore and Mr. Graves had

children together?' Lucy asked. 'And that's who the children are?'

'I think it's a possibility,' Dan replied. 'I know Eleanore said that wasn't the case, but... well, I don't really think we can believe anything she says anymore.'

While Emily couldn't argue with that, the comment still made her sad. Eleanore had given them all a good home and a safe environment after the heartbreak of losing their families. She'd shown them love. It was hard to imagine that same woman would lie to them or do anything to hurt them.

But then Emily realised there had been clues all along that things weren't right, such as the vehement opposition to letting them go down into the cellar, the woman's strange insistence on taking their blood herself rather than letting a doctor or nurse do it, and her creeping around in the night.

The woman obviously had secrets. Could the people in her photo really be her own children?

If they are, what happened to them? Emily wondered.

Eventually, towards the back of the stack, she came across photos of a man who she immediately recognised from the portraits downstairs.

Jasper Graves.

She handed over several more photos. 'Do you think there's a similarity between the kids to Eleanore or Mr. Graves?'

'Maybe,' Dan said as he studied another of the photos. 'Can't say for certain, but... it wouldn't be a total shock if these were their kids.'

'Do you think that's why they really started this home for orphans?' Lucy asked. 'Because they lost their own children?'

'Possibly,' Emily replied. She had been thinking the exact same thing.

After she'd handed off the last photo, Emily bent down and retrieved the manila folder. Inside, there was a single sheet of paper, which she read through:

THORNS OF ERṢETU.

The Ouroboros have already been set. Everything is marked. The three stages can be executed.

1. The black.

Call them. Refer to the texts and the rite. They will observe and form the circle. Form the night.

2. The white.

The offering in thorns. Be strong.

3. The red.

The binding.

Then... it is time. And remember... be wary of the white flame.

SHE FROWNED. *What the hell was that?* Emily took a few moments to read it again, yet wound up no closer to understanding it.

'What do you make of this?' she said as she gave Dan the note, watching as his eyes scanned over it. She wasn't surprised to see a look of confusion form over his face.

'It reads like gibberish,' he said. 'Utter nonsense.'

Ollie took it next. 'I always thought Mr. Graves wrote it,' he said. 'I mean, I don't know for certain, but that was my gut feeling.'

'Given we know next to nothing about the man,' Dan

began, 'we can't rule it out. It's as good a guess as any. But it still doesn't help us make sense of any of it.'

Lucy took longer with the note, however. 'The red,' she mused.

'What?' Dan asked.

Lucy pointed up to the lights. 'The red,' she said again. 'Every light in the house is red. Is that where we are now, in the 'red' the note talks about? The part with the binding?'

Dan shrugged. 'I have no idea.'

'If it is,' Lucy went on, 'then maybe it's a clue about what's happening.'

'Perhaps,' Dan said. 'But we still need to know more.'

'The cellar!' Ollie then explained, eyes widening in realisation. 'There's something down there. *Under* the cellar. I'm sure of it. That's what Eleanore was hiding all along. It might still be down there now, and it might help us understand what's happening.'

'I still think we look for Eleanore,' Emily eventually replied. 'I understand what you're saying, Ollie, but surely it will be easier and quicker if we just get her to talk.'

'I agree,' said Lucy. 'Plus... who knows *what* is waiting down there. Isn't that where that thing came from?'

Emily's thoughts flashed back to when the huge man had first burst through the cellar door.

'Let's take the key with us, then,' Dan suggested. 'Couldn't hurt. If we need to get down there later, at least we'll be able to. Plus, if we have it, that means Eleanore can't use it to get inside. So one less place to search while we're looking for her.'

Emily nodded. Then a thought struck her, and she slowly shook her head and let out a humourless laugh.

'What is it?' Lucy asked.

Emily shook her head. 'Just the thing with the key,' she

said. 'If Eleanore is right, and we are all... you know... dead, then it's ironic we're *still* spending our time obsessing over a key to the bloody cellar. It just seems...' She paused for a moment. 'I don't know... bizarre. But I guess this whole thing is bizarre.'

'Yeah,' Dan said. 'I hear you.' He gazed around the room. 'But then again, this place seems to be an *exact* replica of where we lived together.' His brow creased in thought. 'I wonder how deep that goes.'

'What do you mean?' Ollie asked.

'Well... just... is *everything* the same? Like... words on the pages in the books we read, are they the same? Is it the same mortar in the blocks, or the same screws in the floorboards? How far down does it all go, provided we're actually dead like she said?'

Emily glanced around the room, considering Dan's words. 'Who knows?' she eventually said. 'But let's hope it goes deep enough to replicate whatever was under the cellar, just in case we need it. I mean, the box and keys were still under the floorboards, just like they were back then. That's something, right?'

'I guess so,' Dan said. 'That was what got me thinking.'

There was another brief silence.

Lucy let out a sigh. 'I still can't believe it,' she said, looking at the others with big, desperate eyes. 'Do you think... Eleanore could be wrong? Or if she isn't, do you think there's a way to fix this?'

No one had an answer. Lucy gazed down again, looking to Emily like she was about to break down.

'Maybe she is wrong,' Emily quickly said. 'Maybe there *is* another way to explain everything. We'll find out together.'

Lucy gave her a sad but appreciative smile.

'Should we go find Eleanore, then?' Ollie asked.

Emily glanced down at the boy. 'I guess so. Are you... okay? I know this is all a lot to take in.'

He gave a stoic nod. 'I just want to know the truth.'

She smiled and put a hand on his shoulder. 'Me too.'

The group walked out from the room, Dan and Emily in the lead. He leaned in close to Emily. 'You really think Eleanore might be wrong?' he whispered.

Emily shook her head. 'I don't know, Dan. But I *really* fucking hope so.'

CHAPTER
THIRTY-SEVEN

Lucy made sure to stay close to Ollie as the group slowly made their way along the hallway. She was thankful Dan and Emily had decided to take the lead, allowing her to stay back, which made her feel just a tiny bit safer.

She also hoped that by staying close to Ollie, she could help make him feel a little safer as well. The woman couldn't get over Ollie now being the youngest among them. It felt so strange, and one of the things she found hardest to deal with—which was crazy, given they'd been told they were all actually dead. Her thoughts turned to the monstrosity.

Lucy couldn't help but shudder as she remembered the attack for what had to be the dozenth time. It had been *so* painful. The entity's grip had been impossibly strong, and the feeling of the thorns cutting through her skin was pure agony. No matter how much she had silently prayed for it all to end, her body just kept getting carved and ruined, over and over again—she'd felt every laceration. After he'd discarded her, Lucy didn't remember anything until she came to, lying on Eleanore's bed and looking up at the others while still in tremendous pain.

And somehow younger.

It was like the attack had stripped away her age. She then wondered, *Was that the point of it? To make me younger?*

Lucy shook her head. *That doesn't make sense.* But then... nothing about what they were going through made sense.

As they walked, Lucy's eyes were drawn to the wall near Emily's room. She remembered being dragged through it, but there was no hole anymore, and it looked completely normal.

'What happened there?' she asked as she pointed over to it. 'The wall was destroyed... right?'

'Yeah,' Dan said. 'After the attack, one of those things we used to see appeared. A watcher. It just stared at the hole, which then kind of... repaired itself. It's hard to explain. But you'd never tell you'd been yanked clean through it, right?'

'No,' Lucy replied. 'You wouldn't.'

As they moved, Emily suddenly split off and approached the open door to her room.

'What are you—' Dan began.

'Just seeing if she's inside,' Emily explained as she leaned into the room, the light in there already on. 'All clear.' Emily then pointed to Lucy's room, where the door was closed. 'Should we check in there too?'

Lucy felt her chest tighten. She hadn't been in her room since coming back. The idea of seeing it again after so many years felt... significant. Part of her didn't even want to go in, for fear of how it would make her feel.

But Lucy knew they had to check, just to be sure. And despite being nervous, a huge part of her really wanted to see her old room once more.

'Can't hurt,' Dan eventually replied. However, Lucy noticed he was keeping his eyes on her, as if waiting for her permission.

She nodded. 'Yeah, just a quick look,' she said.

'Want me to go first?' Dan asked.

Lucy was about to nod, but then shook her head. 'No, I will. Just... stay close, okay?'

'I promise,' Ollie said from beside her. She felt him take her hand and squeeze it. Lucy looked down at him and smiled.

With that, she approached her room and pushed open the door. The red light from the hallway forced its way in, fighting back the shadows; Lucy reached inside and flicked on the light. A red glow flooded the space.

She brought a hand up to her face. It was *exactly* the same. The urge to cry started to wash over her in waves, but she fought against it and slowly stepped inside, Ollie squeezing through the doorway with her to stay by her side. Dan and Emily remained close behind as well. Lucy felt a hand on her shoulder.

'It's a lot to take in, isn't it,' Emily asked her in a gentle voice.

Lucy could only nod. If she tried to speak, she knew she'd just break down crying. It didn't take long to realise Eleanore wasn't there—Dan even checked the dressing room and en-suite to be sure. Lucy also opened one of the wardrobes to search inside, and then came face to face with all her old clothes, just dangling there. Now the tears came. She'd actually forgotten about many of the items in the wardrobe, and seeing the clothing again caused it all to come back, hitting her like a truck. Emily walked up beside Lucy and put an arm around her, hugging the woman as Lucy fought to get her sobbing under control.

'We should check the rest of this floor while we're up here,' Dan said. 'Once we know for certain Eleanore isn't here, we can move down and clear off the next floor.'

It sounded like a good idea to Lucy, as it meant they wouldn't be rushing down to the ground floor, where she just *knew* that thing would be waiting somewhere, likely back in the cellar. Therefore, she wanted to keep as far away from the cellar door as she could, at least until they absolutely *had* to go near it.

Their search on that top floor turned up nothing but old memories. It was weird seeing all the rooms again, especially given they were now all bathed in an eerie red hue.

Then it was time to travel down to the mid-floor. Once there, they checked all the rooms, and again came up short. Lucy forced herself to take a steadying breath, knowing that only left the ground floor and cellar.

And outside, she reminded herself, realising there were many places around the grounds Eleanore could have hidden. Everyone walked over to the stairwell and peered down the stairs.

'Everyone stay close together,' Dan said.

'What... what if we see something?' Lucy asked, unable to hide the worry from her voice. 'What if that thing comes back?'

'We run,' Dan replied.

'But we run together,' Ollie added. 'No one gets left behind.'

'Agreed,' Emily said.

Dan nodded firmly. 'If we're quick, we should be able to outrun the entity,' he said. 'At least... I hope we can.'

'Do we run back up here?' Lucy asked.

'I'm... not sure,' Dan replied. 'We could get stuck up here if it blocks off the stairs, just like it did the first time.'

'What about running to the garden?' Ollie suggested. 'Plenty of room out there to outmanoeuvre it.'

'But those other things are out there,' Lucy replied. 'Those four... whatever they were.'

'Plus, it's dark out,' Emily added. '*Really* dark. We couldn't see much beyond our own noses before.'

'Let's just see how it goes,' Dan eventually said. 'If the creature returns, we'll run wherever we're able to, just make sure we stick together.'

Lucy continued to stare down the stairs. 'What if it comes for me again?' she asked, her voice little more than a whisper. 'It wanted me before. What if... what if it wants me again?'

Ollie took her hand once more. 'Then we won't let it get you. Not this time. I promise.'

The young boy spoke with such confidence and resolve it took Lucy aback. The need to protect them all was clearly still with him. 'You're so brave, Ollie,' she said. 'You always were.'

The group slowly made their way down, stairs creaking under their feet, everything else completely silent. It didn't take long before they emerged out into the entrance hallway. Lucy held on to her locket as they walked to the centre of the space.

'Library first?' Dan suggested, keeping his voice low. Emily gave a shrug as if to say, '*might as well.*'

The room was empty, but everyone started to filter farther in to look around, with Emily approaching one of the bookshelves, pulling free one of the books there. She began to flick through the pages.

'It's all here,' she said.

'What's all there?' Ollie asked.

'The words,' Emily confirmed. She then held the book out towards them, pages pulled open so they could see. 'This is the book Eleanore liked. *Bleak House*.' She turned the book back to herself and flicked through more pages. 'Everything is here as it should be.'

'Okayyyy?' Ollie said, clearly not following.

'Well,' Emily went on, 'remember when Dan wondered how accurate this place was compared to the real house?' She waggled the book in one hand. 'I'm thinking it's pretty bloody accurate.'

'Looks that way,' Dan agreed. 'I think—Jesus!' he exclaimed as he jumped in shock, eyes fixed firmly on the window to the room.

Lucy jolted and turned to look. She then drew in a gasp as she saw a featureless face staring back from the bottom of the window. It took Lucy a moment to realise it was one of the small, twisted things they had seen outside earlier.

The group backed away from the glass and pulled themselves closer together. 'Was it watching us the whole time?' Lucy asked, shuddering as a creeping sensation washed over her.

'I have no idea,' Emily said, narrowing her eyes and leaning forward to take in the details of the thing that watched them. Not that there was much to see. From what Lucy could tell, it was just a small, misshapen head with dull, grey skin. The head was devoid of eyes, a nose, or a mouth. It didn't move at all.

Though there were other things that *did* move behind it, coming closer into view. The other three entities shuffled forward, pressing against the first, fighting for a view.

Lucy took half a step back. 'Are they watching us?'

'How can they even see?' Ollie asked. 'They don't have eyes.'

'Can we be done in this room now?' Emily added, setting the book back on the shelf but keeping a close eye on the window the whole time.

'Yeah, I think we're definitely done in here,' Dan agreed. Everyone quickly backed out of the room, the four heads outside following their every movement. Once back out in the hall, Emily pulled the door shut and shuddered.

'What the hell *are* those things?' Lucy asked. She didn't expect an answer. She knew no one had one.

'I don't care,' Emily said. 'As long as they stay out there.'

Lucy heard a *tap, tap, tap* coming from inside the room and froze. She quickly realised one of those things was knocking on the window. 'Are they trying to get our attention?' she asked the others.

'Ignore them,' Dan said. 'Let's just focus on finding Eleanore.'

They searched the drawing room next, where Lucy saw all the old board games stacked up just as they'd been years ago; after that, they started to walk over to the den on the opposite side of the hallway. Just as they were midway across, Dan spoke. 'Guys... hold on a second, will you?'

Everyone stopped and turned to face him. 'What is it?' Lucy asked, noticing he was frowning while gazing at them all.

'Just... wait there,' he went on as he continued to stare, like he was studying the rest of the group. Then he turned his back on them.

What is he doing? Lucy thought.

'Dan,' Emily said. 'What's wrong?'

'I... I can't remember what any of you are wearing,' he said, still looking away.

Lucy turned to face Emily, eyebrow cocked in confusion.

'You don't... *what?*' Emily asked. 'Dan, what are you talking about?'

'I can't remember what any of you are wearing,' he repeated, back still to them. 'I realised it as I was walking. I was thinking about what happened to Lucy upstairs, but when I tried to focus on the image in my mind, I realised I couldn't remember what clothes she was wearing.' He finally turned to look at them once more. His eyes ran over them all, Lucy especially. He nodded, then turned around yet again. A second later, he sagged in defeat. 'What the fuck is happening?' he asked, sounding angry. 'I *just* looked and still can't remember?!'

Lucy met Emily's eyes again. Emily shrugged. She then looked Lucy up and down, turned, and after a moment exclaimed, 'Oh my God. I... I can't either!' Emily whipped around, eyes wide, staring at Lucy.

'How can you not remember?' Lucy asked. 'Of *course* you can. You have to.' She wondered if the others were losing their minds... but when she turned away and tried to focus on the other's clothing, she realised nothing was coming to mind. While she had no doubt everyone *was* fully clothed—Lucy had the faint impressions of shoes, trousers, tops—she couldn't focus on any specifics or colours.

What the hell?

She spun back to the others. They all shared looks of utter astonishment.

'Why is that happening?' Emily asked.

Dan ran a hand through his hair. 'It's insane,' he said.

'It's like we know we *should* be clothed,' Lucy said, 'so our minds are filling everything in for us without giving us details. Just giving us impressions of what we *think* should be there.'

'I remembered Lucy's locket,' Ollie suddenly said. All eyes fell on him. He pointed to the piece of jewellery around Lucy's neck. 'I could picture that part, just... not anything else she was wearing.'

'Yeah,' Dan said, nodding. 'Yeah, that's right.' He lifted his arm. 'The watches too, that me and Emily are wearing.' He closed his eyes tightly. 'Yeah, I can still picture these.'

'Maybe the clothes aren't real,' Lucy suggested. 'Which is why we can't get a clear picture of them.'

'And the locket and watches?' Dan asked.

Lucy shrugged. 'I don't know. Maybe we were buried with them or something, so they stayed with us.' She hated thinking like that; admitting that their being dead was actually a possibility. After a moment, she looked down and pinched her locket between her thumb and forefinger, and popped it open to stare at the small pictures of her mother and father within. A wave of relief hit her—she'd been worried the photos wouldn't be there anymore.

'More questions without answers,' Dan said. His hands were crossed over his chest now, and he stared down at the floor. Eventually, he looked back up. 'Come on, let's just find Eleanore and hope she can fill in more of the gaps.'

Just as they began walking closer to the den, a tremendous roar boomed out, coming from beneath them.

Lucy's heart seized.

CHAPTER
THIRTY-EIGHT

'No!' Lucy exclaimed in panic.

Her hand shot out and grabbed Ollie's shoulder, her grip tight and painful. 'It's... it's *him!*'

Ollie knew she was right. The roar had sounded *exactly* like the one from before. The boy's heart hammered in his chest. The thought of seeing that thing again made him want to drop down and curl up. Ollie thought of his parents, imagining being in their safe and warm embrace, not trapped in the purgatory at Erimus House.

But he also thought about his promise to Lucy. Despite being the youngest there now, he still didn't feel it; to him, it was still his job to make sure everyone was safe.

He took one of Lucy's hands in his own.

'It's okay,' he said, trying to keep his voice steady.

Thud.

'He... he's coming!' Lucy shrieked and took a step back. Ollie could see her trembling.

'We'll protect you,' Ollie said, staying close. He then

looked to the others. 'We need to find somewhere to run to,' he said. 'Back upstairs!'

Thud. Thud. Thud.

The heavy footsteps were getting louder, the hulking entity clearly lumbering up the cellar steps.

Ollie gently pushed Lucy towards the stairs, taking charge as Dan and Emily just stared ahead in horror.

'Let's go!' he snapped, grabbing Emily and pulling her along as well. 'Dan! Let's move!'

Eventually, Dan turned to him and nodded. 'Yeah, okay,' the man said. 'But we still need to find Eleanore. She's the only one that knows—'

'Later,' Ollie interrupted. Then, everyone started running.

Yet before they'd even reached the staircase there came an almighty crash, followed by the squeal of wood splintering. Ollie turned back and saw the cellar door slide into view across the open dining room doorway. Just as it had last time.

Ollie was initially confused, but then remembered what had happened with the watcher upstairs, with it resetting things to how they were.

Thud. Thud.

Ollie tried to make sure he was the last one into the stairwell, but Dan stood firm and forced the boy through first instead. Ollie couldn't help but bristle with anger, finding himself annoyed that Dan now saw himself as the leader. The boy knew there was no malice in what Dan was doing, and the man just saw himself as the adult and Ollie the kid.

Which... was true. Ollie *could* understand it. But he hated it, regardless.

Still looking back, Ollie soon saw the huge being step

into view, wrapped in the awful vines and thorns. The monster had to again duck down to squeeze through the opening as it moved into the hall. As he watched in fear, Ollie noticed a figure flash past the dining room doorway.

'Eleanore!' Ollie shouted, pointing. 'She's heading for the cellar. I just saw her!'

'We need to run!' Lucy shouted, already heading up the stairs.

'She's right,' Dan agreed. 'We'll worry about Eleanore later.'

Thud. Thud. Thud.

The hulking man drew closer. The entity gave another angry roar, and that spurred Ollie into action. He sprinted through the doorway to the staircase, with Dan following close behind.

The group shot upwards, their footfalls thundering as they ran, Lucy at the head, with Emily and Ollie close behind. In a matter of moments they broke out to the mid-floor hallway, all panting and panicked.

'Do we go up again?' Lucy asked, wide-eyed. Ollie shook his head and pointed to the snug at the head of the corridor. 'In there,' he said. 'If it comes for us there, we can go left or right, then work our way around the rooms.'

'But we can't keep running in circles forever,' Dan said.

'What other choice do we have, Dan?' Ollie shot back. 'It's this or we try our luck outside.'

Or try to reach the cellar, he suddenly thought. *See what Eleanore was so eager to get to.* He then admonished himself for the idea, realising it was far too dangerous.

The group quickly started forward, following Ollie's suggestion and rushing to the snug that looked out over the front of the house. Once inside, they kept the light off and swung the door closed, but not fully, leaving just enough room to peek out.

Lucy was breathing heavily, and Ollie could see she was shaking, clearly fighting not to start sobbing. Emily quickly moved next to the woman and hugged her. Ollie and Dan both peered out into the hallway, with Ollie bending down and Dan standing over him.

The booming footsteps started up the stairs. Even from this distance, Ollie could feel the vibrations under his feet.

Thud.

Thud.

Thud.

It was hard for the boy to keep his composure. When he'd been scared back before this nightmare had started, he'd always been able to focus on his role of looking after the others. That had given him a purpose and managed to draw his mind away from the fear. Suddenly, he realised that was why he valued the role so much—that and the guilt he felt for failing his sister all those years ago.

But now, even if he tried to concentrate on keeping the others safe, he couldn't stave off the terror. He watched with held breath and wide eyes, waiting for the monster to appear.

He didn't have to wait long.

CHAPTER
THIRTY-NINE

Dan had to fight from gasping as the huge man slowly walked out into the corridor. The entity was just as immense and menacing as before.

Another roar erupted from the monster. Even from such a distance, Dan was able to make out the horrific face through the torn skin at the front of the fleshy cowl. The eyes glinted, staring madly, and a breath later the monster screamed yet again, the sound deep and primal.

Dan turned to glance at Lucy, who shook uncontrollably as Emily held her. He prayed she could stay silent. He was holding his breath, hoping the monster would head to the next stairwell and keep going up. But his heart dropped as the thing immediately turned to face the exact door they were peeking out of.

The monster roared a third time.

It knows where we are, Dan realised. *Jesus fucking Christ, it* knows!

'It's coming,' he managed to whisper to the others, voice full of panic. The entity's booming footsteps came closer.

Thud, thud, thud, thud.

'Run!' he shouted.

Everyone bolted to the side, sprinting through the side room and then looping around and ahead into Dan's bedroom. As they did, there came a thunderous crash from the snug as the door there was obviously destroyed. Another angry cry echoed out, and the footsteps followed around the outside of the building.

Thud, thud, thud.

'Back out into the hallway,' Ollie ordered. 'Then downstairs. Quickly!'

As good a plan as any, Dan thought to himself, struggling to keep from falling into complete panic. *At least then we won't be trapped up here.*

Plus, Dan knew they would be able to get outside if they *really* needed to. While the four smaller entities were likely still out there, Dan knew they were far less of a threat than the hulking creature.

Everyone sprinted from the room and out into the hallway again. They were about to set off towards the staircase when the huge pursuer suddenly came crashing through the wall, stumbling as plaster and blockwork exploded outwards around its bulky frame.

The creature strode forward, cutting off the group's escape route. The face, partly hidden by the hood of skin, glared at them. The monster opened its mouth and let out another cry of rage, the sound almost deafening. Dan pushed himself to the front of the group, making sure everyone else was behind him, his eyes frantically searching for somewhere to run.

The monster advanced.

In response, the group backed up and Lucy shrieked in fear. The only thing Dan could think to do was to duck back into one of the rooms again, then circle the perimeter of the house once more. If the monster gave chase, maybe they could get it far enough away from the stairs to be able to finally make it back down.

'Into Ollie's bedroom!' he whispered to the others, keeping his voice low. As if it had heard him, the creature started to make a beeline for Ollie's door to cut that off as well.

What the hell?

With no other option, the group turned and ran deeper into the hallway. Dan suddenly felt a stabbing pain around his waist and something pulling him back, forcing him to stop in his tracks.

He gazed down as the others continued forward. A vine was wrapped around his waist, pressing its thorns deeper into the flesh of his stomach.

'Dan!' Emily suddenly shouted. He looked up to see her staring back at him, face locked in horror. As if things were now in slow motion, Dan turned his head to look back over his shoulder.

The entity was still about ten feet away, with its thick arm held out before it. Even so, a cluster of vines ran from the outstretched arm and over to Dan.

Dan was about to shout for help, yet his words were cut off—the entity yanked its arm back, pulling Dan through the air with savage force. Searing pain cut across his stomach as the thorns dug in deeper.

After landing painfully, he was dragged backwards across the rug. He fought against the restraints, utterly terrified, then looked up to see the hulking creature slowly pulling the vines, arm over arm, drawing Dan ever closer.

There came hurried footsteps as the others quickly rushed to him. Ollie and Lucy grabbed his shoulders and pulled, while Emily got to work on the vines around his midsection. A second later Emily cried out in pain and pulled her hands away—blood leaked from her palms.

At almost the same moment, Ollie and Lucy toppled forward as the hulking creature before them yanked Dan closer again.

Dan realised it was no use. The entity was just too strong.

'Go!' he shouted to his friends. They didn't listen and continued to pull on him, with Emily now joining them at his shoulders. But when their attacker yanked once more, Dan was pulled as if they weren't helping at all. 'Just go!' Dan screamed again, then actually started to fight against his friends, trying to squirm free of their grip. As much as it filled him with terror, Dan knew there was no escape for him now, and he didn't want the others to get hurt by helping him. His hands found Lucy, who he pushed away, sending the woman toppling backwards. Then he pushed Ollie clear too.

Dan was yanked forwards yet again, but Emily held on and came with him, both of them drawing close to that thing. Dan quickly grabbed Emily's head and looked up at the woman with pleading eyes.

'Go!' he said to her. 'Just go!' Dan shoved her with all he had... but she clung on.

No!

With a final yank from the entity, both he and Emily slid towards it, finding themselves at the feet of the nightmarish monster. It gazed down at them with a wild look in its eyes, face twisted in anger.

A massive hand reached down for Dan.

Dan tried to kick and punch against it, but the entity's huge mitt quickly found his throat, squeezing so tight he thought his neck was going to snap. The entity swung its other arm and struck Emily, who let out a cry as she flew to the side, rolled twice, and came to a dead stop.

'Emily!' Lucy cried from behind. 'Dan!'

'Keep... away,' Dan managed to croak out as the hand compressed tighter around his throat, the touch was cold and clammy. Dan saw that the vines around his waist emanated from the forearm in front of him, now so close he could see the angry torn flesh where they had ripped through.

The pressure around Dan's waist eased, and for a moment he thought the vines were going to release him... but then he felt the spiked tips of the vines thrust forward, ripping through clothes and flesh, forcing themselves into his gut.

He clenched his teeth together and clamped his eyes shut as burning agony tore through his stomach. He could feel the worming vines push farther inside, cutting and tearing his intestines. He tried to yell out in pain, but the hand around his neck squeezed tighter, cutting off the cry. There were suddenly hands on Dan's legs, pulling at him—Ollie and Lucy.

No! Stay away!

To his relief, the entity seemed content to ignore the other two, at least for the time being, and it slowly raised its free arm. Its palm then came down over Dan, engulfing his face in its cold touch with fingers long enough to circle over the top of his head. At first, he thought the hulking thing was simply going to crush his head completely, but he found himself just held in place for a moment.

Soon enough, he felt more of the vines start to scratch and poke at the side of his face. Eruptions of pain then bloomed as they forced their way through the flesh of his cheeks, working from outside to in, while those in his gut continued their torturous attack. He kicked and fought instinctively, his legs yanking free of Ollie's and Lucy's grip.

Dan wanted to cry out, *needed* to cry out, just to distract himself from the pain in some way, but the grip around his throat was simply too tight—air refused to enter his body.

Then, Dan felt himself flying through the air, his body swinging upwards and over, arcing over the top of the monster, legs hitting the ceiling. His back slammed into the ground, knocking any remaining wind from him. The hand that held his head then released, and as it pulled away, the vines in his mouth shot free, ripping his cheeks to shreds. His mouth filled with blood. The vines in his gut retreated as well with the same savageness as the ones from his mouth. Dan had never felt agony like it and could only look up in horror at the huge man that towered over him.

The creature slowly raised its fists as Dan gazed upwards. It paused for a moment... then slammed its hands down on Dan's head.

The first strike hit his face, causing Dan's nose to crumple completely and his cheek to crack. The second blow came from the side, and Dan felt teeth fly from his mouth. With every blow, the vines that coated the man's arms and fists tore away more of Dan's flesh, thorns ripping through them like tender meat.

Dan couldn't cry. He couldn't move. He couldn't do anything but take it. Another direct strike came straight down onto him and Dan felt his skull fail, crack, and buckle inwards.

Only then did he finally black out.

CHAPTER
FORTY

Emily pushed herself up.

Her mind swam and her vision was blurry. She managed to get to all fours but struggled to hold herself in position, pain throbbing in her head. It felt like she'd been struck by a sledgehammer.

Distantly, she was aware she could hear screaming. After forcing herself to glance to the side, she was then able to make out what was happening.

Dan was lying on the ground, unmoving. Instead of a face, all Emily could see was a gory and crumpled red mass. Crimson also coated the rest of Dan's body, and his clothing had been torn and ravaged.

The huge thing that had attacked them was standing above Dan, but it looked forward at Lucy. She was on the floor, trying to crawl away, with Ollie standing before her, desperately pulling at her arm. Emily was confused as to why Ollie needed to pull—and why Lucy was moving so slowly—but then noticed lengths of vines run from the hulking man's arm and wrapping around her lower leg.

Emily tried to move, but her arms gave out and she fell

face-first to the floor. She then rolled to her side, blinking frantically to try to clear her vision.

'Get... away!' she tried to scream, but her voice was weak and her words were slurred.

More screams. Emily saw the monster bat Ollie away and moved next to Lucy. It started to attack.

No!

Emily heard the sicking sounds of flesh tearing as well as the dull, wet sounds of impact. Lucy's flailing arms eventually fell by her side.

So much blood, Emily thought, terrified, still unable to command her body to move. Eventually, the violent noises died down.

Thud.

Emily forced herself to look over again. The monster had left Lucy's motionless and ruined body and was now approaching.

Thud, thud, thud.

'Leave her alone!' a voice shouted. It was Ollie, who was somewhere behind Emily. Despite his brave words, he was sobbing.

She tried to reach up and ward off the towering entity as it came to a stop before her. It regarded her for a second, then reached down, taking hold of her outstretched wrists. Its grip tightened. Emily let out a cry of pain as she was violently yanked up like a doll. The creature quickly wrapped both of its arms around her, engulfing her in a tight bear hug. She kicked her dangling legs, yelled out frantically, and then begged. The vines and thorns that coated the entity scraped against Emily's skin, moving and writhing beneath her. It felt like barbed wire was cutting across her. The vines then started to penetrate her flesh, yet all she could do was gaze at the ruined face inside the cowl.

There was no compassion there. No empathy. Only anger.

Emily screamed as the pain increased. There was no stopping what was coming, she knew that, but she pleaded for Ollie to run.

Then... the attack became more savage.

CHAPTER
FORTY-ONE

'Please, just stop,' Ollie begged, tears streaming down his face. He saw what was happening to Emily and was finally forced to look away. The boy desperately wanted to jump up and run to help, but his body was wracked with pain, and he couldn't summon the strength to move.

The sounds of carnage continued. Emily's screams, however, did not. She eventually gave a wet cough, then fell quiet. After what seemed like an eternity, the other noises finally stopped as well.

Is she dead? Ollie wondered in fear. *Are they* all *dead?*

Given Lucy's recovery before, he hoped not. And then he remembered what Eleanore had said. That they were all already dead. *Can the dead die twice?*

The silence continued. Ollie drew in a breath and forced himself to roll over, which allowed him to gaze over at Emily's body. Even at that distance, he could see it was a gory mess. The entity stood above her, but was now facing Ollie, glaring at him. It took a step forward.

Thud.

No!

Ollie started to scramble backwards. 'No! Don't! Don't!' he cried out.

Thud. Thud. Thud.

The huge entity strode over and came to a stop, standing above him, looking down. Ollie tensed up as he sobbed, waiting for the inevitable.

Yet the thing didn't attack. It just stared at him for what felt like forever... then slowly turned and began walking away.

Ollie watched it, breath still held, terrified it would come back. But the towering monster continued over to the staircase, ducked through the open doorway, and started to descend. Ollie heard its footsteps get lower and lower.

He started to cry, still on his back and looking up at the ceiling. He then rolled back to his side, pulled his legs up and hugged himself in a foetal position.

The boy continued sobbing for the longest time, utterly terrified, too scared to even move. But through the tears he noticed something at the end of the hallway, where the monster had broken through the wall.

A watcher was standing there, gazing at the hole, which was slowly closing up. Anger filled Ollie, focused on the strange and seemingly benign entity. *That thing is part of whatever is happening here. It has to be.* He balled his hands into fists and finally found the strength to stand. Ollie made sure to keep his eyes away from his fallen friends, all of whom were still unmoving, and started to advance towards the watcher. Though he was still scared, anger was overriding everything.

'You!' he screamed just as the wall became whole again. The creature didn't turn; he wasn't sure it had even heard him. 'Hey! Look at me!'

Once he reached it, Ollie lifted an arm and grabbed its shoulder—an ice-cold shock suddenly exploded in his hand and ran up his arm, causing him to backpedal and cry out. At the same time, the creature spun, finally facing him, emitting excited chirps and clicks. Its head flicked from side to side, its movements jerky, and it stared at him, the scores of eyes on its face all fixated on his.

Ollie continued to stagger backwards, suddenly regretting what he'd done, arm still tingling. The entity didn't advance on him, however. It just stared ahead, watching.

Ollie shook his arm, trying to get the feeling back as wild *clicking* and *chittering* continued to come from the being. *Have I made it angry?*

As he kept retreating, Ollie's feet collided with something. He fell backwards, finding whatever he'd landed on to be firm but wet under him. He quickly rolled off, and to his horror saw that he'd tripped and fallen over Dan. Ollie's hand shot to his mouth as he gazed at Dan's ruined form. His bum and back slick with his friend's blood, and Ollie could smell nothing but copper.

He scrambled away in horror, feeling guilty for landing on his friend, though he didn't know if Dan was aware of *anything* at the moment.

Please wake up, Ollie begged. *I need you all to come back.*

But they all remained motionless, their bodies ruined.

Why didn't it attack me?

He remembered it had attacked Lucy first, not long after she had entered the house, and she had been the oldest at the time. And just now, it had attacked Emily, Lucy, and Dan, who all appeared to be similar ages. All older than him.

Was I spared because I'm the youngest?

Ollie then wondered if the other three would de-age

after the attack. If so, how young would they get? *And what happens when they're the same age as me?*

Though he was terrified, he still held on to his anger—anger at what was happening, anger at how unfair everything was, and anger towards Eleanore.

She's behind all this. She has to be.

His eyes flicked up, searching for the watcher once more, but he found it was gone.

The boy pushed himself up fully to his feet. He considered waiting by his friends until they woke—*if* they woke—so he could be there when they came to. But another idea came to him. Instead of waiting, he could *act*.

Eleanore was down in the cellar. He was certain of it. While the cellar door might have been repaired by a watcher, that didn't matter... they had the key.

The idea of going alone did give him pause. To his best guess, that's where the hulking monstrosity had retreated to. But if Eleanore felt safe enough running down there, maybe Ollie would also be safe. After all, the monster had left him alone thus far.

His thoughts focused on Eleanore. *Why is she safe? She's the oldest of all of us.* If the creature attacked based on age, surely she should have been a prime target.

It was another question without an answer. And Ollie wanted answers. He *needed* them. They all did.

He knew there was nothing he could do for his friends by just waiting with them. But if he went down there, maybe he could uncover something. Or even confront Eleanore.

Besides, it was still his job to make sure they were all safe. So far, he'd failed.

But hopefully, there was time to set it right.

Ollie moved over to Emily; he bent down, keeping his

gaze away from her face, and rummaged through her pockets to feel for the key. It didn't take him long to find it.

As he stood, a swell of determination flooded up from his belly.

'I'll be back,' he whispered to Emily. 'And I'm going to get us out of this. I promise.'

CHAPTER
FORTY-TWO

In the depths of unconsciousness, Emily's mind swam, searching for memories, desperately trying to pull back *something* that she knew was there but was blocked off.

Nothing came. Nothing concrete, anyway. Just... notions. Feelings. Impressions.

Of a family: husband, children. And of a good friend. Then... betrayal. Sudden heartbreak. Pain. Agony radiating from her throat.

Yet Emily could summon no images to match these impressions.

Eventually, her mind plummeted into the abyss again and everything was lost.

The black was quickly replaced by light. A red light. Then came the sensations. Pain ravaged her body. It was agonising. Emily couldn't move. She could see now, though everything was still blurry. Emily realised she was staring up at a ceiling.

A ceiling at Erimus House.

Some memories came back, of her and the others being attacked and torn to ribbons.

Ollie! she suddenly thought.

She remembered being terrified that he was going to be next. Emily desperately wanted to get up and see if he was okay, but moving was impossible. She simply had to lie there and endure.

CHAPTER
FORTY-THREE

O llie stood just outside the cellar door.
It *had* reformed, as he'd expected, and the padlock was in place. It felt so strange to be looking at something as mundane as a lock, considering the circumstances—and weird to think that if this *was* some kind of afterlife, everything seemed to operate exactly as it had in normal life.

With some trepidation, he inserted the key into the padlock and turned it. Though he was initially worried it wouldn't work, the lock easily popped free.

The last time that had happened, Ollie had been filled with excitement at finally being able to get down into the cellar. Now, though, there was nothing but apprehension.

Well, not *just* apprehension, he realised. *I also have to confront Eleanore.*

He removed the padlock, placed the key into his pocket, set the lock on the floor, then opened the door as quietly as he could. He took a moment to gaze down into the darkness. All was quiet. Ollie reached inside the opening and flicked on the light switch. As expected, red light filled the stairwell.

Keep going, he told himself. Though it took some effort, he forced himself to descend the stone steps, moving carefully, listening intently for any sound.

Eventually, he reached the bottom, where he walked forward a few steps before pushing open the next heavy door. The light was already on inside. The machines and equipment were all there as he remembered, with naturally formed walkways between them. At the far end, he could see that one of the units had been slid away, and the trapdoor in the floor was open.

She's down here, he told himself. *I know she is.*

After making his way over to the opening, Ollie peered inside, half expecting to see another watcher looking back up at him again, like last time. However, he breathed a sigh of relief to see the coast was clear. There was more red light inside, illuminating what looked to be a concrete corridor, which ran back under him, beneath his feet. There was also a ladder traveling down from the hatch. He hesitated, thinking again of the monster that had attacked the others.

Come on, you can do this.

After taking another steadying breath, Ollie lowered himself down to the passageway. Once there, he turned to see it stretch off in only one direction. The surfaces were all bare concrete, with only strip lighting fixed to the ceiling and small electrical wires running between each one. Other than that, it was just a mass of smooth concrete.

Apart from the metal door at the far end.

Ollie judged the length of the passageway to be around twenty meters. The metal on the door at the far end had rusted, and though Ollie couldn't be sure, the flaking paint across its surface might have once been red. The door was also slightly ajar.

He could hear something coming from inside: a gentle sobbing. Ollie crept forward, taking slow and steady steps, keeping his footfalls light to avoid making a sound. As he drew closer, he became certain the light crying was coming from Eleanore. She sounded like she was in anguish.

Good.

Ollie then paused just outside, trying to decide what to do next. While he knew he had to go in, he was torn on whether he should just barge straight inside or try to gently open the door wider and peek in. Eventually, he settled on the latter option. He raised a hand to the door and gently pushed—it gave a long, metallic *creak*, and he winced. Eleanore's sobs immediately ceased.

So much for being sneaky.

With nothing else for it, he pushed the door open completely. Eleanore was seated inside, looking back over at him in shock.

'Ollie!' Eleanore exclaimed.

His eyes opened wide and he stared ahead, not quite believing what he was seeing.

CHAPTER
FORTY-FOUR

When will it stop?

Dan tried to roll to his side, but the pain prevented him from moving. It was like nothing he'd ever experienced before. However, it *was* starting to recede. His insides, which had been torn up when he'd awoken, didn't throb as much.

While he wasn't able to roll over yet, Dan was still able to glance to his side, where he saw Emily. She was breathing, but her body was a mess.

It got her too, he realised with despair.

After looking at her, something flooded back to him from when he'd been unconscious. Not full thoughts or memories, but glimpses of things hidden behind the fog.

Pain. Hurt. Even anger.

Though he couldn't make sense of it, he knew there were more important things to focus on at the moment. After what had happened to Lucy, Dan had a feeling his body was healing itself, but he had to wonder if he would find himself younger afterward.

He tried to search the rest of the hallway, but he wasn't

even able to turn his head, so he couldn't see anyone else. He tried to call out, yet that just made air escape through the lacerations in his throat and force out wet bubbles of blood. Pain ravaged his neck.

So he waited. He could do nothing else.

CHAPTER
FORTY-FIVE

'What are you doing down here?' Eleanore asked.

Ollie ignored the question, instead just gazing around the room. While there was one thing in particular that drew his attention, he still took in the cursory details beyond the door.

There was a large space, and while the ceiling and floor were both exposed concrete, the floor itself was covered in a large, thick rug that lay across most of the expanse. The walls had dark oak timber boarding on the lower half, with dark green wallpaper above, embossed with a pattern of small golden crests.

All the furniture in the room was oak, consisting of cabinets and desks, similar to what was up in the living areas, as well as cupboards and wardrobes. There was another door at the opposite end of the room, thick timber with a brass handle.

But all of those cursory details were overshadowed by what was in the centre of the space. It was a hospital-style bed, with a metal frame underneath a thick, stained mattress.

There was a dead body on top of the bed.

The body was pale and painfully thin. Bizarrely, it was wrapped in thorn-coated vines, and was hooked up to dialysis machines and drips, though there were no signs of life in the husk. As Ollie gazed at the gaunt face, recognition flashed within him.

Jasper Graves.

The man looked different from his portrait, clearly ravaged by illness, and his beard was gone too.

As with the rest of the house, the entire room was bathed in red light, coming from circular, ceiling-mounted light fittings above.

It suddenly occurred to Ollie that if the house was *indeed* an exact replica of what came before, that meant the man on the bed must have been down there the whole time as well.

'What... *is* this?' Ollie eventually asked in horror.

Eleanore was seated on a high-backed chair just next to the bed. She slowly got to her feet and spoke. 'You shouldn't be down here, Ollie! It isn't safe. Go back upstairs.'

'It isn't safe up there either, Eleanore,' he said coldly. 'Do you know what just happened to Emily, Lucy, and Dan?' He waited for an answer that didn't come. '*Do* you?!'

Eleanore looked away, unable to meet his furious gaze. 'I... I'm so sorry,' she said. 'It wasn't meant to be like this. I... I didn't *know*.'

'You didn't know *what?*' Ollie demanded. 'What have you done to us here, Eleanore? Tell me. Tell me everything.'

Yet the woman just shook her head. 'It... it will all be over soon,' she said. 'Just... trust me.'

'No!' Ollie shouted, letting out his building anger. 'Of course I won't trust you! That thing up there tore up my friends. My *family*. And it's your fault! I know it is. You have something to do with it.' His rage was growing stronger every second.

Even though Ollie was smaller than the woman, he dearly wanted to run over and attack her for what she'd done... but he knew that wouldn't help get any answers.

Eleanore glanced over to the body next to her, then looked back to Ollie. 'Please, just go. You *have* to.'

'He's been here the whole time, hasn't he,' Ollie asked, pointing. 'Even before. You kept a dead man down here while we were living in the house upstairs.'

'No!' Eleanore quickly exclaimed. 'No, it isn't like that. He *wasn't* dead then. Not... not at first. I was caring for him, Ollie.'

'Caring for him?' the boy asked in confusion. 'What do you mean?'

Eleanore sighed. 'He was sick, Ollie. I was... treating him the best I could. Or rather, making him as comfortable as I could. There was nothing I could do—nothing anyone could do to stop it.'

'Comfortable?' Ollie asked with a frown. 'He's wrapped up in thorns, Eleanore.'

She hung her head. 'That was... necessary,' she said. 'And something *he* wanted as well, before he passed.'

'That makes no sense,' Ollie argued. 'How could he *want* that? To be covered in those things while he was dying. *No one* would want that.'

'But... he *did*,' Eleanore insisted. 'The pain he felt from them... that was all part of it.'

'Part of what?' Question by question, Ollie was growing more frustrated with her evasiveness.

But Eleanore shook her head. 'Just go,' she pleaded. 'Before he wakes up again.'

Ollie paused. 'What... what do you mean, 'wakes up again'? He's dead.' The boy gazed at Jasper Graves. Something clicked in his mind. 'Wait... *He's* the thing that attacked us... isn't he?' While the body of Mr. Graves was thin and malnourished, a far cry from the towering monstrosity they had encountered earlier, the vines and thorns that entombed him made everything come together in Ollie's mind. He then regarded the corpse with much more apprehension.

'Just go, Ollie,' Eleanore stated again, her voice now taking on more of the authority Ollie remembered. 'It isn't safe.'

The words stuck in Ollie's mind. *How many times did she use that line on us when she didn't want us finding out the truth?*

'I'm not going anywhere,' the boy said. 'Not without answers.' His eyes bored into her. He remembered all of her subterfuge, and her sneaking around. 'That's why you kept coming down here at night, wasn't it?' he asked. 'With the tray. You were bringing medicine for him.'

Eleanore slowly nodded. 'And water,' she admitted. 'I kept as much medicine and equipment as I could down here but had to restock often.'

'Why wasn't he in a hospital?'

'A hospital couldn't help. His condition was terminal, so he wanted to stay here, in his home.'

'Down in a dingy basement? Why wasn't he in one of the bedrooms?'

The woman gave another sigh, this one tinged with annoyance. 'Because we couldn't run a children's home if he was up there, Ollie. So, he agreed to stay hidden while I handled things.'

'He stayed hidden down here all this time?' Ollie asked in shock. 'That must have been awful for him.'

'It was,' Eleanore said. 'Even when he had most of his mobility, it was difficult. He felt cooped up. But then the disease got worse, and in his later months he couldn't leave his bed.'

'So he didn't get to go outside in all that time?' Ollie asked. Eleanore shook her head. 'What about food?' Ollie went on. 'We only saw you take water.'

'I snuck food down at night,' she explained. 'But eventually his appetite faded. I tried to keep him eating, but he couldn't hold it down after a certain point, so I just took water.'

'You're a monster,' Ollie stated in disbelief.

Eleanore shook her head again. 'No! It's what he *wanted*. What we both wanted. It *had* to happen.'

'What are you talking about?!' Ollie screamed, unable to keep a lid on his anger any longer. '*What* needed to happen? Why would anyone ever want to go through all that?'

'He went through it to get all this,' Eleanore said as she held her arms out around her, looking around the room. 'He needed to make that sacrifice, Ollie, and it was his choice. He insisted on it. The vines, the thorns, they were needed. He had to be wrapped in their embrace, to feel the sting of the thorns when the time came.'

Ollie's mind was reeling. The things Eleanore was saying were utter madness, but even so Ollie tried hard to commit everything to memory in order to tell the others about it when they healed.

If they healed.

'And... after death, he became that monster? Did you know that would happen? Did *he?* That he would become that... that...'

'The Guardian,' Eleanore said with a slow nod. 'He knew. That is to be his role now: the protector of this reality we're all living in.'

'*Living?*' Ollie asked, his voice thick with scorn. 'We're not living. This isn't living. This is hell!'

Tears came from Eleanore, rolling down her cheeks. 'I didn't know it would be this bad,' she said, sobbing. 'It wasn't supposed to be this way. I'm sorry. I'm so, so sorry. I... I should have been stronger that night. I should have seen it all through.'

'That night?' Ollie asked, confused. 'You mean the night of the fire, don't you?' She didn't answer. Ollie's eyes then widened in horror. 'We were supposed to die, weren't we.' He clenched his teeth together. '*Weren't* we,' he repeated darkly.

The woman nodded, still not looking at him. 'But... I couldn't,' she said. 'I was weak, so I came to get you all. But... it's caused you so much more suffering.' She looked up. 'I didn't know that would happen, Ollie. You have to believe me.'

Ollie balled his fists. He shook with rage. 'How?' he simply asked, teeth clenched. 'Tell me how you did all this. *How* did you bring us here after we died?'

Eleanore just shook her head. 'No,' she said, 'I won't. You don't need to know. It won't make any difference.'

Ollie took a slow and deliberate step forward, moving into the room. 'Tell me anyway,' he demanded, his voice cold.

Eleanore hesitated, shrinking back a little, but then

straightened up with a defiant glare on her face. 'No,' she said again.

'You evil bitch,' Ollie snarled. Eleanore's face fell in shock. 'How could you do this to us? I thought you were supposed to care for us. I thought you *loved* us?'

'Oh, Ollie... I did. I *do!*'

Something else suddenly clicked in his mind. 'Wait... I... I know why you did this, why you brought us here.' His rage built. 'You want to keep us here with you forever, don't you.' He couldn't stop shaking. 'The children in those photos,' he went on, taking another step. 'They *were* yours, weren't they. Yours and his.' He pointed to Mr. Graves.

Eleanore's bottom lips started to tremble. Eventually, she nodded.

'Did they die?' Ollie asked.

More tears came from the old woman. She nodded again.

'So we're the replacements,' he said. 'That's why you started the children's home in the first place and took us in. You lost them, and you wanted to make sure you didn't lose us.'

Eleanore's body shook uncontrollably. Her sobbing intensified. 'It... isn't like that,' she managed to say in a soft, trembling voice.

'I think it is,' Ollie replied, tears of his own forming as the weight of the realisation overwhelmed him. 'You wanted a little family forever, didn't you? And you decided what our fate would be, whether *we* wanted it or not.'

'You don't understand,' she said, voice full of pain.

'I do,' Ollie told her. 'I understand completely.' He found himself wondering what else she was hiding from them. 'Do... do you know *how* we died?' the boy eventually asked.

'No!' she exclaimed. 'That's the truth. I can't remember anything after that night. None of us can.'

'But *look* at me, Eleanore,' Ollie said. Now it was his lip that trembled. 'Everyone else is... different, older.' His voice cracked. 'But I'm just like I was. I haven't aged at all. Does... does that mean...' He had to fight to stop from breaking down completely. 'That I didn't grow up? That I died as a kid?'

Eleanore just stared at him with sad, tear-filled eyes. 'Oh, Ollie,' she said. 'I'm so sorry.'

He couldn't hold back anymore. The dam burst and he broke down crying, hugging himself as he hunched over and wailed.

He soon heard Eleanore approach and felt her arms wrap around him and pull him into a hug. His instinct was to fight her off, but he was so overwhelmed he let it happen, *needing* the comfort, despite hating the woman.

'Why did you do this?' he wailed. 'Why?'

'I'm sorry,' she said, squeezing him harder, pressing his head into her chest. 'I'm so, so sorry.'

As much as he despised it, being held by the woman was strangely comforting. But then his anger returned, partly focused on himself for falling into her embrace so easily. *She doesn't deserve that! She doesn't deserve to be forgiven!*

'No!' he shouted and pushed her away. He stood up straight, fists and teeth clenched again. He pushed her a second time, causing the older woman to topple onto her back. She looked up in shock.

'Ollie!' she shouted.

'No!' he yelled again. 'You don't get to *scold* me ever again!'

He gazed down at her, eyes blazing with fury. She actually looked scared of him in that moment. *Good,* he thought, breathing deeply, trying to stave off the mounting aggression. As Ollie glared at the woman, something else then clicked in his mind. She *looks like she did back then too.*

'You died soon after that night as well, didn't you.' Ollie said.

Eleanore's look of fear softened. She nodded. 'I think so, yes,' she said. 'But I can't remember how, or when, exactly. I'll *never* remember. None of us will. And it's better that way.' The woman stood up, but moved away from Ollie. 'Now go. You should head back upstairs.'

'For what?' Ollie shouted. 'If this is how it is now, do you expect us to just live up there while you stay down here?' He then jabbed a finger at Mr. Graves. 'And will *he* just keep getting up and coming to kill us again and again?'

'No!' she exclaimed. 'No, he won't. It'll all be finished soon. But just... go, Ollie. Before he changes again. I mean it.'

Ollie tilted his chin up and curled his lip. 'Make me,' he simply said.

Eleanore frowned. '*Excuse* me?'

'You heard me,' he replied. 'If you want me to go, then make me go.'

Her frown of confusion turned to anger. 'You always were too defiant, Ollie. You could never just let things *be.*'

'And I'm not going to change, you made sure of that,' he shot back, folding his arms across his chest. 'So if you want me to stop being difficult, I need more answers.'

'I've told you enough.'

'You haven't! Not *nearly* enough. Like... how did you even make all this happen? How did you get the power to control things like this?' He hesitated. 'It has to do with that note in your wardrobe, doesn't it?' No answer. Ollie then pointed to the door on the opposite side of the room. 'What's through there?'

He noticed Eleanore tense up, yet she quickly replied, 'Nothing. Just a storage space.'

'Liar,' he shot back. 'Even now, after everything, you *still* won't be honest with me.'

Eleanore's hands curled into fists and shook with anger. 'Ollie,' she said, teeth clenched, eyes still tear-filled. 'You're making this too hard.' She took a step forward.

'*I'm* making it hard?' Ollie took a step forward as well. 'Look at where you brought us! Look at what you've done! This is Hell, Eleanore. Now tell me how to fix it!'

'There is no 'fixing' anything, Ollie!' Eleanore screamed.

'I don't believe that!' Ollie shouted back. He pointed again to the room behind her. 'Now *what* is in there?'

Eleanore paused. After a moment, her tense body slowly relaxed. She looked down, shook her head, then sighed. 'I'm sorry, Ollie,' she said in a soft voice. 'But you need to leave.' The woman suddenly advanced on him so quickly that Ollie only had time to flinch before she grabbed him with both hands, surprising him with her strength. She then started to force Ollie backwards and out into the passageway.

'What are you doing?!' he shouted, trying to dig in his heels to arrest the momentum. But the taller woman was just too much for him.

'I'm *making* you listen,' Eleanore said as she kept grappling with the boy and forcing him back.

'Let go!' Ollie yelled. He swung his arms across himself, successfully breaking her hold, but he'd over compensated and spun all the way around, which allowed Eleanore to grab him from behind. She wrapped both arms around him, gripping him tight. Eleanore then twisted them both around again and started to drag Ollie out of the room.

'You're going back up there to stay with the others.'

Ollie kicked and fought, trying to pry himself free. It was useless. The door before him was getting farther and farther away. Ollie knew there were answers in there, he just *knew* it. Yet he was being pulled away from them.

No.

He suddenly stopped fighting and allowed himself to be dragged. The action clearly surprised Eleanore, who stumbled at the change in weight.

Ollie used the opportunity to lift his leg and thrust his foot down, aiming for where he hoped Eleanore's foot was. He felt his heel make contact and there was a sharp pain, but the blow hurt Eleanore far more—she yelled out and began hopping on one leg.

He felt the hold on him relax. Thinking quickly, he then thrust his head up, the top colliding with Eleanore's face. She grunted and let go completely.

Now free, Ollie spun and pushed the woman as hard as he could, sending her sprawling to the floor.

My chance!

Ollie didn't hesitate. He sprinted forward again as fast as he could.

'Wait!' Eleanore shouted, yet Ollie didn't look back; he just steamed ahead and shot through the open doorway.

Once through, he turned and swung the door closed, catching sight just before it shut of Eleanore getting back to her feet and starting to run towards him. Once the door was closed, he noticed a thumb-turn lock on the inside, which he quickly rotated until there was a dull *clunk*.

'No!' he heard the woman cry from the other side. She

then began to bang on the door repeatedly. *Boom, boom, boom.*

Ollie stepped back, seeing the thick door shake in its frame, but he could tell it wasn't going to budge.

'Open up, Ollie! Let me in!' she screamed.

'No.'

'You don't know what you're doing!'

'Maybe,' Ollie said to himself as he turned around. 'But neither do you.'

She continued to bang frantically, but Ollie ignored it and focused on the room ahead.

'Ollie! Open the fucking door!' Eleanore screamed.

That caused Ollie to pause. He'd never heard her curse like that before and felt a small sense of pleasure at being the one to drive her to it. *Fuck you, Eleanore,* he thought, allowing himself a smile. Then he proceeded to the door ahead.

CHAPTER
FORTY-SIX

Lucy's body shook. She was crying. *Wailing.*
Why does this keep happening?
She'd finally forced herself up into a sitting position, with her back pressed against the hallway wall. Her body had healed a second time, though she was still coated in drying blood. Lucy could see Emily and Dan farther down the corridor, and each of them was moving now. To her astonishment, the two of them appeared younger, looking somewhere in their twenties.

Lucy looked at the back of her own hand before wiping away some of the blood. She noticed the flesh was smoother, the veins beneath the skin less visible.

Lucy slowed her breathing, trying to calm herself.

'Emily, Lucy!' Dan called as he pushed himself up to his knees. 'Are you both... okay?'

'No,' Emily replied flatly. She was in a sitting position, knees pulled up to her chest, staring straight ahead. 'That was... that was...' Her voice cracked, and she broke down crying. Dan shuffled to the nearest wall and used it to climb to his feet. The now-young man looked quite a bit lighter than he had earlier.

'Where's Ollie?' Lucy called over to them.

'I... don't know,' Dan shouted back, sounding worried.

Get up, Lucy told herself.

She felt no pain, but she *did* still remember the absolute agony of the attack. The temptation to just lie down and give up was strong.

No, get up!

She pressed her hand against the wall and used it for leverage just like Dan had. Once upright, Lucy gave herself a moment.

Emily was still sitting on the floor, crying. Lucy lifted her head and shared a look with Dan. They both then made their way over to their friend.

Once there, Lucy crouched down over Emily and hugged her, feeling Dan wrap his arms over them both.

Lucy had always been the one the others looked out for, that they hugged when she was upset. Now she wanted to be strong for them.

She also knew there was work to do. They couldn't just sit and feel sorry for themselves.

They had to find Ollie.

CHAPTER
FORTY-SEVEN

Ollie kept a watchful eye on Mr. Graves as he walked by the bed. The vines around the body were wrapped tightly, and Ollie could see the thorns from the vines still poking into the pale, sunken flesh.

Mr. Graves had a sheet over his lower half, but Ollie could tell by the shapes under the thin material that the vines ran down the man's legs as well.

The body was painfully thin, with Mr. Graves' ribcage stuck out above a sunken-in stomach. The dead man's shoulders and collar bone pushed out against thin flesh that clung to the bones like shrink wrap.

It was hard to imagine that the huge creature from before had come from this husk.

Ollie stopped at the dark oak door. It looked heavy, with brass hinges and a knob handle, but no lock. Ollie took hold of the handle and pushed the door.

His eyes went wide.

Inside was a smaller room. There was light, but

different from the other areas of the house. It wasn't red; it was white, and it came from a burning white flame.

The glow pushed back the red light that tried to invade from outside, giving the inner room a ghostly feel.

The white fire was burning inside a large, concave metal plate, and that plate sat atop what looked to be an altar, consisting of an ornate wooden base and flat, polished surface. Ollie gazed closer at the fire, which was about the size of a small campfire, looking for any kind of fuel source at its base. Yet there was nothing: no wood, no paper, no coal.

There was only the white fire.

No, Ollie soon realised as he leaned closer. There *was* something. A small amount of congealed black residue sat at the very bottom of the bowl, right at the centre.

Strangely, the fire burned silently and radiated no heat. The only thing it gave off was the flickering white glow.

The sounds around Ollie brought his mind back to the present. Eleanore continued to pound frantically on the outer door, screaming for him to open up, but the boy ignored it. He knew he had work to do.

The altar and fire were situated straight ahead, pressed against the back wall. To Ollie's left was a desk, and on top of that a stack of aged papers with a binding to the left-hand side, holding them all together like a book. The paper of each page looked thick, like they were formed from parchment. As Ollie stepped closer, he saw the top page had a handwritten title:

Thorns of Erṣetu.
&
Crimson Threads of Anum.

Ollie realised he'd read that title before, at least part of it, on the note in Eleanore's room. The handwriting looked the same as on the note as well.

Mr. Graves wrote this, Ollie guessed.

There were a few other cabinets in the room, and a chest of drawers. The walls were again timber cladding with wallpaper above. There was no rug underfoot, only bare concrete. Ollie glanced at the flame once more, then stepped closer to the bound stack of papers on the desk. He reached down and flicked through, coming across pages upon pages of handwritten notes and sketches. Ollie guessed there must have been close to a hundred sheets in the stack.

This is it, he thought to himself. *There are answers in here, I just know it! But there's too much for me to go through on my own.*

Ollie bent down and started to dig through the drawers to see if he could find anything else of interest. In the very top drawer was a leather-bound notebook, which had a length of packaging tape across the cover. Something was written on the tape in marker, acting as a title. *Children of the New Sun.*

Ollie pulled out the notebook and opened it up, seeing the same handwriting inside. He read the first page:

THIS IS everything I know about the family.

No, not family. It isn't a family. I need to stop thinking that way.

It's a cult.

Even so, it was somewhere I felt I belonged. I know Eleanore feels the same, having been a part of it for much longer than I was.

But they took from us more than we could bear to lose.

And so... I have compiled everything that I know. All that both of us know. I want it written down in case something happens to us too. There has to be a record of what they've done.

- Jasper.

Ollie frowned, confused. *The family?*

While not understanding it, Ollie felt the notebook was important, so he set it near the stack of pages.

I need to get these back to the others.

However, he knew getting out with both documents would be hard given Eleanore was still outside, screaming desperately and continuing to strike the outer door.

Ollie tried to think of a way forward. He was again drawn to the white fire, so he slowly approached it, remembering the words from the note in Eleanore's room: 'Be wary of the white flame.'

Looks like I've found it, Ollie told himself.

He'd never known a fire to burn white before, or to burn in complete silence. It confused Ollie, as did the fact the fire didn't generate any heat. He carefully raised his hand and moved it closer, trying to pick up on any warmth at all.

Nothing.

As he continued to stare, Ollie considered moving his hand across the very top of the leaping flames, like he had done with candles. Those times had never hurt, and he wanted to know more. *If there's no heat, surely it can't actually burn me.* Curiosity got the better of the boy, so he inched his hand forward, bringing it closer to the top.

Then... he moved his hand sideways, palm down, cutting through the leaping flames.

An explosion of cold erupted from his palm and his body went rigid, eyes going wide.

Suddenly, Ollie wasn't in the same room anymore—he was lying on his back, pain shooting through his head. He looked up at the night sky and saw the front of Erimus House loom over him, completely ablaze, the front porch a collapsed heap. Lucy was above him, howling and crying in desperation, her broken locket clutched in her hands. Emily and Dan were there as well, sobbing hysterically as they knelt over him, yelling Ollie's name. All three of them were younger again, how he'd always remembered them.

The pain in his head was overwhelming. He could barely move. His vision was fading. *No, hold on! Hold on! This can't be it!*

'Ollie! Please be okay!' Lucy cried out through her sobs. 'I'm sorry! I'm so sorry!'

It's okay, Luce. It wasn't your fault.

Ollie's vision soon faded to black.

Then he was back in the room again, staring at the white flame, his hand beside it having passed through. His hand and lower arm felt numb and he was breathing heavily, panting. Tears welled up in his eyes.

That's... that's how I died, he told himself with horrible realisation. Then he broke down completely.

Cellar

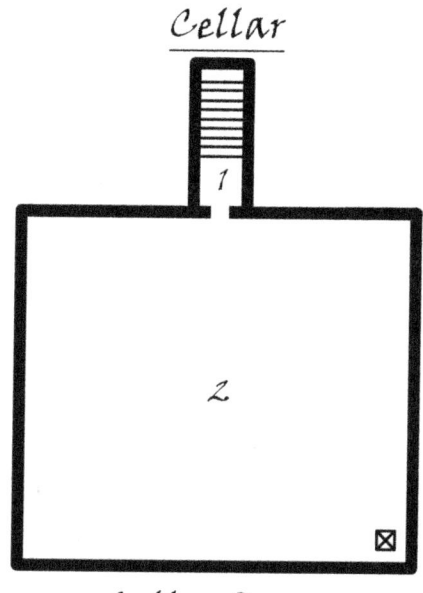

Cellar Rooms

1 - Stairwell
2 - Machine Room

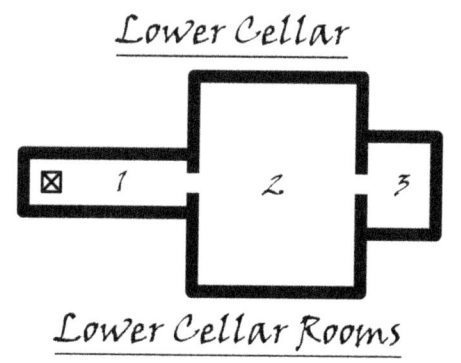

Lower Cellar

Lower Cellar Rooms

1 - Passageway
2 - Main Room
3 - Inner Room

CHAPTER
FORTY-EIGHT

'Yeah, I can hear it too,' Emily said.

She, Lucy, and Dan stood at the top of the stairwell to the ground floor, looking down. Emily was still struggling with the memories of the attack, and the pain she'd endured, but she'd managed to push that aside enough for them to begin their search for Ollie.

But just as they'd reached the stairs, the group stopped —Dan had claimed he'd heard something, which the other two had quickly noticed.

'Someone's banging,' Lucy realised aloud.

'And yelling,' Dan added. 'Sounds far away, though. Like... *really* low down.'

'Definitely in the cellar,' Emily said. 'Do you think Ollie is down there?' Panic flooded her, and she worried about what might be happening. She then remembered the key and quickly started to pat herself down. 'Wait,' she said. 'It's gone! The key is gone. Someone must have taken it.'

'Ollie,' Dan suggested. 'It must have been.'

'But that thing,' Lucy said. 'The monster. It was right

there with us. How would he have had time? Surely it would have tried to get him as well?'

'We don't know that,' Dan said. 'The first time it came, it only went for you. Maybe this time it didn't target Ollie and just took out the three of us.'

'So... he just grabbed the key and took off?' Lucy asked.

Emily nodded. 'Makes sense,' she said. 'He said he saw Eleanore head down there, remember? Him going down there on his own seems like a pretty 'Ollie' thing to do.'

'Then... is *he* the one banging?' Lucy asked. 'Is he okay?'

'We need to find out,' Emily said. 'Come on.'

The three descended the stairs, with Lucy leading the way, which was something of a surprise to Emily.

The faint shouting below continued, though Emily didn't think it sounded like Ollie. Despite it not being clear, the voice sounded feminine, yet it was hard to be certain.

Eleanore, she guessed. Internally, she cursed Ollie for being so bullheaded, but quickly caught herself, realising if that wasn't what had happened and something bad had happened to him, she would feel terrible.

Once they reached the ground floor, the trio sprinted across the main hallway. It shocked Emily just how different she now felt compared to before the attack. Her limbs moved with much more freedom, and her energy was notably improved.

Dan had been the first person she'd seen after coming to, and she was surprised at his appearance. Then she'd gotten a look at Lucy, who looked even younger and more beautiful, despite the miserable and horrified expression the woman had worn. Emily hadn't gotten the chance to see her own reflection yet and had to wonder what she looked like, given she couldn't even remember her own young adult years to know for sure.

After running through to the dining room, they saw the door to the cellar was open, padlock lying on the floor, which confirmed Emily's suspicion Ollie had taken the key. It also became clear now that it was Eleanore yelling, somewhere deep inside.

'Ollie! You open up right now! Let me in! Let me in!' She sounded utterly desperate.

Dan didn't hesitate and shot forward, heading for the stairs; the two girls quickly followed him. Once at the bottom of the stairs, they found themselves in a large room dominated by metallic equipment and machinery. At the far end, Emily immediately spotted an open floor hatch, just like what Ollie had described back in the day. The banging and shouting echoed up from the hole.

'Quickly!' Lucy said and took off forward. Emily and Dan followed, racing over to the hatch and peering down. There was a concrete passageway underground, again soaked in that familiar red light.

'I'll go first,' Dan whispered. He moved to the ladder and started to descend, climbing down steadily and quietly, though any noise was drowned out by the constant banging and yelling of Eleanore. Once he was on the ground, he stared deeper into the passageway, then signalled for Emily and Lucy to follow. Emily let Lucy go first, then climbed down straight after. All three then gazed ahead, where they saw Eleanore standing outside a rusted metal door, pounding furiously on its surface.

'Ollie! Come outside now! Please, I'm begging you!'

Emily cast a look at Lucy, then Dan, before stepping forward. 'Eleanore?' she called out.

Eleanore jolted in surprise and spun around, quickly pressing her back against the door behind her. The old woman looked shocked, eyes wide. But more than that, there was a desperate gaze there Emily had never seen in Eleanore before.

'Emily?' Eleanore's eyes flicked over to the others. 'Dan? Lucy? What are you doing—' She stopped for a moment. 'You all look so young.'

'I know,' Emily said. 'Thanks to the *thing* that keeps coming for us. Where's Ollie, Eleanore?' She already knew the answer, though; her eyes focused on the door.

'You can't come down here,' Eleanore said. 'You shouldn't be down here.'

Yet again, Emily was reminded of their life before, when they'd been forbidden from venturing down to the cellar. *Some things never change*.

'We need answers from you,' Dan said to her. 'You ran off before we got any last time, and you left us to be attacked again. Do you know how *painful* that was?'

The woman's tense body eased a little. Her expression softened, eyes growing sad. She said nothing.

'Why does it keep happening, Eleanore?' Lucy asked, stepping forward and moving past Emily. 'What does it want from us? Why do we keep getting younger?'

Eleanore slowly shook her head. 'I... don't know.'

The lie was obvious. 'Come on, Eleanore,' Emily said. 'That isn't true. You *do* know. Why does it keep attacking us?'

Eleanore looked down. Her silence held for the longest time, and Emily assumed the woman wasn't going to answer. Eventually, almost half a minute later, she said, 'I don't know *how* it's happening, and I didn't know it would be like this for you all. But... it's pulling you back to how you were that night.'

'That night?' Emily asked. 'You mean the night of the fire, don't you.'

The other woman nodded in response.

'But *why?*' Lucy asked.

'Because that's how things need to be,' Eleanore replied, her voice flat. 'Everything needs to be how it was at that point.'

'At that *point?*' Dan asked. 'What do you mean? What point? When the house burned down?'

Eleanore took in a deep breath. 'Not when the *house* burned,' she said. 'But something else.'

Dan then threw his hands up in the air. 'Jesus Christ, Eleanore, enough! Just tell us, stop with the vague answers! When *what* burned?'

Eleanore's eyes came up to meet the young man, but her expression was now blank. 'The blood,' she said. '*Your* blood. Our blood. I burned it. I had to.'

'Our... blood?' Emily asked, feeling a frown of disgust cross her face. She was suddenly reminded of Eleanore taking her blood when she was younger. 'Is... is that how the fire started?' she asked. 'When you were burning the blood?'

Another shake of the head. 'No,' Eleanore replied. 'I started that in the kitchen afterwards. I wanted to... to... finish it all that night. But I couldn't.'

Emily clenched her fists.

'So, is that when our memories stopped?' Lucy asked. 'When the blood burned up?'

'Yes,' Eleanore admitted, her voice little more than a whisper. 'That's when everything was finalised. Made permanent.'

'Burning blood... that sounds insane,' Dan said. 'Like some kind of God-damn ritual or something.'

Eleanore actually nodded. 'Yes,' she said. 'That's right. A ritual.'

'Rituals are just make believe,' Dan scoffed. 'They don't really work.'

Considering the situation they were all in, Emily was surprised Dan was so dismissive.

'That's what we read on the note in your room,' Lucy said. 'Right? Thorns of... what was it?'

'Thorns of Erşetu,' Eleanore confirmed.

'This is so fucked up,' Dan exclaimed, shaking his head and exhaling.

'There were three steps there,' Lucy went on. 'Colours. White, black, and red.'

'Yes,' Eleanore said. She sounded broken, defeated. But Emily didn't care—the woman was finally talking.

'And it mentioned things being marked. The Ouro... Oru... Ourob...' Lucy frowned, obviously trying to remember.

'Ouroboros,' Emily corrected. 'Circles. They signify eternity.'

Dan's eyes narrowed. 'There were circles carved all over the house,' he said, looking at Emily. 'Remember?'

'We marked everything before any of you got here,' Eleanore said, voice still flat. 'Those markings set the boundaries. Then... it was time for the first step.'

'The black, right?' Lucy asked. 'That was the first step.'

'Yes,' Eleanore said. 'We summoned the watchers. The things you all used to see in the house. They... observed everything. That's what made this reality possible.' She held her arms out by her side. 'It's taken from what they saw back then. And they could see *everything*.'

'What *are* they?' Emily asked. 'Ghosts? Demons?'

Eleanore shook her head. 'No. They're from a place that's hard to describe. Another plane. That place is powering all of this.'

'So how is that the black?' Lucy asked. 'I don't get it.'

'The eternal void,' Eleanore said. 'Everything outside the house is everlasting dark. *That* is the black. The first matter. The place our reality exists in.'

'You're talking gibberish,' Dan said.

'I know it sounds that way,' Eleanore said. 'I can just stop if you don't want to hear it.'

'No!' Emily replied quickly. 'Keep going.'

'Why are you suddenly being so talkative?' Dan asked her. Emily grimaced. *Don't derail it. Just let her talk.*

'What is the white?' Emily said before Eleanore could reply to Dan. 'What is the second step?'

'That was the offering,' Eleanore answered. 'The white it refers to is a soul, which was needed to anchor everything here. A soul purified by thorns.'

'Jesus Christ,' Dan uttered. 'This is absolute insanity. You *sacrificed* someone? Are you fucking serious?!'

'No!' Eleanore shot back. 'He offered *himself*. And then he became... became... the Guardian.'

'The what?' Emily's eyes then widened in realisation. 'Wait, the thing that keeps attacking us.'

Eleanore nodded. 'Yes. He protects this place, makes sure there is order, and that everything stays the same. So you see, when you are all young again, like you were, everything will stop. The pain will stop, Emily.'

Dan threw his hands up in the air and drew in a deep breath; Emily knew he was about to explode in frustration. Before he could, Emily grabbed his shoulder. She understood his anger. She felt the same way, but for whatever reason, Eleanore was talking, and Emily knew they needed to hear everything while they could. Dan looked at Emily, clenching his teeth together, but nodded and exhaled slowly.

'And the red?' Lucy asked.

'Rubedo,' Eleanore explained. 'The binding. The blood I burned, mine and all yours, it ties us to this place forever. That's what brought us back after death.'

Dan ran a hand through his hair. 'So just burning a bit of blood brought our souls back here? Gimme a break.'

'Not just that,' Eleanore replied. 'There were incantations and rites.'

'Of course there were,' Dan said, sarcasm filling his voice.

Emily understood how he was feeling, especially considering how outlandish everything sounded. But to Emily, it sounded as plausible as anything she was likely to hear.

'Say you're telling the truth,' Emily said. 'Say that's how all this came to be... how the hell did you learn it all? And why do it in the first place? Why condemn us all to this?'

This time, Eleanore stayed quiet.

'What? Now you've gone all shy on us?' Dan asked. 'You were happy to talk before. Why?'

Eleanore glanced back at the closed door behind her. 'Because what does it matter anymore? None of you will even *try* to understand me.'

'Of course we won't!' Dan growled through clenched teeth.

Emily again placed a calming hand on him.

'Tell us how to undo it,' she said. 'There *has* to be a way.'

'You can't undo death,' Eleanore said as her eyes fell to the floor.

Emily paused.

The words hit her like a truck. *Of course we can't,* she realised. Because if they *were* all dead, then that was it.

Their bodies in the real world were dead. There would be nothing to go back to. While that should have been obvious, only then did it really hit Emily.

No way back, she told herself, the realisation sinking in more and more with each passing second.

'How could you do this to us?!' Dan screamed, his roar full of unbridled rage. Eleanore jumped and flinched away.

There were a few moments of silence as Dan's scream echoed to nothing. Then...

'Hello?' a voice called from behind the door.

'Ollie!' Emily called out. 'Is that you?'

'Yes!' he shouted back. 'Are you all okay?'

Emily hesitated. She doubted there was ever a way she could be 'okay' again. 'We're fine,' she eventually replied, not knowing what else to say. 'We're all here. What happened?'

'Long story,' Ollie shouted back. 'You all need to get in here. Quickly.'

Emily cast a glance at Dan. The man nodded and took a step forward. 'Out of the way, Eleanore,' he said.

The older woman straightened up. 'You aren't going in there,' she said defiantly. 'You can't. Ollie, out of there now. Everyone upstairs.'

'There's four of us, Eleanore, and I'm not a child anymore,' Dan replied. 'You can't stop us.'

Eleanore scowled at him. It looked like she was about to lunge, but then obviously thought better about it and shuffled to the side, again looking down at the floor.

'We're coming,' Emily shouted as the trio made their way close to the door. She heard the metallic *thunk* of a lock releasing from the other side, and then the door opened inwards, revealing Ollie to them. The first thing Emily noticed was that the boy's eyes were red, like he'd been crying.

'Are *you* okay?' she asked, immediately worried.

'Fine,' he said, not sounding fine at all.

'You ran off without us,' Lucy said.

'I had to,' he said. He then frowned. 'You all look... different. Younger.'

'Yeah,' Emily said. 'So we've noticed.'

Ollie stared at them for a second, then shook his head. 'You all need to come and see what's in here,' he said, beckoning them all inside.

'Wait,' Dan said, glaring at Eleanore. 'What if she locks us in or something?'

'The lock is on the inside,' Ollie said. 'She can't, don't worry.' He opened the door wider.

Emily's mouth fell open as she saw what looked to be a dead body wrapped in vines.

'What the hell?' she uttered.

'Say hello to Mr. Graves,' Ollie said.

Emily looked at him. 'I... don't understand.'

Then they all listened as Ollie filled them in.

He explained about Mr. Graves being the Guardian that now stalked them. About Eleanore and Mr. Graves being together. About the children they both had and lost. And about how the four of them—Ollie, Emily, Dan, and Lucy—were now destined to be replacements.

With every word, Emily's anger grew.

CHAPTER
FORTY-NINE

Lucy was the last to enter the room to join Ollie. Before crossing the threshold, however, she looked to Eleanore, who had pressed herself into the corner of the passageway, allowing everyone to pass her. Strangely, Lucy couldn't help but feel for the older woman.

Dan's anger was justified. Lucy knew that. But at the same time, it was still *Eleanore*, the woman that had cared for them all and created a loving home.

The older woman couldn't meet Lucy's gaze, however, and just continued to stare down. It looked like she was on the verge of crying. Lucy had an urge to reach out, embrace her, and tell her she was forgiven.

But I can't forgive her. Not after all that. Can I?

Eventually, she followed the others inside, leaving Eleanore alone, with the woman nearly catatonic, lost in her own world of grief and pain.

Once inside, Lucy couldn't help but stare at the body. It was astonishing to think that, according to Ollie, Mr. Graves had been down there the whole time they'd lived in the house, being cared for by Eleanore before finally passing.

No, not 'passing'. Being sacrificed, she reminded herself, focusing on the thorns that punctured the dead flesh.

'I can't believe she kept a dying man down here,' Emily stated in astonishment to no one in particular.

'There's more to see. The important part,' Ollie said. He then pointed to a door at the back of the room. The door was open just a crack, and through it, Lucy could see a flickering light that looked odd against the red above.

Ollie then led them through, and everyone squeezed into a smaller adjoining room. All eyes immediately fell on the white fire that burned atop a large metal dish, casting the room in a cold, ghostly glow.

'What *is* that?' Lucy asked, staring at the flame.

'Careful with it,' Ollie said. 'It isn't hot but... it does things.'

Everyone turned to him. 'Does things?' Emily asked. 'What does that mean?'

'I'll explain in a second. But first...' Ollie motioned to the desk at the side of the room. 'You need to see these.'

Lucy noticed a bundle of bound and aged papers on the top of the desk, with a small leather-bound notebook next to it.

'I think there are answers in these,' Ollie continued. 'It's all written by Jasper Graves. I think it has to do with how we ended up here—how it all happened.'

'Well, I think Eleanore just gave us the abridged version of how it all happened,' Dan said.

Ollie frowned. 'Abridged version?'

Now it was the others' turn to bring Ollie up to speed, retelling everything Eleanore had shared. As they spoke, Lucy heard the old woman sniffle outside, as if still holding back tears. Again, Lucy couldn't help but feel bad for her, crazy as that was.

When the retelling was done, Emily had a little more to say. 'Ollie,' she began, sounding hesitant. 'Eleanore said something that... kind of hit hard.'

Ollie cocked his head to the side. 'How so?'

The woman pointed to the books on the desk. 'I just... I don't want you to get your hopes up with what's written in there, that's all. I'm... not sure there's anything that can fix what actually happened to us.'

'There might be,' Ollie said.

'I...' But Emily hesitated. 'Ollie, if we *died*, there's no going back. I'm really sorry to have to say it. But no one comes back from that. They just don't.'

'*If* we actually died,' Dan quickly said. 'We don't know for certain that's what's happening here.'

'But how else would you explain it?' Emily replied.

Dan shrugged. 'I can't, but that doesn't mean it's true.'

'Actually,' Ollie said, his voice sad. 'It is true. I... I *know* it is.'

Dan looked at him, eyes wide. 'How?'

Lucy saw the boy take a breath. Ollie nodded over to the white flame. 'Because I saw it,' he said. 'I saw how I died. The very last moments.' His eyes welled up.

Emily moved closer to him and bent down, taking his hands in hers. 'What are you talking about, Ollie?' she asked in a gentle voice. 'I'm not following.'

Ollie drew in a breath. 'I ran my hand over the fire,' he explained. 'It was cold. *Really* cold. Even hurt a little. But as soon as I touched it, everything changed. I was back there that night, lying on the ground just outside the house while it was burning.' Another breath, clearly to fight back tears. 'You were all there as well,' he explained. 'Crying. My head was hurting. A lot. *Something* happened, I just... don't know what, exactly. But a few seconds later I felt myself... die.'

Lucy felt numb. Her mouth hung open. All eyes turned again to the flame.

'You're telling me this thing unlocked your memories?' Lucy asked him.

'Only a tiny bit of them,' Ollie said, eyes wet. 'It was brief. And I still can't remember anything between sitting on the grass with all of you and what happened in the vision a few minutes later.'

Lucy took a step closer to the fire, entranced.

'Careful,' Ollie warned. 'It's really cold. My arm still doesn't feel right.' He then raised the limb to the others.

Emily gently took hold of Ollie's wrist. 'Your arm... It's really pale,' she said.

Ollie nodded. 'I know.'

Lucy gazed over as well. It was difficult to make out, especially given the bright white light from the fire, but the skin tone on the boy's hand and forearm *was* lighter.

'It still tingles,' Ollie said, clenching and unclenching a fist and wiggling his fingers.

This can show us how we die, Lucy realised. She didn't know how to feel about that. *Do I even want to see? Do I even want to know?*

Lucy had obviously been the oldest of the four to return to the house. It hadn't escaped her notice that that meant she was the only one among them to have lived a long, full life. Poor Ollie had still been a child, and both Dan and Lucy had still been relatively young.

Given her advanced age, Lucy knew there was a good chance natural causes had taken her. So... was there really anything to see? Any real reason to look?

Is curiosity enough of a reason?

She slowly stepped closer, realising it was.

'What are you doing?' Dan asked her.

'I... I need to know,' she said. Then she looked at Ollie. 'It was just a brief touch, right?' she asked.

He nodded. 'Yes, but... are you sure you want to do it? It isn't pleasant.'

Lucy hesitated. Eventually, she moved her hand towards the flame. *Strange*, she thought, *there's no heat at all*.

Not allowing a moment to second-guess herself, she quickly ran her hand across the flame that jumped up to her. She felt an ice-cold blast shoot up her arm and gasped...

Lucy was then lying in a large, soft bed. She was covered by a thick duvet that came up to her chest. She felt weak. *So* weak. Her heart ached, every beat causing pain. Breathing was hard. Every exhale was raspy and rattly.

She wasn't alone. As Lucy looked up, other faces gazed back down at her. They were smiling kindly, though none were crying. They didn't seem to be doctors or nurses. Lucy had an impression she knew them but couldn't remember how. Someone held her hand, stroking it.

Her vision started to fade as her breathing slowly stopped.

'It's okay,' a male voice said. 'Let go, Lucy. Go to where you're needed.' Then, Lucy felt... lighter...

She was back in the room with the others. Her hand and arm burned with an intense cold, and she quickly cradled the limb close to her chest, gasping and panting. The others ran to her, putting their arms around her.

'Are you okay?' Ollie asked.

'Is your arm hurt?' Dan followed.

'Talk to us, Lucy,' Emily added urgently.

Lucy felt weak. Her legs started to give out, but fortunately the others caught her, lowering her down to a sitting position. She realised she was weeping.

'Are you okay?' Ollie repeated, moving in front of Lucy and peering into her eyes.

She continued breathing heavily, trying to get her sobbing under control. Eventually, she managed to do it.

'I'm... I'm fine,' she said, though she knew she wasn't. How could anyone really be 'fine' after reliving their death? A flood of questions circled her mind: *where was I? What happened to me? Who were those people?*

Lucy had to wonder if more exposure to the white flame would unlock more of her memories. However, given how numb her arm felt, she didn't want to expose herself to the fire for any longer than she had. At least not yet. Lucy looked at her arm, seeing it was pale, like Ollie's. There was also faint scarring across the skin.

'Can you stand?' Dan asked. Lucy took a moment before nodding. 'I think so.'

The others helped her back to her feet.

'What did you see?' Emily asked.

Lucy hesitated. 'It's... hard to make sense of,' she said. 'I was in a bed, surrounded by people. I didn't recognise them, though.'

'Maybe it was family,' Dan suggested. 'Were you in a hospital?'

Lucy shook her head. 'No. I don't know where it was exactly, but definitely not a hospital. A bedroom, I think.'

'Perhaps you died at home, then,' Dan suggested. 'Maybe the others were your loved ones. If so... that's not such a bad way to go out, Luce.'

'I... suppose not,' she eventually replied. 'It didn't feel nice, though. It was... strange. Awful.'

'I don't suppose dying is ever easy,' Dan said.

'We need to think about getting out of this room,' Ollie interrupted.

'Why?' Emily asked.

Ollie pointed to the open door. 'In case Mr. Graves changes again. We need to take the notebook and papers somewhere so we can look through them. Preferably away from here, so *he* can't get us.'

'But I'm not sure there's anywhere to run,' Emily explained. 'That thing keeps finding us.'

'That doesn't mean we should make it easy,' Dan said. 'I think Ollie is right. We should take what he found upstairs. The space here is too cramped to lay everything out.'

'But... wait,' Lucy said. 'Dan, Emily... don't you both want to know?' She nodded to the ghostly flame.

There was a pause.

'No,' Dan said, shaking his head. 'No, I don't. Definitely not.'

'Why?' Lucy asked.

Another pause. 'I just... don't.'

But Lucy knew why. If Dan relived it, then he'd have to acknowledge that it was true, that he really *was* dead. *I don't think he's ready to do that yet.*

'Emily?' Lucy asked.

The other woman looked long and hard at the fire.

'We don't have a lot of time,' Dan said. 'Maybe we should just go.'

'Not yet,' Emily stated. She took a breath. 'I... I want to know. Lucy only had her hand in the fire briefly and the memory came back to her. I'll be quick.'

'Are you *sure* you want to do it?' Ollie asked.

Emily nodded. 'I'm sure.' She looked at Dan. 'We'll get out of here as soon as I'm done, okay?'

'I understand,' Dan said. Lucy then saw him give her a sad smile. 'Hope it's not too bad for you.'

The other woman chuckled. 'Thanks.'

She approached the fire and slowly held out her arm. As she did, Lucy saw the flames start to reach up, as if sensing Emily's hand was near and wanting to claim it. Emily passed her hand through the blaze.

CHAPTER
FIFTY

Pain. Shock. Anger. Betrayal. All those emotions coursed through her.

On top of all that, Emily's throat hurt a *lot*—she felt pressure around it.

Her heart hammered in her chest, and she tried to desperately pull in much-needed breaths. There were hands around her throat.

Above her, she saw Dan leaning over her, arms reaching down, hands on her neck. Something burned in his eyes. Hurt?

No! I don't want to die! Emily thought to herself in panic.

She tried to move but couldn't, feeling far too weak. There was a sharp pain in the side of her neck, which she assumed was from Dan's thumb pressing down on it.

Images popped into Emily's mind. She had children: Beth and Adrian, the twins. She pictured them as they were, both now in their twenties, but memories of them crawling around as babies soon took over. Emily clung to those thoughts as her life began to ebb away.

She was scared. Terrified. I *don't deserve this. Why is it happening?* She couldn't understand how someone she cared for, someone she loved, would do this.

Dan's hands tightened around her throat. She saw tears in his eyes.

Then... she was back again, standing in the room below Erimus House.

She was breathing frantically, sucking in the air she couldn't get when dying.

Her legs gave out and she fell to the floor. *No! No, no, no. It* can't *have happened like that!*

She remembered the images of her children. There was still much missing from her memory, and she only had what she'd recalled at the time, but the realisation she actually *had* children was overwhelming.

As was the knowledge that she'd never see them again

'Are you okay?' Ollie asked in panic. Everyone rushed over to her.

Emily felt a hand on her shoulder. An arm also fell over her. At first, she thought it was Lucy, but soon realised it was Dan—the last person she'd seen before she died.

The person that had killed her.

She quickly flung him off and scrambled out of the way. 'Don't you touch me!' she cried out. 'Don't you *fucking* touch me!'

'Emily,' Lucy said, hands up. 'It's us. Let us help.'

But Emily jabbed an accusing finger at Dan. '*You,*' she snarled. 'You keep away from me!'

Dan's face fell in shock. He looked to the others, confused, then back to Emily. 'What... what are you talking about? What's wrong?'

Tears came, yet Emily did her best to fight through them, teeth clenched. 'You killed me!' she screamed. 'You fucking killed me!'

Dan recoiled, eyebrows suddenly raised, holding up his hands in shock. '*What?* Woah, Emily, that's not... what are you *talking* about?' He again looked to the others for help.

'I *saw* it!' Emily screamed. 'I saw it! You had your hands around my neck, squeezing the life out of me. I looked into your eyes while I died. You... you... you strangled me!'

Dan went white. He shook his head. 'No, Emily, no. I would *never*. Something's wrong. That isn't what happened. It can't have been.'

Emily flinched back when he took a small step forward.

'Get away!' she shouted.

'Emily,' he said. 'I... I would *never*...'

It was all too much for her to comprehend. This was *Dan*. Little, shy Daniel. She'd considered him her brother. Always kind, always helping. The boy who'd gone to fetch her a towel when she'd cut her hand, wandering off in the dark despite being terrified.

She couldn't comprehend what could have happened to make him do what she'd seen in the vision. Then she remembered the hurt in his eyes.

Did I hurt him somehow? Emily couldn't imagine how—it wasn't in her nature to treat people badly. And besides, *nothing* would have warranted what Dan had done to her.

Not a fucking thing.

As she glared over at him, she felt revulsion and rage, which replaced all the fondness she'd previously carried for him.

Shy little Daniel, who grew up to be a murderer.

Emily felt nauseous. She started to gag and dry heave.

'Emily,' he said again. 'You have to believe me. I would never do that.'

She wanted to believe him, yet she knew what she'd

seen. Unless the memory was wrong somehow, a lie planted in there somehow, then there could be no doubt.

'Just keep away from her, Dan,' Ollie said.

Dan whipped his head around to the boy. '*What?*' he asked, incredulous. 'Ollie, you can't believe I'd do that.'

'I don't know what to believe,' Ollie said. 'But Emily saw what she saw, so just give her space, okay?'

Lucy hugged Emily, who allowed herself to break down crying.

How could he do that to me? Why *would he do that?*

'We need to get out of here,' Ollie said. Emily looked up to the boy through tear-filled eyes. She didn't want to go anywhere, least of all with Dan. 'The body back in there might change back soon,' Ollie went on. 'We can't be down here when he does. We'd have nowhere to run.'

'I'm not going anywhere with *him*,' Emily snarled as she jabbed a finger at Dan again.

Ollie bent down in front of her. 'I don't know what you saw,' he said, taking hold of her hands, 'and I don't know what actually happened. But I know we can't stay down here. None of us can. We need to look through what we've found and try to get answers. There is a lot there, so it'll take *all* of us to do that.'

Emily's stomach churned. She hated the idea of Dan going with them, acting as if nothing was wrong. She wanted to lunge for him and choke him, just to see how he liked being strangled to death. Even so, she knew Ollie had a point. If there *were* answers in the papers or notebook, then the group needed to find them. It was worth a try. Anything to get out of this place and away from Dan.

Having to live for eternity alongside the man who'd killed her would be worse to her than any hell.

'If we go, he keeps away from me,' Emily said through gritted teeth, glaring at her former friend.

Ollie nodded. 'That's fair. But... I think we need to go right now. I kind of feel we don't have a lot of time.'

Emily kept her eyes on Dan, who looked shell-shocked, standing away from the others. Emily got to her feet and straightened up her body, fists clenched by her side. 'Just don't come near me,' she ordered to Dan, her voice cold. 'Understand?'

'I...' But then Dan paused, head falling. He nodded. 'Okay, I won't,' he said. She knew he had wanted to argue back, to insist on his innocence, but he thankfully fell silent.

Ollie and Lucy quickly gathered up the papers and notebook, then they all filtered out of the room in silence, Emily in the lead and Dan at the rear. They headed out into the passageway to find Eleanore still sitting on the floor, knees tucked up to her chest, pressed into the corner next to the door.

Another one that betrayed me, Emily thought. She barely cast the older woman a look as she led everyone forward, where they ascended the ladder and moved up out of the basement.

Emily took them up to her old room, hoping to feel some kind of comfort there. Once inside, she sat on her bed and pointed over to the corner on the far side of the room. 'You can sit there,' she said coldly to Dan. 'Out of the way of the rest of us.'

He just nodded solemnly.

Ollie handed him the notebook. 'Here, read through this,' the boy said. 'See if there is anything we can use.'

Dan took it wordlessly and moved over to the corner as

instructed. He looked crestfallen, and Emily wondered if he was finally accepting what she'd told him.

Accepting that he's a killer.

Ollie set the papers down on the bed and unbound them, splitting the top half of the stack into three and handing them out.

They all began to peruse the notes. Emily knew Ollie and Lucy had questions, but they stayed quiet, obviously unsure what to make of the whole thing.

Emily didn't look at Dan. She couldn't. She just read through what had been handed to her, trying hard to concentrate.

An awful, heavy silence reigned over everyone as they read.

CHAPTER
FIFTY-ONE

Eleanore stood before the white flame, gazing at it intently.

She'd been desperate to keep everyone away from it, but Ollie had already been inside with the fire anyway. Plus, Dan had been right: she wouldn't have been able to stop all four of them.

So, she'd had no choice but to relent, even though she'd been terrified they would use the flame. Which they did... but only briefly. She'd heard what the others had said afterward, and was completely in shock to learn what Dan had done.

Eleanore had already known the white flame had a great deal of power—it was fuelling their reality, after all—but she hadn't known it could unlock memories.

Now, the urge to know how *she* had died filled her.

So... she held out her hand, the flames rising to meet it. A blast of painful cold ran up her arm...

Eleanore was outside in the night. Blood oozed from her inner forearm and wrist, which burned with pain.

She was kneeling away from the four children, as Emily,

Lucy, and Dan all gathered around Ollie, who lay on the ground, unmoving.

Memories of the last few moments replayed themselves in her mind: them all sitting on the grass only minutes ago, then of Lucy screaming that she'd lost her locket, realising it must still be inside. The young girl had bolted off towards the house.

Everyone had moved to stop her, but no one had been quick enough. Ollie had given chase. Eventually, Lucy came to a stop just outside the porch door, the flames ahead holding her back. Ollie drew to a stop behind her as Lucy pointed inside.

'I can see it! Through there, in the hallway! I can see it!'

'You can't go in,' Ollie said to her, holding her back.

'I *need* it. I need it!' she'd said while she struggled against him. 'I have to get it. Let me go!'

'Lucy, wait!' Eleanore had shouted.

'I'll get it,' Ollie had replied. 'Just... wait here.' He'd then dashed inside.

'No!' Emily had yelled after him.

By the time Eleanore had caught up, Ollie was already moving back towards them, locket in hand.

However, just as the boy moved into the porch and was about to step over the external threshold... the porch had collapsed.

A portion of the external wall dropped and landed on him, smashing Ollie to the floor, blocks and rubble bouncing heavily off his head.

Everyone had screamed. Eleanore and the others managed to grab the boy and pull him out. She saw blood.

Lots of it. Running from the side of his head.

The children had gathered around him, crying and

wailing, and Ollie had reached up towards Lucy, locket in hand.

The frantic cries of the children had flooded the air.

No... no, no, no!

Eleanore couldn't take it, couldn't accept what she'd caused. She noticed a loose bit of metal in the rubble, jagged with a sharp end.

She'd then acted, not giving herself the chance to think it through, grabbing the metal and quickly thrusting it into the sensitive flesh of her inner forearm. She'd then grimaced in pain and yanked the shard down towards her wrist, severing the blood vessels.

Blood had flooded out of the wound. Eleanore had quickly dropped to her knees, watching the children continue to cry in despair, feeling overwhelming guilt and anguish.

What have I done?

Though blood gushed from her arm, she didn't put any pressure on it and let it flow. Eventually, Eleanore fell to her side, keeping her eyes on the children.

I'm so... sorry.

CHAPTER
FIFTY-TWO

First pages from Children of the New Sun:
In these notes, I will go into as much detail as I'm able to remember, outlining everything as I see it. But first, I think it prudent to give a quick overview of exactly what happened to us.

For me, it started in my late twenties. For Eleanore, however, it began at birth, because she was born into the family.

While Eleanore always knew who her biological parents were, in the Children of the New Sun, she wasn't seen as the offspring of those two people. They had simply been chosen to birth a new member.

That's because children there were actually seen as a child of the 'family', especially of the elders, and they owned all new life that was created in their ranks.

As I understand it, Eleanore was a long and loyal servant to the elders and became a valued follower, entrusted with more responsibility than most her age ever got. She had even been allowed to glimpse some of the ancient texts—texts the family had acquired generations ago. Indeed, these documents were the very foundations the family built their belief system on.

However, there was a problem with the texts, which I long suspected were stolen. Much of it was unreadable to the family, written in a language long considered dead by most scholars.

Most... but not all.

There are a select few of us that could translate it, experts in ancient languages. And that is why I was sought out.

I'm not sure how they became aware of me, but given I have a reputation in my field, it wasn't surprising. Rather, I *had* a reputation, until I turned my back on my peers, drawn to the family by promises of something greater.

Eleanore was used as bait to initially lure me in.

And it worked. I fell for Eleanore in a big way. Once I had, she introduced me to the rest of the family. At first, they presented as merely a social group that had bonded over a shared interest in the occult and mysterious. And though it took a number of years, I became drawn to the things they spoke of; I soon learned what the group *really* was, yet I yearned for the forbidden knowledge they seemed to possess. Eventually, I agreed to become a full member, and in exchange I was to work on translating the texts.

Unfortunately, in the Children of the New Sun, it was forbidden for people to fall in love and couple up. Eleanore had been used to snare me, but once I was inducted, we were expected to quash our feelings. There were no attachments allowed, and you were supposed to love all members equally. Yet I couldn't see past Eleanore.

And she felt the same.

It soon became clear Eleanore and I couldn't remain

there. We couldn't deny how we felt any longer, and we both desperately wanted children of our own together. That just wasn't possible in the family.

So... we fled. And when we did, I managed to steal away my translations. It wasn't everything from the original texts, but I couldn't completely let go of what I'd learned; I felt I had ownership of the translations anyway, so I took what I could.

We managed to stay hidden for a while. I often wonder if things would have been different if I'd just left my notes. Perhaps then the Children of the New Sun would have just let it all lie and accepted our departure.

Probably not.

I still had two properties in my possession that I'd inherited through my real family, being the last in my lineage, so Eleanore and I took up residence in one of them.

Soon after, Eleanore fell pregnant. We ended up having four children together. Those years were the happiest time of my life.

But then... the family found us. They came to claim what was theirs. Not just the translations, but ourselves and the children as well.

The night those people came will live with me for the rest of my life.

I still do not know how they found us, but a select group from the family descended on our home in the night. They demanded we come back with them, children and all. Eleanore and I were outnumbered, the children were scared, so initially I'd agreed, if only to buy time. When they again pushed for the translations, I told them the documents weren't in the house and that I kept them in a safe deposit box in the city. This was true, yet my answer angered them.

Tensions rose. The leader of the party became more distressed, worried about going back empty-handed. I wasn't able to calm him. Eventually, chaos broke out.

I was knocked unconscious in the fight.

When I woke, agony in my groin was the first thing I felt. I soon realised I was tied to a chair as my house burned around me. Eleanore was opposite me, bound as well, looking terrified. She was already working on the restraints that held her hands behind her back. Thankfully, she freed herself and me soon after.

The pain was because they had castrated me while I was unconscious. Rather sloppily as well, though they had dressed the wound. Another symbolic act of revenge by the family for wronging them.

I forced myself to move, though it was painful. We searched the house for our children... and found them.

Their bodies were in their beds, made to look like they were sleeping. There were no wounds or injuries; they'd been poisoned.

Now, thinking back to it, I just hope it was painless for them.

Eleanore and I managed to flee the house and went to the police, desperate. Yet it turned out the family had vanished without a trace. Eleanore and I were even investigated. It was a long and drawn-out affair. We were eventually cleared, though many in the police force still suspected us.

Our lives were hell after that. I had one last property farther up north, so we moved there. But we were both lost and rudderless in life. The loss of our children, well... it broke us. We would have considered trying again, but given what happened to me, that was impossible.

But... we do have a plan now. A new purpose. All thanks

to my translations. There are two in particular that I think will help us. I took them to the house with us and left the rest of my notes in the city.

The only wrinkle is that I don't have much time left. Another cruel joke played by fate. But still, if we're brave enough, there is a way for Eleanore and me to have that eternal family we so desire.

I mention all of this only because, if we are successful, then it will not matter to us if people find out. Nothing can be done to change things, so judge us all you want. I leave this information to point the finger at the family and hopefully draw attention to them. Everything I know about them lies on the following pages.

The Children of the New Sun are still out there. If whoever is reading this wants to focus their attention somewhere, it should be on finding them, not on what Eleanore and I have done.

Because the family can still be stopped.

- Jasper Graves

CHAPTER
FIFTY-THREE

Dan set the notebook down after reading through the first few pages. The story within was almost an unbelievable one, though Dan didn't doubt it was *actually* true.

It was a lot for Dan to take in, but in truth, he was having trouble concentrating anyway.

All he could think of was Emily.

His first instinct had to assume she was mistaken when she'd told them how she'd died. She *had* to be wrong. It never crossed Dan's mind that Emily was lying, just that she could have been... mistaken.

But the way she'd acted after having come round, being so angry and hurt and betrayed... It gave him pause. And hearing *how* he did it, by *strangling* her, had floored him.

Dan looked down at his hands, which were shaking. It was hard to imagine they were capable of taking a life, much less the life of someone he cared so deeply about. His mind searched for explanations on *why* he might have done it—if it was even true. But he didn't search for long; he knew there was simply *no* justification for it, no matter what had happened.

As much as he wanted to cling to the hope Emily might be wrong, the self-doubt in him continued to rise. He glanced over to the others, all of them sitting on the bed and poring over their pages. He knew he should tell them what he'd just read, yet he struggled to find the words. Speaking would cause them all to look at him, and Emily's hurt and furious gaze would fall on him once more.

He didn't know if he could face that kind of judgement.

However, he also knew he couldn't withhold what he'd learned. While it didn't offer any insight into what they might do next, it would still be useful knowledge, especially if they had to deal with Eleanore again.

'Guys? You... might wanna hear this,' he eventually said. As expected, all eyes fell on him. As also expected, Emily's eyes were filled with scorn.

'Go on,' Ollie said.

Dan looked down before speaking again, not able to hold their gaze. Not even Lucy's. Her expression had thus far been unreadable since the revelation, and Dan hated the thought that even Luce might be disgusted by him.

'I... found out what happened to Eleanore and Mr. Graves' children,' he went on. 'And I know where they learned how to, you know, do all this. Bring us back and everything. They were in a cult. Children of the New Sun, like what was written on the note in Eleanore's room. *They're* the ones that knew about the rituals. Mr. Graves actually translated things for them. And they're also the ones that killed Eleanore's children. Eleanore and Mr. Graves were both part of the cult to begin with and tried to get out, but the cult didn't want to let them go. So they killed Eleanore's children.'

'That's awful,' Lucy said. 'Those poor children.'

'Does it say anything about the rituals specifically that we can use?' Ollie asked.

Dan shook his head. 'No. Not yet, anyway. But I've only just started. Are your notes giving anything away?'

Ollie took a breath. 'I... find it hard to follow,' he admitted. 'It's full of words I don't really understand.'

'Yeah,' Lucy added. 'It's at a pretty advanced level.'

'Wait, can you understand it?' Ollie asked her.

Lucy nodded. 'Yes, but I'm a little older than you.' She then paused as Ollie looked down, embarrassed. The comment clearly reemphasised the change in dynamic in the group. When they were all younger, their reading prowess had all been roughly equal, with Emily being slightly ahead of everyone and Lucy slightly behind, purely because of her age.

Now, things were different.

'Did you find anything, Luce?' Dan asked, moving things on. He didn't dare ask Emily.

'Some,' Lucy said. 'There's a bunch on shapes.'

'Shapes?' Ollie asked.

'Yeah,' Lucy said. 'The first step is linked to a circle. The prima material. The eternal. The second step is a triangle. Then last is a square. After that, there is a symbol drawn of all three symbols together to form one: the circle is on the outside, and the triangle sits inside it, then a square in the triangle, and another circle inside the square. It says something about squaring the circle, but I'm not sure what it means. Also,' she continued, 'I think the white fire below the cellar is important as well. When Eleanore completed the second step, the 'white' stage, that's also when the white flame was formed in this reality. It's actually imbued with Mr. Graves' soul and fuels everything. Apparently, souls themselves are white. Though... it's kinda hard to follow. White in this instance means pure... or something. It's gobbledygook. There's more I need to read about it, but... that flame seems vital.'

'Can it be put out?' Ollie asked. 'And if we do that, will all of this end?'

'I'm not sure yet,' Lucy answered. 'But if we *do* put it out and it does end this reality, then... what will happen to us? Where will we go?'

There was a brief silence. 'I'm not sure,' Ollie eventually admitted. 'Keep reading, see what you can find.'

'The title on the cover sheet made it sound like there were two separate rituals,' Dan then said. 'One about thorns and one about threads, correct?'

Lucy looked down and lifted the first page. 'Thorns of Erṣetu and Crimson Threads of Anum,' she said.

'Right,' Dan said. *Whatever those mean*. 'So... are you all just going through the first bit? The part about the thorns?'

Ollie nodded. 'So far, yeah. There's a *lot* here.'

'Plus,' Lucy added, 'the ritual with the thorns was covered in Eleanore's note as well and looks like it outlines how this place came to be. So it seems the most important.'

'Maybe,' Dan said. 'But the other one might—'

'Just go back to your book, Dan,' Emily interrupted, her voice firm and cold. 'We've got this.'

Her words stabbed straight through Dan's heart. Silence filled the room. Lucy and Ollie both began reading their notes again after a moment, turning their eyes away from him. Emily, however, held Dan's gaze for just a second longer, not hiding her disdain, before going back to reading as well.

Dan's bottom lip trembled. It took everything he had to keep from crying.

Everyone froze when a terrifying roar came from below.

CHAPTER
FIFTY-FOUR

Eleanore's arm was numb. She held it with her other hand as she stared at the white flame in shock, tears in her eyes.

Ever since she'd returned to the Erimus House and walked down its drive alone, she'd periodically felt a burning sensation down her inner arm and across her wrist. Now it made sense.

You need to go.

She knew she had to leave the basement at some point soon. She didn't have the key to the padlock, the others did, so if they wanted to, they could lock her down there and keep her trapped.

Eleanore realised she'd actually been lucky Ollie had shown up. She hadn't been aware the watchers made things reform, and if the boy hadn't come down with the key, she might have been completely stuck—the door had materialised again with the padlock on the outside.

She knew she couldn't let herself get stuck again, even if hiding away was an appealing thought.

No, she had to get upstairs. She *had* to get that key.

There came a gasp from behind her. She spun around, startled, and stared at the body of her husband over in the other room. It was twitching.

The change had begun.

First, the vines that surrounded him started to move and slither, dragging their thorns across his flesh. The sharp ends of the vines pushed into his skin and burrowed inside. Jasper's hands clenched and gripped the bedsheet, his expression turning to one of agony, his teeth gritted together and eyes screwed shut. Then, the man's frail frame started to expand, slowly bulking up and pushing the vines taut. They then had to wriggle and shift to compensate. Jasper rolled to his side and groaned, sounding inhuman. A moment later, he dropped to the floor with a heavy *thump*.

Eleanore ducked down and pressed herself against the wall behind her, slipping down to her rear, eyes wide and heart thumping wildly in her chest. Though she didn't want to, she forced herself to keep watch, just in case the Guardian approached her.

Jasper's body continued to grow, bulking up and lengthening, with the shoulders and upper chest rising upward, actually overtaking the man's head and swallowing it completely. It made Jasper look like a headless monstrosity. Eleanore noticed the flesh soon healed over, congealing together like liquid over where the head should have been.

The entity stood up and stumbled forward, its huge hand desperately flapping at the area above its shoulders. Its body shook, as if in anger. Something started to slowly push up from above the shoulders. She soon realised it was the head rising again, though it couldn't break through the skin, instead stretching it upwards from the shoulders.

Eventually, the thing brought up its hands and dug thick fingers inside the flesh hood, tearing through the skin at the front. It yanked its hands apart, causing a vertical tear to appear down the front of the cowl, revealing the reddened face underneath.

Eleanore could see the entity's wide, glaring eyes, which had no lids. The face was red and raw, missing layers of skin, with some tendons in the cheeks and jaw visible.

A roar of anger exploded from the Guardian. It was deafening, causing Eleanore to shriek and clamp her hands over her ears. She continued to scream, unable to help herself, but the sound was drowned out, only audible once the monster had finally ceased its angry bellowing.

The Guardian's eyes settled on her.

No! Keep away!

The creature paused, standing motionless, watching her as it was drenched in the red light from the outer room. Eleanore felt small under its penetrating gaze.

It took a slow step forward, drawing close to the doorway, and Eleanore held her breath. But the Guardian remained quiet, regarding her like a curiosity, as the vines around it continued to worm their way across his body in endless loops.

Now that it was closer, Eleanore could make out its eyes more clearly, and she had to stifle a gasp.

They were still Jasper's eyes. That shouldn't have been surprising, but since everything else on his body had changed so drastically, the familiarity there was startling.

It then clicked in her mind as to why it was watching her. *He... he recognises me.*

She took a steadying breath. 'J-Jasper, honey. It's me. Do you... do you know who I am? It's... Eleanore.'

The thing continued to stare. Eleanore couldn't be

certain, but she thought she saw something in its eyes. An expression of pain and anguish.

The monster bellowed again, and she jumped out of reflex. She tensed and cowered, expecting the thing to lunge for her, but instead the creature just turned and bounded away, the sound of its heavy footsteps traveling out into the passageway. She heard the scraping of its vines and thorns along the concrete surfaces.

Eleanore continued to cry, horrified at what her dear Jasper had become. *We didn't want this,* the woman told herself. *We didn't know it would be like this!*

She continued to sob.

CHAPTER
FIFTY-FIVE

'No! Not again!' Lucy cried out. They all knew what that roar meant: the Guardian was coming.

'What do we do?' Emily asked, yet Lucy had no answers. She looked to Ollie, then to Dan, desperate for a suggestion. Her gaze lingered on Dan for a moment. She still couldn't believe what Emily had told them about him. It seemed so impossible, yet Lucy didn't doubt Emily was telling the truth about her vision.

But even so, despite all that, she couldn't bring herself to hate her friend. She was shocked, of course, even appalled and confused. But she couldn't find it in herself to resort to hate.

Ollie quickly gathered the papers back together and bound them once more. 'Dan,' he said urgently. 'Keep the notebook with you. We all need to move.'

'But where?' Lucy asked. 'There's nowhere to go!'

'Maybe we can try outside again,' Dan suggested.

'Why?' Ollie asked.

Dan shrugged. 'I don't know, maybe search the outer

wall, find out if there is a place we can get over? I mean, we've only really seen the main gates.'

'There's nowhere to run,' Emily said, her voice flat, almost detached from reality. 'There's nothing out there beyond the walls. We all know that. We're stuck here.'

'It doesn't mean we have to just lie down and accept what's coming,' Ollie replied, pushing himself off the bed to his feet, the bundle of papers still wrapped in his arms.

'But we'll just end up running around the house again,' Emily said. 'Just looping around until that thing gets us. It's pointless.'

Lucy felt a wave of sadness—Emily seemed utterly broken. She couldn't help but cast a judging gaze at Dan. Not only had the man taken Emily's life, but he'd also crushed her spirit in the ever after. Dan could only gaze down in shame.

But she quickly caught herself, feeling a stab of guilt. Dan looked distraught as well and she just wanted to go and hug him.

'Everyone get up!' Ollie ordered. 'We're not just sitting in this room, waiting to be caught.'

A fresh howl of anger came from below, causing Lucy to jump up to her feet as well. 'You're right.' She rushed around the bed to Emily. 'Let's go,' she told her friend, holding out her hand. Emily looked up to her. All the fight in the woman's eyes seemed to have gone. Lucy took hold of Emily by the shoulders and forced her to stand. 'We're not leaving you here,' Lucy said. 'So you need to find the strength to push on and come with us.'

After what seemed like an eternity, Emily gave a slow nod. Her eyes drifted over to Dan. 'And him? Is he coming with us?'

'Well... yeah,' Lucy replied. Despite everything, she couldn't just leave Dan behind to be slaughtered alone.

'No. I'll stay,' Dan said, tears streaming down his cheeks. 'You all go.'

Silence fell. Eventually, Ollie shook his head. 'No,' he said. 'We all go. No one is staying on their own. We need everyone together to figure out a way to get free of all this.'

'There isn't a way,' Emily replied, jaw set. 'When you're dead, you're dead. This is it for us.'

Ollie shook his head again, more firmly this time. 'No,' he said defiantly. 'No, there *is* a way. I know it. But we won't find it just waiting here to be attacked again. Now come on, let's go!'

Lucy guided Emily to the door as Ollie hurried over to Dan, who was still sitting. 'Get up, we need to be quick,' Ollie said, though Lucy noticed there was a distinct lack of warmth in his voice.

Lucy again felt for Dan. It was clear none of them trusted him anymore, yet with Dan not remembering anything about his former life, it must have been hard to deal with.

Impossible to deal with.

'Just go,' Dan said, looking down. He handed the notebook up to Ollie. 'I'll just head down on my own,' he went on. 'See if I can head it off.'

'But you'll get hurt again!' Lucy exclaimed. She heard the heavy footsteps grow louder.

Dan just nodded solemnly. 'It'll give the rest of you the chance to keep running.'

Ollie didn't grab the book. Instead, he took Dan's hand. 'Get up and come on,' the boy said. 'We're *all* going to get away. Together. There is a way out of this. I know there is.

We just need to find it. But first, we need to put some distance between us and that monster.'

Dan tried to pull his hand away, but Ollie held on tight. 'Come on, Ollie, let go of me,' Dan said.

Ollie shook his head in annoyance. 'Just get up. We don't have time for this. If you don't come, then I'm just gonna stay here with you, and it'll be your fault when I get torn up.'

Lucy saw surprise wash over Dan's face, soon replaced by annoyance... then finally acceptance. He sighed, then started to get up.

'Come on,' Lucy urged. 'I can hear that thing on the stairs now!'

Everyone piled out into the hallway. A second later, Lucy heard the Guardian thump out into the corridor below them.

'Do you think we can fight it?' Dan asked.

Lucy, Ollie, and even Emily turned to him in shock. 'What do you mean?' Lucy asked.

'I mean... fight it. So far, we've only tried running.'

'It's too strong,' Lucy said. 'It threw me around like a doll. We can't fight that. We just *can't*.'

Dan looked around the corridor. 'We need a weapon,' he said.

'Don't remember too many machine guns lying around the house, Dan,' Emily quipped with cold sarcasm.

'It doesn't matter,' Lucy interjected. 'There's no time. We need to run!'

They soon heard the footsteps start to ascend the next set of stairs.

'We need to draw it to the other side of the house,' Ollie said. 'Away from the stairs. Then we can loop round and run down.'

Lucy nodded her agreement. She couldn't see any other option, though she still couldn't shake Emily's words. *Is running pointless?*

The group slowly moved backwards, waiting with bated breath for the Guardian to emerge through the stairwell doorway. When it finally did, it swung its huge arms forward, smashing the walls to either side of the opening and roaring before it stormed into the corridor. The wall around it crumbled and rubble dropped to the floor, the door itself also falling away and landing heavily.

The Guardian turned to them, fists clenched, spiked vines slowly moving around its form. Another bellow sounded as it brought its clenched fists out to its sides, shaking with rage.

As scared as she was, Lucy couldn't understand the apparent anger that always seemed to consume the entity.

Anger toward the four of them.

Wait... maybe it's just the three of us.

She realised it hadn't attacked Ollie yet. Lucy was reminded of what Eleanore had said: about the Guardian needing to strip away their age so they would be young again, like the night of the fire. It was protecting their current reality, keeping things as they should be.

Clearly, she, Emily, and Dan weren't as they should be.

Is that why it hates us?

She then pondered how young they might get after the next attack. *Will we be kids again? Kids forevermore, to live here with Eleanore like she wanted. Will that make the attacks finally stop?*

Ultimately, though, none of it mattered in that moment. They just had to flee.

All four of them kept shuffling back, waiting for the entity to stride towards them. It took one slow, deliberate step, which made them back up even quicker. But then... the monster stopped. It just stared, standing motionless.

'What's it doing?' Lucy asked, terrified.

'It's trying to figure out our plan,' Ollie replied as they still backed up.

'It knows we're trying to bait it,' Emily added.

'So... what do we do?' Lucy asked. 'Just wait here in a standoff?'

But then she noticed something change with the entity. Or rather, with the vines that moved across it. The mass of slithery, ropey lengths started to congregate on the creature's left side, swirling around its arm, almost hiding the skin completely, until there was a thick cluster around the hand. Before she could call a warning, the entity flung its arm forward and the thorn-lined vines shot towards Emily. Lucy gasped, frozen in horror, but turned her head just in time to see Dan dive into Emily, knocking her out of the way.

The vines wrapped around him in an instant, curling like they were alive, pressing their thorns into his flesh and causing him to cry out in pain.

'Run!' Dan shouted to the others.

Everyone hesitated, completely shocked—Lucy saw the creature begin to move in her peripheral vision. It swung its arm holding the now-rigid vines to the side, flinging Dan into Lucy, the vines scratching at her. She was knocked to the floor, where she looked up a second later to see Dan get swung the other way; helpless, he collided with Emily next, hard enough to topple the other woman. Dan was then forced on top of her, the vines still holding him, which soon ran down to embrace Emily as well, forcing their way through her skin.

Both Dan and Emily started to cry out as the vines and

thorns ravaged them. The creature's heavy footsteps quickly thudded closer. Lucy could barely move, locked in horror as she saw Ollie run over to his friends. He tried to help, but as soon as he grabbed one of the vines, he was forced to pull his hand away in pain with a yelp.

Lucy got back up, tempted to run, but she knew she couldn't leave the others behind. Though that meant she was probably going to face unrelenting agony like the two times before that. Even so, she rushed over to help Ollie with tears streaming down her cheeks. She copied Ollie and tried to grab the vines with shaking hands—the thorns on them seemed to actually thrust themselves up to her hand, as if in response to her presence. She recoiled in pain.

The woman then gazed down in revulsion as she saw a strip of flesh torn from the back of Dan's head, the hairy flap of skin sticking to the vine and leaving some of the skull beneath visible.

It was enough to make Lucy want to bolt... yet it was too late. The huge entity reached out a thick arm and grabbed her around the throat so suddenly Lucy didn't even have time to scream. She was hoisted up and thrown onto her friends. The vines quickly moved around her as well, tightening and cutting into her, embracing her into the stack of bodies. She fought and kicked and screamed, yet there was no point. The pain continued as her clothing was torn away.

The agony she'd feared returned yet again. Her cries of pain joined those of Emily and Dan, and their blood melded together as it pooled on the floor under them.

CHAPTER
FIFTY-SIX

Ollie was desperate to help his friends, but the horrific cocoon of vines that held them looked impenetrable. It tightened around the trio, cutting into them more, causing cascades of blood to stream from the wounds.

The boy couldn't help but watch with revulsion as their skin was ripped, with vines forcing their way inside. Some even slithered into their screaming mouths.

Run! his mind cried at him. But he couldn't. He couldn't leave them.

Instead, he lunged forward again, ignoring the agony in his palms as he tried to fight his way through the cocoon. He held on tight, blood dripping from his hands in the struggle, but he simply didn't have the strength to force his way through.

Eventually, he let go. His friends' screams growing in intensity. Palms still stinging, Ollie made an angry beeline for the creature itself. Just as he reached it, though, its other hand shot up and wrapped around his neck, grip like iron. He fought against it, pounding on the thick, hairy forearm, yet the entity didn't budge. It didn't attack the boy either, just held him there, stuck in place while its thorns continued their work on the others.

And the Guardian didn't let Ollie go until the thorns were done.

When Ollie was finally dropped, he saw the vines start to slither away, showing him what was left of his friends.

Unable to help himself, he leaned to the side and heaved. He was so repulsed he needed to vomit, but nothing would come up. It was like there was nothing inside of him.

His friends were a mess.

The thorns had desecrated their bodies far more than before, leaving large swathes of their forms completely skeletal. All three were unmoving, and the amount of blood that clogged the carpet was astonishing.

After he stopped heaving a minute later, Ollie leaned back on his haunches, threw his head back, and howled in anguish. He glared at the entity that simply stood and looked back down at him. The hatred and anger it had shown before were gone. It seemed... calm.

After a moment, the great thing turned and walked away, footsteps still heavy; the vines behind it scraped along the floor as they retreated back towards it, eventually wrapping around its body again.

The boy was then left alone with his friends.

Ollie wept. He was tired of this nightmare. *I can't exist like this anymore.* The crushing knowledge of their eternity made him sob even more.

CHAPTER
FIFTY-SEVEN

It took Eleanore a while before she was brave enough to move again, having witnessed the awful transformation of her dear Jasper. When she eventually did leave the room, she found the concrete passageway largely dark, with most of the lights having been smashed. The red light that bled down through the hatch from the machine room helped her find her way, but at the end of the tunnel, she saw the ladder was ruined as well.

Climbing up to the machine room was difficult, and she'd only just made it up into the room above before she heard the Guardian start to return. She hid away behind a piece of equipment, not wanting to see its eyes again, horrified by the idea that Jasper was suffering.

She cursed them both for not waiting longer, for not trying to find out more about what this reality would *actually* be like. After a moment, she stopped berating herself. *We didn't have time. Jasper was dying.*

Plus, the texts could only tell them so much, could only instruct them how to bring this pocket purgatory about. It couldn't tell them what it would be like. That was because anyone that *had* experienced the rituals were dead, so the experience couldn't be relayed.

Eleanore thought about the idea of being stuck there forever and realised that didn't *have* to be true, but she pushed the thought away. *I have to stay and see through what was promised.*

It would be worth it in the end. She kept telling herself that. *It has to be.*

The entity soon returned to the machine room, lumbering towards the hatch. Eleanore cowered, but noticed the Guardian pause for a second mid-way across the room; it turned to her briefly before moving on again.

It knows where we are. It always knows.

She watched as it squeezed itself down through the hatch and moved deeper into the passage, back to where it could rest again. The entity's moments of existence seemed brief, only long enough to fulfil a task before it was time to rest again. Eleanore wondered if it would be that way permanently.

What kind of existence is that for Jasper?

He'd sacrificed his very soul to make all this happen, so she hoped he would get to see the fruits of their hellish labour.

Soon... It'll all be worth it soon.

In fact, she realised that 'soon' might actually be upon them already. Given the Guardian had returned, she guessed it had finished its work. That meant Emily, Lucy, and Dan would become young again.

Maybe young *enough*. Maybe it was time to start the eternal life she'd dreamed of for so long.

Eleanore knew the children upstairs would hate her, but everything she was doing was for the best.

She slowly made her way up to the ground floor and

looked around the space. It was mostly quiet, but she could hear a distant sobbing from upstairs. *Ollie.*

She hesitated, knowing she should go—*had* to go—but was terrified to. She didn't want to see them in whatever state they were in. Seeing Lucy after her attack had been bad enough. So Eleanore waited. Five minutes. Ten.

The sobbing above eventually died down. *Come on, you need to go,* she told herself. She glanced at the front door, knowing what was out there, then forced herself to head upstairs. The middle-storey was clear, so Eleanore continued up to the top. Once out in the hallway, she stopped and drew in a sharp breath.

Oh God... What... have I done?

The bodies of Emily, Lucy, and Dan lay clustered together. Their forms were still ruined, but Eleanore was certain they were healing, with stretches of undamaged flesh now in amongst the ravaged areas. She also noticed each of them was smaller now. Much smaller, looking similar to Ollie. However, their facial features hadn't fully reformed yet, so she couldn't tell if they were *exactly* the right age again; at the very least, they had to be close. Eleanore just needed to see them again whole to be sure.

Ollie was sitting near his friends, eyes red, staring over at Eleanore.

'What do *you* want?' he snapped angrily. Eleanore felt her body sag in shame. On the ground near the boy were the bundle of translations and Jasper's notebook. She wondered just how much Ollie had learned.

'I'm so sorry you all had to go through this, Ollie,' she said as she drew closer.

'You're not sorry,' he shot back through gritted teeth. 'You wanted this. This is all happening because you *wanted* it. Just so you can keep us here forever as a new family.'

Eleanore hesitated for a moment before continuing down the hall.

He doesn't know everything, she realised. *Poor boy.* But she felt no small amount of relief—they obviously hadn't read about the *Crimson Threads of Anum*.

Good.

Not that it would change anything. But it was for the best. Eleanore finally reached Ollie and stood over him, keeping her eyes off the others.

'You're such a fighter, Ollie,' she said. 'So loyal. So eager to protect everyone.'

He didn't answer, just looked away. She then stepped past him, towards the translations and notebook. He glanced up and a look of realisation washed over him. Ollie tried to react, but she was quicker, and snatched up both documents, cradling them in her arm. She then tossed them farther down the hallway, towards the stairs. Ollie made as if to sprint around her, but Eleanore stepped in the way and pushed him back. She then held out her hand.

'The key, Ollie,' she said. 'To the cellar. Hand it over.'

He snarled. 'No! Get away from me. Get away from *us!*'

'The key,' she said again, more sternly this time. She didn't want the children down in the cellar with her. She didn't want to have to witness what came next for them.

'No!' Ollie shouted again. He tried to dart around her once more, but she caught him and wrapped him in her arms, turning him away from her amidst the struggle. He was strong for his age, and it took everything Eleanore had to keep him under control, trapping his arms to his sides with a one-armed bear hug while her other hand rummaged in his pocket. Luckily, the key was in the first pocket she tried, and she pulled it free before pushing the boy away from her.

'Thank you, Ollie,' she said, then walked away to pick up the translations and notebook again.

'Give them back!' Ollie ordered.

'No,' she simply said and turned to him. 'I know you won't believe me, Ollie, but I really am sorry. About everything. I... I wish there was another way.'

'There was another way!' Ollie shouted, fists clenched by his side. 'You could have just *not* done this, let us move on to whatever should have been next after we die. And if it wasn't for you, then I wouldn't have died when I did. I would have had a life, instead of being stuck here forever with a woman I *hate!*'

When the boy started crying again, it made Eleanore realise there had been more tears in their short time together in this purgatory than all the time they'd spent together in the house while alive.

But that would soon end. And she knew the boy deserved to hear the truth. She owed him that much. Yet before she began, she cast a glance at the others. The healing was speeding up now, and she could make out everyone's faces again.

The sight stole her breath away. They looked *just* like they did before. Just like that night.

Which meant it was time.

She took a slow breath. 'You won't be here with me forever, Ollie,' she explained.

He paused his crying and frowned. 'What... what do you mean? Are you letting us go?'

She shook her head. 'Not really, no. But... you won't be here. None of you will.'

'I don't understand,' Ollie said.

Another breath. '*The Crimson Threads of Anum,*' she went on. 'I take it you didn't get to that part when reading Jasper's notes?' When Ollie shook his head, Eleanore went on, 'That rite contains its own rituals. When I burned our blood that night, I burned the blood of four others as well, blood that I had kept for a long time. They became part of the ritual too, part of the *Thorns of Erṣetu*. The threads act as a link to make a transfer, but pulling souls from the heavens carries a price. The one below that reached up to the skies to take the souls for us also demands others to be pulled down as payment.'

'What are you talking about?' the boy asked. 'You're talking gibberish again.'

Eleanore offered him an understanding smile. 'I know it sounds that way, but it's true. *The Crimson Threads of Anum* is like a... contract... with Ereshkigal. It *has* to be honoured.'

'*Ereshkigal?*' Ollie asked with a frown, his lip curled. 'Listen to yourself! Who the hell is Ereshkigal?'

'It doesn't matter,' Eleanore replied, knowing it was pointless. If he wasn't following so far, then how could she expect him to understand how Ereshkigal would then offer the souls to the child-devourer, Lamashtu? She carried on to the main point. 'The other blood I burned... it belonged to my children.'

Ollie straightened up, his frown deepening. 'You kept their blood as well? For all those years?'

Eleanore gave a slow nod. 'Blood is important, Ollie. It is our life force, and it can do amazing things beyond what science understands.'

Ollie shook his head. 'You really were in a cult, weren't you. You sound brainwashed. I'm just surprised you hid it from people, from *us*, for so long.'

'The family was despicable in many ways,' Eleanore

confessed. 'But they found truths that were almost lost to time. Powerful truths.'

'If they're anything like you, then they're all crazy,' Ollie shot back, fists still by his sides.

Eleanore knew he was trying to lash out and hurt her. She didn't blame him. 'The threads aren't quite complete yet,' she said. 'Though now that you're all as you were that night again, we're close. Very close. I just need to let in the four things outside the house. They carry the souls of my children deep within them, you see. And unfortunately... those things will come for you and the others, Ollie. Once they take you, I can finally have my babies back, exactly as they were before. And then they and I can live here forever, and no one can ever take them away from me ever again.'

Tears spilled down her cheeks. *Stay strong. It will all be over soon.*

Ollie's body froze and Eleanore realised the truth was finally dawning on the boy.

'But... what will happen to us?' He looked over at the others, who were whole again now and starting to stir. It broke Eleanore's heart to gaze upon them. Emily's blue eyes opened, her auburn hair framing her freckled face. Dan's big brown eyes looked around, dazed, and Lucy once more was the youngest of them all. Eleanore had to fight from breaking down.

Stay strong. This has to happen. You've always known this is how it has to be!

'What's going to happen to us, Eleanore?' Ollie repeated. His voice had lost its defiance and was now tinged with fear. 'Will... we go up to Heaven in place of your children?' He sounded hesitantly hopeful.

Eleanore sobbed as she shook her head. 'I'm... so sorry. But that's not how it works.'

'So... where?' Finally, it clicked for the boy. His mouth fell and eyes widened. Eleanore had to focus on her own children—keeping memories of what they looked like at the forefront of her mind.

'I'm so sorry,' she said yet again. It struck Eleanore that she'd been saying that an awful lot. She knew it wouldn't bring her forgiveness. Nothing would. But then, that didn't matter. Given she was going to exist in Erimus House for eternity, she would face no judgement for what she'd done, even if she deserved it.

'You can't!' Ollie screamed, fists and teeth clenched. 'You can't do that to us!' He was shaking. 'You... you can't! You were supposed to care for us, look out for us. You were supposed to *love* us!'

More tears flowed from Eleanore. 'I know,' she said. 'And you won't believe this, but I *did* love you all—I still *do*. I tried not to, to keep you all at arm's length as much as I could, but it happened anyway. I... I think that was my biggest failing. It's making things so hard.'

'Hard? For who? *You?* We're the ones going to Hell! Please, Eleanore, don't do it. Stop all this! I know you can.'

Eleanore took one last look at the children on the floor, then gazed at Ollie. He'd been the first to arrive at the house, so it was somewhat fitting he'd be the last one she'd speak with. 'Goodbye, Ollie,' she said, then turned and walked away.

'No! Don't leave me!' the boy called, sounding more desperate than Eleanore had ever heard him. She didn't look back, however, and just continued downstairs, sobbing.

Keep going. They're waiting for you: Arthur, Elizabeth, Tommy, and Susan. I'll see them all again soon.

She held their images in her mind, letting memories of

them all as a family wash over her. Soon, that family would be whole again, and her never-ending heartache would be over.

Finally. After so, so long.

Eleanore eventually made it to the door on the ground floor. She opened it and gazed into the covered porch just ahead.

She heard them outside—the Alû, waiting to be let in. She even caught glimpses of them through the window.

The husks weren't small anymore, nor were they giggling. She could hear them growl, the sound deep and terrifying. She took a breath and put her hand on the door handle, then slowly turned it and pulled the door.

Eleanore didn't have the chance to open it fully before the door burst inwards. The Alû swept inside, snarling and screeching. Eleanore was forced back by their huge bodies, making her drop the notes, notepad, and key. Her head crashed against the jamb of the inner doorway. The woman didn't have time to cry out before the huge form of another Alû slammed into her, smashing her head *through* the wall behind her.

Eleanore felt an explosion of agony, and her world swirled into darkness.

CHAPTER
FIFTY-EIGHT

We're children again, Emily realised.

She gazed over at Dan and Lucy, who pushed themselves up to a standing position, like she was.

Her eyes lingered on Dan—his hair a dark mop and brown, eyes blinking unbelievably as he stared at his hands. Looking at him, it was hard for Emily to still think of him as a murderer. *But he is.*

Lucy was just like Emily remembered her as well, down to the dimples that formed on the panicked girl's face a second later.

What's more, Emily recognised the clothes they all wore, including Ollie's. It was the clothing from that night: pyjamas and dressing gowns. She could take in the details and commit them to memory, unlike before.

Ollie sat on the ground, watching them with worried, wet eyes. *He's been crying again.*

Not surprising, Emily realised, considering what he must have witnessed.

Emily was still terrified, but the pain had thankfully

subsided. It had been the worst attack yet. Every nerve ending had screamed in agony before she'd finally been allowed to fade away.

And now she was a child again. Forevermore, locked in an adolescent body. Trapped in a nightmarish version of her old home with both the woman that had caused it all and the boy that had killed her.

A prisoner in an everlasting purgatory from which there was no escape.

As far as Emily was concerned, there was no possible way the situation could get any worse.

Then she heard a commotion downstairs, accompanied by wild roars and screeches. Her body locked up. The sounds weren't from the Guardian; she was sure about that. These weren't as deep or guttural, but they certainly weren't human.

Everyone quickly pushed themselves up. 'What's going on?' Emily asked Ollie, hoping the boy had more knowledge of the situation.

Ollie looked utterly terrified. 'It's those things,' he said. 'From outside.'

Emily paused, then remembered the giggling creatures they'd met out front of the house. Yet she was confused. Those things had sounded eerie, but not monstrous.

'Eleanore came up here after you were attacked,' Ollie went on quickly. 'She took everything off me: the key, the notebook, the notes, then went downstairs. She said she was going to let them in. They're... they're...' He took a breath. 'We can't let them get us. We *can't!*'

'Ollie,' Lucy said, 'what's going on? Why will they get us?'

'They're Eleanore's children!' Ollie exclaimed, then quickly shook his head. 'Well... not exactly, but they're carrying the souls of the children. We were never meant to be a replacement family for Eleanore. We're supposed to *be* replaced.'

'You're not making sense,' Dan said—there came crashing from downstairs, accompanied by more screeches and howls.

'They're looking for us,' Ollie said, staring off at the stairwell door.

'Ollie!' Dan snapped. 'What do you mean we're the replacements?'

'If those things get us,' he said. 'It'll bring her children back. We'll get swapped out. And we'll be sent to... to... hell. All of this, the whole thing, it was all about her getting *them* back. She... used us for that.'

A stunned silence fell over everyone. Emily couldn't believe what she was hearing.

That had been Eleanore's plan for them the whole time?

Emily stumbled to the side, letting herself fall against the wall near her, legs weak. 'That can't be,' she said, looking again to Ollie, but deep down she knew there was no way he was lying.

'We need to get away,' Ollie said. 'We can't let those things get us.'

'The cellar,' Dan said, voice full of panic. 'If we can get down there and lock the door behind us...'

'Eleanore took the key,' Ollie explained.

'When?' Dan asked. 'How long ago?'

'Just now,' Ollie replied. 'She's going down there, I think.'

'Then we need to move. We need to get to it before she does.'

'But... those things are down there,' Lucy said.

'Yes, but they aren't coming up yet,' Dan went on.

'What does that tell you?' Lucy's expression was blank. 'Think about it. Mr. Graves, he always knew where we were and came straight for us. Listen to those things downstairs, though. It sounds like they're tearing the place up looking for us. Which means we might be able to sneak and hide and stay out of sight.'

'Even if we did get down,' Lucy began. 'Would a locked door be able to hold them? Wouldn't we just be trapping ourselves?' The young girl's hands were trembling.

'We have to try,' Dan said. 'I don't see a better way.'

They heard the chaotic sounds below build, then the sound of something bounding up the bottom flight of stairs.

Ollie pointed to Emily's room. 'Run,' he called.

Everyone bolted, with Emily letting Lucy sprint into the room first. In truth, Emily wanted to turn and block Dan from getting in behind her, telling him to stay outside and face whatever was coming, to face what he deserved... but she couldn't.

There was no time for that. And also, he was just a boy, not the man that had killed her. It was hard to put into words, as it wasn't like they were two different people. She knew that. Yet when she looked at him now, she saw the Dan of old. The conflict in her tore at Emily's soul, though she didn't have time to dwell on it.

Once everyone was in the room, Ollie closed the door as quietly as possible. The four of them backed away, huddling together. They heard the snarling things on the mid-floor, searching in rage, their animalistic sounds absolutely savage.

'We need to get downstairs after they come up to this floor,' Ollie whispered.

'What if they look in this room first?' Lucy asked.

Emily froze as she heard the sounds of scampering up the next flight of stairs. They reached the top incredibly quickly, and the noises emerged out into the hallway. From the sound of it, it seemed like they were running over to the spare room, where they began to attack the door—likely to break it down and get through.

They really don't know where we are, Emily thought.

Everyone looked at each other in horror. Emily then saw Ollie's eyes fall on the window.

Lucy quickly shook her head and mouthed, *No.*

Ollie gave a firm nod in reply. Emily's stomach sank. Climbing down the vines and thorns outside would be incredibly painful, but she knew getting caught by those things and dragged to hell would be far worse.

Dan seemed to be thinking the same, and he quickly moved to the window, pulled it up, and released the safety latch to slide it higher. The movement of the sliding sash thankfully wasn't loud enough for the creatures to hear over the sound of their own snarling.

Dan turned to the others, but Ollie pointed forward and mouthed, *You first.*

Dan looked terrified. He truly was the boy of old again. Ollie gave him a sad smile, then spoke, voice deathly quiet. 'You gotta lead the way for Emily and Luce. I'll go last.'

There was a pause, everyone waiting for Dan's answer. The sound of those things crashing into the door of the spare room over and over caused Emily's heartrate to spike. A look of resolve fell over Dan and he quickly moved to the windowsill. He sat on it and swung his legs over the side, out into the night. Emily held her breath, terrified he was going to fall, all thoughts of what he'd done as an adult now gone.

She realised the fall might not kill them—after all, they

really couldn't die in this place—but it would certainly hurt like hell. *We've suffered enough in here already.*

'Be careful,' Lucy whispered to her friend, who was now looking back as he lowered himself down, fear still in his eyes. He glanced down, then moved his hands carefully below the line of the sill. He winced and gritted his teeth while taking in a sharp breath.

'It hurts,' he seethed. 'Holding the vines *really* hurts.'

Emily's heart flooded with worry—she'd have to face the same thing. *Can I do it? Can I bear it?*

'I know,' Ollie said quietly. 'But keep going. It's the only way. I believe in you, Dan.'

Dan replied with a nod and a determined, tight-lipped smile. He then moved down, completely out of view. Emily and Lucy immediately rushed over, leaning out.

The boy was working diligently, pressing his feet flat against the wall and pushing through the vines, while his hands held onto some of the organic ropes. It was slow going, but he was methodical, looking for other vines to reach for that would take his weight—and there seemed to be no shortage of them. He continued to climb lower.

Emily saw droplets of blood all over Dan's hands.

'Are you okay?' Lucy called down to him.

Dan didn't look up when he responded. 'Yes. It stings a *lot*. But... just try to ignore it when you come down.'

The fact he kept going, likely pushed on by the horrifying alternative, gave Emily hope that the rest of them could too.

The boy started to move to the side, making sure to keep away from the window directly below where there were no vines to hold.

Unlike the vines on the boundary wall, the ones that lined the house didn't move or writhe; they appeared normal, though far denser than back when the four of them had lived here.

'Hurry,' Ollie whispered to Emily and Lucy. 'Who's next?'

Emily looked up at Lucy. The girl looked just as terrified as Emily felt. 'We'll do it together,' Emily said. 'I'll go first, then you come straight out after. I'll climb down next to you.'

Lucy nodded with a grateful grin.

Emily sat on the sill and swung her legs out, just as Dan had. Looking down, she was overcome with vertigo and clenched her teeth together to hold her nerve. She knew she didn't have time to think things through, which was good, as she had no doubt she would easily talk herself out of following Dan. She turned her body and lowered herself down, keeping her eyes on Lucy above. When she was low enough, Emily looked down at her feet, which were pressed against the wall to give her purchase. Thorns scratched at her ankles and lower calves, but she ignored the pain, ready to grab hold of the vines.

When she did, she felt stabbing pains explode in her palms and the inside of her fingers. She hissed and her eyes started to water, but Emily held on, actually gripping tighter.

Keep going!

She jolted at the sound of those things starting to attack the door to her room. It almost made her fall, but she managed to hold on. The noise spurred her on, holding her weight with her feet as her other hand searched for more thorn-lined purchase next.

'You can do it,' Lucy said from above, still leaning out the window and looking down, panic in her voice as she kept glancing back at the door.

Emily was confused as to why the creatures didn't simply open the door, given it wasn't locked, but she put it out of her mind.

There was more pain as Emily took another handful of vines, and she felt like her teeth were going to crack from clenching them together so hard. Her hands were on fire. Regardless, she held on and started to move lower.

'Lucy, come on,' she called as quietly as she could, but looking up, she was surprised to see Lucy had already begun climbing out.

Emily waited until Lucy climbed down close to her, the girl working slowly but steadily, making pained noises with every new grab of a vine.

She saw Ollie then appear up above them. He swung his legs out to follow suit. But just as he started to lower himself down, the bedroom door above burst open. Loud, excited growls rolled out of the open window. Ollie screamed, and she saw his body tense. Emily heard the sound of things scampering closer to the window.

Ollie lost his grip and fell.

CHAPTER
FIFTY-NINE

Lucy could only close her eyes as Ollie's body fell towards her. She braced for impact, and a second later felt her friend slam into her.

'Ollie!' Lucy heard Emily scream.

Lucy's grip on the vine loosened... but only for a moment. The girl squeezed both hands tighter, pain shooting up her arms again. After hitting her, Ollie pitched to the side, but the impact with her had arrested his fall for a moment—long enough for his hand to find a vine. As his body fell beside Lucy and spun—his legs hitting her as they did—he was able to grab another handful of the planting with a groan of pain.

'Are you okay?' she asked desperately, clinging on for dear life herself.

Before he could answer, sounds from above caused both of them to look up to the window; two of those hideous creatures were leaning out, having pushed their upper bodies through the opening. There wasn't space for the others, but Lucy heard them just behind the first two.

They looked different from the giggling things near the

main gate. They had the same dark, leathery flesh, but it was now lined with tooth-like spines, especially around the shoulders and collarbone. Their faces were mostly blank, and at first Lucy couldn't understand where the awful sounds they emitted were coming from, but then she saw a series of vertical slits across where the mouth should have been—they vibrated every time the creatures roared or growled.

They reached their long arms down and swung misshapen claws across the surface of the wall, cutting the vines, but not quite able to reach Ollie or Lucy. One of them stopped swinging and leaned out more, pushing its arms farther down towards Lucy, who cowered back, just out of reach. She saw the ends of the frighteningly close claws change, the tips widening and forming what looked like puckers.

Both Lucy and Ollie screamed.

'Keep going!' Dan yelled up from below. Though Lucy was terrified, she started to move again, finding the panic helped her ignore the pain from the thorns.

Ollie was moving as well. The creatures above continued to desperately sweep their hands across the wall, hoping to claw the pair. Yet they seemed reluctant to climb out, and she could easily see why: their clawed fingers didn't look dexterous, so grabbing the vines to climb would have been difficult.

'You okay?' Ollie asked her as they kept going.

Lucy's heart hammered in her chest. 'Yeah,' she lied. 'You?'

'Yeah.'

Another obvious lie.

The group continued their long climb. Lucy found it difficult moving sideways to avoid the window directly below, though eventually was able to navigate it. The monsters above continued their desperate growling. When Lucy glanced up, she gasped in horror—one had actually started to climb out.

Her heart seized.

'Go!' she shouted to everyone. 'Quickly! They're coming!'

The monster was hanging halfway out of the window, tentatively moving its claw into a thick cluster of vines.

Far below, Dan had almost reached the ground, then jumped the rest of the way. After landing, he quickly wiped his hands on his gown, which smeared blood across the material.

Lucy glanced up again to see the creature above still struggling; it kept pulling back inside the window before trying to climb out again, trying to come at things from a different angle. She heard the other three roar with impatience.

Next, Emily reached the bottom and hugged her bloody hands to her chest, weeping, as she stepped away from the wall.

'Keep going,' Ollie said to Lucy. 'We're nearly there.'

She didn't answer but continued anyway, soon coming to the top of the ground-floor window. Her arms and legs burned fiercely, and her hands were almost completely numb from the constant pricking and stabbing. She looked down and realised she could probably jump.

A loud screech came from above, this one different, more... panicked. She looked up and saw the monster was plummeting down, arms waving frantically as it dropped.

It fell past Lucy and Ollie and landed on the ground with a heavy *thud*, just as Dan and Emily jumped out of the way.

'Let go!' Ollie cried. 'Jump!'

They both leapt from the wall together. Lucy felt a jolt of pain shoot up her shins as she landed before toppling to her side. Not letting herself have a moment to think, she pushed herself back to her feet, ignoring the pain.

The monster was starting to slowly roll to its front, dazed, but unhurt.

'Run!' Dan screamed.

All four of them took off towards the front corner of the house, Lucy limping a little, pain still throbbing in her legs.

She glanced back to see the creature starting to stand, reaching around seven feet tall when fully upright. Three other dark forms dropped from the bedroom window.

That's one way to get down, she couldn't help but think.

Thump, thump, thump.

The four children raced around the corner and sprinted to the main door just as the first monster started to give chase, resuming its savage growling.

'Go!' Ollie screamed, making sure he was behind Lucy. She heard the thing coming closer and closer as they all darted to the main entrance of the house. Dan shot inside the open door first and held it, letting the others rush in after him. The moment Ollie broke through, he slammed it shut. A split-second later, the monster crashed into the closed door and forced Dan back, but thankfully the door held.

'We need to block it!' Dan shouted.

Lucy looked around the small porch, but there was nothing to use. However, when she gazed deeper into the main hallway, she saw Eleanore. The old woman was stumbling forwards, cradling the documents in her arms and heading to the dining room. The hair on the side of her head was thick with blood.

The monster on the other side of the door continued to bang and strike at it, but strangely didn't go for the handle.

'It's just an animal,' Lucy said as everyone backed up.

'What do you mean?' Dan asked, his eyes wide.

'It's not intelligent. It's like a lion or something. It can't actually work the door.'

'You're right,' Ollie said as the door continued to rattle. Through the side-porch window, they saw the other three entities approaching, bounding on all fours like chimps.

'Eleanore is over there,' Lucy told the others, pointing off to the hallway.

'After her!' Ollie ordered.

Just as everyone turned to move, one of the approaching monsters launched itself straight for a side window and came crashing through in a shower of glass.

Emily let out a shriek and everyone ducked down, then sprinted through. Dan slammed the inner door shut, and everyone backed up in horror. They heard the sounds of more windows breaking as the other three creatures got inside the small porch; a moment later, the beasts all started to attack the inner door.

'It won't hold for long,' Emily said.

Lucy knew the girl was right. While the creatures didn't appear to have the strength of the Guardian, they were still relentless; after a few seconds, a long crack appeared on the surface of the door.

'Eleanore, wait!' Ollie shouted and took off. Everyone followed, sprinting after the older woman. Whatever had happened to Eleanore's head, Lucy realised it was affecting her equilibrium, as the woman stumbled again before falling to the floor.

When Ollie reached her, he quickly snatched the papers and notebook from her in anger. Lucy saw the key to the cellar was still in Eleanore's hand, and the boy forced that out of her grip next. He glared at her with his teeth clenched, then raised his eyes to the others.

'Everyone down in the cellar!' he commanded.

'What about her?' Lucy asked, pointing to Eleanore, who was fighting to get back to her feet. Now that Lucy was next to Eleanore, she saw a dent in the side of the woman's head, though the gash around it seemed to be reforming.

Ollie was already running for the door. 'Leave her. Come on!' Everyone took off again, but Eleanore stumbled to her feet and lumbered after them, unsteady and obviously weak.

When at the cellar door, Ollie fumbled with the padlock, but eventually got it open and off the latch. Yet the delay had given Eleanore time to catch up.

'Nooo,' she slurred. The woman then lunged forward at Ollie, tackling him, sending both toppling inside the doorway. Lucy held her breath, thinking the pair were going to fall down the stairs, but Ollie managed to shift to the side and spun Eleanore off him, sending the woman falling on her own instead. Lucy let out a gasp as she saw Eleanore fall head over feet, arms flailing helplessly as she tumbled down the concrete steps. She eventually came to a stop at the bottom, groaning and barely moving.

'Inside!' Ollie told the others. Before Lucy took off, she cast a glance back to the main door and saw the top corner had been forced from its hinges; one of the creatures had its head pushed inside, facing her—*watching* her—as she took off and ran through the cellar doorway with the others.

It knows where we're going.

'The lock!' Dan shouted as they heard the main door

splinter again. Ollie quickly reset the padlock on the latch inside.

While it would buy them some time, Lucy knew it had also trapped them down there with no way out.

'They'll get down here eventually,' she said in panic.

'Then we need to find a way to put an end to all this,' Ollie said, waving the papers he held. 'Come on, let's get as low as we can.'

He led everyone down the stairs to where Eleanore lay at the bottom. The boy unceremoniously stepped over her and pushed open the next door.

The others followed. Lucy went last yet couldn't help but gaze down at the fallen woman in pity. There was anger in Lucy, but she still couldn't bring herself to completely hate Eleanore, she just didn't have it in her. As Lucy went to move, Eleanore's hand found her ankle.

'Noooo,' Eleanore weakly groaned, starting to roll to her front, still holding on. 'You'll... ruin... it.'

Lucy shrieked and kicked Eleanore's hand away before running after the others. 'She's getting up!' Lucy cried. When she turned back again, she saw Eleanore fall through the door into the machine room. The woman forced herself up, grimacing in pain.

'Keep going,' Ollie shouted to them. He pointed to the hatch ahead. 'Dan, you first.'

Dan didn't even attempt to use the ladder and just jumped; Emily followed suit. Ollie motioned for Lucy to do the same, and she did, feeling herself fall the several feet down. More pain shot up her shins, and she cried out, but Dan and Emily took her weight and helped her move away as Ollie dropped down next.

'Go,' Ollie said, and the group took off again. Lucy

heard a *thump* from behind and turned to see that Eleanore had jumped through and landed on her feet.

They all broke through to the first room and Ollie tried to slam the door closed. However, Eleanore lunged forward and was able to force it open enough to squeeze her top half though. She grabbed Ollie's hair, teeth clenched, upper lip curled in anger.

'Help me!' Ollie shouted, and the others rushed over. Yet before they could get there, Eleanore managed to slither through completely and the door *clicked* closed behind her as she fell sideways into the room.

'Leave us alone!' Dan cried.

'You... need... to leave... here,' Eleanore said again, her voice starting to lose some of its sluggishness. Lucy noticed the awful dent in the side of her head wasn't as severe as it had been.

'Why are you doing this to us?' Emily screamed. 'You evil bitch!' Lucy had never seen such anger from the other girl, yet Emily continued her tirade: 'You caused all of this! It's all your fault!'

Lucy saw shame and fear in Eleanore's expression. It became clear to Lucy that, despite what Eleanore was planning, the woman *was* struggling. *Maybe we can convince her to stop?*

But then Eleanore screwed her face up in anger. 'I *have* to do it!' she screamed, then charged forward, grabbing Emily in rage. Emily tried to fight back, but Eleanore forced her deeper into the room, where they crashed into the bed that held Mr. Graves. It shunted to the side but didn't topple. 'You need to stop!' Eleanore cried out. 'You all need to stop this! Why can't you be good children and do as you're told!'

Ollie dropped what he was holding, and he and Dan rushed over to join the fray. As they barged into Eleanore and Emily, everyone stumbled awkwardly into the back room.

'Stop it!' Lucy cried. 'All of you, stop it!' She followed them in, grabbing the transcriptions and notebook on the way. In the distance, she heard pounding on the door at the top of the cellar steps.

They're coming.

She closed and locked the inner door to the passageway as the others continued their struggle, with Dan and Ollie grabbing Eleanore, trying to force her down. Eleanore lashed out in anger and let out a roar, pushing Dan and Ollie away and forcing Emily back once more. Lucy saw wild, uncontrolled rage in the woman's eyes.

However, Lucy could also see what Emily was stumbling back towards. Eleanore pushed the girl hard in anger, and Emily went crashing into the altar, falling to the floor directly in front of it. She'd hit the altar so hard it sent the metal bowl skittering backwards, where it struck the back wall and rebounded forward; the metal slid across the surface to the front of the altar.

Eleanore's eyes suddenly went wide, gaining focus once more. 'No!' she cried out in terror.

The bowl containing the white flame tilted to its side, dropped from the altar, and landed on Emily.

The girl was immediately consumed by the fire. It enveloped her and wrapped around her body, as though alive and claiming its prey.

Dan yelled out and quickly reached for her, but Lucy could only watch in horror. She knew how much the flame had affected her after just a brief touch, yet now Emily was *coated* in it, flailing and clawing as the white fire consumed her. Dan eventually grabbed a fistful of Emily's gown, his own arm deep in the flames, and tried to pull her away.

CHAPTER
SIXTY

Everything came flooding back in a wave. Emily was reliving her whole life, all at once, experiencing each lost memory again as if it was real.

She remembered them all gathered around Ollie, realising he was dead, with Eleanore close by, bleeding out as well. It was madness. Emily was in hysterics in that moment, along with Dan and Lucy.

Eventually, help showed up... but it was all too late.

Not long after the fire, the news story broke about the crazy lady and her house of death, where a dead body had been found beneath the cellar, wrapped in thorns, along with some satanic notes and writings. 'Devil Worship,' the newspapers had called it, with the notes referencing a cult and ancient rituals, which had led to the death of a young boy. It was big news, stretching to the surrounding areas, even being mentioned on national television stations.

The days, weeks, and months that followed were a whirlwind of police investigations and the re-homing process. The trio managed to get a place at another children's home together, which was something. It was fine there... but different. And they missed Ollie. The group promised to all be there for each other when they left, no matter what.

Thankfully, all three also got into the same university later in life and dormed together, staying close. Emily truly saw Lucy as a sister.

She didn't look at Dan like a brother, however.

As they both entered adulthood, it became obvious they had begun looking at each other in a different light. Things developed, even if both tried to ignore it at first. In their final years of education, however, they decided to give things a try, and soon fell madly in love with one another.

While the trio remained close, the new relationship did change things, and Lucy mentioned on numerous occasions how she was starting to feel like an outsider. Emily had always promised that wasn't the case.

Around that time, Lucy had managed to uncover more about the cult that had been responsible for what had happened.

The Children of the New Sun.

The trio promised each other they would expose the cult and get justice for Ollie.

They tried to uncover as much as they could, but after years of limited success, Emily and Dan started to focus on their relationship more and more. Emily remembered one anniversary where they each bought the other a modest watch, with an engraving on the back. Neither had been aware of the other's intention and the watch she received became really special to Emily. Then, the day after, she found out she was pregnant. It was twins.

After the children were born, she and Dan saw less and less of Lucy.

Life just... got in the way.

They tried to make time for Lucy, who kept pushing to see them, but there always seemed to be a reason to put the visits off. Raising a new family was hard, and eventually more and more distance grew between the couple and their friend.

Lucy turned up at their house one night distraught, saying she felt like she'd lost her family. Emily and Dan invited her in and they talked things through; the couple told her they would try harder, but things *were* different now. They had different responsibilities and priorities in life.

Lucy argued that the memory of Ollie was just as important. She left that day after their discussion with nothing really resolved.

A whole decade later, Lucy came to see them again. She said it would be the last time: she had to cut them off for her own wellbeing.

Emily and Dan were shocked—guilt had surged through Emily. As they spoke more, Lucy mentioned she'd had a new family thanks to her investigations. It soon became clear she was talking about the Children of the New Sun.

She'd found them. Or rather, they'd found her, becoming aware of her investigations, and they'd welcomed Lucy in, telling her she was special.

Emily and Dan tried to talk Lucy out of it, telling her to run far away. But she wouldn't. She said she'd found what she'd always been looking for: a real family.

It was all she had, since Emily and Dan hadn't been there for her.

Emily brought up Ollie, saying Lucy would be betraying his memory. The other woman wouldn't listen, insisting *they* were the only ones guilty of betrayal. Countless birthdays had been missed without even a card, despite Lucy always sending one.

The argument intensified, with Emily finally telling Lucy she was going to call the police because she wanted that damn cult exposed.

As she got up to get her phone, Lucy rushed her; they fought, slamming against the dinner table, sending cutlery flying.

Emily dropped to the floor and felt Lucy fall on top of her. Something sharp pierced through Emily's neck.

Emily gasped, wide-eyed, and realised a knife was sticking out of her throat. Lucy yelled in horror. Emily grabbed the handle instinctively and yanked the knife out, but blood began flowing freely from the wound. Lucy slunk away, crying and apologising, a desperate look in her eyes.

'I'm sorry, I'm so sorry, I didn't mean it!'

Dan rushed over to Emily and took hold of her throat, putting pressure on the wound. 'No! Emily! No!'

Emily fought for her life, but could feel herself slipping away.

'Jesus Christ, no!' Dan screamed. 'Lucy, call an ambulance!'

'I... can't!' she sobbed. 'It'll... lead people back to the family. I... I *can't.*'

'Lucy! For God's sake, I'm losing her! Do it!'

Emily felt a swell of emotion as her life slipped away: pain, shock, anger, betrayal.

Her throat burned. Her heart pumped frantically. She couldn't get her breath.

I don't want to die!

But she did.

The last thing she saw was Dan looking down at her in anguish and horror. He was frantically applying pressure to her throat, trying to stem the never-ending flow of blood. Nothing seemed real.

What happened? How did everything spiral like this?

Emily's eyes lost focus.

∼

'No!' Dan screamed. *This can't be happening! It can't be happening!*

He felt a shadow fall over him and had just barely turned around when he saw Lucy holding the bloody knife... which she sunk into his side. Dan gasped in pain and fell to the floor.

Lucy was wailing hysterically, like a madwoman. 'I'm sorry. I'm so sorry! I'm so, so sorry!'

She stabbed him again.

'Lucy... stop,' he begged and began to crawl across the tiled floor. He put a hand to his side, where slick blood flowed out, coating his palm in an instant. Lucy moved away to a corner, dropped to her behind, and started to sob, wrapping her arms around her legs to rock herself.

'I'm so sorry,' she said, again and again.

'Lucy... help...'

Yet Dan's friend didn't look up. She didn't even look at him as he bled out.

CHAPTER
SIXTY-ONE

Emily inhaled sharply, feeling like she'd just been pulled out of water while drowning. Her body was numb. She could feel nothing but cold, and she gasped over and over. Her eyes soon came into focus, with Ollie and Lucy standing over her, looking down in panic. Dan was beside her as well, cradling his arm.

What happened? What happened?

'Are you okay?' Ollie asked, squatting down to her. 'You... God, you look so pale!'

'There are scars,' Lucy said in shock, lowering herself as well. 'Can you see them, Ollie?' Emily saw the girl point down to her face.

'Emily, can you hear me?' Ollie asked.

She flicked her eyes to the side and saw Eleanore with her hands over her mouth in shock, breathing frantically. Emily looked back at Lucy once more, remembering everything. Anger flooded her, yet that was quickly replaced with guilt.

She felt terrible for Dan and how she'd treated him, thinking the worst. As it turned out, he was a good man—a *great* man—and she loved him completely. He was her soulmate. Emily remembered the message from him engraved on the back of her watch: *All my love, for now and forever*. She clung to that.

She also thought of her children, feeling sick knowing she'd never see them again.

Lastly, she felt awful for what Lucy must have been going through. Things must have been really bad for the girl if she'd sought solace in a cult.

Emily wondered if the faces Lucy had mentioned looking down as she died were the Children of the New Sun, seeing her on to the next world.

I could have stopped her from joining them. All it would have taken was a little more effort. Lucy deserved that much.

Her eyes again fell on Dan, and she saw how he was also looking at Lucy. Emily remembered his hand reaching into the fire to grab her just before she'd jumped back. She knew he'd seen his death as well, and it suddenly struck her that in her vision, he looked exactly the same as when he'd come back to the house just a little while ago.

He died just after me, she realised. *Maybe that same night.* She couldn't be certain, but somehow just *knew*.

The only thing Emily could move at the moment were her eyes, and they roved around in panic as her whole body throbbed with an icy-cold ache. She gazed at the altar behind her, which was now askew. The bowl lay on the ground across the room.

But it was the white fire that drew her attention. It looked exactly as it had before, but now burned from a spot on the floor. It didn't seem natural that a fire could slip from one point to another and continue just as it had, though she knew perfectly well it *wasn't* a normal flame.

Regardless, it still burned brightly, unrelenting, casting its ghostly hue.

Emily tried to move again, but it only resulted in her muscles spasming.

'Easy, easy,' Ollie said. Dan moved over and gazed down at her, still holding his arm.

'Emily... I...'

He knows, she realised. She couldn't be sure how much, but she could tell from Dan's expression that he knew he hadn't killed her. She tried to force a smile towards him. Judging by his reaction, it felt like she had succeeded.

She then met Lucy's concerned gaze. Despite everything, she couldn't bring herself to summon the same kind of rage and hurt she'd initially felt towards Dan—especially knowing how much she'd let her friend down. All she could think was: *how did we mess everything up so much?*

Eleanore suddenly stomped over and grabbed Emily by the ankles. 'Get her away from that!' she shouted and dragged Emily across the floor, farther from the flame. Emily jolted as she was moved, and the pain that surged through her seemed to kickstart her nerves—her fingers twitched.

'Leave her alone!' Ollie screamed. He lunged at Eleanore to push the woman away, but she fought him off and quickly moved over to collect the fallen metal bowl. The woman then carefully angled it so she could slide it under the flame; Emily watched as the fire held its form while still slipping back to the centre of the large plate. Eleanore then carefully lifted the bowl and sat it back on the altar. That done, she turned to the others, shielding the altar from them.

'Don't go near it,' Eleanore said, teeth clenched. 'I'm warning you.'

Emily could hear the things upstairs attacking the cellar door. There was more cracking and snapping of wood —they would soon be through. While there were still another three doors to go, the other ones wouldn't be as much of a barricade as the one with the padlock.

They're going to get us, Emily thought to herself. *We're stuck with nowhere to run.*

CHAPTER
SIXTY-TWO

Lucy killed me.

Dan was still grappling with his restored memory.

In an instant, he'd gone from hating himself for what he thought he'd done to Emily, to realising he and Emily had actually been married and Lucy was the one who'd been responsible for their deaths. Both in the same night.

He didn't remember anything before that, nothing from his life prior to Lucy coming to see them. But he did remember feeling awful when Lucy had explained that night what she'd been going through, how lost and alone she'd been. How much they'd failed her by letting her drift away, despite her trying to keep them in her life.

As he now looked down at Emily, he saw there was no scorn or hurt in her gaze anymore. She knew.

He wanted to reach down and take her hand, but refrained, not knowing how much pain she might be in right then. His own arm was tingling with sharp, stabbing pains, so he couldn't imagine how she was feeling.

She looked awfully pale, like the colour from her skin

had been seared away, leaving hundreds of little, delicate scars, each one like the partially healed remnants from small cuts. He wondered if they would disappear or if she'd have them forever.

The crashing from the door above made him realise there probably wasn't going to *be* a forever. Those things would be down soon.

'We need to read through this as quickly as we can,' Ollie said as he took the transcriptions from Lucy and unbound them. 'There is a way to end all this in here. I guarantee it.'

The space on the floor was cramped, but each of them managed to sit and take a handful of the sheets, all crowding around Emily protectively. Dan noticed her fingers were moving, and she was rotating one of her wrists, as if trying to force her body to respond.

Eleanore maintained her position in front of the white flame. 'There's nothing in there,' she stated. 'There's nothing you can do.'

Dan gazed at her, studying her face. *She's worried.* It looked like she was torn between running over and snatching the papers, or defending the fire.

'You're lying,' he told her. 'There's something here, isn't there.'

Eleanore's jaw clenched, but she shook her head. 'No.'

Emily rolled to her side, causing Dan to look down. He laid a hand on her shoulder as she breathed deeply.

Everyone jumped at the sound of the cellar door finally failing. The things raced down the stairs and started attacking the next door.

'They're close,' Lucy said. She looked at Dan. When he gazed back to her innocent brown eyes, he saw nothing of the woman that had reacted in such panic with the knife.

She held up the stack of papers in her hand. 'We don't have enough time to read all this.'

Dan knew she was right. But maybe they didn't have to. He got up and stepped closer to Eleanore, who regarded him with suspicion.

'Eleanore,' he began. 'Just tell us.'

He knew it could all end right there if she was *finally* honest with them—for once. He just hoped the solution, whatever it was, could be carried out in whatever time they had left.

'There's nothing to tell,' the woman replied. She gazed at the papers in Dan's hand. He could tell she dearly wanted to take them, but given she would have to fight three of them for the notes, she was refraining. Dan's attention was briefly diverted as Emily pushed herself up to a sitting position, helped by Ollie and Lucy, who both had their arms around her.

Dan turned back to Eleanore. 'Is this really what you want for them?'

She frowned in confusion. 'Who?'

'Your children,' he explained. 'If you're bringing them here to replace us, is this really where you want them to be trapped forever?'

Eleanore tensed up. '*Don't* talk about them. You don't know them. You have no right!'

'I know they're stuck inside those monsters up there,' Dan said. 'That can't be nice for them. I also know you plucked them from whatever afterlife they were already in to imprison them here. Do you really think they'll be grateful?'

'You have no idea what you're talking about,' the woman spat back, face screwed up in rage.

'Really?' Dan asked. 'Because I've only been here a little

while and I hate this place. I hate everything about it. I hate the never-ending redness; it's like there's no other colour here. I hate that outside the boundary walls it just seems like an eternal darkness. It's terrifying, Eleanore, and makes me feel like I'm trapped outside of reality. It's lonely. It's soulless. And most of all, it isn't *real*. All of this is just a lifeless copy, a photograph, that we're stuck inside.'

He saw Eleanore's eyes well up. There came the sound of another door giving way, and the savage beasts drew closer, snarling in anger. Soon, they started to attack the door to the outer room, having made it through the underground passage.

Ollie and Lucy helped Emily to her feet. 'He's right,' Ollie said to the older woman, one of Emily's arms over his shoulder as Lucy took the other. 'And you know it, don't you?'

'I... I know what I'm doing,' Eleanore replied.

Dan shook his head. 'No, you don't. You've *never* known. Not really. You said it yourself: you had no idea what this place would really be like. You *kept* saying it.'

'Eleanore,' Lucy started. 'You can't bring them here. Your children, I mean. They'll hate it. And it'll be forever. You just... *can't.*'

Dan saw the conflict etched on the older woman's face. Her teeth were still clenched, and her hands were balled into fists by her side. But her eyes flowed with tears.

Please, Eleanore, just listen to us.

CHAPTER
SIXTY-THREE

They're trying to manipulate me, Eleanore told herself. *Don't listen.*

She knew she couldn't turn back now. They'd come too far; she and Jasper had sacrificed too much. It was like he'd said: once they started down the path, there was no turning back. He'd made her promise that.

And the man had given his very soul to this place, literally, all so they could be with their children again. *I can't betray that.*

But then... she couldn't shake what Dan and Lucy had said. Ever since returning to the house after death, it had been clear things were just... wrong. The things Dan had said about what Erimus House had become were completely correct.

It felt cold, detached, soulless... uncaring.

The idea of having her children back but making them exist in Erimus House tore at her. What was more, Jasper wouldn't be around. Not really. He'd exist there as the Guardian, but he would never be able to truly be with his children.

While Eleanore and Jasper had always known the sacrificed person would become the Guardian while their soul burned in the white flame, Eleanore had never expected it would be anything so... horrific. There was *nothing* in the texts that predicted that. But again, she was reminded that the texts only told them how to create their own purgatory, not what would lie within it.

Not that any living person would know. She wondered how many souls from the old, lost civilisation were now suffering, having completed the ritual themselves.

Unless they took the way out. And there *was* a way. The children in the room with her had seen through Eleanore; Ollie had been right all along. There was a failsafe for the trapped souls to use in order to cross over, to then move on to whichever afterlife they were destined to go to.

It was incredibly simple, which was why Eleanore had performed the rituals all the way down below the cellar. And why she'd kept it all locked up.

Though the children were waiting for an answer from her, Eleanore couldn't speak.

The Alû continued their assault on the outer metal door. While the sliding lock would help hold them off, they sounded even *more* savage now, more desperate, and she could hear the door bounce and rattle.

The lock wouldn't hold for long, then they would be through. They would take the kids in front of her, and free her own that were currently inside of them. Finally, her children would be with her again.

Maybe I can let them see this place, she thought. *Maybe we can live together for a little while, see if they adjust. If not, the way out was always there for them.*

Not for her, however. She knew she wouldn't be able to leave with them. Her soul was bound to the underworld—

and not just because of what she'd done in condemning Ollie and the others. Some of the atrocities she'd carried out while in the family had been truly horrific, all to please the elders.

That was why she was so desperate to make her own afterlife work. To make it a forever home for her and her family, and to escape an eternity of punishment.

'Eleanore, please,' Lucy begged. *Poor, sweet, innocent Lucy.*

Eleanore knew she'd let herself get too close to the children. She'd tried to walk a fine line between staying detached but still providing them a nice life, knowing they at least deserved that.

But she hadn't been able to stay distant enough. She'd proved that the night she'd completed the *Thorns of Erşetu* and *Crimson Threads of Anum*. She should have left the children locked in their rooms and let the conflagration consume them. Consume *her*. Then there would have been no need for the Guardian to strip away their age, and the Alû would've carried out their work immediately. Eleanore could have just stayed hidden in her room and not even laid eyes on the four of them again.

But she'd been too weak.

And that weakness had ruined everything. Forced her to see the others again, spend more time with them, and build upon the doubts. Just like they had back then, where Eleanore had spent countless nights in tears, caring for her dying husband, wracked with guilt, unsure if they were doing the right thing.

Eleanore was in floods of tears now. She brought her arms up and hugged herself just as she heard the outer door break open and the Alû surge through. In short order, the door behind them started to shunt and rattle. They were just outside, in the same room as Jasper.

The roaring and snarling was even louder now. The last remaining door was the weakest—Eleanore knew it wouldn't hold for long.

I just need to stay strong for a little while longer. She heard Jasper's words in her mind: *Don't waver, Eleanore. Don't ever waver. I'm giving up my soul for this. Don't betray me.*

In an effort to keep herself focused, she thought of her children. Faces she hadn't seen in so long. She imagined how those faces would look at her when they saw her again.

They'll be elated... won't they?

She then remembered what Dan had said about their souls being plucked from whatever afterlife they'd been in. *What if that was bliss to them? What if I'm taking them from where they* want *to be?*

She thought about them always being in Erimus House, constantly bathed in ominous red light. Nowhere for any of them to go outside the grounds ever again.

Restricted, trapped... imprisoned.

Her heart broke. *How could I condemn them to that?*

She wondered if their souls knew they were currently trapped in the Alû. Would they be scared? Even aware? Eleanore's wails increased. *Oh God, what have I done?*

If she helped the other children now, the souls of her own biological children would go back to where they'd come from. *But* there would still be penance to be paid. Ereshkigal would take the one responsible for breaking the *Crimson Threads of Anum*.

Eleanore wouldn't just go to the underworld. She'd go *beyond* it, to a deeper, darker place.

The door to the room continued to bounce and shake. A

large crack formed down its centre. The latch started to come away.

'Eleanore!' Lucy cried. 'Please, help us!' The children were all crying, utter terror etched on their faces.

That terror is because of me.

The woman finally got control of her sobbing. She took a breath, resolve hardening.

'There... is a way,' she finally admitted, and turned to the white flame.

CHAPTER
SIXTY-FOUR

Emily still needed Lucy and Ollie to hold her weight for her, but slowly felt her strength returning. The things outside smashed onto the door over and over, throwing themselves against it in a bid to get through.

The four children all watched as Eleanore took hold of the large bowl and, with quite a bit of effort, lifted it from the altar and placed it on the floor before stepping back.

The woman was still in tears, but her expression had changed from one of anguish to sad acceptance.

The angry growls from outside the door grew in intensity as the wood around the latch cracked.

Everyone watched Eleanore as she stood back up.

'The fire,' she explained after taking a steadying breath. 'That's the way out. It will burn away your spirit, purify you, absolve you of this place. It can... send you on to the next plane.'

'Heaven?' Lucy asked, her voice full of hope.

Eleanore sniffed. 'Well, I don't call it that but... yes, that's the idea.'

'Wait,' Ollie said. Emily felt his body tense up beside her. 'That... means we stay dead.'

Eleanore nodded. 'Of course.'

Ollie shook his head. 'No! There has to be a way to send us back to when we were alive, send us back to that night, *before* we died.'

Emily turned her head to Ollie, who was looking ahead with wide, frantic eyes.

'Oh, Ollie, no,' Eleanore said. 'That's impossible. That night was so long ago now. Time has moved on.'

'She's right, Ollie,' Dan said. 'We all woke up again when Lucy came back here after dying, remember. She was an old woman then. That night must have been sixty years ago now, maybe more.'

It was only then Emily realised she'd probably been dead for twenty or thirty years—her own children would be middle-aged now. The realisation momentarily sapped the strength in her legs, but she remained upright.

'There has to be a way!' Ollie said. 'I've... I've missed out on everything. My *whole* life. It isn't fair. I want my life back. I don't want to move on!'

Emily unhooked her arm from over Lucy's shoulder, now able to take most of her own weight, and she cupped Ollie's cheek, turning his head to face her.

'Ollie,' she said. 'It *isn't* fair. I know it isn't. None of this is. But when I was in that white fire, I remembered everything from my life. Everything.' She glanced at Dan before looking back. 'I had kids with my husband, you know. Twins.' She saw Dan tense up, but went on. 'Those kids were happy and they grew up to be good people. Even if it was possible to go back, I wouldn't. I *couldn't*. It would mean wiping out everything good I left behind in the world.'

Ollie held her gaze as the door continued to weaken behind them. 'But I never got any of that,' he said. 'For me, I was sitting on the grass with all of you and then... I was at the gate, facing the house, all in the blink of an eye. In *my* head, we were literally sitting on that grass yesterday. And now *she*'—he pointed at Eleanore—'is telling me I have to cross over. That's it. All done. No growing up for me.'

'I'm so sorry, Ollie,' Emily said. 'I know it's a lot to accept. We all have to accept things we aren't ready for.' She thought of Lucy and what the woman had done, as well as her own guilt for playing a part in that. 'But we need to make peace with as much as we can. We need to move forward.' She took his hand in hers. 'And we can do that together.'

There was another smash against the door. A few more and Emily knew it would fail completely.

'We need you with us, Ollie,' Dan said. 'We can't leave you here. We all go together.'

Ollie's bottom lip trembled. His jaw was clenched. 'But... I'm scared.'

Dan put his arm around Ollie, Lucy leaning into him as well.

'It's okay,' Lucy said. 'We're together. We'll cross over together.'

'But what will happen on the other side when we cross?' he asked. 'Will we see each other again? Will others be there waiting?' He looked at Eleanore. The woman had moved away from the fire, but just shrugged.

'I don't have an answer to that,' she said.

'So we might just wake up alone... forever?'

'Or we might get to see everyone we've ever loved,' Emily replied. 'Our family could be there.'

Ollie's wet eyes locked onto hers. 'Grace?' he asked.

Emily smiled at the mention of his sister. 'Maybe. But we can't stay here. We can't let those things pull us down. This is our only choice.'

Ollie took a slow breath, then nodded. 'You're right,' he said, then regarded the ghostly fire wearily. 'Okay, let's go.'

Emily squeezed him tight, and they all started to move forward, with Emily finding she could walk unassisted now. Eleanore watched them, her expression unreadable. For a moment, Emily thought the woman suddenly might have a change of heart and try to stop them all—or worse, the girl wondered if this was all a trick and walking into the white flame was going to somehow make things even more horrible. But Emily quickly remembered how vehemently Eleanore had previously guarded the fire.

No, this isn't a trick. This is the way out. It has to be.

Even so, she shared Ollie's fear and apprehension. She didn't really think she was ready either. She suddenly squeezed Lucy's hand, realising there was one more thing that needed to be said.

'Luce,' she said as the young girl turned to her. 'When we... step in there, you might... remember some things. You might see things you don't really like.' Emily leaned down a little to bring her eyes level with the smaller girl's. The door shunted again, the latch just hanging on.

'What do you mean?' Lucy asked.

Emily gazed at the door again before looking back. 'There's no time,' she said. 'Just know that I love you. I always have and always will. And... I'm sorry I wasn't there for you.'

Lucy's brow deepened. 'There for me? I don't understand what you—'

'Just remember that,' she said, and glanced over to Dan, who gave her a nod of approval.

The door exploded inward.

'Go!' Ollie shouted and pushed them all forward, slipping as he did.

Everything seemed to slow down for Emily. She, Dan, and Lucy all stumbled closer to the flame, and mid-step Emily turned to see Ollie tumble and fall just as the four creatures leapt into the room.

No!

Emily knew there was no time for the boy to scramble over to them—the reaching monsters were going to snag him. Her heart leapt into her mouth when she realised that Ollie, their protector, the boy who had died alone all those years ago, was now going to get pulled down to an eternity of damnation.

All alone yet again.

Outstretched claws reached out for him. Emily tensed.

Then she saw Eleanore leaping forward, crying out in anger, throwing herself into the first of the monsters. The woman collided with it and was knocked backwards, the momentum carrying both of them into Ollie and sending the boy sprawling forward, closer to Emily and the others.

Emily grabbed his hand, Dan his arm, and they quickly yanked the boy to them as the other three entities swooped around Eleanore, who was still grappling with the first.

Emily had no idea how they were all going to fit onto the bowl. It looked barely big enough for a single one of them to stand atop, and she knew they didn't have time to go individually. So she pushed Ollie forward first. The flames reached out for him and swallowed the boy when he fell into them, still keeping tight hold of Emily's arm. The fire consumed him and swelled, expanding over the edges of the bowl. Emily felt his flame-coated body pull her to him. She grabbed Dan, who had hold of Lucy, and they all fell into Ollie, pressing close to him just as Emily felt something claw at her back.

A blast of ice-cold pain seized her. It flooded her veins, just like it had when the fire had consumed her before. Only this time, she wasn't immediately dragged away from it. The coldness increased, becoming white hot, and pain rippled through her. She was able to see Ollie, Dan, and Lucy, all inside the white embrace, their bodies locked in pain, grimaces on their faces. Beyond the fire, she could also see the four creatures shriek and cry, flailing their arms around in anger but seeming to shy away from the fire.

The pain continued to build.

Should it hurt like this? Emily was confused. *What's happening? What's happening?*

White built around her until she could see nothing else. It felt like her nerves were being scorched away. The pain grew more and more intense.

Did we get it wrong? Did Eleanore trick us?

Then... there was nothing.

FOREVER...

CHAPTER
SIXTY-FIVE

Eleanore fought against the Alû in desperation. She knew she couldn't stop the savage beasts, yet she had to try.

The pain was overwhelming. One of them buried their fingers deep into her skin, pulling at her flesh and stretching it like putty as the fingers extended. The other three things seemed happy to just claw and tear at her, inflicting terrible pain as she felt her insides liquify and seep up into the invading hands.

The beast was claiming her, she realised. Ready to take her back. If Ereshkigal couldn't have what was promised, she would have Eleanore.

She kept her eyes on the white flame even as the attack continued. Ollie, Emily, Dan, and Lucy were gone now.

Eleanore felt more of herself siphoned through the claws and into the form of the Alû, more of her soul stripped away.

The woman then noticed white smoke drift off all four of the creatures. The smoke was thin, but the ghostly glow from the white flame somehow made it stand out, and it drifted over to the flame itself in four distinct streams.

Eleanore realised what she was looking at: the souls of Arthur, Elizabeth, Tommy, and Susan all being pulled back to the white flame so they could be released back to where they'd come from.

At least they're safe, she thought joyfully.

Eleanore couldn't move anymore. There was only pain and agony she couldn't withstand but had to. After what was likely less than a minute, she felt herself drawn completely inside of the Alû above her, utterly consumed by it. There was only darkness as she was carried away.

Eleanore didn't know how much time had passed until she was conscious again, though she knew as soon as she stared around in abject horror that time had no meaning anymore.

The landscape around her was wet, organic, and dark. Her flesh screamed and burned. She had no skin, only exposed meat, and it was fused to the landscape. Other souls were stuck to the ground as well, their arms reaching up in desperation to a skyline that almost broke Eleanore's mind.

Multi-legged monstrosities scattered about from person to person, devouring them like a spider would its prey. After one was finished, the creature moved onto the next, and the meal they'd just consumed slowly started to reform. Those people were then duly attacked again by another entity and feasted on once more.

Eleanore screamed in horror, her mind breaking. She heard an awful scuttling sound and saw the face of one of those things appear above her, its features like that of an arachnid. It had a mass of eyes and two enormous, hairy chelicerae, but the mouth below them was wide and filled with small teeth, closer to the mouth of a shark. The front legs of the entity were spider-like for the most part, but they ended with clawed hands, which reached down and gripped Eleanore's exposed flesh, digging in.

The spider-like creature then thrust its mouth down and began to feed, cutting off Eleanore's pained shrieks.

The pain was indescribable, yet with every bite of flesh taken from her, Eleanore felt herself knitting back together. Though she tried to fight, she couldn't get her lower half free of the organic ground. It was like she was part of it, growing out of it, ready to sprout again like a weed after each time she was consumed.

All she could do was to listen to the countless screams of others around her as the entities excitedly continued their work.

CHAPTER
SIXTY-SIX

Emily, Ollie, Dan, and Lucy stood together, the world around them nothing more than a white mist.

It was warm, and Emily realised she felt no fear. No worry. The previous searing pain was gone. All her anxieties had been scrubbed clean as well. She felt fresh and light and full of hope and optimism, which was hard to explain given they were surrounded by what looked like a never-ending white mist.

'Where are we?' Dan asked.

'I don't know,' came Ollie's response.

'Is it... Heaven?' Lucy added.

Their voices sounded... odd. Emily was overcome by a sense of purity, like she was hearing each of them for the first time. *Truly* hearing them, their words stripped of all the masks and protections people threw over themselves to hide their *real* selves away.

What was more, it was like Emily was looking at each of them through every stage of their lives all at once. She could see them as infants, young adults, full adults, and in Lucy's case, an old woman. It didn't make sense, and yet at the same time, seemed perfect—how they all *should* be seen.

Ollie didn't show as much variation, of course, but the life-force that seemed to radiate out of him was no less strong.

'People are coming,' Ollie said, pointing ahead.

Emily saw figures approach through the mists. Dark, shadowy outlines set against the fog.

'I'm... I'm so sorry,' Lucy said. The others all turned to her. She was looking at Emily and Dan. 'I know what I did. I was scared and alone and confused. I was so hurt...'

'No,' Emily said and hugged her. The woman felt warm. 'We shouldn't have abandoned you like we did.'

She carried no hate for the woman. No ill will. All of those emotions were gone from her. She felt only empathy and love.

No more needed to be said. Lucy seemed to sense it too and just hugged Emily back.

'Grace!' Ollie exclaimed.

Emily turned to see a young, blonde-haired girl with a striking resemblance to Ollie step out of the mist. She was smiling.

Others moved through as well.

'Mom! Dad!' Lucy then exclaimed.

'Hi, honey,' a woman replied. 'We've missed you. It's all okay now.'

She saw Dan rush over to two other figures, who embraced him. Then... she saw her own parents. They were just as she remembered them in life, at every stage she'd known them. But also younger, before she'd been around. It was like she was seeing them in a different way, not through her mortal eyes, but finally seeing their true selves.

Their souls.

'I'm so sorry we left you,' her father said. 'But you're safe now.'

'Safe forever,' her mother added. Emily bolted to them, leaping into their arms as they both pulled her into a fierce embrace.

Emotions overwhelmed her: happiness, sadness, relief, wonder, and much, much more.

'It's okay,' her mother said. 'We're so proud of you. So proud of everything you did. It's all okay now. It'll all be okay.'

'But... what about Beth and Adrian? The twins?'

'They grieved you,' her mother said. 'Of course they did. But they're living happy, full lives now. You can still connect with them. They won't know it, but you can.'

'We can *see* them?'

'Not see, exactly,' her father said. 'But feel them. And when the time is right, you can come meet them, like we're doing for you. We're here to take you further on.'

'On where?'

'To where we all come from,' her mother explained. 'It won't make sense until you experience it, but when you do, you'll realise you're home. We all are.'

Emily didn't fully understand, but she didn't question it. She felt Dan move by her side. Reflexively, she lunged out and hugged him. Her old friend, her husband, her love, all of it returned to her, all those happy memories back where they should be.

Soon, Ollie and Lucy approached them both as well. All four hugged each other. Emily didn't want to let go.

'The mists will clear soon,' a young voice said. Emily realised it was Grace. 'Then... you'll be home. Are you ready?'

The four friends—the four *siblings*—looked at each other.

'Are we?' Ollie asked.

'Yeah,' Emily said. She felt at peace, holding no guilt for what came before or fear for what lay ahead. 'Yeah, we're ready.'

Their embrace tightened as the mists cleared. The gentle warmth around them intensified.

'Love you all,' Ollie said as they were filled with a pure and radiant light.

CHAPTER
SIXTY-SEVEN

Jasper Graves was in control now.

He had been for... how long was it now?

Initially, after first waking in his new form, he had been a passenger, acting out of a purpose that wasn't his own and filled with a rage that wasn't his own.

He had to put things right, make them how they should be. The souls had needed to be hunted and purified. After each purification, he had to return to the flame to draw more energy. Then, he hunted again, and again, until everything was as it should be.

Finally, his work was complete, and he was able to control the hulking, pain-filled body and wander Erimus House. He was still constantly drawn back to the flame to rest, so he could only get so far at any one time, but he'd spent longer than he could imagine wandering the house and the grounds.

All alone.

Eleanore was no longer there. He didn't know what had happened to her, nor to the other children from the house.

His offspring were not with him, either.

Something had gone wrong. He didn't know what, exactly, but the plan had failed.

As he'd done many times already, he wandered outside and let out a pained roar. It was all he could do in this nightmarish form. He couldn't speak, couldn't cry, couldn't sob or whimper.

The pain was constant as the punishing vines moved around his body in their endless exploration of his skin and his insides, tearing through him over and over again.

Eleanore... what happened?

He'd *told* her not to waver, made her promise she wouldn't. This place was to be their salvation. A way to avoid their fate after some of the things they'd done while part of the family. Those acts meant they were cut off from Anum and the sky heaven, so Erimus House was supposed to be a way to escape an eternal damnation and be reunited with their children. *Has Eleanore condemned me to isolation forever?*

It felt like he had been wandering the house alone for an eternity. Each time Jasper woke, he had the hope he would see his beloved and his children, all together again. Every time, he was crushed.

Every time, he was alone.

More than once he'd tried to enter the white flame himself, just to bring it all to an end, yet nothing happened; it was a phantom flame, not affecting him at all, like brushing his hand through air.

Strange, considering it was formed from his very soul. But then, he wondered if that was *why* it had no effect on him.

In his form as the Guardian, Jasper was able to see the true reality of the house as well. He could see the normal walls, rugs, furniture, ceilings of the house, but he could also see *through* them, understanding their very make up. So while he stood outside looking at the house, he was able to see the thorns and vines all laced together. Not the ones on top of the walls, but the ones deeper in the walls, the ones that made up everything, all masked by a phantom covering made to look like what came before. Even the books and the pages within were formed by these vines and thorns, some thin and small enough to be almost imperceptible. Everything in the reality around him was formed by this latticework of vines.

Jasper had previously taken to destroying some of the house, just to take out his rage. Every time, the watchers had appeared shortly after and restored everything. One time, he'd grabbed a watcher and torn it apart as it gazed at him in confusion. It didn't make a difference. It just reformed as well.

While outside, Jasper looked up to the sky. He didn't want to, but couldn't help it, taking in what was above him. What was around him. What was around *everything*.

It wasn't a dark void to him. The prima materia was alive. He could see it all. Huge structures dominated the visage, like towering tusks, though he suspected they were actually teeth. There were more of them in the distance, getting smaller the farther away they were—long canines, bigger than continents, lines of them running off into the eternal distance. All of them were bedded in some hideous and terrible lining: a dark flesh, like the inside of a monstrous gullet.

But the gullet *wasn't* eternal. In fact, in the distance, almost perfectly above him, Jasper could see out *beyond* the gullet, through a vast and cosmic opening that showed colourless eyes filling the space beyond. Between those lifeless eyes were wide, cavernous mouths, all filled with teeth similar to the titanic ones closer to Jasper. Each mouth seemed like it could swallow a planet.

Jasper was certain his reality existed in one such mouth. Deep inside it, adhered to the flesh.

There was no sound above, only the horrific visage.

Jasper felt himself called back to the fire. He often prayed for his mind to break, but it never did. Time after time he arose, all alone, left only to wander the house again.

Forever more.

THE END

WHAT TO READ NEXT...

Eager or more?

Haunted: Perron Manor

Book 1 in the Haunted Series.

Sisters Sarah and Chloe inherit a house they could never have previously dreamed of owning. It seems too good to be true.

Shortly after they move in, however, the siblings start to notice strange things: horrible smells, sudden drops in temperature, as well as unexplainable sounds and feelings of being watched.

All of that is compounded when they find a study upstairs, filled with occult items and a strange book written in Latin.

Their experiences grow more frequent and more terrifying, building towards a heart-stopping climax where the sisters come face to face with the evil behind Perron Manor. Will they survive and save their very souls?

Buy Haunted: Perron Manor now.

FREE BOOK

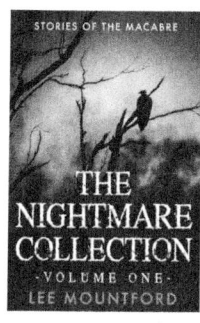

Sign up to my mailing list for free books...

Want more dark stories? Sign up to my mailing list and receive the free ebooks: *The Nightmare Collection - Vol 1* as well as *Inside: Perron Manor* (a prequel novella to *Haunted: Perron Manor*).

The novel-length short story collection and prequel novella are sure to have you sleeping with the lights on.

Sign up now.

www.leemountford.com

OTHER BOOKS BY LEE MOUNTFORD

The Supernatural Horror Collection
   The Demonic
   The Mark
   Forest of the Damned

The Extreme Horror Collection
   Horror in the Woods
   Tormented
   The Netherwell Horror

Haunted Series
   Inside Perron Manor (Book 0)
   Haunted: Perron Manor (Book 1)
   Haunted: Devil's Door (Book 2)
   Haunted: Purgatory (Book 3)
   Haunted: Possession (Book 4)
   Haunted: Mother Death (Book 5)
   Haunted: Asylum (Book 6)
   Haunted: Hotel (Book 7)
   Haunted: Catacombs (Book 8)
   Haunted: End of Days (Book 9)

Darkfall Series
   Darkfall: Deathborn (Book 1)
   Darkfall: Shadows of the Deep (Book 2)

Darkfall: Crimson Dawn (Book 3)
Darkfall: Orchard of Flesh (Book 4)

Short Story Collection
Wanna be Scared?

ABOUT THE AUTHOR

Lee Mountford is a horror author from the North-East of England. His first book, Horror in the Woods, was published in May 2017 to fantastic reviews, and his follow-up book, The Demonic, achieved Best Seller status in both Occult Horror and British Horror categories on Amazon.

He is a lifelong horror fan, much to the dismay of his amazing wife, Michelle, and his work is available in ebook, print and audiobook formats.

In August 2017 he and his wife welcomed their first daughter, Ella, into the world. In May 2019, their second daughter, Sophie, came along. Michelle is hoping the girls don't inherit their father's love of the macabre, but Lee has other ideas...

For more information
www.leemountford.com
leemountford01@googlemail.com

Acknowledgments

Thanks first to my amazing Beta Reader Team, who have greatly helped me polish and hone this book:

James Bacon
John Brooks
Nicole Burns
Mary Cavazos-Manos
Karen Day
Jim Donohue
Sally Feliz
Doreene Fernandes
Domenic Fiore
Jenn Freitag
Ursula Gillam
Vicky Gorman
Larry Green
Clayton Hall
Emily Haynes
Dorie Heriot
Lucy Hughes
Monica Julian
Marie K
Dawn Keate
Jon R Kraushar
Paul Letendre
Katrina Lindsay
Diane McCarty

Leanne Pert
Cassandra Pipps
Janalyn Prude
Carley Jessica Pyne
Gale Raab
Laura Rafferty-Aspis
Justin Read
Emelie Rombe
Nicola Jayne Smith
Crystal Mirja Tyrell
Rob Walker
Sharon Watret

Also, a huge thanks to these fantastic people:

My editor, Josiah Davis (www.jdbookservices.com) for such an amazing job as always.

The cover was supplied by Debbie at The Cover Collection.

(www.thecovercollection.com).

I cannot recommend their work enough.

And the last thank you, as always, is the most important. To my amazing family: my wife, Michelle, and my daughters, Ella and Sophie—thank you for everything. You three are my world.

Copyright © 2025 by Lee Mountford

All rights reserved.

No part of this book may be reproduced in any form or by any electronic or mechanical means, including information storage and retrieval systems, without written permission from the author, except for the use of brief quotations in a book review.

❦ Created with Vellum

Printed in Great Britain
by Amazon